PRAISE FOR

# THE INFECTION

## AND THE WORKS OF CRAIG DILOUIE

"With *The Infection*, Craig DiLouie takes readers on a wild ride into the darkest regions of zombie territory. Brilliant and terrifying!"

—Jonathan Maberry, New York Times bestselling author of *Rot & Ruin* and *Patient Zero*

"This is not just another zombie story ... DiLouie takes everything you know and love about the world and turns it into something else entirely. Unflinching horror and surreal, almost dream-like imagery combine to make *The Infection* a disturbing, nightmarish read."

—David Moody, author of *Autumn* and *Hater*

"Craig DiLouie drives his readers along at a nail-biting pace. His stories pull you in and refuse to let go."

—Joe McKinney, author of *Dead City* and *Apocalypse of the Dead*

"Action-packed zombie mayhem that you won't want to put down. Just when you think you've got *The Infection* figured out, DiLouie takes things to a whole new level."

—Tony Schaab, author and creator of *TheGOREScore.com*

"Craig DiLouie is an impressive storyteller."

—*The Writer and The White Cat*

"Dilouie's thoughtful and unusual approach to the material had me turning pages. Recommended."

*rarian*

# T H E
# INFECTION

## Craig DiLouie

Permuted Press
The formula has been changed...
Shifted... Altered... Twisted.
www.permutedpress.com

## Acknowledgments

Special thanks to Randy Heller for all his editing support over the years and to Chris Arnone for his superior knowledge of all things mechanical.

Scripture quotations are taken from the Holy Bible, New Living Translation, ©1996, 2004, 2007. Used by permission of Tyndale House Publishers, Inc., Wheaton, Illinois 60189. All rights reserved.

A PERMUTED PRESS book
published by arrangement with the author
ISBN-13: 978-1-934861-65-3
ISBN-10: 1-934861-65-0

For Christine and Mieka.

# PROLOGUE:
# FALLING DOWN

Ethan was at the end of his patience trying to explain using factoring to solve equations to his high school algebra class when everybody started falling down.

Hacking at the blackboard with a piece of chalk to guide his students through a third example, he heard the first distant scream. The chalk broke in his hand and he accidentally scratched the board with his fingernails, sending a shiver of revulsion through his body.

"Let's try that again," he said, peering at his class over his rims of his glasses.

Some of the kids smiled back, suddenly engaged by his personal tone, while the rest slouched at their desks and continued to stare out the window—some longingly, some vacantly—at the green lawn washed in spring sunshine.

Finishing the example, he slapped chalk dust from his hands and said, "Okay, who wants to take a crack at this one? Where would you begin to solve for $x$?"

"Wow," several of the students shouted at once, sitting up straight in their desks. Two of the boys stood up, looking out the window.

"Come on, guys," Ethan frowned. "Butts in seats. We've only got fifteen minutes left."

"But there was an accident," one of the kids told him, his eyes gleaming with excitement. "A bunch of people are lying on the ground."

A second scream rang out in a classroom down the hall. Ethan wondered what was going on and took a few steps towards the window. Following his cue, all of the kids got out of their desks and stood to get a better look outside.

Another scream. Shouting in the distance. Footsteps pounded the hallway outside. Ethan turned just in time to see two teachers jog by his classroom. A door slammed.

He took several steps towards the hallway, wondering if there was some type of emergency, if he should be doing something special to protect his kids.

"What is that sound, Mr. Bell?" one of them kept saying.

"I don't know," Ethan murmured.

"It's horrible!"

Another shiver ran through his body. He knew the sound. Why did he deny it? It was screaming. Screaming that would not stop. Screaming that just kept going on and on and on. Whoever was screaming was in extreme, unending pain—strong enough to make them howl at the top of their lungs for minutes. And there seemed to be a lot of people doing the screaming—some outside and some inside the school, in the classrooms down the hall.

He suddenly wondered if he should be here at all. His wife was at work. Their toddler, Mary, at daycare. He took another step towards the door. Would he get fired if he left the school?

Trevor Jackson's face contorted and he fell down screaming, cracking his nose on the floor, blood spurting. The other students jumped back with yelps of surprise, transfixed by the real drama unfolding in front of them. Ethan took several steps back into the classroom and watched helplessly. Trevor was lying on his side, his back arched, his arms outstretched with his hands splayed into claws. His eyes were bulging, leaking tears, while his mouth screamed at a volume Ethan had not thought possible. The sound assaulted him with an almost physical force, pushing him away. He felt the urge to run as fast as his legs would take him. The other students felt it, too, wavering, suddenly aware of the choice of fight or flight.

"Do something!" Lucy Gall shouted at him.

"I'm going to call 911—"

Lucy fell to the ground, her body jerking in little spasms and the crotch of her jeans flooding with piss. Moments later she started to scream loud and shrill enough to damage eardrums. The students shouted at each other to do something. One of the boys got down on his knees and tried to shake her, but then he fell over as well, his eyes rolling back into his skull.

It's in the ventilation system, Ethan thought. Something is in the air all around us.

Five more kids fell down within seconds of each other, spilling desks and scattering their notebooks.

They began to scream.

Ethan was suddenly outside of his body, watching himself push his way along with the remaining students in a blind stampede to get out of the school. In the hallway, they raced over the trembling, screaming bodies of teachers and students as if they were parts of an intricate obstacle course, and then bolted out of the school's steel doors and into sunshine and relative quiet.

He froze in his tracks, amazed. The street beyond the lawn was a tangled mess of crashed vehicles. Plumes of smoke rose above the city in the distance. Now new waves of sound assaulted his ears: car alarms, horns, sirens and, rising up above it all, the distant sound of thousands upon thousands of mouths screaming in unison like an auditory glimpse of hell.

This is everywhere, he realized.

He ran as fast as his legs would go, oblivious to the students toppling around him as if cut down by an invisible scythe. The screaming filled him with blind panic now, an irrational fear of the supernatural, as if actual demons were at his heels. A motorcycle roared by, its rider spilling and cartwheeling through the air. In the distance, planes were falling out of the sky. These things barely registered in his consciousness. All he could think about was Mary's safety. He had to get to her. Please God, spare her, he thought. Take these kids. Take Carol. Take me. If anything happens to my little girl, I will have nothing.

He got into his car and started the engine. The radio began sobbing hysterically at him. He turned it off and that was when he noticed the screaming had stopped. Looking out his window, he saw the lawn covered with bodies, jerking and quivering, while those who escaped Infection walked among them mindlessly, trembling and hugging their ribs and moaning in shock.

So rapid was the transmission of the mysterious virus that swept the world over a period of just forty-eight hours, so sudden the onset of disease, that scientists would later claim that it must somehow be linked to human-engineered nanotechnology. Some kind of weapon that escaped the lab. The government traced the origin of the pandemic to a village near secret facilities in China, but they would never find out the truth. And Ethan would never teach again.

After three days, the screamers woke up.

# THE SURVIVORS

They are refugees forced from everything they consider home, searching for a safe place. They have become nomads, living on whatever they can find. But mostly they are survivors. They are good at surviving because they are on the road and they are still alive. They have done the things one had to do to survive. They have all killed people or they would not be here.

They have not lost anybody since Wednesday, when they lost Philip in Wilkinsburg. There are five of them now sitting ramrod straight in the loud, hot, dim passenger compartment of the armored personnel carrier, passing around a bottle of water, their rifles between their knees. They sit in a tense silence, their mouths slack, sweating in air that is twenty degrees hotter than the unseasonably warm May weather outside, air that stinks of sweat and grime and diesel combustion. Between the engine, the squeal of the treads and a steady drumming sound, they have to shout to make themselves heard, and nobody has the energy to do that. The drumming grows louder, punctuated by sharp metallic taps, until it drowns out the Bradley's five-hundred-horsepower engine. The survivors are perpetually one second away from screaming.

The tapping sound is from jewelry. Bracelets and watches and wedding rings.

The survivors wonder if they have killed everything for which they want to live. Wonder if it might grow back again, given enough time, if only they can find sanctuary.

◆

4

The survivors are adaptive. People who will do whatever it takes to survive naturally do not trust other people. But to travel the road one must be with a gang, and to survive the experience day after day, as they have, that gang must function as a single protective organism. Each of them has been tested by violence and if they failed, they all would have died. They know this. At this point, after what they have seen and done, this sense of responsibility to each other is what keeps them from collapsing into hysteria or catatonia. Fear, sorrow, guilt, rage: These and other emotions are just as dangerous as the Infected outside, and must likewise be killed.

They are going to the Children's Hospital based on a theory. They have the Bradley, weapons, and the illusion of safety as long as the rig's engine keeps humming and its treads keep moving. They need supplies, though, especially water and diesel. They need to find a place unspoiled by Infection, where they can rest. The simple fact is they cannot keep fighting like this. You can only win so many fights before it starts to feel like you are losing.

They sense a subtle shift in the atmosphere, a sudden drop in temperature. Outside, it begins to rain. The drumming gradually fades as the Infected lose interest in pounding on the vehicle with their fists. They fill the air with their plaintive cries as they melt away into the rain.

♦

Anne alone does not appear to be stripped to a single, bare electric wire. She sits in the back near the exit ramp, across from the cop, a place of respect among the survivors as whoever sits there is the first to leave the vehicle and the last to reenter. The others admire and try to imitate her cool. Sarge may be the commander of the Bradley, but they consider Anne to be their leader because without her example and unfaltering aim with the scoped rifle, they would all be dead.

She has two long scars on her left cheek and a short one on her right, still fresh. The survivors assume that she is ex-military, imagining a romantic and violent past. Anne does not tell them that she has an overwhelming feeling that once they finally stop moving and find a place of rest where they can be truly safe, she is going to burst inside out with one long, deafening scream of guilt, terror and anguish.

♦

Hours earlier, they found Sarge's infantry squad in the parking lot of a Wal-Mart, mangled like road kill around a large, strange device and surrounded by a carpet of dead Infected tangled up in a line of concertina wire. The dead stared wide-eyed into oblivion. Many of the bodies were badly burned and emitted a sickening sweet barbecue odor. Bits of charred clothing, stuck to the concertina wire, trembled in the light breeze. A few Infected stumbled blindly among the remains, gnawing on human meat from a dismembered arm or leg. Crows shrieked in protest as the Bradley approached at forty miles an hour. At the last moment, an enormous flock of the birds exploded into the air, dribbling morsels of flesh from bloody beaks as they filled the sky.

Sarge cut down the few Infected in the area with several bursts from the Bradley's coaxial machine gun. Outside, he warned the survivors not to step on any of the bodies.

Of course we won't, they told him. We will respect your dead.

"It's not a matter of respect," he said. "These people are rotting. Gases are building up inside their bodies. See how bloated they are? They can burst and spray fluids. You could get sick."

Six days ago, the Bradley dropped off the squad of six soldiers—who were supposed to operate on their own in the field for three hours—and then withdrew for badly needed repair of a steering problem. The soldiers were testing a non-lethal weapon against the Infected that used active denial technology. They deployed a line of concertina wire, set up their device and blasted a klaxon to attract the attention of any Infected within hearing range.

The device, shaped like a large hoe attached to the face of a basketball backboard, is a transmitter that beams energy waves which penetrate the skin and produce an intense burning sensation. The idea is whoever is subjected to this reflexively tries to avoid the beam and submits. It did not work on the Infected. The Infected only became enraged and attacked until their flesh began to sizzle and even then they still attacked until they fell down.

Another Bradley was going to pick up the soldiers, but it never came because by the time it left on its mission to recover the squad, the soldiers were already dead and the vehicle became reassigned. Sarge knew this but he had to see for himself that it was true. These dead boys were his people. They had served together in Afghanistan. He placed his hand over his heart, a gesture of respect he picked up from the Afghans, and collected their dog tags.

"The device is supposed to be angled to trigger a burning feeling from the neck down," he told the others. "See how it's angled up? That's not an accident. They were desperate. At the end, they tried to burn out the corneas in the eyes of the Infected. They tried to blind them."

Is it okay to take these guns? they asked him. Will you teach us how to shoot them?

"I heard about another test of long-range acoustic weapons, over in Philadelphia, that also failed," Sarge went on. "The device was supposed to cause intense pain in the ear using a certain frequency of sound, but it actually attracted the Infected. They came in hundreds, destroyed the device and killed the unit that deployed it. Pointless."

A pack of dogs yelped in the distance. Somebody, far away, fired an automatic weapon, setting off a brief, crisp flurry of gunfire that sounded like the crackle of firecrackers.

"None of the non-lethals worked," Sarge added. "The only thing that can stop these motherfuckers is a rifle and the will to use it."

♦

The armored personnel carrier smashes into the abandoned traffic jam on squealing treads, its twenty-five tons shouldering aside a minivan and crushing the front of a sports car into metal pancake in seconds. The words BOOM STICK are neatly stenciled in white paint on the side of the turret, near the gun barrel. The rig plows into a pair of Infected and flings them down the street in a fine red mist. The machine emerges from the intersection and grinds to a halt, its engine idling. The Bradley fills the street, flanked by stores topped by low-rise apartments. Using the vehicle's periscopes, its three-man crew scans the bleak, shattered landscape visible through a smoky haze. The rain has stopped and the sun is shining again.

In the back, the survivors cringe and blink. Stopping is bad. They finger their weapons, paling, as Sarge wedges his way into the back and squats, sweating in his ACUs and helmet. The commander is a large man and makes the cramped passenger compartment appear even smaller. As always, he looks at Anne when he wants the civilians to do something. They appear to have some sort of unspoken agreement about the sharing of authority.

"Drugstore," he says. "Once you're out, it's on the left."

"Locked up?" says Anne.

"Not that we can see."

"Any signs of forced entry?"

"The door looks fine and the windows are all intact."

"No damage, then?"

"I saw no vandalism, no fire or water damage."

"Cleaned out already?"

"No, that's the thing. From what I could tell, there's still some stuff on the shelves."

Some of the survivors allow themselves to smile. The store has not been looted or damaged. They will be able to get supplies. Not everything they need, but something. Every useful item they can find is a puzzle piece that must be fitted with everything else.

"How many Infected on the street?"

"None living."

"It's worth the risk," Anne says, and Sarge nods.

"Show time," he says.

♦

Ethan takes a deep breath to steel his nerves, fidgeting with his M4 carbine and trying to remember what Sarge told him to do if the weapon jams: slap the magazine, pull the bolt back, observe the firing chamber, release the bolt, tap it and squeeze off the next round. If a double-feed, detach the mag and drop the rounds. Assuming he has time to do all this while a swarm of Infected are racing hell for leather at him, shrieking their inhuman cries of recognition and rage.

He is certain that he is living on borrowed time and that one day he is going to be killed or Infected. He was a math teacher; he understands probabilities. Every day, just to live, he has to give it everything he has. If just once he is a little slow or takes a wrong turn or is in the wrong place at the wrong time, they will catch him. How many days can a man go on like that? Never be a little slow, never take a wrong turn, never be in the wrong place at the wrong time?

It is true that his body and mind are rising to the challenge. But while his body is dropping fat and becoming more toned, he often feels stabbing pains in his neck and back, especially after sitting in the Bradley for hours. The truth is he is a middle-aged man and not in very good shape. His mind similarly has sharpened, constantly vigilant for threats, completely purged of the pop culture nonsense and old petty worries that plagued the middle class in the Time Before. But the stress is slowly damaging his mind and steadily shaving time off of his lifespan. Ethan is rising to the challenge, but he does not know how long he can keep this up before he will finally break down.

In the end, he knows, the odds are stacked against survival. The Infected spread disease through violence. Possessed by their aggressive virus, they are meat puppets, totally expendable and intent only on finding new hosts. They drink from gutters and toilets. If they get hungry, they eat the dead. They have nothing to lose. They run through fire and bullets to reach their prey. If you are standing, they punch you. If you are down, they stomp you. When you stop fighting back, they bite you and infect you. The virus penetrates the blood through saliva in the bite, enters the central nervous system, and from there is mainlined into the brain, where it proliferates in the limbic system, producing rage. The virus is so strong, so virulent, it paralyzes you in seconds and takes total control in minutes.

And then you become one of them. In the beginning, there were not as many of them. Ethan never imagined how terrifying another human being could be in a world where all people had become predators or prey. Now the predators appear to outnumber the prey, as least in downtown Pittsburgh. Either that or, just as likely, the prey is hiding. The power has been out for days and it is already hard to imagine how people are living behind their locked doors and drawn shades without food or plumbing. In just a few more days, this city will be unlivable.

It is horrible to think that his students are out there, somewhere, hunting him.

"I'll drop the ramp and then we're going to move the rig about twenty meters down the street and park it in the first alley on the right," Sarge tells them. "You'll have to put your own eyes on the street. There are a lot of buildings, a lot of windows."

The survivors not only have to watch out for the Infected, but also other survivors living in the neighborhood, who might be willing to fight to protect the store.

The cop, gnawing a wad of gum, says, "Sarge, we didn't get a chance to tell you. We're all sorry. You know, about what happened to your guys back there."

The survivors nod in sympathy, but they are clearly uncomfortable. They are sorry they did not find the soldiers alive, partly because it would have been a relief to turn over responsibility for their safety to somebody more qualified. On the other hand, if they had found the soldiers alive, Sarge would probably have left them stranded, and gone off with his infantry to fight.

Sarge gives the cop a sharp glance. She blushes, stammering a little, and adds quickly, "If you need a friend, you can talk to me. That's all."

"I have no friends," Sarge says. "All of my friends are dead."

The ramp eases to the ground on whining hydraulics, flooding the compartment with sunshine and the harsh, acrid smell of burning chemicals.

♦

The survivors exit the Bradley and fan out, establishing three hundred sixty-degree security as Sarge taught them to do. Anne says she will clear the store of Infected before the group enters. Wendy, the cop, says she will provide backup. Then the Kid insists on coming, but Anne tells him to stay and watch the street. They disappear into the store guns first.

The Kid grins, dressed up like something out of a reality show about teenage bounty hunters with his black T-shirt tucked into urban BDU pants, bullet-proof vest and SWAT cap. He chews on a toothpick as he peers through the close combat optic of his M4, scanning the street for Infected.

"Is the end of the world not killing you fast enough, Reverend?" he says.

Paul pauses while lighting a cigarette, then finishes and takes a drag. He sighs happily and picks up his shotgun, exhaling a long stream of smoke. "This makes the apocalypse just a little rosier for me," he explains.

"Isn't that God's job?"

A shadow flickers across the Reverend's face, but he says airily, "God sent us you, my boy."

The Kid stops grinning. He is not sure, but he believes the old man just zinged him. He is easily zinged. Even the slightest remark makes him anxious, confused and angry. Oblivious, Paul takes another drag, then coughs into his fist. He has already forgotten the exchange. The Kid envies that kind of cool that comes with age. For the Kid, every interaction has enormous stakes.

"I hope it rains again, a really big rain, that washes all this shit into the gutter," Paul says.

"Me, too, Rev," the Kid says, admiring the thought.

Wendy appears at the door, giving the all-clear. The survivors enter the store and the Bradley promptly pulls away in a cloud of exhaust, crumpling another car like tin foil before staging an abrupt ninety-degree turn into a nearby alley.

Inside, Paul marches to the nearest secluded corner, drops his pants and craps loudly into a five-gallon bucket covered with a toilet seat, clutching a roll of toilet paper and finishing his cigarette. Next to him sits a bag of lime, which he will dump into the bucket to cover up the smell. The Kid envies the way the others can eliminate their waste so casually. He needs privacy to be able to go, but privacy is currently not a preferred survival trait. Privacy means clearing a room that might be occupied by the Infected, a move the others would consider an unnecessary risk. It means being vulnerable. And it involves the risk of being left behind if the group is forced to bug out.

Anne touches the Kid's shoulder and tilts her head towards the door. She has chosen him to stand guard and be their lookout. He whines briefly but does what he is told, asking her to find him some batteries and candy. Oh, and a new toothbrush.

♦

The survivors picked up the Kid three days ago. Cut off from the Bradley by a large swarm, they were saved by the sudden ring of an old metal wind-up alarm clock on the next block, which distracted the Infected long enough for them to escape. When they returned to the Bradley, they found the Kid there, grinning like the proverbial cat. He refused to give his real name, Todd Paulsen, because Todd Paulsen was a loser in high school suffering a grinding avalanche of petty humiliations. Todd Paulsen is dead; the Kid killed that loser himself. The apocalypse, for some, is turning out to be filled with second chances. The survivors were grateful and admired his ability to innovate. They invited him along and he accepted. Everybody else that he knew was dead or Infected. He felt safe alone and had done very well for himself but it wasn't fun if nobody saw him doing it.

Growing up outside cliques, the Kid wondered what it would be like to be one of "us" instead of "them." Even among this tight-knit tribe of survivors, he was the newcomer, and he thought he would have to endure some type of hazing, particularly since he was the youngest among them. But nobody cared, too occupied by their own survival. Then a magic thing happened. Two days ago, driving in the Bradley, Anne cleaned his glasses for him, a touching maternal gesture that made him feel like a full citizen of this group.

Last year, John Wheeler, a giant senior, picked him up in the cafeteria during study hall and dangled him over a garbage can in front of forty other students who watched with a mixture of tension, *schadenfreude* and blunt relief that Wheeler was not doing it to them. The trick was always to stay in the middle of the herd. The trick was never to stand out. They were good at that. But with his good grades and clumsy adolescent skinniness, Todd Paulsen stood out. The teachers called him smart and some of the other kids hated him for it. Then other kids hated him, too, without knowing why, just to be safe.

John Wheeler fell down during the Screaming and that means he is one of the Infected. Many of the kids who were in study hall that day, the ones who cheered and the ones who did nothing out of fear, are either dead or controlled by the virus. For all the Kid knows, he is the sole surviving witness of what happened to Todd Paulsen during those terrible five minutes. And yet he cannot stop reliving it just as he cannot stop reliving all of his other minor humiliations. It is easier to shed your name than your baggage.

He wishes they were all alive just so they could see him now: The Kid, driving with a group of adults armed to the teeth, fighting his way through an apocalyptic wasteland. They would absolve him of his humiliations with their admiration and respect. They would know that they would never be able to fuck with him again because this time, he has a gun.

◆

Wendy finds some plastic bags at the cashier and hands them to the others. Panic buying cleared most of the shelves before Infection put an end to consumerism, but there are still useful things here. Wendy discovers a squashed plastic container filled with packages of beef jerky on the floor behind the open register, a great find. Some idiot rifled the register for its cash but left food on the floor. It goes into her bag. She finds a full pack of matches, large bag of salt, children's vitamins, scotch tape, mosquito repellent, box of condoms and bottle of sunscreen. It all goes into the bag. She finds a bottle opener, which she puts into her pocket. A pack of Bazooka gum, which she immediately tears open with pleasure, spitting out her old wad of gum from her aching jaws and popping in a fresh piece. She finds a box of tampons and displays it like a trophy to Anne, who merely nods and moves on, scooping cans off of the floor.

Ethan pauses in one aisle and picks up a three-subject spiral-bound notebook. He turns the blank pages, leaving dirty fingerprints, as if skimming an old love letter. He brings the book to his face and breathes deep. When he lowers it, Wendy sees tears streaming down his face.

"You okay, Ethan?"

"No," he says. "I mean yes."

She reaches out to touch his shoulder, but suddenly cancels the gesture. Leaders in a crisis are not tender. Leaders in a crisis are strong. She has to be strong.

He adds, "Where would you begin to solve for $x$. I remember now where we left off."

"You're sure you're okay?" she says.

"Yes. Sometimes I forget where I am. I'm fine now."

"Why don't you go see if you can find something worth taking in the pharmacy?" she says. "Especially tranquilizers and sleeping pills. Prazosin for the bad dreams. Look for vitamins, gauze, antibiotics, swabs, Benadryl, Ibuprofen—hell, anything that looks useful."

"All right."

Wendy still considers herself a cop, which is why she still wears her uniform and in particular her badge. To her, symbols matter, especially in a time of crisis. The other survivors agreed at first, looking to her as an authority figure, but not anymore. To them, she is a valuable member of the team but otherwise just another refugee, no different than them. She cannot understand why they put so much trust in Anne when she fights even harder and takes even bigger risks for the group. Wendy just wants to help. To serve and protect. The fact is a lot of cops died back at the station so that she can go on doing her job. She owes a debt to the dead.

They have witnessed the end of the world one horrible scene at a time, each as potent as the last. Pillars of smoke rising from burning communities. The sprawling wreckage of a crashed 727 scattered for miles along the Parkway among blackened, half-melted cars driven by charred skeletons. The Infected feeding on the dead. Screaming on the radio instead of music and commercials. For Wendy, the most crushing thing she has seen is all of the abandoned police cars once manned by people sworn to protect life and property, but now swept away in the violence. The breaking of the Thin Blue Line signaled the collapse of law and order. It means every man for himself. The Infected took only minutes to virtually wipe out her entire precinct. The other cops saved her life, which now she must earn.

Strangely, the uniform probably extended her lifespan. The survivors all wear dark colors, various shades of black, tan and gray. Paul wears his black clerical suit with its white collar, for example. They are sharp, they are the best of what is left, but they are largely here by accident. In the early days of Infection, they would spill out of the Bradley and the Infected would rush straight at anybody wearing bright colors. Red excites them most. And everybody who wore red died or became Infected. Those wearing orange and yellow and green were next. It was Philip who figured this out, the corporate executive dressed in a grimy black suit and gray tie, that they were all alive because they picked the right clothes the morning the slaughter began.

"There's something coming," the Kid cries out from the door.

♦

They hear a low rumble they can feel as a subtle vibration in their feet. The survivors gather around the Kid. Anne increases the magnification on her scope and aims the rifle down the street. The sense of vibration migrates up to their knees.

"It's a tank," she says in wonder, lowering the rifle. "A really big tank. Coming fast."

The tank smashes through an abandoned police barricade, scattering garbage and rats, now close enough for the survivors to take in the scratched and blood-spattered composite armor and massive barrel of the tank gun. They feel the roar of the engine deep in their chests. The treads shriek like a massive bird of prey.

"Um," says Ethan, frowning.

"That's an M1 Abrams," the Kid says, filled with admiration.

"Does that mean the government is still functioning?" Paul asks.

"I think we might be saved, folks," Wendy says, grinning.

"Get down," says Ethan.

"Hey," the cop calls out, waving her warms. "We're in here!"

Their teeth are vibrating. Bottles of household cleaner topple off of the shelves. The windowpanes rattle in their frames. The dust dances on the asphalt. The tank's turret swivels, aiming its massive gun directly at the store.

"*GET DOWN!*"

The tank's machine gun fires a series of short, staccato bursts. The survivors throw themselves onto the floor as bullets crash through the windows, puncture shelving and products, and clatter against the far walls.

*Dot-a-dot dot-a-dot dot-a-dot*

"Stop shooting at us!" Ethan screams.

Wendy buries her face in her arms, listening to the bullets rip the air, destroying everything in their path. It sounds like somebody rattling screws and pieces of glass in a metal can next to her ear. Pieces of plastic and cardboard rain on her like confetti. Then the firing stops.

"Is everybody all right?" she calls out.

The tank turns onto their street and roars by the store on its steel-clad treads. The ground shakes. Shards of glass from the broken windows tinkle to the floor. The air is thick with glittering dust and particles.

"Everybody stay down," she says.

Wendy stands and creeps to the door, where she peers out at the rear of the tank, now already two blocks away, just in time to see small arms fire open up on it from apartment buildings on both sides of the street. A Molotov cocktail streams down from a third floor window, bursting on the rear of the tank and briefly setting it on fire. She flinches, wondering about her safety. Why are those people shooting at the tank?

The Abrams grinds to a halt in a cloud of dust, returning fire with its machine guns while its turret swivels and raises the main gun to aim at one of the apartment windows.

The tip of the 105-mm barrel erupts in a blinding flash. Wendy gasps and jerks her head away as the heat and light strike her with an almost physical force. The apartment building abruptly sneezes its contents onto the street in a massive explosion of wreckage and dust and swirling debris: plastic bags, gum wrappers, bits of foil, flaming clothing. Wendy catches a glimpse of people and furniture flying. The massive cloud of smoke ripples and seethes down the street, obscuring the tank from view and plunging the survivors into virtual darkness.

"What the hell is going on?" the Kid shouts, still on the floor.

"I don't know," Wendy answers.

"Change of plans, I think," says Anne.

"Why is that?"

Anne replies, "That tank is going in the same direction we are."

♦

The atmosphere is still filled with soot and ash from fires burning in the city, making the sunset spectacular with lurid alien colors. The survivors camp for the night in a service garage at a car dealership. After clearing the building, they black out the windows with paint and make sure all of the doors and windows are locked up good and tight while ensuring proper ventilation for their cook stove. Every nook and cranny of the Bradley's interior is filled with the tools of survival, which they carefully unload to establish their camp: flashlights and batteries, Coleman stove and propane tanks, waterproof matches, utensils, bedrolls and gallon jugs of water. They set out a chemical fire extinguisher and battery-operated carbon monoxide and fire detectors.

Cockroaches scuttle from the light into dark spaces. Empty cans, wrappers and rotting food litter the floor. Others have used the garage as a refuge before them, fellow nomads who left behind graffiti messages and photos of loved ones covering part of one wall. Paul and the Kid explore the wall with their flashlights. The light beams play across the photos of the dead and missing, smiling in happier times before Infection.

IF YOU SEE THIS MAN DALE, TELL HIM JESSE IS ALIVE AND HEADING NORTH TO THE LAKE. THE INFECTED ARE NOT PEOPLE ANYMORE: KILL THEM OR BECOME THEM!! IF YOU ACT LIKE YOU ARE INFECTED THEY WILL NOT ATTACK YOU. ←THIS IS A LIE!!! IF YOU SEE THIS BOY, PLEASE TAKE CARE OF HIM AND TELL HIM MOMMY'S OK AND LOVES HIM VERY MUCH!!! INFECTION TAKES LESS THAN THREE MINUTES. THE ARMY IS SHOOTING ANYTHING THAT MOVES SO KEEP YOUR HEAD DOWN! KILL THEM ALL!! YOUNGSTOWN IS FREE OF INFECTION. ←LIE!! REPENT, FOLKS, THE END IS ~~NEAR~~ HERE!!!!

The survivors often have access to information such as the messages that others have scrawled on this wall in fear and boredom and need. As usual, almost none of it is useful.

"Do you think it's true, Reverend?" the Kid says. "Are the Infected not people anymore?"

"I don't know."

"Do they even have souls? Or have they already crossed over?"

"I don't know that either, Kid."

"What are they, though? Are they still men? Or animals? Machines?"

This time, Paul does not answer. His flashlight illuminates the faces on the wall, some of whom are dead, others Infected. It is hard to say what they are, he thinks. Whatever they are, they are not human, but they are still our loved ones. We still love them, perhaps even more than before Infection. When somebody is gone, it is easy to remember only the good things about them. No wonder so many people can't pull the trigger, and accept death or Infection themselves. When Sara came at me, I couldn't do it either.

"Is killing them murder, Reverend?"

"No," Paul says.

◆

Ethan takes out his dead cell phone and stares at it intently, wishing it would ring, before returning it to his pocket. He thinks of Philip, sweaty and grimy, sitting in the back of the Bradley with his tie neatly knotted at his throat and his briefcase open on his lap. As the disaster unfolded, the businessman tried for days to call his broker to buy stock in home security and healthcare companies. He drooled over the killing he would make shorting the airlines. He saw home-based power generation as the next big thing. He speculated about pharmaceuticals and trucking and water and agribusiness. The other survivors listened politely, blinking.

Philip's broker in New York would not answer the phone, making him steadily more anxious. Philip said economics was simply the study of who got the pie. Infection, like the Screaming, was just another economic shock creating new winners and losers, and those who could shift their investments from the losers to the winners quickly would earn the biggest return. But that required a broker who would answer his goddamn phone. It seemed particularly important to him that he convince Anne of his theories, but Anne would listen wearing the expression one usually brings out when rubbernecking a crash, and say nothing.

Philip started shouting into the dial tone, demanding share prices in Remington and Glock and Brinks. Then the grid failed and he lost his signal. He was cut off now and became quiet and morose. In Wilkinsburg, while picking through the ruins of a convenience store, he saw a copy of *The Wall Street Journal* with the wrong date, sat in the ashes, and let the Infected take him.

♦

They found the dead man in a dark corner, his feet sticking out from under a tarp, which they now pull back to reveal a desiccated corpse sitting with its legs spread and the top half of its head exploded up the walls behind it. The corpse wears a brown uniform. This man was an employee of the Allegheny County sheriff's office. His gun is missing. Somebody has taken his shoes.

Killed, or killed himself.

Wendy kneels next to the corpse and unpins the man's star-shaped badge.

"What are you doing?" Sarge asks.

"Collecting dog tags," she says tersely.

The soldier nods.

Anne approaches, her rifle slung over her shoulder, and tells them dinner will be ready in a few minutes.

"Does this place remind you of anywhere in particular?" Sarge says, watching her closely.

Anne looks around at the garage as if seeing it for the first time.

"I think I was born in a place like this," she says.

Sarge nods.

She adds, "We need to talk about that tank."

"We should have followed it," Wendy says.

"The tank was going to the Children's Hospital," Sarge tells them. "Just like us."

"An isolated unit, then," Anne says, nodding. "Just trying to stay alive."

"That tank was the first evidence of a functioning government we've seen in days," Wendy cut in. "It was a patrol. We could try to find the base where it came from."

"No," Sarge says. "The tank has no base. It is going to the hospital to shell it. That tank is going to rain fire on it with every bomb and bullet it's got."

"That can't be true." Anne is at a loss for words, it's so absurd. "Why?"

"Containment. They were ordered to do it. You have to admire the dedication even while you laugh at the stupidity. The hospital was overrun nine days ago and Infection has already spread far and wide. But just a few days ago the military shifted from containment using non-lethals to use of deadly force, so they ordered the hospitals, the source of Infection, to be attacked. The tank commander is only carrying out his orders, even if they came a week too late. Its infantry escort is gone now, its base has probably moved and every resentful shit-bird in the city is apparently trying to kill it, but that tank is going to complete its mission."

"How sure are you about this?" asks Anne.

Sarge shrugs. "I know how the military has been responding. It fits."

"So what do we do?" Wendy says.

"We find another hospital. Preferably one that isn't being bombed."

"There's Holy Cross, across the river," Anne offers.

"Which river?"

"The Monongahela. In the south."

They have already previously decided that a hospital is the ideal place to settle for several reasons. First, few people would even think to enter one. They are taboo places. Charnel houses. Unclean. After the Screaming, the Infected were picked up from the ground one by one and brought to hospitals, but there was not enough room, so the government requisitioned schools, hotel ballrooms, indoor arenas and similar spaces to accommodate the millions who had fallen down. The hospitals were filled to overflowing. The screamers were stacked like cordwood in the corridors. So many people required care that medical students were handed licenses and retired healthcare workers were drafted. When the Infected woke up three days later, they slaughtered and infected these people, making the hospitals epicenters for death and disease.

The hospitals are rich in resources, however, and they are defendable. Specifically, they have medical supplies, food and water, lots of space and emergency power. And most of the Infected are long gone, compelled to search for fresh hosts for their virus.

Anne adds, "It's worth the risk."

The three nod. The group's next move has been decided.

♦

Wendy touches Anne's elbow and motions her aside. The two women walk through the service garage, seeing everywhere the evidence of work abandoned suddenly by the mechanics.

"What branch did you serve in?" Wendy says.

Anne shakes her head almost imperceptibly.

"I appreciate your service," Wendy continues. "But I am the highest civil authority here. It would help if you acknowledged me as such in front of the others."

Anne regards the cop in the gloomy half-light from the camp's LED lanterns.

Wendy clears her throat and adds, "We have to function as a team."

"You know, I didn't believe in evolution before," Anne interrupts, inspecting a car muffler lying on the floor like the bone of a giant animal. "But now I do. We are natural selection in action. So many other people died because they wanted to die. They fought tooth and nail to survive but they didn't want to live while everybody they knew and loved died or became Infected."

"You're talking about survivor's guilt," Wendy says, nodding.

"Yes. We all have it. The question is whether you're going to let it kill you."

Ethan calls out to them, telling them supper is ready.

Anne turns to go back, pausing to add, "You go on taking crazy risks like you have to prove your leadership, and you will let it kill you."

Wendy stares at the woman for a moment, unable to speak.

"I'm just doing my job," she says finally. "I'm responsible for these people."

"That's fine with me. I don't care who's in charge. I'm just trying to find refuge and help the group find it, too."

"So you will acknowledge me then," the cop presses.

"No," says Anne.

♦

Before the world ended, the cop woke up alone at five each morning in her small apartment in Penn Hills. She showered, ironed her uniform and wolfed down an energy bar. She put on her crisp short-sleeve black shirt over a clean white T-shirt, then stepped into her black pants. She attached her badge and pins before pulling on her bullet-proof vest and Batman belt.

She reported to work at six in the morning carrying a tall cup of coffee. After roll call, she started up her patrol car, told the dispatcher she was in service, and drove to her patrol territory. Most of the time, the dispatcher called her about dogs barking, suspicious characters walking through backyards or hanging around playgrounds, loud music and domestic violence. She pulled over speeders and drunks, wrote up accidents and graffiti, gave people lifts to the nearest service station when their cars broke down. She isolated crime scenes and canvassed homes for witnesses to murders. Every so often she did a "park and walk," where she left her squad car and patrolled on foot for ninety minutes. Some days, she was so bored she could barely stay awake. Other days, so busy she ate nothing but donuts and Slim Jims. She watched other cops act aggressively to control every encounter, and tried to imitate that impersonal, in-your-face attitude. After several months on the job, she began to view most people as idiots who needed to be saved from themselves. She wrote tickets, threatened wife beaters, ate dinner in her car, waited for the next call on her radio. After a twelve-hour shift, if she did not have to work late, she went home.

Even though a large part of her job involved either cleaning up or eating other people's shit, she was proud of being a police officer and loved her job. Then the world ended and she never felt so important or needed. A part of her rejoices in being a cop in a lawless world. In the land of the blind, the one-eyed man is king.

◆

The survivors share corned beef cooked on the Coleman stove with stewed tomatoes and served on paper plates on a hot bed of cooked brown rice, with canned pears for dessert. As much as they are sick of food out of cans and crave fresh fruit and vegetables, they wolf down their meal. The Kid feels a sudden piercing stab of regret as he realizes he will probably never eat Buffalo wings again. It is odd to focus on such a trivial thing when faced with so much loss but he realizes that he is going to have to mourn the lost world one little bit at a time.

After dinner, Paul lights a cigarette and smokes in silence while the others take turns having sponge baths behind a nearby car. Wendy, breathing angrily through her nose and holding back tears, gets the solar/crank radio working.

"—not a test," a soothing, monotone, mildly British-sounding voice says. "This is the emergency broadcast network. This is not a test. Today's Homeland Security threat level is red for severe risk. Remain indoors. Obey local authorities. Avoid individuals displaying suspicious or aggressive behavior."

One by one, the survivors chime in with the announcer, almost chanting, "When encountering military units or law enforcement officials, place your hands on your head and approach them slowly and calmly. Do not take the law into your own hands. Respect life and private property—"

Sarge turns off the radio. "I think we can all agree that today was as bad as yesterday."

They nod glumly.

"On the other hand, Sergeant," Paul says, "I think we can also safely say that we're all still here. I would consider that one for the win column."

"Amen, Rev," the Kid says.

Anne returns from her sponge bath and nudges the Kid's shoulder.

"Here's that new toothbrush."

◆

Outside, they hear the howl of the Infected and the tramp of hundreds of feet. Distant gunshots and screams. Then it is so quiet they can hear the blood rushing through their veins. In the dim light of a lantern, Ethan accepts a sleeping pill from Wendy and dry swallows it. He lies on his bedroll in a T-shirt and shorts and relives his last conversation with his wife and child, and then becomes groggy. His last coherent thought before falling into a deep sleep is a vague recollection of a Greek myth in which sleep and death are brothers.

His nightmares are exhausting trials of lurid colors and feelings, extremes of good and evil, and symbols of guilt. He finally dreams of a warm evening at home, his wife pink and happy in a cherry bathrobe, holding their daughter on her lap in a rocking chair next to the toddler bed. The familiar ritual of getting ready for sleep. But the walls turn dark and sooty with ash and cluttered with graffiti tags and photos of missing children. A bullet hole appears in the window behind his wife's head. She is still smiling as she smells her daughter's hair, but her face has turned gray, her mouth and chin stained black. His little girl is not moving. He does not know if she is breathing.

His wife licks the back of her head, as if grooming her. As if tasting her.

# FLASHBACK: ETHAN BELL

Nine days ago, Ethan woke up in an empty bed with his heart pounding against his ribs. He found his wife in the bathroom, putting on mascara in front of the mirror with her mouth open, while Mary sat on the floor imitating her. Ever since the Screaming three days earlier, he found himself panicking when he did not know where his family was. He suffered nightmares in which they fell down screaming. He tried not to think of his students who actually did.

"I need coffee," he said. "Where are you going, hon?" He added a quick wave and grin at his daughter. "Hi, Mary!"

"Work," said Carol. "I have to work today."

"Hi Daddy," said Mary.

"But you weren't going to go to work until Thursday."

"Uh, today is Thursday, Ethan."

"No," he said, then smiled broadly for Mary, who was suddenly staring at him acutely, worried that he was upset. "You should stay home again today. A lot of people are doing that."

"Ethan, we talked about this," his wife said, her own smile genuine. "We're all still freaked out but the country has to get moving again. Too many things are up in the air. And we need money coming in. We have to eat."

Mary said, "No talking."

"The schools are still closed," he pointed out.

"They need room for the screamers."

"Don't call them that."

Carol snorted. "You actually want me to call them SEELS?"

"We should show a little respect, that's all," he grumbled.

Sudden Encephalitic Epileptic Lethargica Syndrome, or SEELS, was the more formal, if overly broad, term popularly used by scientists to describe the mystery disease. Other than naming it, scientists knew very little about it. Some said it reminded them of Minor's Disease, with its sudden onset of pain and paralysis caused by bleeding into the spinal cord. Some wanted to explore exploding head syndrome, others frontal lobe epilepsy, others maladies related to the functioning of the inner ear. A group of scientists wrote a letter to the President demanding widespread sampling of air, soil, water and people for novel nanotechnology agents, warning that the worst may be yet to come.

Equally puzzling was the ongoing exotic symptoms exhibited by some of the victims of the new disease. Echolalia, for example, the automatic repetition of somebody else's sounds. Echopraxia, the repetition of other people's movements. And, in some cases, "waxy flexibility," the victim's limbs staying in whatever position they were last left, as if made of wax. Nobody could explain why some people had these symptoms and others did not, just as they could not explain how the disease chose its victims, nor how it spread so quickly around the globe in a single day. There were very few real facts, only hundreds of theories that tried to force these facts to make sense.

"Look, Ethan. They'll reopen the schools soon. In the meantime, why not go to the school and see if you can volunteer at the clinic? A lot of people need care around the clock."

"Maybe," he said.

"It might do you some good," she said tartly, cutting him down with a single a glance at his tangled, curly red hair and stubble. "Get out in the sunshine a bit. It's time, Ethan."

"All right, I probably will," he lied. He had no intention of leaving the house. "Leave Mary here, then. Last night, when I was up watching some TV, there was some kind of rioting going on all over the west coast. I'd like to keep her close to home."

"We live in Pennsylvania. And Mary misses her friends at daycare. They're holding a special candlelight vigil today for the SEELS."

"No talking!" said Mary, upset that her parents were talking to each other and not to her. "My talking!"

Carol got down on one knee to talk things out with their two-year-old, asserting their adult right to have a conversation, but the fact was the conversation was over.

Ethan made a cup of coffee, kissed them goodbye, and went back to bed.

He woke up, feeling uneasy, to the sound of sirens in the distance. Sitting up, he yawned and pulled on a T-shirt and a pair of sweatpants.

Sunlight shined into the second floor bedroom picture window, which offered a spectacular view of downtown that had cost them an extra twenty thousand dollars on the house list price. Ethan and Carol moved to the city from Philadelphia during the previous summer, and she insisted on having a view. It was early afternoon. He needed another cup of coffee. Then he glanced out the window and saw plumes of smoke rising up from downtown, over which helicopters swarmed. There were a lot of sirens.

"Goddammit, I knew something bad was happening," he said, searching frantically for the TV remote before finally finding it under the bed. He clicked the television on and pulled on his glasses, blinking.

Riots spreading throughout the country, across the world in fact, focused on the hospitals and the clinics, following the same path as the screamer virus. Panicked mobs firebombing the clinics. Families of victims arming themselves and taking up positions outside the clinics. And the screamers, who had lain in a catatonic state for three days, were waking up and apparently committing acts of violence.

"Holy crap," Ethan said, his heart racing.

He dialed his wife, but all circuits were busy. Should he drive to the daycare and get Mary? Then drive to the bank and get Carol? What if she were already driving here? What if she were trying to call him right now? He hung up the phone and paced, racked by indecision.

He needed a moment to think. He tore off his sweatpants and put on a pair of jeans and socks. He went downstairs, turned on the TV in the living room and made himself coffee, which he drank scalding. Some anchor on the TV was sobbing through evacuation instructions.

"Nobody knows anything!" he shouted at his empty house.

He made another coffee and drank it in front of the TV, hitting redial on his phone repeatedly and continually getting an all-circuits-busy signal. Then the news cut to video recorded by a helicopter accompanied by the breathless monologue of a reporter describing the scene.

A group of people surrounded a family of four in a tightening circle in the middle of a busy downtown intersection, blocking their escape. The man stepped in front of his wife and kids. The other people rushed in. The man punched one and then they beat him and his family to the ground and kicked them for a while and tore the children limb from limb, stunning the reporter into shocked silence. The screamers began to eat their remains while the man and the wife lay on the ground twitching.

"Jesus Christ," Ethan said, almost in tears.

The reporter was screaming, *The SEELS are changing. Oh God, oh God, they're attacking people, they're attacking everybody they see, they're eating people.*

Ethan turned the TV off and went back upstairs to watch history unfold from his picture window. Towers of smoke dominated the downtown skyline. It was chaos down there. Across the street, he saw his neighbors' houses standing in a neat row facing him. One stood dark and silent, the living room window painted with streaks of dark fluid.

What is that? he wondered. Could they be here already?

Pale faces looked back at him from an upstairs window of the house directly across from his. The three Tillman kids. He could see their father, Roger, pacing furiously downstairs in the living room, holding one of his big hunting rifles. In the distance, an Army Chinook helicopter pounded over the city. Roger had the right idea: bunker down. Ethan stared at their house for a long time, trying to think about what came next: food, water, defense. But everything was fuzzy. He could not focus on these things beyond abstractions. He decided that he would pack some items in an emergency backpack and leave it by the door. He did not think they would need it but when Carol finally came home she would have wanted him to have done something constructive. He pictured himself showing her the backpack. He smiled glassily, taking a little comfort in the thought.

A hole appeared in the window with a sound like a wine glass breaking in the sink, jolting his consciousness. Roger Tillman stood on his porch, lowering his rifle and squinting up at him through a puff of gun smoke. Ethan backed away from the window in a dry-mouthed stupor, occasionally flinching as if prodded.

Why did Roger do that? he thought. Jesus, he could have killed me!

He retreated to the bathroom, locked the door and sat on the toilet, shaking. Long minutes passed and nothing happened. He sat there until he started to feel safe again.

The gunshot made him realize how serious the situation was. What am I doing here? he asked himself. I have to find my family. I have to find them now and get them to a safe place.

Ethan ran out to his car and drove to the bank and then the daycare but both were closed, locked and empty. He saw many terrible things but later he would remember the entire drive only as a blur. As darkness fell, he returned home and paced his house alternating between rage at Carol for not coming home and blind panic that what happened to that family on TV might have happened to his wife and precious little girl. He howled in torment like an animal until he realized that he was starving and needed food immediately. He drank more coffee instead and watched the news in the dark and hit redial on his phone repeatedly until he fell asleep.

He stayed at home for days waiting for Carol to bring Mary home. Each morning, he woke up hopeful and each night, he passed out from exhaustion in a state of near suicidal despair. The days began to blur together until the power failed. There were no more sirens downtown, only sporadic gunfire. He realized that he had plenty of meat in the freezer that he should cook before it spoiled, but the gas stove did not work either. He ate as much as he could from the refrigerator and washed it down with the cold dregs left in the coffee pot and then went back to staring at his cell phone, willing it to ring and feeling sick. He tried to pour himself a glass of water but the plumbing did not work. He had not filled the tub or any gallon jugs, only a few bottles for the backpack. For some reason, he had thought the plumbing did not need electric power to work. He stared at the faucet, feeling helpless rage at his own stupidity.

He tried to call his wife again but his cell phone could not get a signal. The collapse of the power grid had cut off phones, cellular communications and the Internet. Ethan was completely isolated from his family now. He knew all about the mathematics of probability. Finding them at this point would be like finding a needle in a haystack—a haystack soaked in gasoline and blazing. He spent the day overpacking two suitcases with clothes and provisions and put them by the door.

That night, he lay curled up in a fetal ball on the bed, crying into his wife's pillow, unable to even look inside his daughter's room, and smell her in the air, out of fear of losing his mind entirely. A machine roared to life outside and he got out of bed in the utter darkness, grateful for the distraction. Across the street, Roger Tillman had a generator going and the house blazed with light under a beautiful night sky filled with stars. Ethan watched, running his hand over his scraggly new beard, questioning his own manhood. That Roger really knew what he was doing. He had a gun, generator, food, water and his family under wraps. He had prepared for the apocalypse. He had thought of everything, while Ethan had whined and paced.

Black shapes and shadows flickered around the Tillman house. Suddenly a man came running out of the darkness into the pool of illumination created by the bright porch light. He bolted straight into the front door and bounced off it with a startling crash, howling in pain and rage. Then ran back again, and again. A woman appeared at the edge of the light on wobbly legs, dressed in a torn suit and holding onto her purse slung over one shoulder. Her head jerked in little spasms like a bird as she walked to the living room window and peered in as if looking for somebody to ask directions. She began punching the window repeatedly, finally putting her fist through it, her arm spraying blood until she fell to the ground twitching. Within minutes, the house was surrounded by growling people. Some of them began to crawl into the opening. Roger banged away at them with his rifle but now dozens of people, drawn to the light and noise, were pouring into every window and door. Jane Tillman was screaming like an animal, *Don't you touch them you motherfuckers, I'll kill you, I'll fucking cut you.* Roger was shouting, *Get back, get back, there's too many.* Shadows flickered inside the Tillmans' living room and a table lamp spilled, its bulb popping in a flash of light, plunging the room into darkness. The rifle banged several more times, the muzzle flashes lighting up the dark. Then the screams for mercy began.

Moments later, the house was quiet except for the buzz of the generator and the screamers stumbling around the illuminated porch, drawn like moths to the light and noise.

Ethan returned to his bed, curled up into a ball and fell into a deep, dreamless sleep until a crash jarred him awake.

Footsteps clomping downstairs. Somebody was in the house.

He almost called out, but didn't. He knew it was not Carol. He realized then that he had lost hope that she would bring Mary home, and that it was time to get out of this house if he wanted to survive the week. The threat of death was once miles away but now it was crashing through his front door and this fact electrified him. There are people in my house that cannot be spoken to or reasoned with, he thought. Things out of nightmares that are now wild animals and hunting me even though they are not yet aware of my existence. Creatures that will claw and bite me until I am dead or become one of them. Some of them wear faces that I know but they are no longer human.

The first step was to get out of the house.

Stepping quietly, Ethan got dressed. The sun was rising over a smoking America and its first rays provided a dim red light in the bedroom. He stuffed his pockets with photos and trinkets and a hairbrush from his wife's drawers. He found a tiny yellow rubber airplane on the floor, a toy carelessly left there by Mary days ago, and pocketed it. He suddenly wanted to take as much of them with him as possible. The floorboards creaked downstairs. He picked up his baseball bat and felt its reassuring weight in his hands. His suitcases were downstairs by the front door, ready to go. He tried to control his breathing. Here we go, then.

Footsteps in the den, the room he and Carol used as a home office. Moaning in a female voice, sad, plaintive. Whatever it was sounded more like a woman in mourning than a monster. As he descended the stairs, however, he could feel the air thickening around him as the woman sensed his presence and began growling deep in her throat. His heart pounded against his ribs. Books and papers crashed to the floor in the den. The woman yelped and paced, shouldering the walls as she moved. At least there was only one and not a pack of them in the house. He forced himself to breathe in and out, in and out, his bowels liquefying. Feeling the weapon in his hands, he felt a sudden stabbing urge to rush in there and bash her brains out, but the moment passed quickly, leaving him feeling dry-mouthed and drained and even more terrified.

Ethan slipped out of the front door, leaving it open, and began running to the car, which he had left parked on the street. Instantly, people in neighboring yards saw him and began howling, the sound echoing all over the neighborhood. Something snarled and thrashed through the rosebushes. Dropping the suitcases in a blind panic, he ran to the car, started the engine and stomped on the gas pedal just as a man threw himself against it, leaving a massive dent in the door. The car roared, building speed rapidly.

"Get out of the way!" he cried, jerking the wheel.

People were running out of driveways and lawns. The car jolted as a woman bolted directly into the passenger side window, cobwebbing the glass and leaving a red smear clotted with tufts of hair. A man surged into the back door, bounced off, and then ran alongside, pounding on the glass with bloody fists until losing his balance and falling hard onto the pavement. Ethan speeded up but then began weaving erratically, trying to avoid hitting an overturned truck and another man running at him from the open front door of a house.

"Oh God, no, please no," he begged, leaning on the horn.

The sound only attracted more. The shapes burst against the car like human missiles, impacting and bouncing off with heart-stopping bangs, leaving blood and cobweb fractures in the windows and dents in the body. Ethan drove past a burning house with a burning tree in its front yard, screaming his head off and gunning the engine again, plowing into a snarling young woman in a red dress who went flying over the roof. Another blurred against the door on his side, cracking its nose against the window and leaving a long squirt of blood.

"Stop it!" he screamed, almost blinded by tears. "Fucking stop it!"

The neighborhood began to turn from residential to commercial. He glanced into his rearview mirror and saw a horde of his neighbors shrieking at his heels. He suddenly became aware that an old Beatles song was playing on the car's speakers. After a few moments, his pursuers began to lag behind, and gave up the chase, glaring at him.

It's over, he thought, letting out a ragged sound that was part chuckle, part sob.

By the time he glanced back at the road it was too late to avoid the small mob running directly at him from the front. The car plowed into their bodies and flung them over the car like ragdolls. One became stuck like a nightmarish ornament, flailing with its one good arm, the crumpled hood spraying scalding water onto the body and the windshield. Ethan gunned the engine, half blinded, until the man, writhing and shrieking, detached and became caught in the right wheel hub, which ground and broke up the body with an awful cracking sound. The car jerked to the right and everything went black.

Ethan awoke on the sidewalk, stumbling away from his car that rested half-smashed against the wall of a department store. He tried to run, holding onto his backpack, and fell to his knees vomiting. People howled behind him. He heard the tramp of feet. One of the department store's display windows was broken and he climbed in, then began limping through the store past selections of men's ties and belts and leather shoes. Several men clawed their way in behind and gave chase at a loping gait, hunting him as a pack through the cosmetics department.

They steadily gained on him, yelping. They almost sounded happy. He ran blindly now, dropping his pack, seeing stars and gasping for breath. He had left the baseball bat in the car. One of the men appeared at his side, snarling. Moments later, he lunged and tackled a mannequin Ethan just passed and began beating and biting it. Another pushed over a second mannequin and began stomping on its face. The rest snapped at Ethan's heels. Inspired, he saw a mannequin at the end of the aisle and ran straight for it, his legs burning from a lack of oxygen.

The mannequin's fists belched flame and smoke. Ethan threw himself onto the ground as his pursuers toppled around him.

Ethan lay on his back, dripping sweat and gasping, unsure of whether he was going to laugh or cry when he finally caught his breath. He felt like his adrenal glands had been wrung out to the last drop. He looked up at his savior, a petite brunette dressed in a black T-shirt and jeans, her hair cropped in a military-style buzz cut. She had a hard look about her, as if she had been born to kill people and had been doing it for years. Her face was disfigured by fresh scars. Her eyes looked old.

She helped him onto his feet and handed him one of the pistols. She pointed at the wounded men who writhed and keened on the floor in widening pools of blood.

"Finish them and you can join us," she said.

That was how Ethan met Anne.

# THE HOSPITAL

The Bradley mounts the steel cantilever Liberty Bridge and begins crossing its five-hundred-foot main span over the Monongahela River at a careful pace. There are few abandoned cars cluttering the four-lane bridge but Sarge does not want to take any chances. He knows that a National Guard artillery unit destroyed several bridges in the area in a misguided effort to contain the spread of Infection, and does not want to drive through a big hole and plummet more than forty feet into the muddy waters below.

The density of vehicles thickens as they approach the other side of the river, blocked by abandoned makeshift barricades. Piles of stiffening corpses draw flies in front of a machine gun mounted behind a heap of sandbags. The Bradley speeds up and drives through the scene, popping skulls under its treads.

The Bradley enters the South Hills neighborhoods. Sarge opens the hatch for a look around in the open air and sees more barricades and piles of corpses. Some of the barricades apparently held; some were overrun. Either way, it did not matter. Even if they held, Infection was everywhere, eventually making barricades meaningless. Plastic bags and bits of garbage dance in the air, carried on the wind. A shredded T-shirt hangs on the branches of a tree, waving bye-bye at him, while another tree burns energetically like a giant torch, scattering heat and sparks and ashes. A pair of military jets fly high overhead, reminding him that the government is still fighting its own people.

The houses here are covered in graffiti. After the Screaming left more than a billion catatonics twitching on the ground all over the world, volunteers in these communities worked with local authorities to search each house for people and get them to a place where they could receive care. Orange posters are still taped to streetlight poles encouraging citizens to call tip lines to report SEELS for pickup. Black Xs are still sprayed on many doors marking houses that have been searched and cleared of victims of SEELS. The tragedy is that by helping the screamers avoid starvation and dehydration, these good people unwittingly aided in their own destruction. Some houses have other graffiti on them; as people fled their homes, they sprayed messages, and other refugees added their own, using the houses for communication. Names and dates. Missing persons. Directions and wayfinding. *Going south. Avoid the police station. Bill, I'm going to get grandma.* Other messages warn travelers of infestations, give opinions on everything from purifying water to effective killing methods, or offer trade. Some of the graffiti are simple tags. Newly formed militias claiming territory. Boasts of kills and time served. Totemic symbols scrawled by people in a hurry. Arrows. Biohazard signs. Skulls and crossbones.

The Infected stumble and hold their heads, wailing in a constant state of metaphysical pain. They glower and bare their teeth at Sarge as he drives by in the armored vehicle.

♦

The survivors find the tall, muscular man on his front porch wearing a bathrobe and boxer shorts, shouting and waving a pistol in his right hand and a battered, folded-up umbrella in his left. All of the neighboring houses have a large black X painted on their front doors; the Screaming apparently wiped out this community and left this man as its sole survivor.

"This is my neighborhood," he says, firing off a round with his pistol and killing a running Infected, who falls sprawling on the sidewalk, joining another draped over a fire hydrant and a third crumpled in a fetal position on the hood of an ancient Cadillac. "You ain't welcome here!"

The Bradley's gunner, sitting next to Sarge inside the vehicle, sizes up the man through the periscope and says, "I think we found somebody who might be big enough to take you, Sergeant."

Sarge snorts and says, "I like his spunk. He's a fighter."

"Spunk as in crazy," says the gunner. He has the square jaw of an action movie hero and wears a Dora the Explorer Band-Aid on the left cheek of his stubbled face. "Crazy as in a threat to all of us."

"If crazy disqualified membership, there'd be no club in this rig. Ha."

"I thought the plan was we want 'survivors, not fighters.' That's what you said."

"Fighters are useful, too," Sarge says cryptically. "We can't do job interviews, Steve. Let's invite him on. If he blends, he blends."

"You're the boss, Sergeant," the gunner says, shrugging.

The man roars: "Kids used to play on this street!"

*crack crack*

Sarge says, "Something about him reminds me of Randy Devereaux. Remember Devereaux?"

"Not really, Sergeant. I hardly knew him."

"Right," Sarge says. "You're right. That's my bad." Steve and Ducky, the driver, are new to the Bradley, replacements for the previous crew, who fell down during the Screaming nearly two weeks ago. Two weeks and an eternity. The replacements barely had any contact with the Bradley's infantry squad, the boys who survived the Taliban and the Screaming and then flew all the way back from Afghanistan to die in a Wal-Mart parking lot in Pittsburgh.

"This is a nice place to live!"

Sarge calls out to him, but the man ignores him. If he does not trust the military, maybe one of the civilians can coax him. Anne volunteers to get out and do the inviting. While the Bradley stands idling, she approaches with her hands up, palms out.

"What's your name?" she asks.

The man glares at her sideways, frowning, then waves her off. "Aw, you don't live here neither."

"My name is Anne. There are five of us plus the crew—"

The pistol cracks in the man's hand twice, dropping two distant running figures.

"I am making my stand!" he announces to the sky.

"Come on, get in," Anne says. "You can come with us."

"I said, step off, bitch!"

Sarge laughs, shaking his head, while the gunner grins.

"But we want you to come with us," Anne says.

"Too dangerous out there," the man tells her, waving his umbrella. "It's raining zombies!"

*crack crack*

He fires again several times at distant figures running down the street. At long range, barely looking, and does not miss. One of the kills, Sarge saw it clear, was a headshot. The Infected's head snapped back and he was dead in the blink of an eye.

Steve says, "Is he actually hitting anything with that pea shooter?"

"Yeah, he is. In fact, every shot hit a separate moving target and brought it down at between twenty-five and thirty meters."

"You're kidding."

"I'm not a kidder, Steve."

"With a handgun, though? Wow, this guy is amazing."

"No, you're right," Sarge says. "He's crazy. Radioactive."

He calls out to Anne, who jogs back to the vehicle.

"This is my home! My land!"

*crack crack crack*

Sarge lowers the telescopic seat and closes the single-piece hatch.

"How long do you give him, Sergeant?"

"I don't know, Steve. Longer than most. Not long enough."

◆

Paul runs his hand over his salt-and-pepper stubble and takes in the massive hospital looming against the graying sky. The air is cooling and he can feel the tickle of tiny drizzling raindrops on his face. Dull thunder grinds in the distant ether, as if God is moving his furniture across the floor. Now this is good weather for an apocalypse, he tells himself. A gray sky against which black birds swarm. He found the past two weeks of May sunshine jarringly discordant with the end of the world. The diseased walking blindly past flowers in bloom. (Earth abides.) The dead rotting away on lush green grass and overgrown gardens, slowly eaten by bacteria and insects and birds and animals. By the very soil. (Yes, the earth abides.) Paul wonders if God, who also abides, is as impervious as the weather to all of mankind's horrible sufferings or if, like the grass and the animals and the insects, his creator is getting something out of it.

◆

The wind picks up and the drizzle turns into a spring shower. The survivors set out buckets to catch the water and decide to wait out the downpour inside the hospital instead of the Bradley. They navigate a cluster of abandoned ambulances and dead bodies and enter what is supposed to be the emergency room but what instead looks like a burned-out slaughterhouse. Signs of extreme violence are everywhere on this place. The floor is littered with charred bodies under a thick layer of ash and dust. The walls are painted with dried blood.

"When the first Infected woke up and spread out into the city, the first responders brought the victims of the violence here, to the hospital," says Ethan. "Gift-wrapped for the rest."

"It looks like some concerned citizens then showed up and firebombed the place," Wendy says, kicking at the ash and raising a small cloud of black dust.

The place gives them the creeps. The hospital seems eerily deserted except for the charred dead. It is not hard to imagine doctors and nurses hurrying across this noisy room to greet hardworking first responders bringing in broken and dying people for life-saving treatment. But this is where Infection started. After the Screaming, the people who fell down were brought here and to the ad hoc clinics. Three days later, they woke up and slaughtered and infected the people who had been working around the clock to keep them alive. They slaughtered and infected their own families coming to visit. Then they went out into the city in the early morning hours, driven by the virus' simple programming: Attack, overpower, infect.

Now it is a killing floor. A dead place. Sarge regards a wheelchair crumpled in a corner, the walls above it riddled with bullet holes. Wall-mounted electronic medical devices hang uselessly. Disturbed by movement, black ash swarms in drifts in the air, acrid to the nose and bitter on the tongue.

Ethan studies the faces of the other survivors, searching for encouragement and finding none. The others look as damaged as he feels. The place has an almost supernatural aura about it. As familiar as the hospital is in some ways, in many ways it feels like the unknown.

◆

Paul wishes the dead had come back to life to eat the living. That there was truly no room in hell anymore and the end of days had come. Because then there would be evidence of a supernatural cause instead of just a bug created in a lab by men to kill other men. There would be evidence of a hell and true evil and Satan. And if there is a Satan, there is a God, and if there is a God, then death is not the end, but the beginning. Man's suffering over a lifetime is nothing compared to an eternity of bliss in God's direct presence. To see the dead rise is to see the end of days and with it, the end of faith—the beginning of certainty. With such certainty, Paul would willingly walk into the embrace of the dead and let them tear him apart and eat him. Did

Christ not suffer more on the cross? What use is this old fleshly cage when paradise awaits the spirit?

His wife had always laughed at him when he would watch quasi-religious films about Satan visiting the earth and trying to trigger the end of the world, only to be stopped by an action hero with a shotgun. He would cheer for Satan to get on with it. He would yell at the action hero: Why are you fighting God's plan? Let Satan win already so we can all go to heaven!

◆

"We can't stay in this room," Sarge says, finally breaking the spell. He crosses his arms and nods to Anne. "What's our next move?"

Anne shakes her head, looking back at him with raised eyebrows.

"We treat this like climbing a mountain," Wendy says. "It's too big. So we conquer it in stages. But first we need a base camp."

"Sarge has military experience, Wendy," Anne says quietly. "I think we should ask him what he thinks we should do."

Sarge nods at the transfer of authority, which he expected. "There are some simple tactics for taking down a building. Wendy, that analogy of yours was actually very good."

"Go ahead, Sarge," the cop says. "It's your show."

"All right," he says. "Here's how I see it. There are three things we need to do. One: secure a piece of this building for ourselves. Two: strip it down of anything that we can use that will keep us alive. And three: avoid obvious signs that the building has new ownership. We all agreed on that?"

The survivors nod.

"The crew and I will get the rig under cover. Out of sight, but not too far. Anne and Paul, find a janitor's closet and get as much bleach as you can. Then find a broom."

"You want us to clean this room?" Paul says, incredulous. "Just the two of us?"

"No. Later on, we're going to make it exactly as it was before we showed up. We'll need to get rid of our footprints and we'll need the broom for that. Okay?"

They nod.

"And while you're doing it, take a look and see what kind of supplies might be around that we can come back for later," Sarge adds.

"Got it," Anne says.

"Wendy, Ethan and the Kid will go up to the third floor, seal themselves in, and then start clearing it of anything living." Sarge grins. "Then we all get to do some cleaning. We will need to scrub that level from top to bottom with bleach and air it out before we can move in. But only the rooms on the side of the hall away from the windows. Don't clean the rooms with the windows, since again we don't want to advertise to anybody that the building has new ownership. Just seal those rooms and leave them. Okay? Once we get all that done, we can do some exploring."

The survivors agree. It is a good plan.

◆

When Paul's wife fell down during the Screaming, he arranged for her care in their home. The next day he visited the hospital, where exhausted first responders and volunteers were still delivering scores of twitching bodies, and tried to provide counseling and strength to the families of the victims. He expected the Spirit to tell him what to say but nothing came. Feeling hollow, he rolled up his sleeves and helped empty bedpans for hours. That night, he held a special service. The church was filled to standing room only, the few regulars and the many fair-weather Christians he was accustomed to seeing only at holiday services, many of them holding candles. There was no music or singing because the organist had fallen down and Paul had not arranged for a new one. There would be no collection plate because the ushers had fallen down and Paul had not replaced them either. Paul simply wanted to speak for a few minutes, and offer comfort to his flock through the power of prayer. He had no sermon planned. The Spirit would move him, would speak through him. Looking at all the anguished and weeping faces on the benches, he began by asking rhetorically why this happened.

For long, agonizing minutes, the Spirit said nothing. He was on his own.

He cleared his throat and said, "John, chapter thirteen, verse seven: 'Jesus replied, "You don't understand now what I am doing, but someday you will."'"

Several in the congregation nodded, encouraging him to continue, but he fell silent. It was not enough for him to say the Lord works in mysterious ways. Not nearly enough.

Why would God allow this to happen? He could not fathom it. The standard arguments raced through his mind justifying God's existence in a world in which God allows evil to happen to good people. *God's creation has free will and that includes the free will to do evil.* But what evil did his Sara do? *God allows evil to thrive in a world corrupted by original sin.* But were not the sins of Adam and Eve and everybody since, including Sara, washed away by the blood given by the sacrifice of Jesus Christ? *Evil is complementary to good.* But how could Paul see anything good in a world without his beloved wife?

*God is testing us. God is trying to teach us something.*

No, he decided. God is not just teaching.

God is punishing.

Paul told the congregation, "The good book also says: 'And if you fail to learn the lesson and continue your hostility toward me, then I myself will be hostile toward you. I will personally strike you with calamity seven times over for your sins. I will send armies against you to carry out the curse of the covenant you have broken. When you run to your towns for safety, I will send a plague to destroy you there, and you will be handed over to your enemies.' Leviticus chapter twenty-six, verses twenty-three to twenty-five. I intend to learn why these verses were written. I intend to learn the lesson God is trying to teach us through such harsh discipline."

His congregation did not like his message. They did not want to be forsaken. They wanted answers. They wanted comfort and mercy. They stared back at him with terror.

The Old Testament God of justice was back, and Paul, who had worshipped and studied and preached the good news of the New Testament God of mercy and love all his life, did not know what God wanted from him. For two days, he prayed. Sometimes he prayed for understanding. But mostly he prayed that God would show mercy and bring his Sara back to him.

Two nights later, his wife got out of bed in her nightgown, her face gray and her eyes black and cold as a serpent's, and lunged shrieking for his throat.

◆

The survivors climb the stairs to the third floor. Wendy and the Kid volunteer to clear it while Ethan guards the stairs so that nobody can get in or out. They left him huddled in a corner, terrified at being alone.

The Kid walks ahead of Wendy, scoped carbine shouldered and ready to fire, jerking the barrel back and forth as he scans for targets, although he is not paying much attention to what he is doing, instead imagining what he looks like to the beautiful blond cop. He wonders if Wendy is impressed with his warrior skills. He wishes his carbine had a laser sight. She walks behind him, treading slowly, holding her Glock in her right hand and a flashlight in her left. Their footsteps disturb a thick layer of dust carpeting the ground.

The Kid suddenly bends over with an explosive sneeze, followed by another.

"Shit," he says, his face burning. "Sorry about that. That wasn't very *ninja*."

The cop smiles grimly. "We're not trying to be *ninja*. We're here to clean up, not sneak around."

"Oh, right."

"You know, I'm never going to get used to calling you Kid."

His mind is reeling. "You don't like it?"

"I'd rather call you by your real name."

"It's Todd," he says quickly. "But don't tell anybody else."

"I promise," she says with a smile. "It's our secret."

He says nothing, flustered and afraid he might blurt out something stupid and irrecoverable.

Wendy motions for him to stop. "You ready to shoot that gun, Todd?"

He nods.

"Then let's clear this hallway." The cop calls out, "Hey! Hello? Anybody home?"

A woman bursts out of one of the recovery rooms, dressed in hospital scrubs stained with dried blood down the front, and begins jogging towards them with a bark. The survivors flinch, their hearts racing. Immediately, the ammonia smell of piss assaults their nostrils, making their eyes water.

"Who?" says the Kid.

"You," says the cop.

The Kid wishes he could have set his rifle to full auto and let it rip like in the movies, but Sarge said not to do that. Sarge said you do not need suppression. You just need to stop somebody, running right at you, with as few rounds and as little energy as possible.

The Kid does not aim at the woman's head, which offers only a small, lurching target. Instead, he aims at her center torso and squeezes the trigger, firing a single burst of three bullets.

The center of the woman's chest explodes and she stumbles, wincing and smoking, before bouncing off a wall and toppling to the floor.

The man turns the corner and lunges at them from behind. Wendy wheels and fires her Glock. The bullet enters his left eye socket, scrambles his brain and shoots the mess out the back of his head. He collapses instantly without a sound, dead before he hits the floor.

"Nicely done," the Kid says weakly, feeling drained.

"I swallowed my gum," Wendy says.

The corridor suddenly echoes with howls and the tramp of sneakers, dress shoes, high heels, bare feet. Wendy and the Kid freeze, breathing hard, standing back to back with guns ready.

A lot of people are coming.

♦

Sunlight cannot reach this part of the building where it is now perpetual night. The corridor connects the emergency room with the guts of the hospital. Paul and Anne explore its length, searching for supplies, anxiously aware of the sound of their breathing and footsteps. Paul lights the way with a highway flare, revealing bloody handprints on the wall in glaring detail. Beyond several feet, the light is quickly swallowed in the gloom. Bodies lie on the floor surrounded by small clouds of flies. The air reeks of bleach and rot. Water drips loudly somewhere close. A door slams, far away. Paul's shoes crunch on the scattered remains of a smashed jar of tongue depressors. Rats scamper along the walls before disappearing into the dark.

"I made a mistake, Reverend," Anne says, shattering the silence.

"What kind of mistake?"

"The kind you regret."

Paul grunts. He does not know what to say. This is survival. He does not think it is possible for somebody to be alive today without having regrets. He is trying hard to keep his moral compass aimed in the right direction but the harsh truth is morality is a luxury at a time like this. There is plenty of guilt to go around. He wishes there were just a little forgiveness. But even guilt is a luxury reserved for those still alive and feeling safe enough to experience it.

He pauses in front of a door and holds up his flare.

"'Custodial,'" Paul reads. "I think this is it. It's unlocked."

Too late, he realizes that Anne was not talking to him as a fellow survivor. She was speaking to him as a man of the cloth. Sorry, lady, he wants to say, that well has run dry at the moment. He realizes that he knows so little about the people on whom his life depends on a daily basis. He glances at this petite woman holding her powerful scoped rifle and the satchel filled with ammo and thinks, take the gun away and she could be a housewife. A dentist. An actress doing local theater. President of the PTA. The only part of her he has really cared about, however, is her natural talent with the rifle that has helped keep him alive for so long while other men, better men, have died.

"Reverend, did you have to kill somebody you love?"

Paul remembers Sara getting older and how on some level he saw her as a mirror reminding him that he was getting older. He did not like it. Death? Beats getting old, Sara used to say. She had a great attitude about it. He frequently wondered about the strength of his faith if he was afraid of getting old and dying. But even then his mortality was still just a frightening abstraction, not like the past nine days, during which he has been continually, painfully aware of the thin ice separating life and death. You walk along and suddenly you fall through and then either there is a heaven or there is only oblivion. Sara used to joke, if you want to be remembered for a really long time after you're gone, die young.

He remembers lighting a cigarette in the alley behind his house several nights after the Screaming. So late at night it was practically morning. He had tossed and turned and barely slept. The neighborhood twenty-four hour convenience store was open and he bought a pack of cigarettes to satisfy an incredible, sustained craving he felt immediately upon waking up. Now here he was smoking for the first time in years. Beating an addiction takes belief in a higher power, and while his faith in God helped, the strength of his marriage got him to finally kick the habit. Now Sara was lying on a bed inside his house, connected to an intravenous bag, and here he was standing in the alley lighting up and blinking at the immediate head rush. He coughed but by the third drag he was hooked again. Like riding a bike. He enjoyed the quiet. A dog barked and then stopped. For the first time in the past few raw days, he felt something like an inner peace. At least one itch had finally been scratched.

A figure appeared under the streetlight at the end of the alley, a small silhouette. Paul squinted at it for a few moments, unsure it was even a person until he realized it was growing larger. Moving towards him. It passed a light fixture mounted on a neighbor's garage and Paul caught a glimpse of its terrible face. It was breathing hard and running at Paul as fast as the average human being can run. It was doing the hundred yard dash and Paul was the finish line. For several critical moments, Paul was outside his body, watching himself do nothing. He was not sure he could move; his legs had turned to water.

He started to feebly ask, *can I help you*, barely finishing the sentence before turning and sprinting back into his backyard and locking the gate behind him, his heart hammering in his chest. He sensed the man pacing outside the gate, hissing like an animal.

He walked carefully back to his house on wobbly legs, still filled with dread.

Inside, Sara was sitting on the edge of her bed. Waiting for him.

"No," Paul says. "I haven't killed somebody I love. Have you?"

"Yes," Anne says.

♦

The doors at the end of the corridor burst open and a snarling man races through. The Kid fires a burst that obliterates his face and then falls back, continuously firing and dropping bodies as a swarm of Infected pours into the corridor, filling it with their horrible, sour stench.

Wendy keeps pace at his side, the beam of her flashlight glittering across red eyes, covering him with her pistol. The Kid's gun jams and he stares at his weapon in numb surprise. The cop empties the Glock into the snarling faces, drops the mag, loads another. The Kid wrestles with the bolt until a howling woman claws at his eyes. Holding the carbine sideways in front of his body for protection, he slams it into her gray face on impulse, breaking her nose. She falls back howling and a giant of a man in a paper hospital gown stomps towards him with clenched fists like sledgehammers, roaring. The top of his head erupts in a geyser of blood and he disappears. Wendy is still shooting, burning quickly through the next magazine. The first woman comes back and wrestles with the Kid for the carbine, her jaws chomping in a blind rage. He hears a scuffle and the crack of the cop's police baton striking bone. The Kid shoves the woman against the wall and smashes the carbine into her face repeatedly until she slides down the wall leaving a smear of blood. Panting, he turns and sees Wendy fighting two men twice her size and kicking the shit out of both of them with her side-handle baton. He clears the jam out of his carbine and signals to her, murder in his eyes. She backs away just in time for him to gun them down with several bursts from the hip.

They stand quietly for several moments, unable to speak or move, utterly drained. Just breathing. A pall of gun smoke hangs in the air. The cordite bites their nostrils, competing with the bitter smell of blood and the rank stink of the dead Infected.

"You kick ass," he says finally.

"It's the training."

"That was way too close."

"We're going to be okay."

"You'll have to teach me your judo skills sometime."

"Wait," the cop says. "Do you hear that?"

The Kid shakes his head, trying to get rid of the ringing in his ears.

"I can't hear anything," he says.

Ethan, Anne and Paul rush into the corridor, breathing hard.

"We heard the shooting and came as fast as we could," Anne says.

"Sounded like a war up here," Paul says. "You okay, boy?"

"We're okay," the Kid tells him.

"Quiet," the cop says. "Something is coming."

♦

The survivors train their light and weapons on the doors at the far end of the corridor. A strange sound comes to them that slowly reveals itself as something familiar. Chewing. The sound of an animal chewing a piece of meat, oddly amplified.

"What the hell is that?" the Kid says, wincing.

A fresh wave of sour milk stench assaults their nostrils with an almost physical force.

"God, that smell makes me want to puke," the cop says.

"Don't even say that word or I'll actually do it," Ethan says, pale.

"Wait," Anne tells them. "Quiet."

A baby is crying.

Ethan takes two steps forward before Anne reaches out and grips his arm, holding him back.

"It's a baby," he says, his eyes wild. "A little baby. Oh, God."

Paul grunts in surprise, holding his dying flare. A baby in the hospital, alone in the dark. A miracle baby. How did it survive? What has it been eating? Is it Infected?

"That's not a child," Anne says.

The creature pushes the doors open and slithers through. The survivors flinch and take a step back with exclamations of horror and revulsion. It is a giant worm, half as thick as a car and twice as long, with an enormous blank face made up of wrinkled folds of skin. The creature appears to be blind, propelling itself towards them using tiny appendages, something like a cross between giant warts and tentacles, that cover its body. It looks sick, its body pale and grayish and covered in purple bruises, trembling as it slithers, starving.

Ethan sobs in horror, unable to comprehend the existence of such a repulsive thing. His concept of reality is disintegrating. It is as if the map of the world were now blemished with big blank spaces marked with the thickly scrawled warning: HERE BE MONSTERS.

The worm plows into the dead, pushing the corpses against the sides of the corridor.

"Can it see us?" Wendy says.

The monster shivers at the sound of her voice, pausing in front of one of the bodies and nuzzling its hair. The massive blank face cracks open, revealing a gaping black maw ringed with sharklike teeth. It promptly begins to absorb the corpse headfirst with a slurping sound.

"Oh, God!"

The creature shudders, then resumes its feast, cracking bones. Chewing.

"I'd like to leave now," Ethan says, shaking.

"What do we do?" says the Kid. "Anne? What are we going to do?"

The creature shivers again, mewing like a baby wanting milk.

Anne shoulders her rifle and says, "Kill this fucking abomination."

♦

Gunfire instantly fills the corridor as the survivors vent their fear and revulsion, screaming bloody murder and draining their magazines. The worm abandons its grisly meal and lurches forward, its movements jerky in the strobing light of the muzzle flashes. The bullets sink into the mottled flesh of its face with no apparent effect.

Ethan lowers his smoking carbine, feeling helpless. How can it be killed? Does it even have a heart or a brain? Even if it were just a giant worm without a brain or heart, the amount of ordinance they are throwing at it should be tearing it to shreds, and yet here it comes. The creature appears to have some type of bony plate on its face that is thick enough to absorb their firepower. He sees it differently now, not as an aberration but as a form of life perfectly designed for tunnels. That would mean it is vulnerable on its sides but not its front.

What about its other end?

Something whirs in his brain and clicks.

He roars at the survivors, *"GET BACK!"*

The creature's rear end leaps into the air, revealing itself as a second head with another hissing mouth ringed by giant sharp teeth, and lunges forward with surprising speed and force, leapfrogging its front and landing among the screaming survivors, scattering them. Wendy pauses at the top of the stairs, squeezing off a few more shots with her Glock before following the other survivors down.

"Keep going," she calls. "It's right behind us!"

They exit the stairs and enter the emergency room. Anne points to the Bradley parked outside in front of the large floor-to-ceiling windows, the barrel of its 25-mm automatic turret-mounted gun aimed directly at them. Slanted rain pelts the armor. Sarge sits in the open hatch, waving at them frantically.

"Out of the way!" Anne screams.

"Everybody get down!"

The cannon fires, shrouding the vehicle in smoke. The windows burst and the inside of the emergency room dissolves in a series of flashing explosions and enormous clouds of smoke and dust. The survivors are on the ground, their faces buried in their arms and eating ash. The vehicle trembles as the gun fires again: BUMP BUMP BUMP BUMP BUMP BUMP, vomiting empty shell casings down its metal chest onto the ground. And again. And again.

The firing finally stops. The dust and ash swirl in black clouds.

The survivors are screaming.

♦

Sarge climbs out of the Bradley gripping his AK47 rifle, leaps down onto the ground, and races into the hospital, shouting names. The impossible creature he saw is now a quivering, smoking ruin smeared across the floor. He hopes he has not killed the other survivors in the bargain. The Bradley's cannon is a sledgehammer, not a scalpel, and it is best to be nowhere near where its rounds are falling and exploding if you want to live. He had no choice; he heard all the shooting upstairs and revved up the Bradley and brought it back in case the others needed to make a quick exit. He calls the others' names again and is relieved to hear voices shouting behind reception. He finds the others, covered in black ash, ringed around the Kid, who sits on his knees, holding a bleeding wound on his arm. The cop is screaming and pushing her Glock against his head while he pleads for his life and the others shout at her and each other, waving their weapons.

"It's dead," he says, wiping rain from his face. "The thing is dead."

"We've got a bigger problem right now, Sarge," Anne says.

"My point is we're okay now. So let's just be cool and lower all these guns."

"He got cut by the thing's teeth," Anne says. "Wendy is right. He could turn."

"I'm not doing anything unless that happens," the cop says.

"How long is incubation?"

"Somebody his age and size . . . Three minutes, tops."

"Who has a watch?"

Ethan spits on the face of his watch and rubs it with his thumb.

"Counting down," he says.

"I'm just trying to protect us!" Wendy says, panicking.

"You're doing the right thing," Anne tells her. "You're doing fine, Wendy."

"I don't want to do this," she says, tears streaming down her face.

"We know. The Kid knows it, too."

They wait. Ethan marks the time out loud. The survivors hold their breath while the Kid listens to his life ending in ten-second increments. He had pictured a heroic end for himself but this is getting put down, covered in filth, like an animal. After everything he has been through, he will die from a friend's bullet. He wants to remember something important, hold onto a beautiful memory or thought he can take to the other side with him, but his mind is a raw blank. He wants to pray but all he can remember is the one he used to recite each night as a child.

"Now I lay me down to sleep," he rasps quietly. "I give thee Lord my soul to keep."

The survivors slowly back away in a widening circle, coughing and fingering their weapons.

"And if I die before I wake, I pray thee Lord my soul to take."

He clenches his eyes shut as Ethan counts down the final ten seconds of his short life.

"Zero," Ethan says, visibly deflating.

"But I'm still me," the Kid says.

He laughs until it turns into hysterical crying. Wendy drops to her knees and hugs him. Sarge jogs back to the Bradley to get the med kit.

"I'm so sorry," she tells him, her tears joining his. "I'm so, so sorry."

"I want my mom," he says.

♦

Todd Paulsen sits numbly on the floor in the glow of an LED lantern in one of the recovery rooms. Anne unscrews the cap on a plastic gallon jug and pours water into a bucket. Todd wearily pulls off his ruined bullet-proof vest, ripped and slashed by the thing's teeth. He is skinny and normally does not like taking his shirt off in front of other people, but right now he does not care. He peels off his T-shirt and reaches to scratch a spot between his bony shoulder blades. He feels hollow, empty. Completed drained. If he were not so scared of never waking up he would be asleep already. He did not know death was so terrifying. It had always been an abstraction to him, sometimes even a romantic one. He could afford such foolishness before today because he had been immortal. Now death is in his hair and skin. It lurks in the empty space between the beats of his heart. Non-existence. Nothingness. And all the world with its beauty and horrors will go on without him as if he never existed. What was it the preacher was always saying? The earth abides. The earth, in other words, does not give a shit.

Todd takes the sponge from Anne and goes through the motions of washing himself. His arms are filthy with ash, the black dust contrasting strangely against his pale torso, gleaming white like a dead fish. He is ashamed of his body and his weakness. He cried in front of them. The adults. He faced death and he cried. He could not think of even one beautiful memory. And worst of all, at the moment he thought he was about to die, he could not remember his mother's face.

"Would you rather be alone?" Anne asks him.

Todd shakes his head numbly. He is already alone.

Anne says, "Here, let me help you."

She takes the sponge, wrings it out, and begins wiping down his face and neck.

Somebody knocks at the door. Sarge enters carrying his helmet, filling the space with his large frame.

"We need to talk, Anne."

Anne glances at Todd and shakes her head slightly.

Sarge nods. He squats in front of Todd, who cringes, his expression vacant.

"How's the arm?" he says, pointing at the bandage covering the boy's wound, which Sarge carefully cleaned and stitched up with needle and thread.

Todd does not answer.

"Keep it clean, soldier," the soldier adds. "The bug going around ain't the only infection we got to worry about."

"I'll take care of him," Anne says. "You might want to check on Wendy."

Sarge appraises Todd with a hard stare and a tight smile. "I just wanted to say you did real good today, Kid. You're a tough little sumbitch, you know that?"

After he leaves, Anne nudges him and whistles.

Todd smiles.

◆

Wendy sits on a sheet of plastic on the edge of the bed in another recovery room, her hands shaking. Slowly, she removes her Batman belt—heavy with handcuffs, gloves, gun, TASER, baton, leather notebook, extra magazines and pepper spray—and sets it carefully on the plastic beside her. She takes off her badge and pins and places them next to the belt. She unbuttons her uniform shirt, balls it up and puts in a plastic bag. She unhooks her bra, grimy and soaked through with sweat, and hangs it to dry out. After a quick but thorough wash, she examines herself in the mirror, brushing her wet, tangled hair. She recognizes the face and body but her eyes look like somebody else's. Her face and perky chest earned her a lot of attention from the other cops but prevented them from fully accepting her. Wendy knows she is physically beautiful; she heard it said enough times to be sure. She knows it made them want her. She knows it made them angry. Then it saved her life when the man who had hurt her most told her to leave and save herself when the Infected came howling through the door.

She raises her left arm and frowns, inspecting a thin red line across her ribs. The creature's razor-sharp teeth grazed her flesh. Not deep enough for stitches but enough to draw blood. Enough to plant virus and infection.

Christ, she was about to shoot Todd in the head and she was on Infection's doorstep herself.

Would she have done it?

If she had to do it, then yes, she would have. Murder one or help to murder all.

Would she have then shot herself if she felt herself turning?

Yes, she told herself. More readily than shooting one of the others, in fact. The realization surprises her.

Most of the other cops never accepted her and yet she was still a cop. Many cops at the station had an us-against-them mentality about the communities they policed. Wendy was trained in that culture and adopted it as her own. She was still one of "us." Nobody had as much authority as she had when she patrolled the neighborhoods. Up until she held her gun against that teenage boy's head, she saw the other survivors as civilians, people who were not her equals but instead her ungrateful charges. She no longer feels that divide. We are becoming a tribe, she thinks.

Somebody knocks and she tells them to wait a moment while she pulls on a black T-shirt, making a mental note to put antiseptic on the cut given to her by the monster, which carried God knew what germs in its rancid mouth besides Infection.

Sarge enters the room, glancing up and down and nodding appreciatively. It is so subtle that he does not realize he is doing it, but Wendy can read the language of attraction without trying. She pointedly looks away, pinning her badge to her belt. The soldier clears his throat and gets down to business immediately.

"I brought you some more water so you can wash your hair if you want," he says.

"Just did it. See?"

"Roger that," he says. "Well, take it anyway, for later. It's rainwater."

"Does the building not have any water in its tank?"

"It does. A lot, in fact, but we're saving it for drinking and cooking. Tonight, we are washing with good old rain."

"Well, thank you," she tells him. "So what's our situation?"

"Steve and Ducky swept the rest of the floor. It's clear. No Infected and no giant slugs with teeth either. I think we're secure. Now we're clearing out the bodies and cleaning up the place."

"You need a hand?"

"No, no, no. This is just a social call. You rest. You've been through hell."

The cop sits on the bed, sighing. "All right."

"Hey, uh, Wendy . . ."

"Yes?"

The soldier takes a deep breath and says, "I wanted to say thanks."

"For what?"

"For what you said about my boys yesterday. I appreciate what you said. So, thanks."

◆

Ethan, Paul and the Bradley's crew drag the bodies downstairs on plastic sheets, change spilling out of the corpses' pockets. This work done, they mop with a strong bleach solution. The gunner and the driver retreat to one of the recovery rooms to set up the Coleman and try to get supper going. The idea of food makes Ethan want to vomit. Wincing at the sting of the bleach, he and Paul decide to try the roof. The hospital has turned out to be a chamber of horrors, and they are craving some fresh air and a little time and space to wrap their heads around everything they have seen.

He immediately regrets it. The stairwell is pitch black. The air is stale and musty. He cannot remember how high the floors of the hospital go, or what fresh terrors await him up there in the dark. His clumsy footfalls sound like thunder in the stillness. After three flights, his knees and lungs begin to protest.

He cannot stop thinking about the wormlike creature that attacked them. That these things were another of the horrible children of Infection is obvious. But are they a mutation, a freak? Or an entirely new life form? Were they once men? Or has the virus jumped species? He has a terrible feeling that the emergence of this creation may be a sign of a fundamental shift in the ecology of the planet. The Infected violently spread disease and cannibalize the dead; they are a plague and an enemy that has humanity on the run, and that is bad enough. But this is new. The balance of nature is changing. A new world is coming in which humans are no longer at the top of the food chain. The thing appeared to be a bottom feeder, another eater of the dead. There is plenty of food to sustain a large population of these monsters, depending on how much they need to eat. What will happen when they can no longer feed on the dead?

It took a 25-mm cannon to kill it . . .

They reach the top of the stairs and find the door unlocked. Some of the hospital staff must have fled onto the roof to get away from the Infected rising out of their beds. But the roof is bare of the living or the dead. Ethan walks carefully, feeling exposed under the massive twilight sky.

The rain has mostly stopped but the ground is still wet and the air feels heavy and humid. They walk to the parapet. Over the roofs of the houses and low-rise buildings, they see downtown Pittsburgh in the distance, across the river. The tall buildings stand dark and derelict. The Grant Building is on fire and veiled in white smoke, an incredible sight. Pillars of smoke rise up from a dozen smaller fires scattered across the city. They hear the distant crackle of gunfire at the Allegheny County Jail to the east.

"Reverend, why did those people leave their photos in that garage?"

"I don't understand you."

"The parking garage where we stayed last night. People passing through there before us left photos of their families and friends on the wall. Why did they do that?"

"Just saying goodbye, I guess," Paul answers.

"I don't think I want to say goodbye," Ethan says.

Paul shakes his head and says, "I don't even know how."

Bonded by their grief, the men watch the sun go down and the Grant Building burn in the twilight. Even after everything they have gone through, it is still sometimes hard to believe what has happened to the world they once lived in. People and buildings and phone calls and TV shows and grocery shopping and the normal pace of life. The gray sky occasionally spits. Over time, the warm rainwater collects in their hair and on their faces, slowly washing away the ash and the filth. They stand there without speaking for over an hour, Paul slowly chain smoking his cigarettes.

This high up, the apocalypse seems almost peaceful.

"The end of the world doesn't happen overnight," Paul says, nodding. "It takes time."

The sky is quickly turning dark. They decide to turn back. Ethan notices that somebody sprayed the words HELP US in bright orange paint across the hospital roof.

"It may never end," he says, feeling homesick.

# FLASHBACK: WENDY SASLOVE

The Screaming changed everything. Millions of people lay helpless and twitching on the ground. Thousands died in accidents. Fires burned out of control. Entire towns suffered without electricity or running water. Devastated survivors walked numbly through the streets. Distribution of everything from food to Internet access to Social Security checks was completely disrupted. Entire industries such as insurance folded overnight. Government and businesses struggled to continue operating as one out of five people simply fell down, broke everything in the process, and took all their knowledge with them in a massive brain drain. The country reeled from the shock.

Seventy thousand people fell down in Pittsburgh alone. The police department was devastated. Roughly three hundred out of nearly nine hundred police officers had either fallen down or simply taken their guns home, locked their doors and refused to return to duty. Burglaries were up as people broke into homes abandoned by the fallen. Arson was rampant as communities, terrified of another outbreak, burned homes with the screamers still inside. Frightened people were taking their guns to the local grocery store, which devolved into scenes of panic buying and looting. The cops remaining on the job dug in, marked their territory and held it with force. They cracked skulls and exchanged gunfire with street gangs and vigilantes. They cleared the streets and protected firefighters and helped to recover the fallen. The police stations became forts in hostile territory. They were used to dealing with murderers and drug dealers and other criminals. Now everybody was the enemy.

The cops worked around the clock. In just three days, they already made a difference. The power was on, food was being delivered to stores, and the fires were under control. For now, that was enough. They were gearing up for another big push to recover the fallen. Humans can live up to nine weeks or longer without food, but cannot go more than about six days without water. Thousands were still missing and had to be found and transported to one of the new emergency clinics as quickly as possible.

Meanwhile, people continued to gather at the hospitals each day. Most were pilgrims searching for missing loved ones. It was common to find screamers without any identification on them as their wallets were stolen. Sometimes, screamers were found without any clothing at all, as they had been raped while lying helpless on the ground. The pilgrims arrived filled with hope, clutching photos of friends and family, and stood in line all day waiting their turn to go inside, sit in front of a computer, and try to track down their loved ones in the SEELS database. As a counterpoint, several hundred people also arrived each day shouting and carrying angry signs and concealed weapons. Terrified of another outbreak, they demanded stronger isolation measures for the fallen, calling for their removal to quarantine camps outside the city.

These two groups of people naturally hated each other and were kept separated by an aggressive line of police officers mounted on horses. A line of riot police guarded the front of the hospital, intimidating in their black body armor, helmets with clear plastic visors, yard-long hardwood batons and tactical riot shields. Three-man arrest teams formed a second line.

Wendy was in one of these teams. In the old days, the cops used to form a line and charge, bashing skulls until the street emptied, but the tactics changed over the years. Now snatch teams were sent into the crowd to strategically arrest troublemakers and remove them from the scene. The idea was to prevent a protest from turning into a riot that could suddenly rage out of control. They barely had the resources to counter protests. A large-scale riot might spread and become the end of law and order in Pittsburgh. They had arrested eight people already, rushing into the crowd behind her body shield while the two men with her took down the troublemaker they wanted.

Word was being passed down the line that the new Mayor had had enough of the protests and was cutting off all public access to the hospital at four o'clock.

The cop on Wendy's left, Joe Wylie, shook his head and spit.

"Bullshit," he said. "This ain't no Nazi state. Shit, I lost people in the Screaming, too. These people have a right to find their family."

"We don't have the manpower," said Archie Ward. "Or, in Barbie's case here, girl power."

Wendy said nothing, staring forward wearing an expression of sullen professionalism. She knew better than to take the bait. She chewed her gum.

Archie added, "The Mayor's right. These people here tie up how many cops every day? We don't have enough people. We're running on empty, Joe."

"I don't mind the overtime. And right is right."

The sergeant was shouting into his megaphone, telling the crowds to disperse.

They refused, screaming, *No!*

Another sergeant, the overweight old cop they called John-John, sang out in a comical World Wrestling Federation voice, "Get ready to rumble!"

"What do you think, Barbie?" Joe said.

"Doesn't matter what I think," Wendy said, shrugging. "We got our orders."

"Shut the fuck up," Joe said.

"Jesus Christ, rookie," Archie said. "You're either the dumbest broad or the best politician I've ever met. Either way, you'll go far at the Pittsburgh PD."

The words hurt her, as usual, but she would never give the other cops the satisfaction of knowing just how much they did. Her expression never changed just as her opinions were always neutral and noncommittal.

The line of mounted police cantered off of the street. The phalanx of cops in front of the hospital pulled on their gas masks. Some began clashing their batons against their shields, and the rest joined in. Wendy knew these men. Despite their sympathies for one or even both factions, they were hoping the crowd would refuse to disperse and they could let off some steam stomping ass. Joe and Archie were grinning, bashing in a warlike rhythm.

The cops began firing tear gas grenades, which burst in brilliant white clouds. The crowds recoiled from the growing pockets of swirling cloud, people crying and sneezing and gasping and coughing in agony as the gas attacked the mucous membranes in their eyes, nose, mouth and lungs. The cops lowered their visors and crouched, tense, waiting for the signal.

Wendy felt a strong hand grab her ass and squeeze.

"Too bad you're not a screamer, Barbie," Joe Wylie said, his voice muffled by his gas mask. "I'd keep you in the spare bedroom."

Even now, even after the Screaming, even after the thousands of smaller but equally horrible tragedies that followed, some of these men were still trying to break her. She wasn't broken yet.

"If you ever touch me again, I swear I'll fucking take you out," she told him.

Joe grinned. "So there is somebody in there behind the mask. Nice to meet you finally."

Wendy had attended the Training Academy two years ago with forty other cadets. All cadets experienced some type of degrading hazing treatment, and with three out of four police officers being men, they were hard on women—especially a beautiful young woman like her, making her scrub toilets and clean laundry and fetch coffee. She had taken it all in stride, excelling in firearms training, certification with the TASER, CPR and first aid, high-risk traffic stop training and the rest—all of it. The other cadets had constantly hit on her but she'd had neither the time nor interest in taking romantic risks with men. But then she met Dave Carver. Dave was different. He was a detective—older, experienced, adversarial against the world. He smelled like her cop dad used to smell before he retired, like cigarettes and black coffee. Dave was also different than the young men her own age in that he seemed so sure of himself. He could take or leave Wendy's looks while seeming to be engaged by her personality and energy. He told her stories about drug dealers and bureaucratic hassles and the time he used his gun during a liquor store robbery. It was only later that she learned that he was married and that she had a reputation.

Dave's friends were hard men and they could be cruel. After graduation from the Academy, she got assigned to her zone and started doing real police work. But the hazing had not stopped. Instead, it had spread, like infection, throughout Patrol, men and women alike. Through bad luck or somebody's malice, she had been assigned to the same station as Dave Carver and his friends.

Wendy had worn a mask ever since.

The whistles blew. The line of cops surged forward and crashed into the crowd. The batons rose and fell, driving people back or beating them to the ground. The line quickly dissolved as everyone became lost in the expanding white clouds of gas.

Wendy slammed into a man with her shield, knocking him back. She raised her baton at a couple holding handkerchiefs over their faces, warning them off. People were shouting at each other in the smoke. Wendy felt detached, as if moving through a surreal dream. The desperate faces flashed by, weeping and coughing and screaming. She swung her baton at a man who stumbled away, blood pouring into his eyes from a jagged tear in his scalp. He did not seem to be critically injured, so she continued to press forward, quickly forgetting about him.

As far as the police were concerned, she was at the bottom of the pecking order. But she was still better than these fleeing people. In the larger pecking order of society, they were all lower than her. She was cop. They were civilian.

She heard a deafening bang that she instantly recognized as a gunshot. She flinched as the sound was followed by the roar of multiple shots. Moments later, Joe Wylie staggered out of the clouds, his plastic body shield riddled with blackened holes, and crumpled to the ground in a heap.

Wendy pulled him out of the chaos until other cops hoisted him onto a stretcher and rushed him into the hospital. By the time the gas cleared, they found two other critically wounded cops lying on the ground among the moaning protestors. The cops had identified four shooters; they were dragging the one they'd caught behind some nearby bushes for swift justice.

These were not ordinary times.

The sergeant saw her watching them, gripped her arm with a hand like iron, and pulled her roughly away, towards the police station, which was only four blocks east of the hospital.

"I'm assigning you to recovery operations until the end of your shift, Saslove," he barked. "Check dispatch to find out where the teams are going tonight. Now get the fuck out of my sight."

Wendy walked to the police station, dumped her riot gear, and caught an hour's sleep under a desk. For the next twelve hours, she looked for screamers. Her search team found sixteen, half as many as the night before, and one-fifth as many as the night before that. At six in the morning, exhausted but buzzing with coffee, she returned to the police station and entered Patrol. Some of the cops were gathered around a TV set, shaking their heads. Riots in the western states. A wave of violence spreading inland from the coast. Most of the military and National Guard were still deployed overseas and in disarray from the Screaming, with only some units having been flown back to the homeland. The police was the main line of defense and in city after city, that line was breaking. Not here, the officers swore. They were tired and angry but they were holding their ground and they were not going anywhere unless it was on a stretcher.

Craig DiLouie

"Turn that shit off," somebody yelled, and they did. The windows were open and a cool breeze wafted through the big squad room. Somebody produced a bottle of scotch and was sharing splashes in Styrofoam cups. "Get ready," he was saying. "They need you out there. Get ready." Wendy was bone tired and covered in bruises and her jaw and skull still ached from earlier in the night, when somebody clocked her while her team intervened to prevent the looting of the Whole Foods store.

John-John handed her a cup. "You done good, rook," he said, winking and punching her lightly on the shoulder. "Keep it up."

*You done good, rook.*

She smiled, her jaw aching.

"Throw in a blowjob and he'll make you Officer of the Month," one of the patrolmen said, sneering. He flinched as another cop jabbed him in the ribs with his elbow. "What'd you do that for?"

"Lay off," the other cop said. "She's one of us."

John-John had raised his cup and was intoning loudly to all of them, "Sometimes it seems the only time a cop is called a hero is when he takes a bullet. Well, today, we got three heroes. That's right. But I say you're all heroes, every day, and especially right now, in the middle of this goddamn apocalypse. So here's to our guys still in critical condition at Mercy Hospital, and here's to all of you ugly dicks who won't give up. You guys are my heroes. Here's to you, Pittsburgh's finest."

*She's one of us.*

The cops emptied their cups and held them up for refills. Somebody turned a radio on, trying to make it a party. Everybody stood around awkwardly in their uniforms and Batman belts, holding their drinks. The alcohol burned Wendy's throat, making her feel alert and loose at the same time. Bracing. One of the communication dispatchers entered the room, blustering, "I need somebody to take a domestic disturbance and everybody's committed. We're getting flooded with calls."

"Give it to the commander," one of the cops called out, and everybody laughed.

The dispatcher was rifling through his slips. "Sound of breaking glass on the street," he read. "Man heard screaming in alley."

The officers chanted, *Tell it to the commander!* until the dispatcher left, red-faced and roaring. The cops cheered. They were dead tired. They needed a break. Wendy had just finished two twelve-hour shifts back to back. In just a few hours, she and the other police officers in the room would have to pull another twelve-hour shift. Until then, they were officially off duty.

The radio was playing an old song that reminded her of summers as a child. A very old song recorded before she was born. Some of the younger cops were moving to the music, nodding and shifting from one foot to the next, trying to unwind. Wendy could not remember the band but the song took her back to one particular summer when she was ten years old, maybe eleven. She remembered riding a bike down the driveway past her dad, who stood hunched over the open hood of his big police cruiser, working on the engine. Her bike's handlebars had multicolor tassels that streamed in the wind. She remembered the sound of lawn mowers and the smell of fresh-cut grass. A boy kissed her that summer. His name was Dale. There was a tire swing hanging by a thick rope from an old oak tree in his backyard and he kissed her there. The memory gave her butterflies. For a few seconds, she fell asleep on her feet.

She opened her eyes. Men were shouting in the foyer. Several of the officers looked at each other, some frowning, others laughing. A scream pierced the air. Everybody froze and glared at the doors. More screaming. Stomping feet. The cops bristled.

The Raspberries, Wendy thought. That was the band.

The doors burst open and people began running into Patrol, grabbing at the nearest officers, who shoved them back with shouted obscenities. More entered the big room, panting, wearing paper gowns and hospital scrubs. The cops flailed with their batons while others tried to cuff the assailants. More rushed in, howling and baring their teeth. The cops nearest Wendy dropped their drinks and reached for their batons. Wendy did the same.

"Son of a bitch bit me!"

Cops were going down. Wendy saw a man bite a cop's arm and shake his head like a dog. She struck the man with her baton and he stumbled away. The cop sank to his knees, shaking, his eyes glazed, and toppled onto the floor. Everywhere it was hand to hand fighting. The batons rose and fell but for every attacker clubbed to the ground, more took his place.

John-John gripped her arm.

"Go tell the lieutenant we're under attack," he roared. "Go, rook, go!"

She ran down the hall and entered the Detectives section. A man instantly grabbed her in a headlock. She struggled but other hands held her. She heard guns crashing back in Patrol.

"Stop struggling, Wendy," she heard a familiar voice.

She opened her eyes and saw Dave Carver surrounded by a group of burly detectives in cheap suits and bad ties, glaring and flushed and breathing heavily. They reeked of stale coffee.

"Let go of me," she cried. "I have to see the lieutenant."

"He's busy," one of the detectives sneered. "What's going on in Patrol, rookie?"

"They're killing them. I'm serious—they're killing them!"

"What are you talking about?"

"She's drunk. Smell it on her breath."

"Who the hell is shooting in the station, rookie?"

"Just let her talk!"

The detectives released her. Wendy caught her breath and said, "We're under attack. Civilians dressed in hospital clothes. They had no weapons." The truth suddenly struck her. "They're screamers. Probably from Mercy. They've woken up and they're crazy."

Dave nodded. "How many?"

"Forty. Fifty. Maybe a hundred. I don't know. Maybe more. It's wall to wall in there. Every patrol officer was committed."

They suddenly realized the screaming and gunshots in Patrol had been replaced by growling in hundreds of throats. A fist banged on the door, startling them. Then another.

"This is bullshit," one of the detectives said, paling.

The other detectives glared at the door, their fists clenched.

Dave said, "Is everybody armed?"

Multiple fists were pounding against the door now.

"Where's Patrol?" one of the detectives cried, panicking. "Where the fuck is Patrol?"

Dave touched her shoulder and said, "Get behind me, Wendy."

The door began to shake on its hinges, splintering.

The detectives unholstered their guns and aimed them carefully at the door.

"Let's go, let's go, let's get this over with," somebody said.

The door exploded inward and people ran screaming into the room. For a critical moment, nobody did anything; their attackers were just regular people—unarmed, sick people. Some of the detectives yelled, *freeze, police, stop or we will shoot*. A moment later, somebody fired his gun and they all started shooting, roaring like madmen, one running forward and emptying his shotgun at point blank range into the gray faces. But the screamers were already in the room and the fighting quickly turned hand to hand.

Wendy stared, horrified and unable to move. Some of their attackers were police officers. She saw John-John tackle one of the detectives, scattering files and a typewriter from one of the desks. She unholstered her Glock and aimed it at the doorway.

Dave grabbed her arm and began pulling her towards the window. "Get out of here! We're not going to make it!"

"Fuck you, Dave," she said, shrugging him off.

"Wendy, get out now!"

"They need my help!" she screamed back.

"We're done!"

She fought him but he was stronger than her. He began to physically drag her to the window and push her out onto the fire escape.

"Survive," he said.

"Come with me, then," she pleaded.

"All right, babe. I'll be right behind you. I promise."

He turned away before she could respond, blazing away with his hand cannon. She climbed down the fire escape and stood in the vehicle yard, waiting for him. The guard booth was empty. From here, the sounds of gunfire ground together like the rumble of thunder. The muzzle flashes lit up the windows like paparazzi. Dave did not appear at the fire escape. The detectives were backing against the far wall and giving it everything they had.

Wendy stood helplessly, her fist clenched around her Glock, her eyes flooded with tears.

The shooting fizzled out until the windows became filled with dark shapes stumbling aimlessly, silhouetted by the glare of the station's institutional fluorescent lighting.

The entire station was wiped out in minutes and she had not fired a single shot. Her ears were still ringing loudly and the loss of sleep over the past few days suddenly hit her hard, making her feel drained and disoriented.

*Lay off her. She's one of us.*

She raised her pistol with both hands and aimed it carefully at the windows above her.

"Help me! Please help me!"

A woman ran down the alley in a nightgown, waving her arms.

"Stay right there," Wendy said raggedly, extending her palm, her nerves raw and electric. Her training kicked in automatically. "What's the problem?"

"My husband is hurt," the woman said, her eyes wild. "He's bleeding."

"Okay, did you call 911?"

"The lines are all busy."

"Where do you live, Ma'am?"

"Just over there."

You can't do this, she told herself. You need to report what you saw.

Another voice in her head countered: What you saw could not have happened.

"Let's go, then," she said.

They entered the house. Wendy felt dizzy. Details in the scene jumped out at her. A pale man dressed in pajamas lying on the floor, bleeding from the head. A table lamp, still on, sitting on its side on the carpet, casting long shadows. Family photos on the wall. A TV with the sound off, showing a worried anchorwoman. A broken pot and the dirt and scattered remains of a plant. A baseball bat.

"Officer, are you okay?"

Every time she closed her eyes, she saw the mob run screaming into Patrol.

"Tell me what happened here, Ma'am," she said mechanically.

"I hit him on the head. You can arrest me if you want. But take care of him first. Please!"

Wendy inspected the wound.

"What's your name?"

"Lisa."

"Okay, Lisa, come on over here. He's got a scalp wound. That type of wound bleeds a lot. I'm going to elevate his head a little so that it is above the heart. There. He's going to need an ambulance but he should be okay. In the meantime, I want you to sit here and put pressure on it."

Wendy stood, fighting tears, and tried to call 911. The circuits were jammed. She saw the couch and suddenly wanted to lie down on it for just a minute. Maybe five minutes. Just a little while—

"I had to do it," Lisa was saying.

"Uh huh," Wendy said, glancing dazedly at the TV set. The anchorwoman was crying, mascara running down her cheeks in black lines.

"He was threatening our boy—"

"This man—?"

"My husband."

"You say your husband was attacking your son?"

"Then I stopped him. I heard him wake up and I followed him. When I saw him holding Benjamin down and biting him I grabbed the bat and hit him on the head. I had to do it."

"Was he one of the people who fell down? One of the SEELS?"

"Yes. It was a miracle. But he must have been confused because he would never hit Benjamin. He loves that boy more than himself."

Wendy backed away, staring in horror at the sleeping man tangled up in his own limbs. Her hand flickered around the handcuffs on her belt. She unholstered her Glock and flicked off the safety. She frowned, trying to think.

"You can remove your hands now, Lisa. I want you to back away from him slowly."

*Lay off her*

"Okay," Lisa said. "But he's still bleeding—"

*She's one of us—*

The cop raised her gun and fired, the sound of the discharge filling the house. The man's head exploded and splashed up the wall.

The woman wailed like an animal caught in a steel trap, rushing forward to hug the man's broken face against her chest.

"You killed Roy!"

Upstairs, a teenage boy was snarling and banging on a bedroom door.

Wendy holstered her gun and walked out the door into the night.

*"Why did you do that? Why? Why?"*

The woman's screaming followed her down the street until it became just one of many voices rising up from the city in pain like a demonic choir.

# MEMORIES

Todd wakes up in a bed in a warm, windowless hospital room after a long, dreamless sleep. He is still exhausted but his body is telling him he has already overslept. You're still here, Todd old man, he tells himself. Still truckin'. Wrapping his blanket around his bare shoulders, he shuffles blearily to a bucket in the corner and empties his bladder. His stomach growls. Outside, he finds Paul in the hallway, whistling as he mops the floor with a strong bleach solution. He finds the sight reassuring. He is not used to being alone.

"Hey, Rev," he says.

"Morning, Kid."

"Wow, we just got here and they got you mopping floors already. Too bad there isn't more need for preachers in the post-apocalyptic world."

Paul pauses in his work, smiling. "On the contrary, son, a true minister is no stranger to working with his hands. It's a form of prayer. Good for the soul. You ought to try it sometime."

"Are you trying to turn me into an atheist?"

"Ha," says Paul.

"Anyhow, my soul needs some coffee or it's not doing anything today."

"Go around the corner and look for the lounge. We got it set up as a common room. I'm sure Anne saved you something."

"Thanks, Rev," Todd says, his blanket forming a train on the floor behind him.

"Good to have you back, Kid."

Todd turns and grins. "The Kid abides, Rev. The Kid abides."

◆

Ethan plods slowly through the pathology department, marveling at the expensive equipment now gathering dust in the gloomy light of his lantern. Everywhere they go, he sees signs of a world that has fallen down. He is looking for things that they can use but has not found anything. A large centrifuge sits on a laboratory table, its lid open showing test tubes filled with cells, once living and now dead, from an unfinished experiment. People had been working here when the Infected got out of their beds. They left in a hurry. Ethan sees an overturned chair with a crisp white labcoat still clinging to the back. A crushed test tube on the floor.

He pauses in front of a cabinet filled with delicate glassware, test tubes and beakers. They are clean but he feels a primitive fear of touching them. Germs are the greatest threat to his survival right now, and his instincts are not very discriminating. In the corner, an emergency liquid nitrogen tank catches his eye. He stares at it for a long time. The nitrogen is stored under pressure, so they might be able to siphon some of it off into a container to make a crude explosive. If they don't blow their own hands off first. They might dump it on the Infected and flash freeze them. As long as they don't freeze their own arm solid in the bargain.

Liquid nitrogen is a dangerous laboratory material, he reminds himself. Probably best to leave it alone. He considered it worth thinking about, however. In this world, everything must be evaluated as a potential weapon. Out of the five basic survival needs, security now ranks first.

Ethan fiddles with a fluorescence microscope but it sits dark, inert, lifeless without electricity. The room is filled with hundreds of thousands of dollars in deteriorating lab equipment. He recognizes an incubator, decides not to open it. It strikes him again that scientists studied disease here. Not scary diseases like AIDS and Ebola, no, not in a lab like this, but dangerous nonetheless: cancer, diabetes, emphysema, bone disorders. The pathologists examined tissues and blood and urine to figure out what was wrong with people. Doctors used these tests to treat people with all sorts of disorders and extend their lifespan. Researchers looked at the smallest living particles in the human body and tried to understand what hurt them and how they adapted to being hurt—knowledge that could be used to diagnose some diseases more easily, treat others, and even cure. Now the healers have all gone, possibly never to return.

Ethan tries not to think of all the great things they might have accomplished.

♦

He once thought he understood what severe stress was like. He and Carol both worked hard at their jobs. They juggled dinner and daycare and doing the dishes. They survived the dramas of raising a little girl who was deep into her terrible twos. Life was full of responsibilities and bills and little errands and phone calls and annoying bank mistakes and miscommunication and petty conflict. It was hard, but he would consider that sort of stress a breath of fresh air after what he has been through in the past ten days with the Sword of Damocles poised over his head, hanging by a thread. The human body was not meant to experience this level of fear for this long. Getting this close to death for too long can turn your hair white, break your mind.

He and Carol would cope as best they could but every so often their frustrations boiled to the surface and they bickered. They bickered as they prepared dinner and as they ate it and as they cleaned up and put Mary to bed. They each knew how far they could go, and no further, to needle the other person without getting a major reaction that would upset their toddler. Every once in a while somebody would go too far, and there would be hurt feelings. When this happened, the bickering escalated and either Ethan or Carol would storm away from the table out of fear of shouting in front of Mary.

One night, nobody walked away, and, without really understanding what he was doing, Ethan started shouting.

"Carol, stop it, stop it, just stop it."

Carol sat back, stunned, while Mary, busily pouring her glass of water into her mashed potatoes, stared at him with eyes like saucers, her mouth hanging open.

Ethan smiled at his daughter quickly, trying to reassure her.

"How dare you shout at me in front of her," Carol hissed.

"I said I don't want to argue. So stop it."

"I'm not the one shouting."

"STOP IT."

"Why don't you shut up?"

They shouted over each other for the next minute until he could not take it anymore and he stormed out of the house, seeing red. He walked for an hour, his mind boiling as he played the argument over and over in his mind, hating it. As his anger began to dissipate, he felt the first wave of panic over what they had done to Mary. He needed to talk to Carol. He hurried home.

Ethan found his wife and daughter upstairs on the rocking chair in Mary's room. Carol was reading her a story from a hardcover compendium of *Curious George* stories.

"Are you happy, Daddy?" Mary said.

"I'm very happy," Ethan said, close to tears.

They gave her a glass of water and tucked her in with her dollies, then turned out the light and left her to sleep.

Carol went downstairs for coffee and Ethan trudged after her.

"I'm sorry I yelled," he said.

"I'm sorry, too," she said.

The next thing he knew he was bawling with his head bowed and his shoulders shaking and Carol was holding him, telling him everything was going to be okay.

"I didn't like the look on Mary's face," he said.

That heartbreaking look of confusion, fear, guilt that her parents were fighting.

He had surprised himself by crying. He had not cried in at least ten years, when his mother died. But that look haunted him. That look of broken trust and loss.

"Kids blame themselves for everything," he added. "I don't want to fight in front of her. I don't want to ever fight in front of her again. We're supposed to be protecting her."

Carol understood. They promised each other it would never happen again. They made up and went to bed feeling better about their marriage. As Ethan lay in the dark that night, trying to sleep, he vowed to preserve Mary's pure innocence and joy as long as he could. She would slowly learn over time that the world was a hard and terrible place. But he would fight that world as long and as hard as he could to protect his little girl from its dark truths.

◆

In the third-floor lounge, the other survivors sit around a small table and share a breakfast of peanut butter on crackers and wash it down with instant coffee sweetened with honey and lightened with powdered milk. An espresso machine gathers dust in the corner next to a small refrigerator nobody is interested in opening. Corporate art decorates the walls. The stale air smells like dust. The LED lantern casts long shadows behind a fake potted plant.

"I think we can all agree we need to continue searching the building," Anne says. "I'd like to lead a team to look for supplies. Food, water, drugs and anything else we can use."

"If it's all right with you, I need to sit that one out," Sarge says.

"Got to work on the Brad?"

"No, I'd like to take my boys and find the emergency generator. We might get some lights going again. Charge our electronics. Maybe even get some news of the outside world."

"Wow," Wendy says, smiling. "That would be nice."

"Hooah," says Sarge.

"Don't tell me you have to go into the basement," Anne says.

Sarge shakes his head. "There ain't no generator in the basement. If a water main broke or there was some type of disaster where fire hoses or sprinklers would have to be used, it could get flooded out too easy. Hurricane Katrina taught everybody that. No, this hospital has a mechanical penthouse. High and dry on the top floor. That is where it will be. Me and the boys will take care of it."

The survivors eat quietly. Sarge pours himself more coffee, smiles and adds, "So don't you worry about me. The only people going into the darkest, most dangerous parts of the hospital today will be you."

"Don't leave without me," Todd says, shuffling into the room. "But first give me some of that coffee and my pants back."

"How's the arm?" Wendy says.

"Sore as hell, but I'll live."

Anne pats the empty chair between her and Wendy. "Have a seat, Kid."

Todd sits, grinning in his blanket and glasses and battered SWAT cap, and extends his hand to Anne for a shake. "Todd Paulsen. Nice to meet you."

◆

Paul aims his shotgun into the darkness, illuminated by the sharp beam cast by a flashlight wrapped around the barrel with electrical tape. The Remington 870 tactical pump shotgun features a short pistol-grip stock and a recoil pad. It packs seven twelve-gauge rounds. He likes the gun because it is dependable and it will stop anything.

They pass the radiology department. Down the corridor, on the right, they find the chapel. Paul blinks at it in surprise. He had completely forgotten that the hospital would have a chapel. The survivors look at him, questioning, and he nods, yes, he would like to see it.

The small room looks like a miniature church, complete with red carpeting, dark wood pews and a stained glass wall that was probably backlit when the power worked. Hymn books are scattered on the floor. Dead flowers are crumbling in their vases and most of the candles are melted. Ethan takes the candles that are still usable and puts them in his bag. The others stand by the doorway, watching Paul, who picks up the hymn books and stacks them carefully on the lectern.

He looks at the arched ceiling overhead and closes his eyes, remembering the last time he spoke as a clergyman. After the Infected rose, he kept Sara tied to a bed for three days, feeding her, bathing her, changing her bedpan, while the world ended outside his window. He even tried an exorcism, commanding demons to abandon her body while she shrieked and panted, straining at her bonds. Time blurred until he realized that people were probably flocking to his church for comfort and there was nobody there to give it. He had a responsibility to his congregation that was just as great. Exhausted from lack of sleep, he put on his clerical uniform and staggered out into the night. People sobbed and screamed in distant houses as he walked to the church in a daze. The Infected were running howling down streets and alleys, breaking into homes and attacking their occupants. Paul arrived at his church only to find it had been attacked. The dead lay in heaps surrounded by clouds of flies. The streetlights shined through the stained glass windows in a ghostly shimmer. The carpet squished wetly under his feet. The Infected had eaten the children on the altar. And he thought, *Isn't this what you wanted, Paul? The End of Days?*

The signs of violence were everywhere in this place. There were as many Infected lying on the ground as those who were not. His congregation had put up a fight—for their children and their sanctuary. The massive wood cross mounted behind the altar, the symbol of his faith in a divine sacrifice that had made life everlasting possible, loomed without potency over the carnage. Rage boiled up inside him. Infection had invaded and defiled this holy place. Infection had raped his wife's blood. And he, personally, had not been touched.

Dawn brought the singing mob marching down the street out of a haze of smoke, sweeping him along. Middle-class suburbanites carrying shotguns and baseball bats and crowbars and kitchen knives and garden tools. They shouted and sang and waved banners proclaiming: WE ARE THE MAJORITY and DEFEND OUR HOMELAND and WE SHALL NOT BE MOVED. One carried a Bible and a large wooden cross. There were hundreds of them. The vanguard roared and dragged along eight

Infected, who snapped and struggled against handcuffs and ropes tied around their necks. The men stopped in the middle of an intersection, threw the ropes over the traffic signal, and promptly began hauling the Infected kicking and gasping into the air. Paul pushed his way through the clapping mob for a better look until he was satisfied that Sara was not one of the victims. The air smelled like smoke. The Infected hung by their necks, jerking and twitching until they died. The mob cheered, some shooting at the corpses with their guns, others singing "The Star Spangled Banner" until everybody joined in, tears running down their cheeks. Paul was finding it hard to breathe. Several people noticed his clerical collar, shook his hand and began shoving him to the head of the column, chanting, "Bless us! Bless us!" A man with a mullet and a hunting bow, standing on the hood of a car, pulled him up with one hand and clapped him on the back. Paul looked down upon the cheering crowd in anger and did not trust the Spirit. What could he say that they wanted to hear? Should he tell them that God was on their side and approved of them murdering their brothers and sisters in broad daylight? Should he rouse them to torture and murder more of them with a hymn, maybe "Onward, Christian Soldiers"? Then he realized how scared they all were. The faces looked up at him hungrily; if ever they needed the strength and hope of Christ's love, it was now. They were quiet now except for the cries of their babies. A pair of military jets roared overhead in the gray, smoky sky, followed by the boom of distant explosions. His heart opened. He raised his hands and blessed the mob.

"Your war is just," he told them.

For a war to be truly just, its soldiers must kill with love, not hate, he thought. This was perhaps the first war in history where the combatants killed those they loved most.

People at the edge of the crowd began to scream. Infected were rushing out of nearby lawns and gardens into their midst, punching and biting. Shotguns and handguns roared in a motley cluster of shots, followed by triumphant shouting. Several people began trading punches over a bitten and newly Infected teenage girl lying twitching on the ground.

"Brothers and sisters," Paul sang to them. "The Lord is with you. Do not be afraid."

More Infected ran into the crowd, sending tremors of panic rippling through it. Some people ran away while others huddled closer together for protection. They stumbled over the newly Infected that lay twitching under their feet. A swarm arrived howling, and the mob began to break and tear with screams and gunshots and running feet.

The fighting went on and on, the mob slowly dissolving like a wounded whale surrounded by sharks, flailing and dying one bite at a time. Soon, Paul found himself alone, watching the last clumps of people throw away their banners and flee, abandoning dozens of bodies on the ground. A small knot of fighters made a stand in a smoky haze, shouting at each other and firing their shotguns, until the Infected overran them.

Paul opens his eyes and is back in the hospital chapel, his face upturned towards the ceiling.

He offers a silent prayer for the dead and then sings aloud in a rich baritone voice, "Amen, amen, ah-ah-men."

The other survivors stare at him wearing stricken expressions. Wendy wipes her eyes with the palm of her hand. Paul wonders if he said something while reliving that horrible day so vividly. He realizes his own face is wet and that he has been crying. He realizes that he was not singing at all. He was moaning. He did not remember what happened so much as relived it. But he cannot remember what happened afterwards. The fighters made their stand and they died in the smoke. Then nothing more.

◆

They all know about flashbacks. The experiences are so real, so visceral, that they can swear they have discovered a legitimate form of time travel. But unlike the type of time travel one might find in, say, the movies, with this type of time travel, they cannot change the outcome. They are doomed to relive the past repeatedly without being able to change it. And no matter how many times they visit the past, they will never truly comprehend it.

◆

The survivors enter the gift shop guns first, clearing it the way Sarge taught them—fanning out along the walls and circling back to the door.

"Clear," they sound off, then start looting.

Ethan is again struck by the sensation that the world has become a giant museum dedicated to the day the world ended. The magazines and newspapers sitting in their racks still trumpet dramatic headlines about the Screaming. He runs his fingers over the greeting cards, pauses in front of a selection of stuffed animals and shiny balloons that proclaim IT'S A BOY! and FEEL BETTER SOON! and HAPPY MOTHER'S DAY!

Behind him, Wendy opens a dead refrigerator and begins emptying its bottled water and juices into cloth shopping bags packed onto a wheelchair, which they are using as a cart. Paul lights a cigarette with a tired sigh and sits on a stack of magazines. Todd scoops up candy and gum and shoves it into another bag. Anne prowls the other shelves with her flashlight, snatching up aspirin and nail clippers and deodorant.

Todd holds up his bag of candy, shakes it, and says, "Trick or treat."

Ethan says, "Do you think they remember who they are?"

"You mean the Infected?" Todd says.

"Yes. Do you think their consciousness has been replaced, or that they are still trapped inside their bodies, forced to do things they don't want to do by the virus?"

"I would hate to think they were still in there watching themselves attack people and being helpless to stop it," Wendy says. "Either way, killing them is a mercy."

"Maybe when the Infected dream, they remember who they are," Todd says. "It would be nice to think that." He quickly adds, "Or completely horrible."

Ethan picks up a stuffed animal, squeezes it, and drops it to the floor. "I'm wondering if they still love us. If they recognize us and love us while they attack us even as we recognize them and love them while we kill them."

Paul's head jerks up and he stares at Ethan.

Anne says, "Nobody likes these questions."

Paul says, "They're the only questions worth asking."

♦

The door to the mechanical penthouse is locked. Sarge and the crew go out to the Bradley to recover the demolition kit, which contains a few blocks of C4 plastic explosive and detonators. They are going to cut and mold a wad of C4 onto the doorknob, stick a detonator into it, let the wires run out until they get to a safe place, trigger the detonator, and BOOM. The soldiers have a casual but deep appreciation for the stuff. You can throw it and kick it and it will not blow up on you. Light it on fire and it burns nice and slow and you can heat an MRE on it if the area is properly ventilated, as Sarge did many times in Afghanistan. Mold it wherever you want it to go in whatever shape you want it, pop in the detonators, and you can take down buildings.

They move quickly, rifles shouldered and aimed, communicating by hand signals only. Papers and loose trash flutter across the parking lot. The parking garage where they hid the rig under a tarp does not appear to be occupied, but swarms have a way of appearing as suddenly as a flash flood. They are used to playing it safe. Caution is now second nature to them.

Once they are back in the hospital, the soldiers begin to relax a little.

"Are we safe here, Sergeant?" Duck says. "In this building?"

"Safe enough at this moment." This is Sarge's stock answer to that question. He credits staying alive and sane this long with taking this hellish journey one day at a time. One moment at a time. Speculating about what you do not know is a waste of time and energy that you need to stay alive.

"I mean, are we going to stay a while?"

They begin climbing the stairs. Sarge shrugs and says, "I think we should. It's a good place."

"I thought the idea was we would train a civilian combat team and use them as security until we found some friendlies."

"That's still the plan, Ducky."

"The civs seems to think we're going to live here."

"Yes, we are still trying to find the Army," Sarge says. "No, we do not need to advertise this fact to the civilians. Do you even know where the nearest friendlies are? Because I sure as hell do not. Our battalion technically does not exist anymore. We've heard nothing on the net in days."

The soldiers reach the top floor and pause to catch their breath. The gunner drops to one knee and starts rigging the C4 charge.

"There's always the camps," Steve says as he works. "The FEMA camps. The closest one is in Ohio, right?"

"Which we do not even know still exist, Steve. If they ever did. We've heard of lots of refugee camps and Army elements that either moved by the time we showed up or were never there in the first place. I am not interested in risking our safety for any rumors, especially if it means driving all over Ohio on a quarter tank of gas."

"Hey, I'm with you. I'd like to stay. I wouldn't mind if we bunkered down here until the whole thing blows over. Let the gung ho mo-fo's take care of it."

"I don't want to stay here forever. The Army is out there still fighting somewhere and we've got to find them and help. But these people need a rest. We need a rest."

"Roger that," Steve says.

"I look at it this way," Ducky says as they retreat down the stairwell. "Every hour we sit here, more people die that we could be helping. So how long are we staying if we are staying?"

"At least a few days," Sarge says. "A lot can change in a few days. We are still taking this one day at a time." He remembers what the Boy Scouts taught him about having the right frame of mind for survival: Stop, think, observe and plan, or STOP.

"What if we decide to move on but the civs want to stay?"

"I do not know, Ducky. I honestly do not. They're not in the Army."

"Fire in the hole!" Steve announces. The soldiers crouch and plug their ears.

The C4 explodes with a clap of metallic thunder that rolls down the stairwell, followed by a wave of smoke and dust and a strong chemical smell. The warped metal door hangs on one of its hinges, then snaps off and flops to the side.

The soldiers stand and dust themselves off.

"The truth is we really need them," Sarge says. "They've gotten good." He smiles grimly. "In fact, I would hate to piss them off."

♦

God is good, and death is evil, so why does God allow people to die? That was a question Paul had never been able to answer during his ministry. When he was ten years old, a plane crashed, scattering burning metal and body parts across miles of scorched and bruised earth, killing more than two hundred people, including his mother. He experienced the full gamut of grief, from denial to anger to bargaining to guilt. The guilt was the worst. He had been asleep when she left for the trip and it haunted him that she could be taken away so suddenly, without even a final goodbye. By the time he reached the acceptance phase, he had aged beyond his years. He had aged beyond his years because he had become aware of death and the fragility of life.

A minister came to the house frequently in the weeks following the crash, offering consolation to Paul and his father.

"If God loved my mom, why did he let her die?" Paul asked him.

"I don't know," the minister said. "What I do know is that it was her time to cross over."

"To Heaven?"

"To be with God, who made her. Your mother did not die. She underwent a transition. It is painful that you will have to wait to see her again. But you will see her again."

Paul wrestled with his next question, feeling insecure about asking it.

Finally, he said, "Is God going to make me die, too?"

The minister smiled. "We all die, Paul," he answered. "But you won't die for a long, long time. The world is a hard place. But it is also wonderful. You've got a lot of things to do here."

Paul spent the next few days thinking about what Reverend Brown said. By the end, he not only began to accept the loss of his mother, he decided to become a minister. He loved superheroes, could not get enough of them on TV and in comic books. But here was a real superhero, somebody who fought the evil of death every day and helped other people conquer it.

He turned out to be good at being a minister. He spent hundreds of hours in grief counseling with dying people and their families. He offered whatever comfort he could. When they had nobody else, he spent more time with them and even helped with chores and bills. As a minister, this was his mission, to help wherever he could, and he felt he made a real difference in people's lives. He helped the dying accept what was happening to them, and to Paul, there was simply no greater gift than some degree of confidence that they were not dying, but crossing over, not into oblivion, but to a better place, to wait for loved ones they left behind.

And yet a part of him always felt like a sham because he, himself, remained terrified of dying.

Rita Greene was not a regular churchgoer, but when she was diagnosed with bone cancer and rushed into a painful treatment regime including chemotherapy and surgery removing part of her pelvis, her family asked if Paul would visit with her, and he agreed.

He came to her home and sat by her bed while she shook with a fever that was not a fever but instead a side effect of her treatment. The drugs she was taking killed growing cells in her body, both the fast-growing cancer cells and the normal, healthy cells in her mouth, stomach, intestines, hair follicles. Some days, he was told, she felt so well she would be out in her garden working on her daffodils. Today was a bad day. The fact was she was declining fast.

They exchanged small talk while he tried to put her at ease. He gave her a compilation CD of jazz, which her son said she liked to listen to while tending her flowers. He explained to her the reason he was there and that she should consider him another form of support.

Rita said the hardest part for her was the weight loss, her hair falling out, the general sickliness. She hated looking in the mirror and seeing what the cancer and its treatment had done to her. Plus she was a woman who liked to get up and do things. She hated being inside, trapped in bed.

"Are you afraid of what comes next for all of us?"

"No," Rita said. "We all got to go sometime. It's my time, is all."

"How are you feeling about leaving Jim behind?"

"He's a good boy. He'll find his way."

"You're a very strong person," Paul said.

Rita coughed. "I got no choice about it."

"And do you feel you are right with Jesus?"

"I don't believe in Jesus, Reverend," said Rita.

Paul stared at her, stunned. "But of course you do."

"No, I don't."

"You've been worshipping at my church for years."

"That's right. But I never really believed any of it."

"Oh," he said.

"No offense, Reverend."

"You don't believe you're going anywhere special, and yet you're not afraid?"

"Why should I be? Like I said, I got no choice."

Paul regarded her for several moments, unsure of what to say. Based on his experience ministering to the dying as well as the living, he had always agreed with the sentiment that there are no atheists in foxholes. Rita Greene was proving a rare exception.

"Reverend," she said. "Read me that passage from Ecclesiastes. The one about the seasons."

"Um," Paul said. "Of course." He cleared his throat and recited from memory, "'For everything there is a season, a time for every activity under heaven.'"

"Mmmm," Rita said, smiling and closing her eyes.

"'A time to be born and a time to die. A time to plant and a time to harvest. A time to kill and a time to heal. A time to tear down and a time to build up. A time to grieve and a time to dance . . .'"

He stopped. Rita had fallen asleep.

Her son Jim met him in the kitchen. He was a large man who worked in construction. He told Paul that he was taking it hard. They sat at the kitchen table to talk.

"Chondrosarcoma," Jim said with revulsion. "I never heard that word before a week ago. And here it comes, the thing that's going to kill my mom. Goddamn cancer."

Paul nodded.

"Hey, Reverend," Jim added, "what do you say to people when you do grief counseling? What technique works the best?"

"Well, the hardest part is giving our loved ones permission to die," Paul told him. "Some people go on trying to interact with their loved one even after they're gone. They'll go on talking to them because they don't know how to move on."

"So what do you say to these people to help them?"

Paul took out a pen, pulled a napkin from a neat stack on the other end of the table, and drew a thick black line on it.

"It's a line," Jim said.

"I tell people that their past is on one side of the line and their future is on the other," Paul explained. "I tell them they have to acknowledge that they are crossing this line and that things have changed. They've got to let go and begin to accept the change so they can move into the future."

Jim grunted, letting the visual sink in.

Paul looked at the line and imagined that it did not separate the past from the future, but life from death. On the left, a tiny life of joy, hardship, searching and wandering. On the right, either eternal joy in union with the Creator, or eternal oblivion—an endless, mindless, terrifying darkness—each of us alone, each of us forgotten, each of us nothing.

◆

The hospital appears to grow larger and more complex as the survivors explore its depths. They mark their progress with a can of fluorescent paint. All of the phones are off the hook. Ethan picks one up and places it against his ear just to rediscover the old, familiar act. He dials his home number and listens. The phone does not ring. Nobody answers. He places the phone carefully back on the receiver. Then he hurries to catch up with the other survivors, who have stopped in front of a door.

The sour, rancid smell of the dead is strong here. Ethan places a rag soaked in cologne over his mouth and nose and fights the urge to gag.

"We have to check every room," Anne says.

The others nod, reluctantly, and step inside.

Ethan instantly regrets it. He slowly explores the walls with his flashlight. They are covered with crayon drawings on construction paper, crude depictions of homes and mommies and daddies and family pets and suns with big yellow rays coming out of them. Sprayed with dried blood.

"Oh Jesus," he says. "Oh, Jesus."

"This was the daycare," Wendy whispers.

Like a trapeze artist afraid of vertigo and falling a long way, Ethan tells himself not to look down. For some reason, the Infected do not want prepubescent children. They do not try to infect them. It may be that the virus does not see them as viable hosts. Or perhaps the virus places a higher value on them as nutrition, for the Infected murder children and feed on their remains.

He knows the floor is littered with rotting meat and bones. Little skulls.

Ethan suddenly cannot breathe.

Anne shines her flashlight in his face. "Ethan?"

He moans, swatting at the light.

"He's losing it. Get him out of here."

As the survivors retreat from the daycare, Wendy steps on something soft, which pops with an organic squeaking sound.

She aims her flashlight down and illuminates the floor.

"Anne," she says, her voice thin. "Oh God, Anne, come quick."

The floor is littered with translucent, fleshy sacs filled with a mucus-colored slime. As the beam of light from Wendy's flashlight crosses the sacs, pale worms inside the fluid become agitated and thrash, making the sacs wobble and stretch.

The sacs are eggs. The room is infested with eggs.

Anne appears at her side, looks down, and says nothing.

"What do we do?" says Wendy. "If they hatch, we're dead."

For a single long minute, Anne does not answer, holding a bandana against her face, her eyes wide and watery.

"Destroy them," she says finally.

♦

The soldiers sweep the gray concrete walls with light, looking for signage that will help orient them to the layout of the hospital's mechanical equipment floor. The rooms are filled with boilers, pumps, piping and makeup air units used to provide heating and cooling to the building, all of it sitting dormant under an exposed ceiling coated with fireproof foam.

Sarge does not doubt that the hospital has emergency backup power. All hospitals have it because outages can happen unexpectedly, causing monitors, oxygen pumps and other life-saving equipment, not to mention cordless phones and data servers, to suddenly fail. What he does not know is if the generator burns natural gas or diesel.

If gas, it might have a backup propane tank that would be useful for heating water and cooking. But if it is diesel, then they can refuel the Bradley as well as produce electricity.

Sarge stops in front of two bright yellow nine-feet-tall, twenty-ton machines that look like a cross between a tractor and a train locomotive. The hospital has two generators wired in parallel, each rated at two thousand kilowatts, and what appears to be a big backup fuel tank.

"Hallelujah, boys," he says, grinning. "It's diesel."

The soldiers laugh and whoop, then hang their lanterns and get to work inspecting the generators. They are natural grease monkeys and know their way around internal combustion engines. They begin checking the oil and batteries and measuring how much diesel is in the tanks. Each of the generators nominally holds a hundred fifty gallons, while the Bradley holds one-seventy-five. And that does not count what is in the backup tank. It has been ten days since the Infected put this hospital out of business, so the fuel may have deteriorated a little, but it should be all right. Sarge guesses that both generators at full loading would probably operate all the critical stuff in the hospital for about eight hours. With the fuel in the storage tank, however, that could be extended to twenty-four, maybe forty-eight.

"The tanks are at around eighty percent," Steve says, grinning.

"Hot dog," Sarge says.

They are sitting on a lot of fuel.

"It's about time luck got on our side," Ducky says.

Once they get it working, the generator will burn its fuel to generate force that turns a crankshaft. The crank will turn a rotor inside a stator, which will create a steady magnetic field. As the rotor passes through the field, electrical current will be generated in wires that it houses. The current will flow to whatever circuits they assign for loading. If it works, they will have light, refrigeration, cooking, air conditioning, heat and power for electronics.

"All right, let's find the breaker panel and set up our loads," Sarge adds. "Then we can take this baby out for a spin."

◆

Wendy peels off her grimy clothes, dumps them in a bucket and tosses in some washing liquid she found next to a pile of bloody laundry. Anne also strips down until she is naked, then stands under one of the showerheads.

"Wow, it feels good to be out of those clothes," Wendy says. "It also feels scary. I'm not sure I like it."

Anne points to the inflamed cut along her ribs. "Where did you get that?"

"Worm teeth," Wendy says. "I didn't know I had it until after. I don't think the worms are infectious. Either that, or Todd and I are very lucky."

"Well, that cut is infected with something. You got a fever?"

"Honestly, I've felt feverish ever since the Screaming. Almost two weeks ago."

"Make sure you take care of it. Your immune system is weak from the stress and lack of sleep. If your temperature goes up, take some antibiotics."

Wendy nods and for the first time is aware of Anne's nudity. The end of the world and its forced survival diet has been kind to her, burning off her excess fat and leaving sinewy muscle on the woman's petite frame. Anne has the body of a gymnast.

"You're beautiful," Wendy says, smiling.

Anne blinks in surprise. A smile crosses her face, but her hand flickers at the scars on her left cheek, and the moment passes quickly.

"I might have been once," she answers.

"Come on, ladies, let's go," Todd calls out from the locker room. "I haven't touched a bar of soap in two weeks!"

"Don't let him peek, Reverend," Wendy says. "We're counting on you to protect our honor."

"Your honor is in safe hands for exactly three minutes plus drying time," Paul calls back. "Let me know when you're ready so I can start counting down."

Wendy and Anne turn on the faucets, which groan for several moments before spitting out gobs of cold water and then a steady stream.

"You can start it now!"

Wendy steps under the faucet and is instantly electrified by the sensual feel of the water and its cold bite on her skin. Closing her eyes, she finds it easy to imagine being under a waterfall. The building's water was designated for drinking and cooking only but Sarge said very quick showers would be a great way to celebrate their taking the hospital back from Infection and reminding them of what they are surviving for; the others eagerly agreed to the luxury. Wendy closes her eyes and feels the water drumming against her head and shoulders. Lathering up her hands with a bar of soap, she begins to wash herself, laughing.

"Two minutes!"

Wendy pours a handful of shampoo into her palm and massages her scalp. Soapy gray water pours out of her hair and down the drain. She marvels at how precious water is now. Standing under the downpour, she feels rich with its wealth. Drunk on the luxury of being able to use it to wash herself like this.

"One minute!"

"Shit," she says, frantically beating and rinsing her dirty clothes before Paul calls time and they turn the faucets off.

"Now can I peek?" Todd says.

"No!" says Wendy, adding to Anne, "We're going to have to find that kid a girl soon."

The women towel down, put on hospital scrubs and slippers, and hang their clothes up to dry. Then she grins.

"You know, for a few moments there, I actually forgot all about it," Wendy says.

Anne says, "I don't want to forget."

◆

Eleven months after entering the Academy, Wendy was sworn in and told to report to Zone One. The Northside neighborhoods would be her territory for the foreseeable future. Her first day finally arrived. She woke up after only a few hours of sleep filled with energy and too nervous to eat anything. She downed a cup of coffee and took a hot shower. She tied her hair back into a bun and again considered getting it cut short. She carefully laid out and then put on, piece by piece, over black bra and panties, her crisply ironed uniform and pins and badge and Batman belt, conscious of a mundane cop ritual that was still novel to her, fussing over getting rid of every speck of lint. Then she stood in front of the mirror and worked on her game face.

At the station, after orientation, she was told that she would be partnered with a senior officer named Kendrick, a grizzled, overweight cop with a permanent scowl. She held out her hand to shake and he gave her a long, incredulous once-over, which he concluded by shaking his head.

"I hope that fucking Dave Carver isn't the only thing you're good at," he said.

Wendy put on her game face and said, "I'm not fucking Dave Carver."

"If you say so, rook."

"But you're right, I was good at it."

Kendrick snorted with laughter.

"All right, Cleopatra. Let's get going. But one more thing before we go out today. We're going to be in some rough neighborhoods, but remember there are a lot of good people who call those neighborhoods home, so show some fucking respect out there."

Wendy nodded, appreciating the perspective. They reported to the dispatcher and entered the garage, where they found their cruiser.

"I'll drive, rook," he growled. "You don't do anything unless I say so—*what?*"

"I said, 'Okay, Officer Kendrick.'"

"If you think I'm being hard on you because you're a woman, fuck you."

The squad car left the garage. They drove around their territory for a while and then stopped at a Dunkin Donuts for breakfast. Wendy went in and minutes later returned to the car with a box of donuts and two tall Styrofoam cups full of coffee. Kendrick wolfed down the donuts and drank his coffee, then sighed contentedly and settled into his seat. He watched the street with the dull gaze of a basilisk. Wendy guiltily prayed that something terrible would happen and that she could do some real police work on her first day. She pictured the dispatcher calling out, *car crash with injuries*, or *robbery in progress* and *shots fired*. Maybe she and Kendrick would catch a drug deal in progress. Maybe there would be a man on one of the city's many bridges, threatening to jump, and she would have to talk him down. She began to fidget in her seat.

"This is the job, rook," he growled, slurping his coffee. "You hurry up and wait. And wait."

The radio suddenly blared.

"CD to all units."

There had been a break-in and stabbing. The dispatcher gave the location and advised that the suspect was still in the house. He had broken in through a window, punched the occupant to the floor, robbed her, and cut her up. By the time the dispatcher finished, Kendrick had already started the car, turned on the lights and siren, and was now replying that they were en route.

The car lurched into traffic and roared toward the scene on squealing tires.

"Hold on to your ass," Kendrick said.

"Every unit in the zone must be on its way," Wendy shouted over the siren.

"We'll get there first. Excited, cherry?"

Wendy tried not to smile through her game face.

He whistled. "First day on the job and you might get a collar. Lucky kid."

The dispatcher was firing updates over the radio when Kendrick yanked the steering wheel and brought the squad car to a screeching halt in front of the house.

They got out of the car, Kendrick pausing to retrieve his shotgun. Wendy unholstered her Glock, fighting to control her breathing, and ran to the front of the house at a crouch.

They knocked loudly and took a step back.

"Police!"

The door opened and an old woman, leaning on a cane, waved them in.

"He left when he heard you coming," she said.

"Where'd he go?" Wendy demanded.

"Up there," the woman answered.

"Hold it a second, rook," Kendrick said tersely. "Ma'am, are you hurt? Did he cut you?"

"He stabbed me right here. See?"

Kendrick's face turned purple.

"It's all better now. I *refused* to stay hurt. I am quite resilient."

"Which way did he go, Ma'am?" Wendy said.

"I already told you he went up through the ceiling to his helicopter."

Behind them, other cars rocketed to a halt in front of the house, spilling cops.

"What a waste of time," Kendrick muttered.

"Can I get you a glass of milk, officer?" the woman said to him.

Sergeant McElroy showed up, talked to the woman for several minutes with clenched fists, and called the dispatcher to report the call as unfounded.

"Congratulations, Sherlock," he said, jabbing Wendy in the chest with his finger. "You caught your first big case."

She spent the rest of her first day as a police officer filling out reports on the incident in triplicate.

♦

Clean and pink and dressed in plain green hospital scrubs, the survivors wolf down heated cans of ravioli and spaghetti and meatballs in the lounge, washing it down with bottles of red wine that before the world ended would have been considered expensive. The showers washed off the days' old stink of fear and they are beginning to feel human again.

As the time approaches six o'clock, they chant a countdown. When they get to zero, nothing happens. The survivors stare at the ceiling, their hopeful expressions wilting in disappointment.

"Bummer," Todd says.

The fluorescent lights suddenly blink to life, impossibly bright.

The survivors gasp in amazement, then cheer.

"Ladies and gentlemen, I give you civilization," Sarge says.

"Fantastic," Ethan says. "It almost feels normal."

"How much of the building is powered?" Anne asks.

"We isolated the power to a section on this floor that includes this lounge plus the pathology department, brain clinic, OBGYN, nursing administration and all of our rooms."

"How long will we have it?"

"The generator runs on diesel like the Bradley. After topping up the rig, we've got enough fuel to have power for forty days if we use it an hour a day."

"I'm going to try to power up my cell phone," Ethan says.

"There's probably still no service, though," Paul says.

Ethan shrugs with a sad smile.

"Sorry," Paul adds. "That was a stupid thing to say. Anything is possible."

"It's all right. I just want to have the phone ready, just in case. I have to be ready."

"I hear you."

Todd says, "I'm going to juice up my iPod. Shazam!"

"Are there any windows we need to black out?" Anne asks Sarge.

"I think we're good, Anne," Sarge tells her. "We turned off the lights in all the rooms with windows."

"Somebody should go out and check to make sure no light is leaking out of the building."

Sarge blinks. "If you think that's wise."

"If somebody sees the light, we will not be safe."

"True," he admits.

"We're acting like we're safe here but we're not. We've only explored a small part of the building. Today, we found a room infested with worm eggs. There could be more of those things, not to mention more Infected, right under our feet on the second floor, or right over our heads on the floors above. They could be crawling through the air ducts. We can't worry about both them and other people coming in from the outside wanting to take what we have."

"All right, Anne," Sarge says, feeling sour, as if a fine party has been spoiled. "Who do you want to go out and check? The power will only be on for an hour and it's starting to get dark, so whoever is going had better get moving."

"I'll do it."

"Not alone. If nobody else wants to go with you, I will."

"Thanks, but I'd rather go alone," she says. "I'll be fine."

"I'm not at all sure that you are," Sarge says.

"So it's decided."

Anne cleans her hands on her pants, gets onto her feet, and walks out the door. The survivors stare at the empty doorway in a stunned silence for a few moments.

"Are you really going to let her leave like that by herself?" Wendy asks Sarge.

The big soldier shrugs. "She don't belong to me."

"She wanted to go," Paul says, shaking his head. "She practically ran out of here."

"I'm not going anywhere," Ethan says, pouring himself another tall cup of wine.

◆

The television set's large screen flickers to life, filled with snow. The soldiers wheeled it in on a cart and plugged it into one of the power outlets. Sarge fiddles with the antenna. An image begins to resolve: a military officer standing in front of a blue curtain and giant map of the

United States mounted on an easel board. The image lurches for a moment, stretching like a funhouse mirror, then snaps back, snowy, as if perpetually on the verge of disintegration.

"Whoa," Todd says, eating a chocolate bar. "This isn't the usual emergency broadcast crap."

The speakers roar white noise, under which they can hear the officer murmuring like a ghost behind the walls. Sarge gives up and finally turns the sound off, backs away from the TV gingerly, and sits in one of the lounge chairs.

"Who is that guy?" Wendy asks. "Do you know him, Sarge?"

Steve snorts. "He's the chairman of the joint chiefs."

"The who?"

Sarge explains, "The chairman is the highest ranking military official in the country, besides the President. That's General Donald McGregor. Ran the show for a few years in Afghanistan. He's a tough sumbitch."

"Any idea what he's saying?"

"It looks to me like he's giving some type of press conference."

The survivors stare at the unstable image raptly, their brains tickled by the sensation of watching television again. Drunk on the feeling that they are no longer alone.

Ethan finally gets up and stands next to the TV, pointing at the map. "It's shaded. Like a weather map. See? Pretty much all of Pennsylvania is red."

"I guess we're in for some hot weather."

"That's not a good color," Ethan agrees, squinting closely at the grainy image. "Philly and New York are shaded a really dark red. That can't be good either. But eastern Ohio, outside the major cities, is yellow. Yellow's better than red, right?"

The survivors shrug, but nobody objects either.

He adds, "If the chairman would move his ass out of the way, we could see what's going on out west."

"The chairman looks profoundly unhappy about the current state of affairs," Todd says, his mouth full of candy.

"Washington, DC is shaded dark red," Wendy says. "I wonder where the President is."

"At Mount Weather in Virginia, most likely," Sarge guesses. "The emergency bunker. Anybody in government who made it out of Washington when the screamers woke up, that's where they'll be now."

"At least there's still a government," she tells him. "We're still resisting. That's something."

Sarge nods. "Yeah, that's something. We're still in the game. I hope we're winning it."

The survivors pour fresh drinks, lean back on the couches, and watch until they grow bored.

"Is there anything else to watch?"

"When does Jon Stewart come on?"

They laugh.

"Thank you for coming to my important press conference," Todd says in a nasal voice, watching the general talking on the TV screen and imagining aloud what the man is saying. "My strategic assessment is we're all fucked. Any questions?"

◆

Before the end of the world, Todd wouldn't be caught dead watching television, which he considered an opiate for the masses and a big waste of time besides. He grew up on the Internet. He would spend hours staring at his PC, flitting from one site to the next, engaging total strangers in obnoxious debates in message boards and chat rooms about weapons and tactics and rules in *World of Warcraft* and *Warhammer 40,000*, his favorite games. He called this nightly ritual "doing the time warp." He would sit down at his computer screen after dinner and, after several hours that flew by as if only a few minutes, his mother would be nagging him to go to bed.

One night, seven months earlier, as he sat hunched over his keyboard dying to piss, his mother yelled his name from downstairs, which he dutifully ignored, as it was his policy to never answer his parents' first call, only the second. Less than a minute later, she yelled again.

"WHAT?" he roared in a blind rage.

"Come down!"

"I'll *never* finish this post," Todd complained, sighing loudly.

He trudged downstairs and froze in his tracks. Sitting on his living room couch was April Preston, wearing jeans and a sweater and glasses.

April was a senior. April was popular. April was beautiful, even with her glasses on.

"Hey," he said, recovering.

"Hi," she said, smiling awkwardly.

"I thought you might want to say hello," Todd's mom said. "You go to the same school."

"Different grades," Todd said.

"Right," April said.

"April's car broke down," his dad said. "We just called AAA."

"Excellent," Todd said, nodding.

"Do you want a Pepsi or something, April? Something to eat?"

"I'm all right. Thanks, Mrs. Paulsen."

"Do you need to call your parents?"

"I already did, thanks. My dad's coming to get me."

Todd studied April while they talked, feeling nervous. While she personally had never done any harm to him, he considered her an enabler to those who had. She certainly hung out with them. Apparently, she found total jerks irresistibly attractive, because she also dated them. *You're abusive to people who are younger and weaker than you, and you play football? Wow, you're so hot!* Now she was in his house. Should he consider this an invasion? Even his home was violable, apparently. They could just walk right in. He pictured her telling everybody at school what a dorky house he had, what dorky parents. She would imitate them: *I just called AAA. Want a Pepsi?*

She did not look particularly threatening, however. In fact, she looked even more nervous than he was. He suddenly felt an overwhelming need to do something chivalrous. Maybe he could impress her and she would tell everybody how cool he actually was.

He realized his parents had left the room and April was staring at her hands in her lap.

"Must be great to be a senior," he said.

She smiled again and nodded.

"Um. Are you going to college?"

"I'd like to go to college," April said. "I'll probably end up at Penn State. You?"

Todd blinked. "Me? I'm not sure yet. I mean, I'd like to go, I definitely will go, but I haven't chosen a school yet. Graduation seems like an eternity to me."

"Well, you're smart. You'll probably get your pick of schools."

Todd did not know what to say. April had violated the first law of the jungle, which is you never praised above-average intelligence. You could be a great athlete, a great musician, a great consumer of twelve-ounce beers, but never a great student. He began to see her as outside the game, operating by different rules. In her last year of high school, she already seemed like an adult. His ears were ringing and his entire being felt warm and flushed at the compliment. He was used to being complimented, but only by authority figures—his parents and teachers, mostly—never by other students. Never by his peers. He began to see himself as outside the game as well, entering a world where a reputation for smarts would be an asset instead of a source of embarrassment and fear. For the first time in a long time, Todd actually felt hopeful about the future.

He suddenly wanted to talk to her all night.

Just then, his dad returned to tell April that her father was outside waiting for her.

Todd looked at her hopefully, looking for more, but the spell was already broken. Tomorrow, they would both return to the same building that defined their lives, and they would have no relationship. He felt like he had been given an unexpected gift, while at the same time cheated.

"Well, I'll see you around, I guess," April said.

"Good talking to you," Todd said formally, meaning every word.

Months later, the game of high school ended with the Screaming. April was one of the majority that did not fall down. Todd still wonders sometimes what happened to her. He hopes she made out okay. She was one of the good ones.

◆

The survivors drift away one by one. Wendy goes back to her room to clean her Glock and refill her magazines with bullets. Sarge wants to work up a sweat with some exercise. Ethan, drunk and slurring his words, scoops up two unopened bottles of wine and announces that he is going to his room to recharge his cell phone. Todd shows Steve and Ducky his crudely stitched forearm and asks them if they ever heard the story of how he got wounded. He asks them if they had to choose between a pistol with thirty rounds and a *katana*, which would they want to fight a zombie horde with?

The crew shake their heads in irritation and excuse themselves to check on the emergency generator, which they are supposed to shut down in fifteen minutes.

After they leave, Todd grows even more bored. He begins listing all of the things he misses the most. A big, fat, juicy steak, for starters. French fries. Buffalo wings. Anything cold to drink. His PC and his X-box game console. Friday nights at the hobby store. *World of Warcraft. Warhammer 40,000.*

"I wonder how much time we spend each day doing things and not actually knowing we're alive," Paul contemplates, draining the last of his wine.

"So what do you miss the most, Reverend?"

Paul grimaces, shaking his head, and leaves Todd to watch the crumbling, snowy image of the tired general by himself.

♦

Sarge mentally counts his pushups—*twenty, twenty-one, twenty-two*—his shirt off and his thickly muscled torso slick with sweat. A medallion engraved with the image of Saint George, the patron saint of soldiers and Boy Scouts—and the victims of plague—dangles from his neck. He has been sitting reclined in the Bradley for over a week, which is like being forced to sit on a tiny couch playing a violent video game, one in which people actually die, for ten days straight. His brain is exhausted while his body has been going soft. Exercise will reboot both. Rest means refit.

His mind wanders to mountains looming over a sprawling base built of sandbag bunkers and huts and tents surrounded by timber walls and concertina wire. *Chinook helicopters pound over the valley with their Apache escort. A patrol toils over distant hills. Soldiers laugh and clean their gear and piss into PVC tubes stuck into the ground. This is Afghanistan.*

"Forget it," he thinks aloud. "Just forget it."

*The first Chinook falls out of the sky and crashes into the mountain, breaking into pieces and spilling bodies as it rolls down into the valley.*

He quickens the pace of his pushups. His heart is racing.

A knock on the door.

*The soldiers at the base begin falling down onto the crushed stones.*

"Not yet," he says, *thirty-seven, thirty-eight, thirty-nine—*

*The bodies are screaming.*

The person knocks again.

He stops, panting. So close. He had come so close to forgetting.

"Come in," he says.

The door opens and Wendy enters. She watches him wipe the sweat from his body with a towel. She seems particularly interested in the bear paw print tattoo on the left side of his chest. He looks away, suddenly feeling naked.

"Has Anne come back?" he says.

Wendy smiles and nods.

"Good," he says.

She reaches into her mouth, extracts a chewed ball of Bazooka gum, and sticks it to the doorframe.

"Good," she says, staring at him.

"So," he adds, feeling awkward.

"So," she says.

The cop takes a step towards him, holds his face in her hands, and kisses him gently on the mouth.

He forgets everything.

◆

Ethan sits on his bed in the fluorescent light, watching his phone lying inert on the floor and drinking red wine out of a Dixie cup. The phone is connected to a power outlet. The power from the emergency generator will shut off in fifteen minutes and he wants to make sure he has his phone charged. It is starting to hit him that they are safe and that they will be living here for a while. Ever since he fled his home with nothing but a backpack, his every waking thought focused on staying away from the Infected when he could and killing them when he could not. After that: water, food, shelter. Now that all of his basic needs are being satisfied, his mind is already beginning to wander to other needs. New clothes and toiletries. Some DVDs to kill the time. Exercise equipment. Some art on the walls. And, perhaps most important, a project that will give him a sense of purpose, that will allow him to start living again instead of simply surviving. Rescuing other survivors, maybe. Starting a greenhouse. Anything to keep out the other emotions that continually threaten to invade his mind. For ten days, he has felt little other than fear, anxiety and panic. Now he is beginning to feel guilt, depression and boredom. A crushing sense of isolation and homesickness. He misses his wife. He misses his little girl. He misses his old life.

We were lucky, Carol, he thinks, his brain soggy with alcohol. We were stupid.

He takes another long sip of wine. It is a ridiculously expensive vintage but he has put down so much already that his taste buds right now could not tell the difference between a fine Bordeaux and Mad Dog.

Ethan takes out his backpack and carefully places a series of artifacts on the bed. A hairbrush with his wife's hair still tangled in it, which no longer smells like her. A yellow rubber airplane, a promotion from an airline during a family vacation to Florida. Plastic piggy: Mary picked it up while playing in a park and would not part with it. Grimy little teddy bear that squeaks when squeezed; Mary used to make it talk back to her in a falsetto voice during pretend conversations. A hairclip.

A card his wife gave him to express how glad she was that he had not been taken from her by the Screaming. Ethan knows the words, written in her fine handwriting, by heart. A wood spirit carving, the face of a bearded old man. A little blue Buddha on a keychain: Carol frequently toured spirituality but could not commit to religion. A photo of her from before Mary was born. Another of them smiling at their wedding, hastily ripped out of its frame before he fled the house. Several wallet photos of Mary when she turned one. The edges are worn from constant handling.

He has dozens of other photos but they are all on his computer at his house. He wants to think that he can go back there one day and get them. That someday the Infected are all going to drop dead or some scientist will invent a cure, and he can go home.

♦

Sarge returns to consciousness with an intense sensation of butterflies in his heart. The beautiful cop is pulling away. He gazes after her sadly, wondering if he did something wrong.

But she says, "Will you hold me?"

"Yes," he says, surprised at how relieved he feels that she is not leaving.

"Just hold me for a minute?"

"I would like that."

Wendy guides him gently to the bed and pushes him down. She curls up next to him. They lie together on their sides, spooning, his large arm wrapped protectively around her stomach.

"This is nice," she purrs. "Jesus, I feel really safe right here. Oh, fucking yes."

Sarge feels the warmth of her body against his. He smells her hair. The sensations are intoxicating; he has not been with a woman since before his deployment to Afghanistan. A long time. He wonders if he can touch her in other places, but does not move. He is afraid of spoiling the moment.

"Do you mind if I sleep here tonight?"

"You can sleep here," he tells her.

"Sarge?"

He frowns at her tone. The moment was spoiled after all. A part of him expected this all along. She is going to ask him why he prefers Anne as leader. He does not want to have to explain the deal he made.

Instead, she says, "Do you think we have a responsibility to other people anymore?"

He blinks in surprise."What do you mean?"

"You're a soldier. I'm a cop. We swore an oath. We have our duty."

Sarge thinks of Ducky, willing to risk everything to find friendly forces.

"We do," he agrees.

"What if this is really a safe place? Are we allowed to stay here and be happy? Or are we obligated to find others like us and see what we can do to help?"

"I don't know, Wendy," he says. "I honestly do not know."

He wants to kiss her again, but she has already fallen asleep in his arms. She is a different person in sleep, so beautiful and innocent it makes his heart ache. His arm is already hurting from the weight of her body but he does not care.

She moans briefly in her sleep, wincing. Her cheeks are wet with tears.

"I'll protect you," he whispers.

♦

Paul stands in the dark on the roof facing north, gazing into more darkness. The fluorescent lighting had begun to make him feel nervous and exposed. It, or the wine over which he had silently mouthed the Sacrament almost without thinking, was starting to give him a headache. He believes he understands why Anne left. He felt a similar yearning to go out into the night. The dark can be a safe place. In the dark, nobody can see you. Sanctuary is what we all wanted, he tells himself, and now we fear it. We fear its illusion of safety and choice.

He lights another cigarette, careful to conceal the flame of his lighter. He coughs on a cloud of smoke. His throat feels scratchy and raw. He is already planning his next cigarette. He has a fresh pack making a comfortable bulge in the pocket of his jacket. He finds renewing his old habit good for the nerves. A habit is reliable. Right now, lung cancer is the least of his worries.

He thinks about the first man he killed. A woman, actually, in the beverage aisle of Trader Joe's market. The woman came running and the shotgun, held in his shaking hands, suddenly seemed to weigh a hundred pounds. He barely remembers firing it—by that point, his heart rate was skyrocketing and his vision had shrunk down to the size of a small circle. He couldn't control his hands. The roar of the gun startled him and he flew back against the empty shelving; then he ran screaming for help. When he returned with the other survivors, he found the woman lying on the ground, her head splashed down the aisle, stone dead. His legs gave out and he cried. Over time, he has gotten better at killing, but he still regrets every one.

The only man he actually wishes he had ever killed was that first Infected who came running at him out of the darkness in the alley behind his house. When he tries to sleep at night, that hateful face lunges out of the dark, flooding his system with adrenaline. He has killed a dozen Infected, wounded perhaps twice that, but that one man still terrifies him. That one man has become more than a memory; he is a symbol of Infection and the hate and fear it has imposed on his life. If Paul could only go back in time, he would fight and kill the man with his bare hands.

He sighs and wonders what Sara would think about the new Paul if she were still alive. He takes comfort in the understanding she loved him and would want him to survive no matter what the cost. She would tell him to kill the thing in the alley. She would say: You are my man and I love you more than myself. She would say: Survive, baby. She would say: Kill them all.

He cannot remember what happened to her. He remembers the grisly slaughter at the church, and the mob, and the battle with the Infected. The next thing he knew, he was huddled in a corner in a temporary shelter set up by the government. He cannot remember anything else but wants to know what happened. Sara is Infected: Knowing will not affect that outcome. But he would like to know. Or rather, he would like to remember.

The sky is covered with flying clouds that hide the moon. For a few minutes, it is so dark that it is easy to imagine he is in a spaceship hurtling lost through the void. Slowly, his vision adjusts to night until he can make out the details of the urban nightscape. He hears muffled gunfire and shouts carried on a fresh breeze. He sees the headlights of a small convoy of vehicles driving far to the west. A bright red line emerges from the darkness in the northeast, like a glowing cut.

He watches the line grow larger, curving, a glowing red scimitar. Fire. A big fire on the south side of the river. He can already smell the smoke. Around the spreading flames, gunshots and screams. People and Infected alike are in flight. Paul shudders. If the fire keeps going, there will be a bloodbath tonight as thousands are flushed out of hiding onto streets filled with Infected. Many of them will come this way. There are few other directions they can go.

Already, down at the edge of the parking lot behind the hospital, he can see gray shapes moving in the dark, writhing and pushing against each other like maggots.

♦

Ethan's head is reeling from the wine and he cannot think straight. He picks up the cell phone, his heart suddenly pounding loudly in his ears, and turns it on. The image tells him that there is no service available in his calling area, another reminder that the entire power grid is down. Cellular networks use radio base stations and networks enabling voice calls and text and connection to the wider telephone network. All of these systems use power, and there is no power because the people who run the power plants, provide fuel to the power plants, and maintain the power distribution system are all dead or Infected or hiding. He feels a crushing headache coming on.

During his family's last vacation together, they joined a group helping baby turtles make it to the sea. The female turtles leave the sea to dig a hole, lay up to two hundred eggs in it, and refill it with sand, the same as they have been doing for millions of years. After the turtles hatch, instinct draws them to the sea. As they emerge from the sand, predators, lying in wait, devour them. Most die; few survive. Only one in a thousand survive the journey. It is a heart wrenching thing to watch but there is no morality here, no overarching narrative, not even a guarantee that just one would make it. There is only life and death and survival of the fittest. This is nature. As Paul would say, the earth abides. The earth is blind to suffering and justice and happy endings.

A part of him believes his family is alive. He pictures Mary, hiding alone in a closet, scared and crying for her mommy and daddy; the image almost physically rips the heart out of his chest. If she is alive, she is a needle in a burning stack of needles. He would not know where to look and he knows that he would not survive five minutes on the streets without the protection of the other survivors and their big fighting vehicle. One in a thousand survive: They are innocent but so few make it and the rest are culled and there is no reason for any of it. He cannot believe his family is dead even though the rational part of his mind knows that this must be true. Ethan understands that he will spend the rest of his life being broken, stuck in the past, unable to say goodbye.

The lights cut out; the soldiers have turned off the power for the night. He becomes aware that he is on his feet pacing, drinking straight out of the bottle in long, painful gulps, his vision blurry with tears. His organs feel like they are in free fall. Ethan coughs on a mouthful of wine, vaguely aware that his right hand is bleeding and alarmingly swollen and throbbing with pain. *My family is dead.* It suddenly feels good to scream. *What did my little girl think when the Infected beat her to death?* He becomes aware of other people in the room. An LED lantern being turned on. He throws the bottle.

*Did she feel any pain?*

Voices cursing.

*Did she wonder where her daddy was?*

Hands on him, pushing him down.

*Was she still alive when they started eating her?*

Voices pleading.

*WHY, WHY, WHY—?*

Ethan lies on the bed screaming, his eyes wide, arching his back against the hands holding him down. His consciousness swims through a haze of guilt and rage, briefly focusing on Anne's face, hovering overhead, just before he feels a jab in his arm and his vision fades to black.

# FLASHBACK:
# TODD PAULSEN

The government closed the schools after the Screaming. For Todd Paulsen, this meant the possibility of early summer vacation.

Four whole months of freedom. No more furtive darting through the crowds in the hallways between classes. No more ritual humiliations during gym class. No more awkward moments trying to secure a seat on the school bus. No more fantasizing about walking into the school with a machine gun and hunting down every jock asshole who ever hurt him. He prayed the school system would stay screwed up until the end of the summer. The Screaming had culled the assholes; graduation would claim most of the rest. Then next year he would be a senior.

The only thing that kept him sane since entering high school was the Lycans, the wargaming club down at Lycan Hobbies. Most of them were guys attending the local college. He counted them as his only friends. He pretty much worshipped them. They were basically geeks like him, but they were much more self-assured and worldly. In fact, to them, *geek* was not an insult, something to be ashamed of, but instead a simple, apt and mildly amusing descriptor. They even dated girls and discussed their dating casually, without fanfare. They assured him that high school may feel like prison but college would be better, so be patient. This tantalizing thought had kept him sane all year.

That, and Sheena X, the high school chick who worked the register at the store and usually sat with her feet up on the counter, chewing gum and reading comic books. Sometimes, she even participated in the gaming on Friday nights. She would typically show up wearing red skinny jeans, Converse All-Stars, and a black T-shirt with SCREAMO or some band name scrawled on it. Often, she wore a matching studded belt and wristband. On colder days, she wore a tight sweater vest. Her hair, dyed black, fell over one eye. She would show up at the store with an obsession of the week. One week, it was getting suicide scars tattooed on her wrists. Another week, making a movie based on the songs of Island Def Jam and Joy Division and Garbage. For the next three weeks, Johnny Depp, Johnny Depp, Johnny Depp. Todd usually communicated with her in an overexcited, virtually shouted stream of consciousness, but instead of rolling her eyes at him and mouthing *freak*, Sheena X simply stared and nodded sagely.

They accepted him, more or less, as he was. They were his port in the unending storm that was his adolescence.

The club played several tabletop miniature wargames but usually *Warhammer 40,000*, set in a space fantasy universe where the Imperium of Man, far flung across the Milky Way galaxy, was in constant conflict with powerful alien species. For many teenagers, music and fashion were their outlets. For Todd, it was gaming. He had painstakingly collected and painted a company of a hundred Space Marines, war machines and bosses, allowing him to participate in smaller games as well as big games, three thousand points and up, that played out over days. The Lycans had just gotten a new codex for urban warfare and had been trying it out with a game between Space Marines and massive swarms of Tyranids. The table presented the ruins of an ancient city in the middle. The Space Marines' mission was to secure the city within several turns and set up a defense in time for a massive Tyranid counterattack. Todd and Alan had just taken the city before the Screaming, and now that school was canceled, he was itching to get back to the game. Alan had fallen down but his opponents were okay, and so the game could continue.

Lycan Hobbies, however, remained closed three days after the Screaming. Finally, in a state of panic, Todd called Sheena X at home. She explained to him that the owner's wife had fallen down, and that he was out of his wits trying to find his brother, who was missing.

"Wow," said Todd. "So do you know when he's going to open the store again?"

"I don't know, dude. What are you doing up this early? You're *never* up this early."

"Sirens woke me up. It's like non-stop sirens out there. Some kind of fire or something."

"I can hear them here, too."

Fires were a common occurrence since the Screaming. A lot of heating devices—ovens, irons and so on—were left on when the screamers fell down. Natural gas systems were not being properly maintained. Power lines were still falling.

"So anyway, do you think he would just let us in so we could finish up our game?"

"*Todd*, what the fuck?"

He launched into a recap of the first night's gaming. She had not been there that night. Surely, if she knew how great it was, she would understand his impatience at continuing the contest. He'd had a simple strategy, he said. He and Alan had sent armor—two Venerable Dreadnoughts with plasma and auto cannons, flanked by Land Speeders armed with missile launchers and heavy bolters—pushing hard through the city, securing it. When the infantry caught up, he sent about half to mop up the remaining resistance and the other half to establish a defensive perimeter in a horseshoe shape. Then the Tyranid counterattack suddenly appeared, a real party made up of Tyrannofex, Termagants, Tervigons and Hive Guard led by a Swarmlord with three Tyrant Guard—

"*Enough*, Todd," Sheena said tersely.

He felt his stomach fall into his feet. "I'm sorry," he said tentatively, his mind racing to figure out what he had done wrong.

"I don't give a shit about *Warhammer* right now. My dad *fell down*, Todd."

"Now he won't bug you anymore," he offered.

"I know I don't like my dad very much," Sheena X said, her voice strained. "I know he can be a real asshole when he wants to be. But I didn't want *this* to happen to him. I didn't want him to go into a fucking *coma*. I didn't want half his foot to get chopped off by the fucking *lawnmower* he was pushing when he fell down." Her voice became shrill. "*Okay?*"

"Okay, Sheena," he said, feeling chastened and more than a little shocked by her language. "I get it. You know, my mom fell down, too."

"I *know*, Todd. Maybe you should be thinking about her instead of that stupid game."

He recoiled, his face burning with embarrassment while anger flared in his chest. She had made him feel childish for enjoying *Warhammer 40,000* when he had always understood that it was a game that adults played. It was not stupid. And his mom was fine. Dad had put her in a special facility where she was getting around-the-clock care. He also tried to get Todd to see a therapist, but luckily they were all booked up with new patients after the Screaming—indefinitely, it seemed. Why would he need a therapist anyhow? He was at home lying on the living room couch sick when the Screaming happened, fast asleep; he had missed the entire thing and had to see it on TV later. Half the school's bullies were in a catatonic state and the school itself had been closed. His mom was sick like the other screamers but he knew that she would be okay. They would all be okay. He had tremendous faith in the government's ability to solve problems like this. A cure was coming.

Todd said nothing, racking his brain for something to say, maybe something funny that would ease the tension.

She sighed. "I got to go, Todd. My *mom* is yelling for me."

"All right."

"Oh my *God*," Sheena X shrieked happily. "Mom says Dad is waking up!"

"That's great," Todd said, laughing.

"I got to go. Bye, Todd!"

Todd hung up, grinning. If Sheena X's dad was waking up, so was his mom.

His grin evaporated. *And so are all the others.* Like John Wheeler.

And they would reopen the school. Maybe even keep school going past the end of June to make up for the lost time. Todd felt deflated at the thought. God had a crappy sense of humor.

The phone rang. That would be his dad bearing good news. He picked up the receiver.

"Todd, listen—"

Couldn't they all just stay asleep for one more month?

"Hey, Dad. Are you calling about Mom?"

"Listen to me. I don't have much time. That barricade is not going to hold. We have nothing to fight them with—"

"Aren't you at work?" His dad worked in an office as a manager of something. In one of those big cubicle farms like you see in *Dilbert*.

"You need to get my gun. It's in a shoebox on the top shelf of me and your mom's closet. Make sure you get the bullets, too. Don't leave the house. Shoot anybody who breaks in. Shoot to kill."

Todd laughed. "Dad?"

"They're coming in. DON'T RUN! STAY TOGETHER! FIGHT! Todd, I don't know. I *don't know.* We're fucked. I love you, kid. Yeah. I guess that's it. Take care of yourself."

A flurry of screams at the other end of the phone.

"Dad?" Todd said into the dial tone.

He smelled smoke through the open window. Sirens continued wailing from all four corners of the city. Other sounds ripped the air: screams. And splashes of gunfire, startlingly loud. Todd looked out the window but saw nothing out of the ordinary. Just his boring little typical suburban street washed in bright May sunshine. Every lawn was perfectly manicured; even the front yards of the homes abandoned by the screamers had been well tended by charitable neighbors. Looking at this gentle scene, it was hard to believe that even the Screaming had happened.

One thing was wrong, though: The street was empty except for a single distant running figure, which quickly disappeared behind a house. The headlines on the major news sites on the Internet announced widespread rioting in California. Todd wanted to head downstairs and turn on the TV to find out what was going on, but remained rooted where he stood, torn between the thrill of massive developing tragedy and the uncertain terror of finding out that something awful had happened to his dad. He tried calling his dad's office line and got voicemail. He left a message, trying to figure out what to do next to keep his growing sense of panic at bay a little longer.

He looked down at his front yard and saw a big cop in a motorcycle helmet marching purposefully down the sidewalk.

"Hey, officer!" he called. "What's going on?"

The policeman looked up at the window, showing his gray face and wet, blackened chin.

"Are you okay?" Todd said.

The man ran up the front walk of his house, quickly disappearing from view.

"What the hell is he doing?" Todd mumbled to himself, both alarmed and amused.

He heard the front door crash open. Moments later, the motorcycle cop came banging up the stairs.

"Oh, crap," he said.

Todd threw himself onto the floor as he heard the stomping in the hall, and crawled under the bed as his door flew open, knocking half his Space Marines off his dresser.

The cop paced around the room impatiently, sniffing the air and shouldering the walls. Todd lay under the bed and tried not to breathe, flooded with panic and fear. The emotions reminded him of school, the strange feeling that everybody hated him. He watched the cop's boots track blood across his carpet. The minutes ticked by. The cop continued to pace and knock things over. The room began to fill with a rancid sour-milk stench, forcing Todd to breathe through his mouth. After an hour, the cop left. Todd heard him in the bathroom, splashing in the toilet. Then the man came back, coughing wetly, and resumed his march around the room.

After a few hours of this, Todd grew bored and eventually fell asleep.

He woke up dry-mouthed and sweaty and fighting a massive urge to piss. He almost cried out at the jolt of confusion he felt waking up under his bed, but remembered the danger he was in and wisely kept his mouth shut. Thank God he had not snored or farted or laughed or did any of the other things he speculated that he did in his sleep. He had no idea what time it was; the sun had gone down and he could barely see his hand in front of his face. The maniac cop was no longer pacing but was still in the room. Todd could smell his sour stink and hear him breathing in quick, shallow gasps. He wondered if the man was sleeping. Should he risk moving? The thought of leaving the security of his hiding place paralyzed him with fear. He did not know exactly what the cop would do to him if he caught him but just the idea of being dominated physically by a stronger man electrified him with revulsion. He stalled by fantasizing about his dad coming home, and warning him just in time that the cop was there, saving his life. Then he fantasized about Sheena X coming over to check on him, and saving her life, which gave him an erection. An hour went by like this while the night breezes delivered the sounds of screams and squealing tires and gunfire through his window.

He realized that he had to do something soon or he might be trapped under this bed for another full day. He crept towards the far edge of the bed, stopping to listen every few inches. The policeman panted like a dog. Finally, he left the shelter of the bed and wondered what to do next. A part of him wanted to stand up and make a run for it on pure adrenaline, but this notion was quickly overruled by his tiny but growing voice of common sense. Do nothing and you're going to die, Todd old man, he told himself. So do something. The bedroom door was open and the cop was somewhere to his left. If the man was facing the door, he would see Todd. If he was not, then Todd might have a chance.

He slithered forward like a snake and paused at the edge of the bed, peering at the dark form swaying on its feet in the darkness. The cop was facing the corner. The white motorcycle helmet bobbed as the man breathed in his little shallow gasps, his shoulders shrugging in rhythm.

This is really freaking *ninja*, he thought.

Within minutes, Todd was free and gently closing the door behind him. He tiptoed to his parents' bedroom, emptied his bladder quietly into the sink in the en suite bathroom, and began pulling boxes down from the top shelf of the closet until he found a heavy blue shoebox. Inside, he found nestled a small handgun, box of bullets and sheet of paper. He took the sheet to the window and squinted at it under the light of nearby streetlights. It was a note from his dad to him saying the gun was loaded and had no safety, so do not even think about touching it if he ever found it.

Awesome, he thought, picking up the gun.

The gun roared in his hand, punching two smoking holes through the wall. He blinked in the afterglow of the flash, his ears ringing and his nose burning from the cordite.

"Holy crap," he said. His voice sounded muffled in his ears. "Aw, jeez. I barely touched it."

Dad's gonna murder me for that, he thought.

As his hearing returned to normal, he became aware that the cop was roaring and banging on his bedroom door. Todd ran to the hall, braced his legs and aimed the pistol with both hands. Strangely, the presence of the gun made him feel weaker instead of stronger. His hands started to shake. The door was shivering and splintering under the blows. He took a deep breath to try to calm himself. Picture the outcome, he told himself. He envisioned the cop bursting through the door and lunging out of the gloom. He imagined squeezing the trigger and putting two in the chest and one between the eyes. He pictured the crazy cop dying before he hit the floor.

"Screw that," he said, lowering the pistol.

He ran down the stairs, stepped into his shoes at the front entry and bolted out of the house. Almost immediately he collided with a snarling woman coming up the driveway, the gun going off in his hands again and taking the top of her head off.

"Crap, sorry," he said to the crumpling form, and kept running, into the night.

He became winded after a few blocks and slowed down, cradling the gun carefully against his chest. He heard the tramp of feet and quickly hid as a pack of people ran by growling, their torn shirts flapping. People were screaming everywhere. On the next block, a house was burning without a single fireman on the scene; he could feel the heat on his face. He fought the urge to cough on the smoke.

Todd began to feel as if he were moving through a nightmare. Changing direction to avoid the fire, he approached a group of people huddled on the ground near the wreckage of a horrible car crash in the middle of an intersection. He wanted to ask if they were all right but the tiny voice of common sense warned him to stick to the shadows.

One of the cars was on fire, the light glittering on the tiny shards of broken glass carpeting the ground.

As he passed the group of people, he realized they were hunched over a body, pulling out organs and chewing noisily. The light crawled across their gray, bloody faces. He fought the urge to retch.

Picture them eating something nice, he told himself. Fried chicken. They're eating a bucket of fried chicken. Crispy fried chicken with a side of fries. That's all. No big deal.

Bad idea. The contents of his stomach leaped into his throat and he vomited noisily against a brick wall, helpless, his eyes filled with water. When he turned back, he saw that one of the eaters was looking right at him. He knew they were different—crazy, demonic, even—but they couldn't see in the dark, could they? He clung to the wall, trying not to move and yet shaking uncontrollably. The woman was topless, her chest wet and darkly stained, firelight gleaming in her black eyes. Todd stared wide-eyed at her bare breasts. Eventually, she lowered her head back to resume her grisly meal.

People are turning into cannibals, he thought. What the hell is going on? Where am I supposed to go? He suddenly wanted to find a computer or TV so he could see what was happening. Maybe a phone so he could call his dad again. Maybe his dad was dead. He tried not to think about it.

Sheena X. He decided to go to her house, help her barricade the place, and wait out this zombie apocalypse together. He was rolling a fantasy of them sharing the pain of their parents being dead—followed by the realization that that they are in love, and a huge make-out scene—when the Infected came running out of the darkness, howling and reaching for him.

Todd ran in a blind panic. Jesus, he thought. These people want to kill me. The very idea sapped the energy from his legs. Made him suddenly want to sleep. His mind swam in panic. If only, he thought. It's not fair, he thought. His lungs were gasping for air on razor blades. The gun, he thought. He remembered the pistol in his hand.

He slowed and turned as the first Infected bore down on him, a big man wearing a T-shirt soaked through with blood and sweat, emitting a long, terrible shriek. Todd squeezed the trigger on reflex, forgetting to aim. The bullet entered the side of the man's head just above the ear, instantly turning half his skull into a spray of blood and skull fragments. The Infected staggered, shaking his head vigorously as if sneezing, shaking free pieces of brain, and then collapsed. The death of this monster struck Todd as nothing short of a miracle.

"Yeah!" he cried through a haze of gun smoke.

More came howling out of the darkness. He had to wait until they got close so he could be sure that he would hit them. But if they got too close, he would panic and run and then they would get him. Todd blanked out his mind, breathing heavily through his nose and trying to slow his heart rate, and pictured the scene as an online first-person shooter game, letting his hand-eye reflexes take over, shifting his aim and firing as the Infected approached.

"I am invincible," he sang off key, wishing for a soundtrack, then stopped, unable to remember the rest of the words to the song. The fight was over in seconds. He blinked, surveying the bodies of five Infected lying on the ground moaning and thrashing.

He approached the twitching bodies carefully, watching for any who might make a last-second movie lunge and deliver a mortal wound that would be just payment for his hubris. One of them was a police officer. Todd was curious about him because he shot the man three times but the cop kept getting up and coming at him until the last bullet destroyed the right side of his head. The mystery was solved easily; the man wore a bullet-proof vest.

Todd pulled the vest off the man and put it on himself. It was a little big and it was heavier than he thought it would be, but he loved it. He had seen them on TV, of course, and had always wanted one. He thought it made him look bigger, bulkier, tougher than he usually felt when he looked in the mirror. He sensed that he could be good at this—surviving in a post-apocalyptic world.

Looks like school is out forever, he thought. The thought almost made him happy.

He continued his march. After a while, the sky began to lighten; dawn was coming. He had to get off the street soon. His heart pounded as he approached Sheena X's house.

Wait until she sees me in this gear, he told himself. She'll be all over me.

The porch light was on, as if she were expecting him. Lights were on in the house. The door was ajar. He rang the doorbell and waited.

Todd backed away, shaking his head.

"Aw, Sheena . . ."

The screen door banged open and Sheena X stumbled out of the house, twitching and gray-faced, the front of her T-shirt soaked with blood, her hair still combed over one eye.

"No," he said. "Oh, no."

"*Rah, ruh,*" she snarled.

"I'm sorry, Sheena."

Todd raised the gun and fired. The bullet punctured her skull and splashed her brains onto the screen door. She collapsed instantly, leaving a puff of smoke and bloody mist hanging in the air.

The crash of the gunshot echoed down the street and mingled with millions of similar sounds occurring all over the city, rising up to the sky as a single chaotic roar.

Todd sat on the ground in a daze, unsure of what he felt. Then it all suddenly hit him. Within moments, he was shaking uncontrollably and hugging his knees and bawling.

# THE FIRE

The three survivors stand on the hospital roof and watch the growing fire consume western Pittsburgh. The sky over the east glows red as buildings continue to burn downtown, soar up into the sky on powerful convection currents, and rain back down as particulates. The air is thick with heat and smoke and falling ash. The night is alive with gunfire and screams.

"Paul was right," Anne says. "It's huge. And it's moving."

"Gone," Wendy says, her voice cracking. "It's all gone."

Sarge says, "We've got to get out of here. Tonight."

♦

The survivors race in and out of their rooms in the glow of LED lanterns, throwing bags and supplies into the corridor. Their shadows flicker across the walls. Shouts echo in the gloom. A box rips open and cans spill and roll noisily across the floor. A handful of bullets clatter and roll like marbles. The survivors know they cannot stay here and yet none of them want to go outside. They never go outside at night, but they have no choice. The fire has produced a massive migration. Pittsburgh is on the move. The fire is flushing thousands of people out of their hiding places and into the streets to mingle with the fleeing Infected. The numbers of Infected must be increasing exponentially, by the minute, and they are all headed this way in a tidal wave.

"What about Ethan?" Todd says, panting.

Sarge glances at Anne, who shakes her head almost imperceptibly.

"He's coming with us," he growls, glaring at her.

"Goddamn right he's coming," Paul says.

"I got him," says Sarge.

The soldier grabs the front of Ethan's shirt and pulls him to his feet, cursing as the man instantly spews a small bucket of spaghetti and red wine onto the floor. Then he heaves the man up and over one shoulder and his rucksack over the other like a counterbalance.

The survivors hustle down the stairs in a train, moving as fast as they can with as little light as possible, and begin dumping supplies at the entrance of the hospital. Sarge drops Ethan in a heap in the vestibule and turns to scan the outside parking lot using his rifle's night vision close combat optic. The optic amplifies ambient light thousands of times and creates an image rendered in green. He can make out grainy figures marching through the parking lot.

"Where's our ride?" Todd says, his voice edged with panic.

Steve and Duck went to retrieve the Bradley, and if they do not come back, the survivors will be stranded. And probably die.

"It's coming," Sarge hisses. "I'll cover here. The rest of you: Go get the rest of our shit."

Anne touches his shoulder, asking the unspoken question, *Do you need me for anything?*

"Light," he says.

They have flashlights, but turning one on right now would be like ringing a dinner bell. Instead, he needs fire—flares, Molotovs. He does not have to explain this. Anne knows what to do.

He suddenly thinks about Wendy, his heart racing. It was always nothing to take care of himself, but now he is worried about her, too. It is hard to aim a rifle when your heart is pounding in your chest. He pushes his worries roughly out of his mind and breathes slowly and steadily for a few moments until he has regained complete control of his nerves.

Crowds of Infected flow through the cars in the parking lot, squealing and shoving and howling. A pack of them breaks off with strident cries, pounding towards the hospital, apparently curious about what might be inside, their eyes gleaming bright green in Sarge's optic.

They never stop searching for us, Sarge thinks, as he pulls the trigger and cuts them down with several bursts.

♦

Steve and Ducky race between the rows of abandoned cars in the parking garage, guided by their night vision goggles, rifles held in the aiming position.

The sounds of distant fire and chaos, a constant roar filling the air like white noise, is suddenly undercut by the characteristic *ping* of Sarge's AK47. The commander is blazing away at somebody down at the front of the hospital, from the sound of it. Steve takes a moment to look out from the second floor of the parking garage. He sees the muzzle flashes and, beyond, the Infected streaming through the cars towards the hospital, adding their shrieks to the night's din.

"Let's go," Ducky hisses from somewhere ahead of him.

Steve nods. He wants to help Sarge, but the only way he can do that is to get the Bradley down there as fast as possible.

He trained to fight to protect his country, but he never trained for this. Of course, he is scared. They are all scared, all of the time, even in their dreams. But more than that, he hates, with every atom and every fiber in his being, killing other Americans. The first time he did that, he stopped being a soldier. He trusts Sarge and will go on following his orders as long as it helps keep them all alive, but Steve isn't in Sarge's Army anymore.

A noise like a foghorn stops them in their tracks, followed by a deep, rumbling, phlegmy cough. Steve and Ducky crouch behind the hood of a car and scan the area. Something big is moving through the far end of the garage, pushing vehicles out of its way with its lumbering strength.

"What is that?" Ducky says, his voice cracking. "One of those worms?"

"No. Yes. I don't know."

Steve turns on the SureFire flashlight mounted on his rifle and aims it at the thing moving through the gloom. The flashlight has a red lens, making the beam barely visible to anybody not wearing night vision goggles. On NVGs, the light appears a brilliant green. The beam plays along the smooth flank of something big striding ponderously through the garage, coughing deep in its massive lungs.

"Some kind of elephant or something," Ducky says.

"Or something. At least it's moving away from us."

The thing shoulders aside an SUV, setting off a car alarm.

Ducky pats Steve's arm and says, "We'd better get moving."

They find the Bradley where they left it in the corner. Steve pulls at the massive black plastic tarp, exposing a yellow happy face stenciled on the vehicle's side. Moving quickly and expertly, he and Ducky begin folding the tarp.

Another sound distracts them. Something making a wet clicking sound deep in its throat.

The soldiers stop, look, listen, aiming their carbines into the darkness.

"We don't have time for this," Steve says.

"Forget the tarp, then," Ducky tells him. "Just get in the rig."

Steve ignores him, staring intently at the source of the noise, a squat, stumbling shadow. At first, he believes it is a child on a tricycle, the noise a squeaky wheel. He takes two steps forward until freezing as the shadow reveals itself.

"Oh my God," Ducky says.

The creature looks like a little sickly albino baboon wobbling on legs articulated like a grasshopper's, grotesque on something its size. Its little barrel chest heaves as it takes rapid, wheezing breaths. Despite its shocking appearance, it appears almost harmless, a bizarre mutation thrust into a hostile world, barely equipped to survive, a pale and hungry thing.

"Kill it," Steve says, his skin crawling with revulsion.

At the sound of his voice, the baboon thing stops, fixes its gleaming eyes on Ducky, and roars massively, showing rows of teeth like knives. A moment later, its nose wrinkles and the elongated face shakes with a massive sneeze, spraying a cloud of mucus.

Ducky raises his carbine and fires a quick burst but the thing is already flying through the air, shrieking. It lands with a thump on the soldier's chest, hugging his body and champing its teeth down on his Kevlar body armor.

Steve aims his weapon but hesitates. He does not have a shot. Ducky is reeling drunkenly, screaming for help, trying to push the thing off of him.

Steve drops the rifle, pulls out his knife, and closes in, slashing. The thing shrieks in pain and a jet of scalding, oily liquid shoots up his arm.

And then it is gone, vaulting into the air and landing ten feet away, where it briefly whines and hisses before disappearing into the dark in a series of long, flying leaps.

Steve races to collect his rifle until stopped cold by Ducky gasping, "I'm hit."

◆

Sarge drops an empty magazine, pops in a fresh thirty-round mag, and chambers the first round in a single rapid, fluid motion. He fires a quick burst, cutting down an Infected racing at him with a bloodcurdling howl. Sarge had gotten the automatic rifle from a dead Taliban fighter, who had probably gotten it off of a dead soldier during the Soviet occupation, long ago. More than a souvenir, he treasures the rifle for the simple fact that it almost never jams. It is rugged and reliable if a bit inaccurate, but between the close combat optic he had retrofitted onto it and the close range of less than a hundred meters, he is dropping bodies steadily.

He misses a shot and curses. He is tiring, getting sloppy. He fires again, and the snarling man goes down wearing a surprised look on his face.

Sarge knows he cannot keep up this pace. Anne must either show up with the flares and Molotovs or the Bradley must show up to get them all out of Dodge. If neither happens soon, the Infected will take him and that will be that.

His eyes continually sweep the parking lot while barely moving, absorbing every detail and instantly assessing it as a threat, an asset or nothing. The robot has taken over; he is in complete survival mode, every part of him focused on fight and the option of flight. Being under fire in Afghanistan has given him the ability to look at the world as a palette of survival. He finds it bizarrely unsettling to be in combat, firing his rifle steadily at close targets standing out in the open, without worrying about the snap of bullets flying past his ear. When he blinks, sometimes he sees insurgents running at him at a crouch, not Infected. Time is compressing and he has little idea of whether he has been out here for minutes or an hour.

No matter how many of them he kills, they never quite feel like the enemy. Even after all of the atrocities he has seen, he cannot bring himself to hate them.

The worst is when they come at him wearing military uniforms.

The flares go arcing high into the sky, landing among the derelict cars, bursting with a fierce orange glow and revealing scores of moving figures.

Anne taps his shoulder, then raises her rifle, peers into the scope, and takes down a running woman with a colossal bang and flash of light.

"It's about time," he grunts, still firing.

Anne is a different sort than him, he knows. Anne has enough hate for both of them.

The asphalt vibrates with stomping feet.

"Swarm!" says Wendy, standing with her Glock held ready in case any Infected get close.

"I'm on it," Todd yells, lighting his first Molotov.

The Infected bob among the cars, blending into a howling mob racing through the night towards the six survivors.

"Molotov out!" Todd cries.

The flaming bottle soars through the air and hits one of the Infected in the chest, bursting into a wide sheet of fire that turns her and five others into staggering, screeching human torches.

"Good throw, boy," Paul says, yelling, "Molotov!"

The flaming bottle arcs over the Infected's heads, bursting on the roof of a station wagon. A group of Infected races through the fire, the clothing on their arms and legs suddenly igniting with flaming gasoline, and continue running at the survivors until Wendy cuts them down with her handgun. The fire flares briefly, then suddenly ebbs and begins to fizzle out.

"It's starting to get dicey out here, Sarge," Todd says, his voice breathless and panicky.

"Shut up, Kid," says Sarge. "This ain't nothing."

Actually, they are in deep shit. The enemy is relentless and inexhaustible. His own tiny force is tired, scared and fighting with a limited supply of ammunition. In the long run, the Infected will either overrun them or force them back into the hospital, where they will be killed by the expanding fire or stuck barricaded behind some door for who knows how long.

Unless the Bradley gets here first.

He sizes up his next target, the red dot in the close combat optic hovering on the man's chest. He squeezes the trigger, the view shakes violently, and the man drops.

And another. And another. Bankers and housewives and bakers and students and firemen.

Behind him, Wendy and Paul are firing. The Infected press in on the flanks. Somebody throws a Molotov and Sarge hears the bottle shatter dangerously close; he can feel the heat from it.

A loud metallic squealing fills the air.

"What is that?" Paul says, sweeping the parking lot with his shotgun. The gun fires with a deafening roar, cutting a howling woman almost in half.

The squealing grows louder, like a giant eagle descending on its prey.

Sarge grins. That sound, he thinks, is the cavalry arriving in the nick of time.

The Bradley slams through a row of nearby cars on its screeching treads, its main gun blazing like thunder and lightning. Sarge sees the familiar BOOM STICK on the side of the turret. The red tracers stream toward the far end of the parking lot, where the cannon rounds rip apart Infected and cars alike and fling both into the air like confetti in a series of mushrooming fireballs. The survivors watch this incredible violence in silence until the Bradley grinds to a halt nearby.

The tail lights wink and the ramp drops, promising safety in its dark interior.

♦

Ducky Jones sits in a semi-reclined position in the driver's station in the left front of the hull, hands on the steering yoke and foot working the pedals, eyes glued to the center periscope that offers night vision. He removes his right hand from the yoke and shifts into higher gear using the selector lever, engaging the transmission. Building speed, he scans the gauges arrayed across the dashboard with a single glance before returning his attention to the periscope. To his right, the five-hundred-horsepower Cummins engine hums loudly, with heart, propelling the heavy vehicle forward on its treads.

He is working the accelerator and brake pedals with his left foot instead of his right. His right leg is completely numb below the knee. The bruise on his hip is the size of a grapefruit now and continues to throb steadily like a drum made out of pain. The agony is incredible. He wonders if this is what it is like to be shot. To donate bone marrow. He wipes sweat from his face and stifles a moan. Deep down, he knows that he is growing weaker by the moment, that he is, in fact, dying a little at a time.

Ducky was a ten-year-old military history buff when the September 11 attacks shocked the country. He made a decision that day to become a soldier. Years later, he made good on that decision and enlisted. By that time, the ideals of fighting for freedom around the globe had deteriorated into the usual lies, betrayal and corruption. The guy who planned the attack on the Towers got away with it while big business cashed in on the wars. It was a valuable lesson in a fact of life: That which is pure is precious and easily corrupted. But he was still idealistic enough to believe that something could be pure. He loved his country and wanted to serve. Maybe he could do something good. He still believed one man could make a difference. At least he would get to see history up close and maybe make some himself instead of just reading about it.

The Army became his life. He lived on the base and had Army friends and dated women his friends introduced him to. He complained about the Army constantly but he loved it like a second mother, and would deck any civilian (or serviceman from another branch of the military) who dared criticize it. He thought about death philosophically, as young men tend to do, and accepted the fact that one day he might die for his comrades in combat. As he saw war close up in Afghanistan, his ideals faded even further. He watched as the Army built a clinic in a village and then accidentally bombed its school. But he still believed in one thing that was pure and could never be corrupted—the sacrifice of comrades for each other in combat. He believed that dying in combat, fighting for the men next to him, was a truly honorable death, which it was.

Ducky had never imagined he might die of a bizarre, enormously painful infection growing in his body, planted there by a sickly mutant, while driving out of the burning ruins of a major American city. There is no honor in this total war, this war of extermination, only futility and waste. There will be no medal for him. No historian to record his deeds. Possibly, there is not even a country anymore for which to die. Instead, he will die with people he barely knows in the ruins of a country he loves at the end of history. Not what he imagined at all.

The simple fact is Ducky is still fighting the pain and driving the vehicle because he is living on borrowed time and is willing to give that time to help these people stay alive themselves a little longer. There must be some honor in that.

♦

The Bradley rolls into a downed telephone pole, cracking it into splinters and dragging a tangle of insulated cable and chunks of wood clattering after it. The gunner and commander sit at their stations, gripping handles used to maneuver the turret and fire the weapons, the gunner using a periscope with night vision while the commander sees what the gunner sees using an optical relay.

"There's something wrong with the ISU," Sarge says, squinting.

Next to him in the cramped, dark compartment, the gunner shakes his head.

"I can't see shit, Steve," Sarge complains. "What the hell now?"

He taps the display, which accomplishes nothing. Under the familiar reticle, large, flickering pale green blobs glow brightly, which he interprets as fires. Off to the left, he can see little bursts of pale green light, which he knows from experience are muzzle flashes; there are people out there shooting. He can make out a road sign announcing ROUTE 22, 376, the Penn Lincoln Parkway. But the rest makes no sense. His visual is filled with bizarre shapes that seethe across the screen at different speeds in multiple shades of green, as if the relay were on a bad acid trip.

"I saw a sign," Sarge says. He activates the comm and says, "Take the next exit for Parkway West, Ducky."

*Wilco,* Ducky says.

They are almost home free now. Once they reach the highway, they will break west and escape the conflagration.

He adds to Steve, "Not that it matters. We could get on the eastbound highway and still go west. It ain't like somebody's going to write us a ticket for driving the wrong way, right?"

Except maybe Wendy, he thinks, suppressing a grin. He briefly wonders what she sees in him. Aside from the uniform and the values it represents, he does not consider himself to be anything special—a "big lug," the kind of guy that beautiful girls like Wendy would consider a valuable friend, but not a lover. Most girls like that fall for the gunner with his square jaw and surfer build.

Steve says nothing, glued to his periscope.

"All right, Steve?"

"Not now, Sergeant," the gunner says, his voice tight, gritting his teeth.

"What do you see? What's going on out there?"

Steve turns away from the periscope with a wince, making Sarge's heart skip a beat in sudden alarm. His face is taut. Droplets of sweat glisten on his forehead. His eyes are gleaming like those of an animal caught in a steel trap.

"See for yourself."

"But . . ."

"There is nothing wrong with the equipment," the gunner tells him.

"This interference . . ."

"What you are seeing is *real.*"

"Steve . . ."

"Look, Sergeant. Look again."

Sarge concentrates on the images unfolding on the commander's optical relay and gasps as the tumbling, seemingly random shapes begin to coalesce into monsters.

The Bradley hurtles down the road, punching cars out of the way or flattening them, surrounded by a ragged column of creatures joining the exodus out of the burning city. Little baboons hobbling on insect legs. Lumbering and tentacled behemoths. A leathery wall impossibly covered with screaming human faces. Giant balls of flesh, like ticks bloated with blood, strutting on spindly tripod legs. A thing with massive lobster claws where its hands should be. A half dozen other species. And of course, hundreds of Infected marching like refugees in their grimy and tattered T-shirts and uniforms and business suits and jeans and dresses. The murmuring of the Infected competes with the constant roar of the rig's engine.

The fire appears to be flushing everything out of their hiding places tonight. The conflagration soars into the air behind them, flowing into the sky and coming back down in a constant rain of ash on this parade of monsters.

"What are these things?" Steve asks in a childlike voice. "What does this mean?"

♦

The survivors look at each other with gaping eyes in the dark, hot interior of the Bradley, gasping for air and scarcely able to believe they are still alive when so many thousands of people were either claimed by the Infected or burned alive in the fire. Every breath astounds them. Their bodies are slick with sweat and their old street clothes, already damp from washing earlier in the day, cling to their flesh. It is so hot it feels like they are being cooked in a microwave. They can barely move, almost buried in boxes and bulging plastic bags and gallon jugs. Cans and bottles roll around their feet, making a sudden clatter as the Bradley takes a sharp turn. Ethan is stuffed crumpled into a corner, breathing shallowly, ignored.

Anne is experiencing a deep sense of contentment to be back on the road. She finds familiar comfort in the drone of the engine and the smells of fear and body odor and burning diesel. They are safe here, for now, in the Bradley's dark and sweltering metal stomach. She opens a bottle of water, takes a long pull, and passes it on. She welcomes the road. This is where she is meant to be.

Sitting across from her, Wendy covers a private smile with her hand.

Anne stares at her, wondering what could possibly be worth smiling about right now.

Wendy sees her watching and says, "Did you ever do something on crazy impulse and it turned out to be the best idea you ever had?"

"No," Anne says, struggling to remember a time when that might have been true.

The cop frowns and turns away. Anne did not mean to offend her. Sometimes, she feels like she no longer knows how to be a real person and connect with other real people in a real way. Everything she thinks, feels or remembers ultimately winds up taking her to a dark place in her mind where people die over and over. She does not know how to tell Wendy that she lived most of her life obeying her impulses, and that they eventually got everybody she loved killed.

♦

"Ducky's hurt," Steve says. "He says he's okay, but I think he's hurt real bad."

Sarge says nothing. He waits for the gunner to continue.

"There were things in the garage, Sarge. Fucking *monsters*. Dark shapes that flitted around the cars, always just out of sight. Then we saw one. A giant bloated thing covered in elephant trunks that boomed like a foghorn. When it made that sound, the trunks stuck out straight, shaking. Like something out of a nightmare. It pushed cars out of its way. Made you want to puke just to look at it. Then we saw a little white, hairless monkey with thick insect legs, barely able to walk. It was sickly, diseased. It could barely see. It was in pain. It was like a newborn, Sarge. A freak of nature that somehow survived against all odds and was walking along making this bizarre clicking noise in its throat. Kind of sad, like a little kid looking for his family.

"The little bastard jumped on Ducky. The only way I could get it off was to cut it with my knife. Ducky went down, saying he was hit. The thing had sharp teeth and had been biting around Ducky's throat, so I assumed that's where he was wounded, but I couldn't find a wound. His neck was wet but there was no blood. So I asked him where he was wounded, and he said his hip. The little fucker had used his teeth like he used his arms and legs, to hold on. It was . . . I don't want to say what it had been doing to Ducky's hip, but it was unnatural. It . . . stabbed him, with this big stinger between its legs, like a barbed scorpion's tail. The puncture left a massive bruised lump. He insisted on driving. I had to help him into the rig. He could barely walk."

Steve stops talking. Sarge takes a few moments to rub his eyes. Outside, the horde of Infected continue making noise like a house being slowly ransacked, barely audible over the loud hum of the Bradley's engine. He hears no more gunfire.

"Ducky," Sarge says into the microphone attached to his helmet, "do you copy?"

*I'm okay, Sergeant,* the driver answers.

"How's that wound?"

*I said I'm okay.*

"We'll pull over at the nearest safe point and get it looked at."

*By who? Who's going to look at it?*

Sarge does not know how to answer. The fact is they have little in the way of real medical supplies, no medical knowledge, no medevac. They are completely on their own.

*I'm still fit for duty. So let me do my job while I still can.*

Sarge nods grudgingly. He does not know what to say. Perhaps he should just say thanks.

"You sit tight," he says, gritting his teeth. "We're going to try to find help for you."

*Sergeant, I just wanted to say—*

The air fills with an enormous roar of rage so pervasive that at first Sarge is convinced that it originated inside his own head.

♦

The survivors flinch at the sound and stare at each other, their eyes big and watery. The roar stops as suddenly as it began, replaced by pounding footsteps and a sudden *boom* that makes the rig tremble like a gong. The sound rattles through their bodies and hums in their brains, knocking out every thought as effectively as high voltage. They wince and cup their ringing ears in the aftermath. Then another *boom*, jostling them, vibrating deep in their chests.

The roar again, filling the air, followed by another *BOOM*. Something is hitting the Bradley repeatedly. The rig tries to speed up, lurches, corrects itself. Wendy sees Paul huddled with his arms wrapped around his ribs, his eyes clenched shut and his mouth working silently. She never saw the Reverend pray before. She finds it deeply disturbing, the idea that the Bradley is unsafe.

The roar never seems to end. It cascades in waves of endless despair and rage that scrapes its nails repeatedly over the chalkboard of her nerves. It fills the air so completely she finds herself struggling to breathe it. She still has enough sense to understand that whatever is out there, it is big and powerful and angry. She has a moment to wonder about the size of its lungs. Then her mind blanks out completely as the terrible sound of the attack builds and builds. The sound finally punches its way out of the paper bag of Wendy's mind and she screams, the sound tinny and distant and lost like a child shouting in a wind tunnel. She reaches out and Todd clasps her hand tightly before another *boom* jostles them violently against the boxes and each other. Todd lashes out with his other hand, pushing at the boxes in blind panic. Across from her, Anne is shouting angrily and Paul is grimacing and cupping his ears with his palms.

The siege lasts for years; it lasts for minutes. The thing outside suddenly appears to lose interest, lagging behind. The last tremor dissipates through the Bradley's armor and their bones. The last roar fades, leaving behind a deafening echoing ring in their ears and a tingling vibration deep in their chests. The thing cries plaintively in the distance, as if sad to see the Bradley go and calling for its return. Wendy gasps for air, her heart clanging in her chest like a bell. She sees the terrified pale faces crying in the dark and barely recognizes them. She touches her mouth, unsure if she has stopped screaming yet.

The Bradley crashes through an abandoned military checkpoint and then the survivors are free of Pittsburgh at last. Behind them, the city burns like an early sunrise.

# FLASHBACK:
# SERGEANT TOBY WILSON

Combat Outpost Sawyer had all the beauty of a heavily fortified shantytown. But the mountains were breathtaking. This was the roof of the world.

Afghanistan, land of the Afghans.

As the Bradley topped the crest and drove along the escarpment, Sarge, sitting in his telescoped seat with the hatch open, got his first good look at the outpost that was just another island in a vast archipelago of little firebases scattered across the mountains.

The soldiers here called it Mortaritaville.

Sawyer lay perched on the valley's long slope, a sprawling little compound of sandbag bunkers and huts and tents around which sturdy timber walls and rows of C-wire had been erected. From here, on the ridge, it appeared tiny and weak.

Sarge whistled. The base had been poorly sited. A series of ridges commanded the base. From there, Afghan fighters could drop mortar rounds right into the middle of the compound and then drop behind the ridge, disappearing from view. The nearest helicopter support was at least twenty-five minutes away. No wonder the boys here were reported to be so fatalistic, living in this remote place in almost total isolation, with an enemy that could strike from anywhere at any time.

The Bradley began to catch up to a "jingle" truck, a high-axled vehicle painted in bold and bright colors and jingling with hundreds of shiny bangles. Luridly painted female eyes stared at him from the rear bumper, as enigmatic as a cat's. The truck was open in the back and several men sat inside wearing the baggy trousers and loose tunics typical of Afghan men.

Smiling in the dust cloud raised in the wake of their truck, Sarge waved.

The men glanced at each other until one of them nodded, apparently giving permission to another man to wave back shyly.

There we go, Sarge thought. We're making progress now. *Salaam*, bud.

Hares scattered from the road, taking refuge among the rocks.

These men were elders and their retainers from one of the villages in the valley, on their way to attend a pow wow at the base. For several years, the Pashtuns in this wild region of Nuristan Province, so close to the Pakistan border, had welcomed the Americans. The land here was heavily forested, mostly conifers; while a majority of Afghans scratched out a living in farming and herding, the people here had been timber cutters since the days of Genghis Khan. They sold timber to Jalabad, Mehtariam, Pakistan. The jingle truck Sarge was following, in fact, was probably filled from top to bottom with firewood most days. The Taliban were oppressive and bad for business, so the people here celebrated when the Americans threw them out. Soon, however, Kabul began to enact laws restricting trade with Pakistan. The locals grumbled, but cut the Americans slack as the Americans were building roads and schools and regularly sending them gifts—school supplies, milk, prayer rugs.

The Taliban remained active in the area. The region was a corridor for insurgents crossing over to and from Pakistan. Inevitably, the locals got caught in the crossfire. The Air Force dropped a smart bomb onto a village and missed the target, a mid-level Taliban commander, by ten minutes, instead killing thirteen civilians, including several children. As a result, the locals threw their support to the insurgents against a foreign military they now saw as infidel occupiers. Fighting raged in the valley for the past six months, accounting for thirty percent of all combat in the brigade. The Afghan National Police station in the closest village to the east had been attacked so many times that the police were permanently demoralized. Without local support, the Americans controlled nothing outside their compound.

And so this meeting had been brokered in an attempt to stop the fighting.

Two Bradleys loaded with heavily armed combat infantry were sent to the base as a demonstration of strength. Sarge was glad to be in the point vehicle. For most of the trip, he was able to enjoy the beautiful scenery rolling by without eating the other vehicle's dust.

The truth was he loved Afghanistan and had even learned to love its people. The Afghans lived close to life and death. This was one of the places of the world where it was still common to see nomads living off the land. It was a very old place. Numerous armies had marched through it—Greek, Persian, Indian, Mongol, British, Soviet. The Afghans had beaten the British and the Soviets and had nothing to show for it; centuries of warfare had impoverished the country, and many people here lived as they had for thousands of years, in ignorance and poverty.

Sarge had grown up in Los Angeles searching for something he could not name. He spent his teenage years gang banging on the city's hard streets as a corner dealer and later as muscle. He killed a boy three days before his seventeenth birthday, but they never caught him for that. A month later, his girl dumped him and he smashed windshields in a drunken, brokenhearted rage all the way up two blocks of Hillcrest until the cops finally showed up. He took a swing at one and they did a Rodney King on him. In court, he was given a choice of prison or the Army.

Two years later, he was deployed to Afghanistan. Found himself sitting on a Bradley, watching M1 Abrams tanks drive across fields of poppies overlooked by the wild mountains of the Hindu Kush and endless blue sky.

And that thing he'd been searching for? He'd found it.

The column followed the jingly truck into the base in a blinding cloud of dust. The men piled out of the truck. One hoary specimen, his eyes white with cataracts and sporting a long white beard, scowled at everything. The Colonel and his staff emerged from a large tent set up for the meeting and they shook hands all around. The old man with the beard stood off to the side, refusing to shake. Noticing Sarge, he spat and said something in Pashtun, ending with *Yabba dabba doo!*

Sarge knew the expression but had never heard it spoken. It was Afghan slang, roughly translating as, "falling crates that knock down houses." During the invasion in 2001, the Americans dropped boxes of food onto the villages, and some of them landed on huts and destroyed them, a perfect little parable of the trouble with good intentions.

One of the other Afghans, the man who had waved to him from the back of the truck, laughed and said, "Do not take it personal. He thinks you are Russian. He thinks you are all Russians."

"He's got a long memory," Sarge said. "Maybe he thinks I'm British."

"Ha. Perhaps. English and Russians alike died here. I hope you will do better, my friend."

"*Inshallah*," Sarge said. If God wills it.

The Afghan laughed with feeling. "There is a path to the top of even the highest mountain," he exclaimed, quoting an Afghan proverb. Then it was Sarge's turn to laugh.

More jingle trucks pulled up to drop off more village representatives. The squad in Sarge's Bradley dismounted in full battle rattle, showing off their firepower to the Afghans. The place was suddenly swarming with locals and heavily armed soldiers in a melee of salutations and small talk. The Colonel ushered them into the big tent for tea, and then it was quiet again in the compound.

A dollar got you fifty afghanis, the local money. Sarge had seen a lot of Afghanistan and particularly enjoyed visiting the larger bases that had a market day where you could buy local food, crafts, anything. He loved the food, especially the rice *pilau*, and ate it the way the Afghans did, using *naan* flatbread as a utensil to scoop the food into his mouth. But in these smaller bases, there was nothing to buy. And nothing to do except duck bullets.

Sarge talked to Devereaux about the base and its vulnerabilities for a few minutes, and then decided to join a few of the base's soldiers sitting and smoking on buckets and ammo crates in the protective shadow of a concrete bunker. This little nook apparently passed for the base's lounge.

"Welcome to Mortaritaville," one of the soldiers said. "Got any cigarettes?"

Devereaux did, and they all got along fine trading jokes and war stories and cutting into MRE pouches looking for candy. Sarge found a comfortable spot on the ground with his back against a wooden bin holding water bottles. The soldiers were already laughing at Devereaux. The boys in the squad called him "the Afghan" because he loved to tell big stories. The smallest firefight became an epic starring him and the Bradley. Sarge loved this part of Army life. Shooting the shit and occasionally busting balls.

"Black and white don't matter to me, Sarge," Devereaux was saying. "I wouldn't mind being a black dude like you if there weren't so many fucking douchebags. I'd rather be white because there are more white douchebags than black douchebags, and so the odds of somebody being a douchebag to me are less being white. Does that make any sense?"

"At least you're not a jinglie," another soldier said to Devereaux, referring to the Afghans. "Everybody's a douchebag to the jinglies. This place has been douchebagged since the dawn of time."

Sarge laughed.

The meeting dragged on all day until the Afghan leaders piled into their jingly trucks and started the drive back to their villages. They were smiling when they left, which the soldiers took as a good sign. Word went around that the Colonel had made good progress in getting the locals back on their side. Sarge understood that he and his boys would stay the night, and then rejoin his unit near Mehtariam tomorrow morning. The valley filled with a familiar mechanical sound and he looked up, shielding his eyes against the sun's glare with his hand, to see a pair of Chinook helicopters pounding air, escorted by a single Apache attack helicopter.

One of the Chinooks wobbled and abruptly fell out of the sky, crashing into the mountainside moments later and breaking into pieces as it rolled into the trees.

"Whoa," Devereaux said to one of the base's soldiers. "Did you see that?"

The soldier shook his head in wonder. His nose wrinkled and he said, "Man, that smells funny." Then his eyes rolled up into his head and he collapsed screaming.

"Medic!" Sarge roared, kneeling next to the man to check his vital signs. "We need some help over here!"

But soldiers were falling everywhere onto the crushed stones, screaming.

The Colonel came running out of the tent.

"We're under attack! Get to your posts!"

The Apache veered and collided with the other Chinook, bringing them both down onto the mountain in a spectacular, hundred-yard-long eruption of dust and stones.

The soldiers were falling and lay on the stones screaming, their bodies taut with pain.

"Holy shit," Sarge said, and ran for the Bradley.

He sat in the commander's station, panicking, his heart pounding against his ribs. What had happened to those men? Were they dead? If this were a biological or chemical attack, weren't they all exposed? If the Taliban did this, the gloves would come off. They were begging the world's best military for wholesale extermination, and they would get it.

After waiting for several minutes, he shifted into the gunner's seat, working the periscopes to scan the heights for possible enemy attack.

The screaming stopped. Sarge almost cried with relief. After several moments of pure silence, the compound filled with shouting voices. Sarge sat for three hours, talking occasionally to the commander of the other Bradley on the radio, trying to find out what he could. Martinez and Thompson, the driver and the gunner, did not return. He assumed the worst.

Somebody banged on the side of the Bradley.

"You in there, Sarge?" It was Devereaux. "Answer me, goddammit!"

Sarge popped the hatch and emerged blinking into the late afternoon air.

"I'm here," he said. "I'm okay. How about you? Your boys okay?"

His comrade nodded, his eyes glazed and his face pale.

"We're managing," Devereaux told him.

"Where's my crew?"

"They're down, Sarge."

"*Goddammit*," Sarge said fiercely.

Devereaux added, "They're still putting everybody in that big tent where they had the meeting. The base suffered twenty percent casualties from whatever the hell just happened."

One of five men was down. It was incredible.

"What's our alert status? Why is everybody walking around?"

"The Colonel just dropped security to thirty percent," Devereaux said. "I heard somebody say they heard the RTO tell the Colonel that this is happening everywhere, and the Colonel is figuring it's not an attack. Right now he's arguing with the Captain over whether to send a unit out to look for survivors at the place where those helicopters crashed. The Captain is refusing orders. He doesn't want to go. Says we might still be attacked."

"What do you mean, 'everywhere?'" said Sarge. "You mean the whole country?"

"*INCOMING!*"

Soldiers were running everywhere, seeking cover. Devereaux ran and dove into a mortar pit, leaving Sarge to look for the source of the fire. The mortar round fell short, exploding just outside the base's timber walls in a flash followed by a giant cloud of smoke and dust. A machine gun began firing on the rocky heights, sending plunging fire into the compound. Small arms fire flashed across the distant hills. Sarge flinched as he heard the first hissing snap and twang of bullets flying past his ears.

He climbed back onto the Bradley, lowered himself in and began working the control handles to maneuver the turret and align the rig's cannon with the MG position at the top of the ridge.

It's the locals, he realized. They fell down screaming too and they think it's us who did it to them. Christ, there are seventy thousand NATO troops in the Sandbox and nearly thirty million Afghans.

Twenty percent casualties would be fourteen thousand NATO troops but *six million Afghans*. If they think we did it, we're toast. They slaughtered the goddamn Red Army for a fraction of the offense.

He fired, sending rounds arcing to crash into the heights. The MG fire stopped.

*Big Dog 1, this is Big Dog 2, come in, over*, he heard over the radio.

"I'm here, Big Dog 2, over," he said, scanning for another target.

"The Mark 19 is down!" somebody yelled outside.

Mortar shells were bursting in the compound. A rocket propelled grenade hit the Bradley—an amazing shot—and glanced off before bursting in the air, raking its armor with shrapnel.

*Big Dog 1, we've got reports of fire from the police station. Can you confirm, over?"*

"Identified," he said into the mike. "I've got hostile fire from the ANP station, Big Dog 2. The insurgents have taken the building, over."

*They're all yours, Big Dog 1. Happy hunting, out.*

He fired the cannon, dropping a score of rounds onto the building, which crumbled under the fire in a massive cloud of smoke and dust.

"Target," he said.

*Oh my God. Oh my God.*

"Big Dog 2, this is Big Dog 1, over."

Then he saw. The Afghans were sending plunging fire down into the tent where the fallen soldiers had been placed. The radio filled with angry voices.

*We need fire on that fucking hill!*

The human condition is to survive. When a man is just surviving, he has been carved down to the animal he once was. And animals only think of their own survival. It is all about fight or flight and a lot of times the animal in you wants to run blindly to safety. What makes a soldier a good soldier, Sarge knows, is when he is properly trained to control these impulses. What makes a soldier brave, even noble, is when he is willing to sacrifice his own safety for his fellow soldiers.

Soldiers were running into the open to draw fire, trying to distract the insurgents away from shooting at the tent, and were getting cut down. Sarge counted three bodies writhing on the stones bleeding and a fourth lying completely still. Another soldier was standing in the open on a carpet of spent brass and links, firing steadily into the hills. It was Devereaux.

"The Afghan" is going to have one hell of a story to tell if he survives this, Sarge thought. He continued to rain suppressing area fire onto the enemy positions along the ridge.

The radio steadily filled with traffic.

*We got hostiles identified in the open to the north and east. They're crossing the minefield, over.*

The insurgents were launching a full-scale attack, spending their first wave on the minefield. Two additional waves followed closely on the heels of the first. Then it would be hand to hand fighting among the hooches. There were hundreds of insurgents in the assault.

Combat Outpost Sawyer was very close to being overrun. Sarge could hear the distant voices shouting, *Yalla yalla!* One of them cried *Allāhu akbar*, and the rest took up the shout. The volume of fire intensified. Hand grenades began bursting near the bunkers.

*Jalabad says we're getting zero air support, over.*

"Medic!" a man was screaming.

*Enemy in the wire, we got enemy in the wire, over.*

A line of claymores exploded, sending geysers of dry earth and splinters of wood soaring into the air. The soldiers were retreating and blowing up everything behind them.

Sarge could not move the Bradley. He was not a mobile cannon, but instead a pillbox, his own personal Alamo. He scanned his forward sectors, looking for targets, but the air was filled with smoke and dust. Small arms fire crackled around the bunkers. He saw a fireteam abandon a burning building and fall back to the next defensive line.

Grenades began bursting around his rig. Sarge realized that the Bradleys were now in front of the Americans' position, not behind. A Molotov cocktail streamed high into the air and landed on the rear of the turret, shattering and flaring to life.

The first insurgents came into view, firing AK47 rifles and crouching low as they ran.

Sarge opened up with the Bradley's M240 machine gun at close range and cut them down. Small arms fire rattled off the vehicle's armor. He saw an RPG team set up near one of the hooches, pointing at the other Bradley. He quickly switched back to the cannon and armed it.

"On the way," Sarge hissed, pressing the firing switch on the right control handle. The insurgents exploded in a series of bursts.

As his visibility deteriorated, he kept it hot with the cannon, trying to stall the insurgents' advance.

*We got air support.*

It was a single Apache helicopter flying through a hail of fire, dropping Hellfire missiles onto the insurgents running in the open towards the flaming base. The soldiers cheered. Its missiles spent, the helicopter began to set up its first strafing run.

Every man living in this valley must be here, Sarge thought, trying to wipe us out over a horrible misunderstanding. And with the insurgents caught in the open between Bradleys in front and the Apache behind, we're going to wipe them out over that same misunderstanding.

This was war.

The fighting raged into the night. The soldiers shot flares and exchanged fire with the insurgents in streams of tracers. Sarge spent the night in the gunner's station, pissing into a plastic bottle and dying for a glass of water. Outside, the wounded screamed and screamed. By the time dawn finally came, the surviving insurgents had melted away into the dark. More than a hundred bodies carpeted the rocks and were stacked around the scorched and broken bunkers.

The dazed survivors stumbled among the ruins of the base. Sarge found Devereaux and the other boys of the squad, all of them miraculously unscathed, and bear hugged them. Devereaux told him the Colonel had gotten orders to shut the base down and bring everybody to Jalabad, where local American forces were consolidating. He found out that his crew was still in the tent and that they remained catatonic but were otherwise unharmed in the fighting.

"This entire country must hate us right now," Devereaux said. "How do you come back from that?"

"Welcome to the suck," Sarge told him, but the old Army complaint rang hollow. He started walking toward the big tent, wondering what was going to happen next. The war had suddenly changed. Quite possibly, so had the world.

Twenty yards from the Bradley, an insurgent lay dying on the ground, silently praying and choking on his own blood. It was the laughing Afghan who had waved to him from the back of the truck and translated the old man's curses.

Looking at him, Sarge raged at the waste of life.

"We didn't do this to you," he said. "Before you die, I want you to know that. We didn't do it. All of this fighting was for nothing."

"God hates you," the man said. Then the lights in his eyes went out.

♦

Several weeks later, as Pittsburgh burns behind him in a ruined America, Sarge will think about his comrades serving overseas. Only a fraction of the military deployed abroad had been brought home after the Screaming. He will wonder how they are doing over there, the thousands that were left behind in the wild parts of the world. He will wonder whether the boys in the Sandbox ever made it home. Whether they are now shooting at Americans instead of Afghans. If he ever sees them again, he will say, *"Pa khair raghla."* Thank God you arrived safe and sound.

# THE TRUCK STOP

Wendy staggers out of the Bradley's oven heat onto a wide open parking lot under a glaring, overcast sky. The scorched air dries the sweat on her face instantly, cooling her skin while giving her the strange sensation of being baked. She breathes deep but coughs on air heavy with a tangy burning chemical smell.

A large building sprawls in front of her under a massive sign announcing GAS and ALL YOU CAN EAT BKFST and CAR WASH. Two canopied fuel islands flank the building, one promising gas for vehicles and the other diesel for big trucks. Without power, the building appears dark and desolate. The place has been abandoned for some time. The parking lots are all empty, dotted with random litter and fluttering on the sudden hot breezes.

For a moment, she imagines truckers filling up their rigs during their long hauls in and out of the Keystone State, heading into the greasy spoon for coffee and a piss. Then the moment passes. These days, she knows, people can see ghosts. They are all around if you know how to look. All you have to do is remember the past. Conjure up some memory of the dead world.

She gasps on the smoky air. The very atmosphere has been burned. It smells like lung cancer. Impossibly, little gray snowflakes tumble gently across the barren landscape. It takes her exhausted brain several moments to understand that these flakes are hot ash. That they are, in fact, the cremated remains of Pittsburgh, drawn into the atmosphere on massive convection currents, and scattered on the winds. One twirling piece of ash lands on her shoulder and she absentmindedly tries to brush it off, leaving a smudge of gray dust.

Pittsburgh is still burning. Wendy turns and stares at the vast wall of smoke rising up from the smoldering ruins of the city in the east, surrounded by heavy particulates.

"Everything I knew was in that town," she says hoarsely, her throat raw and dry and scratchy from the heat and the screaming. "Everything and everybody I ever knew in the world."

The place where she was born and the place where she was raised. The house where she smoked weed for the first time and the house where she lost her virginity. The school where they educated her about the basics and the school where they taught her to be a cop. The station house where she worked and all of the neighborhoods she patrolled and the mall where she shopped for clothes and the supermarket where she picked up her groceries and bars where she drank a few beers on the weekends. The theater near her house where she watched dozens of movies with various friends and dates, the hospice where her parents died, the hospital where her niece was born, the restaurant where she fell in love with Dave Carver, the squad car that was like a second home to her.

These places, and all the people who filled them with their lives and played a part in hers both large and small, all burned into ash. All lost in the fire. And all of her past lost with it. It is too much to comprehend, too horrifying to even imagine.

"I can't believe it's gone," she says, swallowing hard.

She turns to see if anybody is listening to her, but nobody is there. Each of the other survivors has wandered alone and dazed across the empty lot and stopped as if straining against an invisible leash tying them to the vehicle. They have gone as far as they can from each other without being completely alone. She wants to go even further.

Patting the Glock on her hip to feel its reassuring weight, Wendy begins marching towards the highway.

◆

Ethan wakes up on warm asphalt with a splitting headache. He feels like a piece of chicken left in the oven too long. He opens one eye blearily and clenches it shut as the glaring silver sky painfully blinds him. Blinking tears, he tries again. Slowly, his eyes adapt to the light and he can make out figures on a wide parking area in front of a simple shoebox-shaped building. Truck stop, he thinks. Woods and hills beyond. They have not only left the hospital, they have abandoned Pittsburgh entirely. Just what the hell happened last night?

The last thing he remembers is the sharp prick of the needle sliding into his arm.

He tries to bring the dark figures into focus. His glasses are missing and he has trouble seeing distances. The blurry figures slowly coalesce into the other survivors, scattered around the asphalt. Anne is at the Bradley, ransacking it. The soldiers are dragging the struggling driver into the shelter of one of the fuel islands. Ethan notices their body language and wonders if they are Infected. His immediate instinct is to play possum. He closes his eyes and tries to ignore his aching bladder.

"Where are we going to go?" somebody asks. "Is anywhere safe?"

Ethan knows the voice; it was Paul speaking. He suffers a sudden sense of déjà vu, a flashback to one of the endless nightmares he dreamed last night. Again, that strange sense of disorientation, of not knowing who he is or why he is here. At least he knows now that the others are not Infected; the Infected do not talk. He opens his eyes and tries to sit up. The air is hot and tinged with smoke, stinging his eyes. His shirt is covered with a dried red crust. Not blood; vomit. The acid smell triggers the dry heaves. He groans on his hands and knees, his vision blurred with tears, spitting repeatedly into the dust. He wipes his eyes and notices the other survivors watching him.

"Water," he croaks. His voice sounds alien to his ears. His tongue feels like a piece of leather.

Anne comes out of the Bradley and drops a box onto the ground, where it bursts open, spilling cans across the asphalt. She unholsters one of her handguns and begins marching towards him. The other survivors drift closer.

"Can I have some water?" he says.

Anne kicks him in the ribs, pushing him back down onto the warm hard ground.

"Motherfucker," she says.

The sudden stress makes his stomach lurch again. His body writhes in the soot, struggling to breathe, retching.

Anne kneels next to him, grabs his curly hair in one first, and shoves the barrel of her pistol into the soft flesh under his chin. The sky darkens as the winds shift.

"We were attacked," she hisses close to his ear. "We were attacked and you weren't with us. We had to carry you out of there. We had to *carry you*. You let us down, Ethan."

"Don't you do it, Anne," Paul says, his deep voice angry and commanding.

Ethan regains control of his stomach and breathing and glares up at Anne.

"Yes, do it," he says.

Anne recoils in surprise.

"Are you trying to die? Is that it?"

"I don't care anymore."

"You want me to do it because you can't do it yourself. You're a coward. I could do worse. I could leave you here for *them*."

He hesitates before answering, struck by the realization that she is right. He has no hope of finding his family and without his family he has no hope at all. But he does not know how to die.

"I'm sorry I let you down," he says. "If you want to scapegoat me, that's fine, too. It doesn't matter anymore. So do it, if that's what you want."

"He knows what he did, Anne," Paul says. "What's done is done."

"Who trusts him?" Anne says, glaring at the other survivors. "Who here trusts him now? This is not about justice, Paul. It is about survival."

"We all know what's at stake here. You think we don't know?"

"Leave him alone," Todd says shrilly, his voice cracking.

"It could have been any of us," Paul adds.

He stands over Ethan, holding his shotgun. Ethan realizes these people are not his friends and that he does not really know them.

"Do you want to live or not, boy?" Paul asks him.

"I want to live," Ethan says through gritted teeth. "But I'm sick of surviving."

"That's not an answer," Paul tells him. "We've got to know we can count on you or Anne's right, we've got to part ways right now. It's a simple question. Can we count on you?"

"Yes," Ethan says.

"He's mine," a commanding voice booms.

Sarge pushes his way into the ring of survivors, his helmet off and holding his automatic rifle in his right hand. The soldier glares down at him.

"You come with me," he says.

◆

Anne returns her large handgun to its leather shoulder holster and heads back to the Bradley. The supplies she left on the ground are already gray with a light coating of soot, a depressing sight. She feels an overwhelming urge to hit the road. Paul suddenly blocks her path, cradling the shotgun, glaring down at her from his large, grizzled head. The gesture would be enough to intimidate anybody except her. She sidesteps him and continues to the vehicle.

"We need to talk, Anne," he says. "I have something I need to say to you."

She ignores him, rummaging through the boxes until she finds a battered PHILLIES cap, red paisley bandana and bottle of water. After fitting the cap on her head, she unscrews the cap of the bottle and soaks the bandana before tying it over her face to cover her mouth.

"We all look up to you," Paul says. "If things get really bad, we all look to you to tell us what to do. And even if we think you're wrong, we still do it. Because we believe."

Anne clasps her metal canteen onto her webbed gun belt.

Todd watches her closely. "Where are you going, Anne?"

Paul says, "But there are some things you don't get to decide. Like who stays and who goes. You don't get to make that decision. It's not up to you."

Todd adds, "Why can't we get out of this ash and make some plans? We need a plan."

Anne squints up at Paul's face, sizing him up.

"I'm going to take a walk," she says, picking up her scoped rifle. "You're in charge."

She begins walking towards the distant trees.

"I wouldn't do that by yourself," Paul says.

"You're not me," she says.

"When are you coming back?" Todd asks nervously.

Anne ignores them, marching with a purposeful gait that takes her onto the highway. In the distance, coming and going, she sees tiny figures moving along the road. The only vehicles are abandoned wrecks, their doors hanging open. Her ears still ring painfully from the screaming monster that attacked them.

She needs to be alone for a while. She relishes the sudden sense of space.

They are all going insane one day at a time and each of them—at different times, depending on the individual—will crack under the stress, she knows. This can take many forms. And if one of them cracks, that person could put them all at risk. Like Ethan. He suffered some sort of breakdown and endangered all of them. The man already has a bad habit of firing his rifle with his eyes closed. He is simply not as cool as the others in a fight. Anne was willing to overlook these things, as Ethan has good instincts that warn them about obtuse threats such as the tank firing on them and the worm monster having a second head. He also came up with the idea of the Molotov cocktails. He makes a real contribution. But if he is cracking up, he will be a liability to them. He will take up space in the Bradley, consume scarce resources; worse, he will not cover their backs.

Then they will have to make a tough choice as a group. Anne would rather not wait until people get killed before that decision is made. If it were up to her, the man would have been left behind at the hospital last night. Which would have been sad. But necessary.

About a mile down the road, oily black smoke billows from a burning vehicle in the middle of the highway's westbound lanes. She peers into her scope and sees a pair of olive green vehicles, one a Humvee with its headlights on and behind it, a military flatbed truck, its cab on fire and pumping smoke. Anne squints, trying to see more, but everything is blanketed in ash. Visibility is steadily diminishing. Across the landscape, tons of ash continue to flutter to the earth in drifting clouds of black snowflakes, rapidly turning into a hellish blizzard swirling through the trees and darkening the sky.

Anne slings the rifle onto her shoulder, digs her hands into her pockets, and begins walking west.

Sarge and Paul and the other survivors are getting sentimental, she knows. They are getting to know each other. Becoming friends, even. They are forgetting that being sentimental is a luxury at a time like this. They are forgetting that the only reason they have this luxury is because they have been tough as nails. Because they all pull their weight.

She has a sense that the others are leaving her behind. But they are not moving forward. They are regressing. They are becoming what they were before the world ended.

Anne cannot go back.

As she approaches the Humvee, she shrugs the rifle into her hands and approaches more cautiously, the weapon held in the firing position.

She almost trips over the first body. There are four dead soldiers sprawling on the ground amid broken weapons and scattered empty shell casings, coated with soot. Their heads are eerily missing. Something decapitated them and left the rest for the birds.

Inside the Humvee, a tangle of voices compete for expression across the ether, gradually resolving into a single urgent female voice, *Patriot 3-2, Patriot 3-2, this is Patriot, how copy, over?* The radio blasts white noise for ten seconds. Then the message repeats.

Something rustles in the trees, sighing.

♦

Wendy tramps numbly through the ash along the road, surveying the hellish gray landscape warped by shimmering heat waves. The giant wall of smoke continues to rise over the smoldering ruins of Pittsburgh like a distant storm. Heavy particulates flow steadily up into the sky, riding pulses of heat. The highway races east in a long straight line that dissolves into the smoky haze. Figures toil in the distance—refugees, probably, fleeing the inferno. Tiny headlights glimmer in the ash fall. She wonders what it would be like to lie down in the warm soot in the gulley below the guard rail and surrender herself to the earth. Philip did that, she remembers. He was tough as nails but one day he saw a *Wall Street Journal* with the wrong date and sat in the ashes and that was that. He had become numb, too. He could not handle seeing his world die. When you find yourself envying the dead, you are not long for it.

Stopping at the hospital was a mistake, she knows. They invested their hopes in its promises, believing they found a place where they could at last feel safe. But that is not the world they live in. All of those hopes—of living instead of barely surviving, of having some sort of future after the end of Infection, of being able to dream again—were blindly and cruelly crushed. In this world, giant faceless things haunt abandoned buildings and duel with armored fighting vehicles in the dark. In this world, entire cities burn to the ground and everything you ever knew and loved is converted into tons of ash floating on the upper atmosphere. In this world, the children are dead. It is best not to hope in this world. It is best to keep moving and never stop.

The only thing giving her strength is that brief moment of contact she experienced with Sarge last night. The memory of that contact is still burning in her chest. She had gone into his room on impulse intent on dropping a hint, maybe flirting a little: *I see you,* she wanted to let him know. *You see me and I see you, too.* She found herself kissing him and falling into blissful nothingness. She told herself that the world was ending and love was in very short supply and so you had to grab it where and when you could find it. Wendy and Sarge were made of the same stuff, she thought; that is what attracted her to him. He is a soldier without an army, a centurion still fighting even though his legion is dead; she is a cop in a lawless land. Then she slept in his arms for a short time and had never felt safer. It amazes her how just a simple man could make her feel that safe in a world this dangerous.

Wendy begins to pass a motley group of refugees, mostly young men and women, some of them wrapped in blankets, others carrying backpacks and umbrellas, some decked out in goggles and respirators. All of them are armed with knives and crowbars and baseball bats and even makeshift spears. The soot is beginning to form a paste in her mouth, a grit between her teeth. She spits and wishes she had thought to bring along a canteen.

"Hello," she says, eyeing them curiously. "You all right?"

The people ignore her, walking by in a daze, their hair and shoulders covered in gray-white ash.

"You're going the wrong way," a man says, flashing gray teeth.

One of the women notices her badge and belt and asks her if she is a cop.

"Where are we supposed to go?" the woman says.

Wendy pauses to spit out her gum, which has become gristly with dust. The woman watches it fall into the cinders with longing.

"My advice would be to keep going west," Wendy tells her. "Get as far away from Pittsburgh as you can."

"You mean there's no rescue station on this road?"

A man with a bleeding ear shouts, "ARE YOU FROM THE FEMA CAMP?"

"I don't know of any FEMA camp, sir."

"WHAT?"

"If it's not on this road, where is it?" the woman says, her voice edged in panic.

A small crowd is gathering. The people stare at her with a mixture of hope and resentment and shock, shivering in the heat. The man who shouted stumbles, briefly disoriented, and then shouts again, "THERE'S NO HELP AHEAD? WE'RE ON OUR OWN?"

"I don't know of any rescue station or FEMA camp anywhere. I'm not here in any official capacity. I'm with another group of people leaving the city after the fire."

"We lost everything," the woman pleads. "We have no food. Some guys with guns back there on the road took the last drop of water I had. Where am I supposed to go?"

"Where were you cops when those monsters were ripping my family apart?" a woman says, her eyes glazed with fever. Most of her hair and eyebrows have been burned off and the right side of her face is covered by a filthy, bulky bandage. "That's what I want to know. I called 911 and nobody came. Nobody came and now Edward is dead. Edward and Billy and Zoe and little Paul. Now you show up and try to tell us what to do? Where the hell were you, lady?"

The crowd presses in, angry, its slim hopes dashed and its resentments stoked.

"I'm sorry," Wendy says. She wants to explain her situation—that her precinct was overrun, that she is on her own, that she cannot help them—but these people do not care. She is a symbol to them. They look at her with hungry, feral eyes gleaming from the folds of bundles of rags tied around their heads. They cough into their fists loudly, struggling for enough air to scream.

"Give me something," a woman hisses, reaching out for Wendy's face.

Wendy takes a step backward and places her hand over her pepper spray dispenser. She senses a dangerous line forming—knows it is there because it is about to be crossed. The crowd closes in, muttering.

A man wearing a cowboy hat and carrying a walking stick marches past and yells, "Hey, now! What are you bugging that girl for? There ain't no rescue coming and there ain't no police. She ain't no cop. Get over it."

Wendy bristles, but before she can say anything, she hears the echoes of gunshots back in the smoky haze. All of them turn toward the noise, flinching. A moment ago they were menacing her but the fact is they are terrified and running on fumes.

"There you go, officer," the man says, still walking. "There are a couple of guys back there with a truck robbing people and shooting anybody who fights back. You want to be a cop? Do something about it."

◆

Ethan follows Sarge past the Bradley and pauses with his mouth hanging open in awe. The rig looks like it lost a brick fight. The welded aluminum armor is pockmarked with dents and scratches. Several plates on its side are missing.

Sarge turns and sees him lagging behind.

"You sure you're okay?"

"I could use a drink of water."

"I'll get you water after we do this thing, okay?"

"Okay."

"Anne can be a little rough."

"It doesn't matter," Ethan says, meaning it. The truth is he feels completely numb. He does not feel pain. He does not feel anything. "What happened to your tank?"

"Those plates are explosive reactive armor," Sarge tells him. "It protects the vehicle by exploding outward when something comes at it trying to explode inward, canceling it out."

What could have hit the Bradley with that much force?

"What happened last night?" Ethan says.

"There was a fire," Sarge tells him. "See all the ash starting to rain down on us? That's what's left of Pittsburgh—west of the Monongahela and the Ohio, anyhow."

"What happened to the vehicle?"

"The gates of hell opened. If we hadn't dropped smoke, I don't think we would have made it. That thing was kicking the shit out of my rig. Come on."

Ethan shakes his head in amazement. *That thing*, Sarge said. This was not the average Infected and probably not a worm either. The commander obviously had no idea what he had been fighting in the dark. As Ethan suspected, there are other children of Infection, probably an entire family of monstrosities. If there is something out there that can take on an American armored fighting vehicle, Ethan believes, the human race might have to give up its claim on the planet.

He has often speculated about what could have caused the pandemic. As an educated man, he refuses to believe the cause is supernatural. Infection is spread by a virus, but a virus does not explain these bizarre mutations. In the days following the Screaming, scientists were speculating about a nanotech weapon that escaped the lab. Could nanotechnology create such monsters?

Ethan once again finds himself entertaining an alien colonization theory. Consider an alien race on a distant world that wants to propagate itself across the galaxy. Instead of spaceships, it sends seedlings out across the cosmos, which eventually rain down on Earth to colonize the resident species' DNA, mutating the natives into adaptations of the alien species and its ecology. The creatures are at first sickly because they are still adapting to Earth's environment. They eat the dead but are starving because their alien digestive systems cannot extract nutrition from it. While they turn the dominant species against itself through Infection, they burrow into the darkest spaces in abandoned buildings and adapt and multiply. Over time, they grow stronger until they eliminate the dominant species and complete the conquest of their adopted world. It makes sense, he reasons. Why else would they target our children for immediate extermination?

Or perhaps the aliens are indeed coming in spaceships, but they are terraforming the planet before the ships arrive, eliminating the resident species in the process. Which means humanity is not fighting aliens, but the wildlife of the aliens' home world. These things are repulsive but they are not evil in the sense that they want to hurt humans purely out of malice. They are hunting people for food. In one sense, they might as well be millions of hungry lions roaming the streets, hunting and eating people simply to survive.

The worst part is the human race will probably never truly understand what killed it.

His family needs him more than ever. He will keep looking for them. He wonders if this is why he is so calm, that he has surrendered what is left of his sanity to the delusion they are alive.

I'll keep searching for you, Mary. I'll never stop looking.

They approach a figure sitting on the ground propped against a gas pump. The man is pale, underweight, his cheeks sunken, his eyes dark and bruised. His arms rest withered and useless at his sides. Ethan suddenly recognizes him as the driver—what is left of him, anyway. The gunner kneels next to him, trying to give him water.

Sarge is saying, "You're smart, Ethan. I'm betting you can figure out a way to fix him."

Ducky Jones lost thirty pounds since Ethan saw him the night before. The man is almost visibly wilting in front of him, coughing feebly, his breath rapid and shallow. His dark, intelligent eyes flicker at Ethan with a mixture of fear and hope. There is still a man in there.

Ethan holds his gaze respectfully for several seconds, then looks down at the revolting thing that protrudes from his hip like something out of Ripley's Believe It Or Not.

◆

Todd enters the truck stop cautiously, violating Anne's standing rule of never going anywhere alone. Something could attack him and he would be vulnerable. Anne's rules suddenly mean a whole lot less to him today, however. The monster changed the game last night. How can they hope to survive with horrors like that out there hunting them? Like most victims of bullies, Todd is highly sensitive to what other people are feeling, and the best word he can think of to describe the mood right now in the group as a whole is *deranged*. Deranged and black, raw, angry. In other words, morale is shit. They are becoming people who do not care, people who are losing hope and otherwise have nothing left to lose. Damaged goods.

They are close to giving up.

Inside the lobby, he has a choice of restaurant, convenience store or public restrooms. As much as he would like to take a private dump on a real toilet, there is no way he is going into a public restroom by himself. The store looks interesting. The shelves have been rifled but whoever did it left most of the stuff behind. He might find some good loot in here. He remembers that Wendy wants a pair of toenail clippers.

His nerves are crawling with the oppressive feeling that the group is falling apart. Anne and Wendy wandered off to who knows where, Paul is emptying the Bradley's guts into the ash under the pretense of organizing their supplies, and the driver is dying at the fuel island. Anne was ready to blow Ethan's head all over the pavement. What about Todd? Nobody wants to listen to him. They obviously think of him as just a kid. But he will not abandon the group. He feels a very strong loyalty to it. Groucho Marx once quipped that he would never want to be a member of a club that would have him as a member. Todd wants to be a member of the club almost entirely because they offered him membership. America feels like a distant dream. This tiny tribe is his nation now. These people are not mere tools used to help collect food and stand guard while he sleeps. They are much more than that. They are something like family to him.

It is true that as individuals, while he trusts the other survivors and feels comfortable with them, he does not know them well, even after days of fighting together against terrible odds. All anybody talks about is how they plan to survive the next ten minutes. It is not like people are going to open up during the apocalypse about their hobbies or where they went for vacation last summer or their favorite flavor of ice cream. They have intense flashbacks, but never talk about their separate pasts from the Time Before. The past right now seems less real than the demon that attacked them last night. The past is also too painful to recall willingly, bringing to mind too many lost things. Todd likes the other survivors, but his interactions with them, while intimate, have been largely superficial. He feels his deepest connection with the group itself—feels safest, in fact, interacting with the others through the medium of the group.

But if there is no group anymore, to what or whom is there to be loyal?

A bell tinkles as he enters the store, sending his heart galloping in his chest. The place smells musty. The air feels flat, dead. He accidentally kicks a two-liter bottle of Mountain Dew spinning across the floor. He flinches at the noise, raising his rifle and sweeping the store for targets as he backs against the nearest wall.

Maybe coming in here by myself was not such a good idea, he thinks, gasping for breath. Another scare like that and I'll drop dead from a stroke.

Having a closer look at the shelves brings further disappointment. Most of the merchandise is still sitting on the shelves or hanging on hooks, but there is no food, water, medicine. Instead, almost all of the stuff left in the store are products specifically marketed to truckers who have to live on the road for as long as a month at a time. Movies and audio books, CB radio equipment, hazmat placards, truck stop exit guides, road atlases, electric frying pans, toasters, DC adapters, coffee makers and TV/VCR systems.

Todd wonders what a trucker would do with a coffee maker and then realizes, looking at the packaging, that all of these devices are DC powered. And the DC adapters allow AC devices to run off of DC. He suddenly has an epiphany. Most appliances do not work anymore because they need AC power, and the only way he knows to make AC power when the grid is down is with an emergency generator that runs on diesel or propane or natural gas. But DC comes from batteries.

They could run all this stuff off of car batteries. Of which there are plenty lying around, courtesy of the fact that their drivers are either Infected or dead.

Looks like being a whiz at science has finally come in handy, Todd tells himself. He slowly realizes that he has hit some sort of jackpot.

♦

Wendy marches resolutely through the smoky haze, her Glock unholstered and held at her side. She is a police officer, still on duty, still protecting life and property. Perhaps the last cop left in Pittsburgh. Perhaps the last government employee still doing anything. Once she left, the crowd debated following her to see what kind of loot might become available, but eventually gave up and resumed their long walk west. Apparently, they did not have much faith that she would be able to stop the bandits and recover their supplies. The truck stop is far behind her now, perhaps a mile, perhaps more. The chemical fog hems in on all sides, reducing visibility to less than fifty yards. Ahead, the headlights of a large vehicle wobble in the rising heat waves.

She hears gunshots, flinching at the sound, and then puts on her game face.

The absurdity of her situation continues to nag at her, however. What is she supposed to do, arrest these people? And then what?

There are no more courts, no more judges. No more jails or wardens either. The entire legal system is gone. There is only frontier justice now—the law of the gun, with justice dispensed using bullets. Is that it, then? Is she supposed to kill them? Even sheriffs in the Wild, Wild West had judges and jails and a community they could count on.

She clears her scratchy throat and considers her next move.

Perhaps she should yell *freeze, police* before shooting them, she thinks with bitter humor. Read them their rights before opening fire and cutting them down in cold blood for maybe doing something that used to be illegal when there used to be laws and a government.

*She ain't no cop*, the man said.

Wendy suddenly stops, her mouth hanging open, and returns her Glock to its holster on her belt. *Ain't no cop*, he said. And he was right.

The realization of this simple fact feels as pleasant as her heart being torn out of her chest.

I did my best, she thinks, trying to remember the fallen whom she once considered her tribe, but she cannot recall their faces. Even Dave Carver is just a blur. She has a pounding headache and is starting to feel light headed. She should have brought water.

Time to go back, then.

Wendy slowly removes her badge, runs her thumb over its edged details, and puts it into her pocket. This done, she turns and begins walking back to the truck stop.

In the land of the blind, the one-eyed man is not king. He is not king because nobody recognizes him as king. The others do not even know he is there.

Wendy coughs long and hard on the smoke and soot, her lungs on fire. When it is over, a smile flickers across her face. If you are still alive after part of you dies, she thinks philosophically, it is like being reborn. She will survive this.

The gunshots escalate back at the truck and the headlights shake and blink out. Moments later, the first screams echo across the asphalt. The darkness closes in around her.

Wendy breaks into a run, reeling from the sudden understanding that her decision to stop being a cop probably saved her life.

◆

Anne steps carefully between the trees, her body taut and her rifle shouldered and ready to fire. She blinks away the sweat that is slowly pooling under her soaked cap. Her finger twitches near the trigger.

Each step is planted carefully, one foot following the other, taking her deeper. She is a hunter now. She does not yet know what she is hunting. Her quarry is present, but not known.

Sighing in the trees. She can hear them now, their guttural clicks. Communication that is like ancient speech, but also as mindless as insect mating. The things scamper playfully through the bushes and leap into the trees, releasing clouds of soot that make the little bastards squeal and sneeze.

They're like children, she thinks, and then banishes that painful thought. Unlike the other survivors, Anne does not question why she is here. Does not constantly compare herself, the world around her and what she is doing in it to the Time Before. Anne has survived so far because she successfully locked away her past. She does not need to remember it to continue atoning for it. She has learned to truly live in the moment.

The ash blankets the treetops and drifts in the air, obscuring everything green and creating a virtual twilight. Anne closes her eyes for a moment, and when she opens them, she sees the eyes glimmering in the haze. Dozens of staring red eyes burning in the gloom, the dark spaces of the forest. She takes another step forward.

Foliage thrashes as the creatures scamper across the treed ground. The air fills with guttural clicks and squeals. Even the squeals sound like language. They know she is here. She is no longer hunting, but observing. There are too many to fight; it is not worth the risk.

Anne raises her rifle slowly and peers into the scope, conducting a slow sweep until stopping at a small group clustered at the foot of a massive oak. The crosshairs come to a rest on a blank little elven monkey face, blandly chewing, its mouth stained. As if sensing it is being watched, the creature bares bloody teeth and glares with pure malice, without real intelligence. She moves the rifle and begins watching the others shove handfuls of some furred animal into their mouths.

She cries out, her eyes flooding with hot tears, before she can stop herself. She falls to her knees, weeping openly with racking sobs, her shoulders shaking with each burst.

The forest suddenly comes alive with hoots and shrieks.

"It's just a dog," she says. "Just somebody's old dog."

Anne stifles the next sob, sniffing loudly and wiping her eyes with the back of her hand. Within moments, she regains control of her breathing. She hates them with every ounce of her being. She raises the rifle, aims it at a snarling face, exhales and squeezes the trigger.

The rifle fires with a flash and bang that fills the forest with an echoing, rolling roar. The creatures rush and bound through the undergrowth, hooting and shrieking, gathering for a charge. The acrid smell of cordite fills the air.

She fires again, the rifle lurching hard against her shoulder. She sees the skull explode before the view in the scope jumps in a haze of smoke.

"I'm going to kill you!" she screams at them with incredible volume, her voice ringing through the trees. "Do you hear that, you little freak bastards?"

Her dog had an almost supernatural talent for catching Frisbees.

The creatures try to gather again. Anne shoots another one and the rest leap back into the trees. They appear to be baffled by the distance over which she is reducing their numbers one by one. The little things caper about, roaring and baring their teeth and puffing out their little barrel chests, pointing at her and throwing handfuls of their shit in her direction. She fires again. And again. A group breaks from the woods, leaping at her with their comical insect legs, and she cuts them down. She fires until her rifle clicks empty. They sense her hesitation. With a massive howl, the children of Infection rush at her all together. She drops the rifle.

"God damn you," she sobs, tasting salt and soot in her mouth as they rapidly close the distance in great leaping bounds. "God damn you for what you've done."

Anne raises her handguns in both fists and rains death upon them.

◆

Paul pulls a large sack out of the Bradley and curses loudly as it splits open in his hands and spills cans, bags of rice, water bottles, medical tape, hand sanitizer, tampons, mosquito repellant and a box cutter onto the gritty asphalt. Everything is coated in a sprinkling of soot. He can feel the ash settling on his hair and shoulders, finding its way under his shirt, mingling with his sweat and turning into a grimy paste coating his back. This project is converting him to paganism. Getting these supplies sorted is like something out of a Greek myth expressing the usual cruelty of the gods towards those who worship them.

He reenters the hot, dim interior of the Bradley, his back aching at having to walk stooped, and rummages through the three neatly rolled MOPP suits that he found earlier. The soldiers at the government shelter wore suits like this, and they had respirator masks. He finds one with the filter already attached and pulls it over his head. The inside smells like a men's locker room and it feels mildly suffocating, but it seems functional enough. He no longer feels like he is breathing sandpaper. He raises the mask until it rests on top of his head, sits and lights a cigarette, tossing the match on the floor and coughing.

*Where are you, God?*

Paul has not prayed in weeks, ever since Sara came at him with her hands stretched into claws. He always found conversing with God directly a path to inner peace and unlocking the solutions to problems.

*Why have you forsaken us?*

He wonders if this is some type of test for humanity and possibly for him personally. If it is, it is not a fair test. Imagine a school where the students have to guess what the question is on a test before they give their answer.

*Dear God, help me to remain your servant. I only want to serve you and glorify you through good works and spreading the good news of your son's resurrection.*

He thinks about that. What has he done to help, other than endless work with the shotgun? He wonders if he is still invited to Heaven. Jesus' teachings do not appear to apply to this holocaust. Those who followed to the letter God's prohibition against killing died fast.

He had been so close to giving up entirely. He remembers standing near a wall in the government shelter while the other refugees were being evacuated. The people crowded against the doors while Paul pretended to pray over rows of body bags lined up neatly against the wall. He intended to stay behind after the others left. He wanted to stay behind because he was going to zip himself up inside one of those bags and lie there, pretending to be dead, until God came for him.

Instead, Anne taught his hands to war.

God already ended one wicked age with water, a great heaping flood that covered the earth and drowned it. Then the waters gave and Noah, stepping down from his ark, saw the washed-away ruins of the great cities covered in rags of seaweed, the thousands and tens of thousands of bloated bodies half-buried in the mud.

Noah had been tested. And yet God had talked to Noah.

*Speak to us, Lord. Tell us what you want.*

He steps on his cigarette and thinks bitterly that perhaps there is a Noah out there, building his fortress for the righteous, and Paul is simply not invited.

He is no Noah. He knows that. He feels he has much in common with Job, however.

God asks Satan what he thinks of Job, a truly pious man. Satan answers that the only reason Job loves God is because God blessed him with riches, health and family. God gives Satan permission to test Job. First, all of his property is destroyed. Then a wind kills all of his children. Job continues to praise God, lamenting that as the Lord gives, so the Lord takes. Satan next afflicts him with boils. Sitting in cinders, Job laments but forgives God.

Finally, unable to endure, he curses the day he was born. He realizes his life has no meaning and believes there is nothing for him to do but die. He does not understand why God created man to suffer.

It is a good story. Paul can relate to all of it.

God comes in a whirlwind and tells Job that it is not for him to question God, as God is king of the universe, not accountable to his creations for anything, including their approval.

Paul had always thought that it was a cop-out, that God gave Job a terrible answer that basically boiled down to: I'm God and you're not, so do not ask me to justify myself.

But at least it was an answer.

*Talk to us, God. If you will not even talk to us in this time of darkness and sorrow, why should we give you any allegiance?*

The Jews grappled with the Holocaust for more than sixty years, trying to reconcile their belief in a just and merciful God with the millions gassed and shot and fed to the ovens in the death camps. Paul wonders what humanity will make of God when and if this plague ever ends. If God does not need Man's approval, he may sacrifice it.

The Old Testament God rewarded such waywardness in his creation with pestilence and slaughter. But as Job basically said, what else can you do to me that has not been done?

Paul dons the respirator mask and steps out into the early twilight created by massive smoke clouds slowly writhing across the sky, as if tormented. He spends several minutes watching as the green landscape continues its slow dissolution into a gray wasteland. He thinks of the other survivors wandering across this wilderness, alone and without hope. This is a place where people face themselves and learn what they really are. In war and adversity, we learn our true nature as humans. On our deathbed, our curse as earthly beings. In a place like this, we gaze into a mirror at our image rendered naked in cruel honesty—at who we really are as people.

His knees popping, he bends and begins brushing soot off of the supplies and organizing them for repacking into the Bradley. Lanterns, Coleman stove, propane tanks, rifle bore cleaner and lube, first aid, duct tape, cord, string, roll of sheet plastic, bags of salt, vitamins, toilet bucket, powdered lime, coffee pot, aluminum foil, soap, Ramen noodles, beans, waterproof matches, bolt cutters, energy bars, bedrolls, flashlights, his tattered copy of the Holy Bible.

*Lord, would you have destroyed Sodom if I was there?*

Abraham argues with God to spare Sodom and Gomorrah, saying he should not destroy the innocent along with the wicked. He asks God if he would destroy the city if fifty innocent people live there, and God says he would not. He asks God if he would destroy it if forty-five innocent people live there, and God says he would not. And so he bargains with God, forty, thirty, twenty, finally settling on ten. Paul always wondered why Abraham does not ask for mercy if even one innocent man or woman lived there.

Paul decides that he must make himself a righteous man to save the world from God's wrath, but he does not know how. This is a world where the righteous are easily culled.

He prays for guidance, but again, God does not answer.

♦

"Oh Lord," Ethan says.

He remembers seeing stories on the news about poor kids from the developing world who were flown to hospitals in the United States to have giant benign tumors removed. The kids were grotesques, carrying twenty to third pounds of flesh on their faces. The tumors were large masses of tissue forming as a result of cancer cells reproducing at an abnormally accelerated rate.

Ducky has something similar growing out of his hip, but it is not a normal tumor. It is a monkeylike creature curled up into a fetal ball, breathing, apparently asleep. Ethan can see where the driver cut the pants of his uniform to release the constantly growing creature. Now he understands why the soldiers were carrying the driver here, away from the other survivors. They do not want the others to see Ducky like this.

Sarge asks the driver how he is feeling. Ducky's gaze shifts to Sarge but otherwise his expression does not change.

The gunner shakes his head. "He barely has enough energy to breathe right now," he says.

Sarge looks at Ethan pointedly. "So. You're the smart one. What do you think?"

Ethan examines the thing growing out of Ducky's hip, careful not to touch it. It is like cancer, but more than that: a parasite. He cannot believe his eyes; it appears that the man's entire body has been completely rewired to give everything it has to the growing creature. The thing has apparently reorganized Ducky's organs and is pressing on his bladder, making him piss himself nearly continuously, a sickly, foul-smelling pink fluid.

Fascinating, almost miraculous, from a purely scientific standpoint. Horrific, and utterly revolting, from a human standpoint.

"We don't have much time," the gunner says.

"Time's up, doc," Sarge says. "Can you fix him?"

"I don't understand what it is exactly you expect me to do here."

Sarge extends his service knife to Ethan.

"Can you fix him?"

Ethan almost laughs, but stops himself. Sarge is not the kind of guy you laugh in front of when one of his people is dying.

Sarge adds, "I sterilized it. It's clean. And we got plenty of alcohol and gauze."

"He can't survive an amputation."

"Ducky's a tough sumbitch." He smiles weakly at the driver. "We'll booze you up good, Ducky. You won't feel a thing."

"Sarge, I'm sorry about your man," Ethan says carefully. "But there's nothing anybody can do."

"Did I make a mistake hauling your ass out of that hospital?"

"Sarge, you're not really thinking straight. A procedure like this would take a team of real doctors something like half a day in a real hospital. I'm a *high school math teacher*. I am just smart enough to know that anything I do will kill this man. Look at this small wound here that's still weeping; he must have tried to cut it off himself in the Bradley, and the pain stopped him. At some point, I assume the parasite will detach, as you can see legs forming here, but right now there is an entire system of veins supplying blood to it. I cut into this mass and even if Ducky's heart didn't fail from the shock, the loss of blood would surely—"

"Holy shit," Steve hisses, pushing himself away from the driver, falling sprawling on his ass.

The parasite's eye is open, studying them each in turn. The head, fused to the rest of the body-shaped mass of tissue by a thin film of clear mucus, begins to stir. The men gasp with revulsion. Ducky looks down at it, his eyes wide with helpless terror.

The creature is becoming aware. It is literally being born right in front of their eyes.

"It ain't nothing, Ducky," Sarge says, his voice fragile. "Don't even look at it."

Ethan points to the thing's face and says, "See how it's able to move, but Ducky isn't. The parasite is now stronger than its host, and is—"

He leaps to his feet and bolts across the asphalt screaming.

♦

Sarge chases Ethan under a darkening sky, calling his name, coughing on the smoke and ash that is now falling in a blizzard and almost blinding him. The tiny green figure flickers like a candle fifty yards ahead. The screams ring out across the blank, empty spaces.

Suddenly, Ethan collapses to his knees, gasping. The soldier catches up and drops heavily to one knee next to him, still coughing.

"Let me see it," he says.

Ethan moans, shaking, cradling his bloody hand.

Paul and Todd come running, looking down at him in surprise.

"Is he in shock?" Paul says.

"No," Sarge says. "Not physical shock, anyhow."

"You need help?"

"What the heck happened to him?" Todd asks him, his eyes gaping.

Sarge leans close to Ethan's ear.

"You're okay now," he says calmly and quietly. "Now let me see it."

He is still doubting what he saw until Ethan slowly unravels his trembling hand and shows the bloody stump where the tip of his index finger used to be. *The fucker bit it off. Ate it with a crunch. Its little black eye gleaming with hate.*

Ethan is looking at his hand, his face pale and surprised.

"Somebody, get me the med kit," Sarge says.

"I'll go," Paul says, and starts running for the Bradley.

"And plenty of water, Reverend," Sarge calls after him. He tears a strip from the teacher's shirt and winds it tightly around the wound. "We're going to take care of this," he tells Ethan. "You're going to be okay. We'll put some pressure on it for now, all right? Then we'll clean it real good and I'll sew it up."

Todd drops to one knee next to Ethan and says, "You're alive, man. You're *alive.*"

"You're fine," says Sarge. "It ain't nothing."

Ethan whispers something. Sarge bends closer to hear.

"*Kill. Him.*"

"The hell you say!"

Ethan winces, his eyes clenching shut against the pain.

*"Not murder. Mercy. Quickly, before—"*

Back at the fuel island, Steve's rifle pops once, twice.

"Take care of this man," Sarge barks.

"Sarge?" Todd says.

Sarge jumps to his feet and runs back across the lot. *"No, goddammit, no!"*

He finds Steve standing over Ducky's corpse, his rifle smoking and his eyes wild.

"What happened?" Sarge demands.

"That thing," Steve says, shaking with disgust and rage. "That fucking *thing.*"

Sarge closes his eyes but he can still see Ducky's body lying on the ground, a drained, sightless, empty husk, and the creature splattered across the asphalt.

He can still see where the parasite had begun eating Ducky's leg.

♦

Wendy returns in time to see Sarge carrying Ducky, a limp bundle wrapped in a blanket and light as a child, into a nearby gently sloping field crowned by a stand of oak trees. Paul and Todd and the gunner have gathered at the top, covered in soot, next to a hole they dug. They ask her where Anne is; Wendy shakes her head, staring in horror at the empty hole, feeling death's chill. She tells them the Infected are not far behind. A heavy silence falls on them as they fear the worst has happened to Anne, and turn inward to look at these fears.

Sarge and Steve gently lower the body into the pit.

"He knew he was going to die and yet he kept doing his job to the very end, saving our lives," Sarge says. "That thing was pounding us and Ducky kept on going. He was in an amazing amount of pain, alone and without hope, and yet he kept on going. For us. And for that, Ducky, you have our thanks. Because of you, we're still here, and we will remember you."

He nods to Paul, who intones: "'Our days on Earth are like grass; like wildflowers, we bloom and die. The wind blows, and we are gone—as though we had never been here. But the love of the Lord remains forever with those who fear him.' Amen."

"Amen," the survivors murmur.

Paul lowers his respirator mask to cover his face while the others lift wet bandanas over their mouths. Steve pours gasoline into the hole with the body and Sarge lights it. They step back from the sudden fury of heat and light. Sarge insisted on burning him. That way, he said, nothing will be able to dig him up and eat him.

There is no time for mourning. Sarge knows that grief is a luxury at a time like this. They will just have to try to find Anne on the road, if they can. After several minutes, the survivors plod back down the slope toward the Bradley, now completely inventoried and repacked, everything in its place. On any other day, they might admire the view from this hill, but not today. Not this wasteland across which distant tiny figures toil. Sarge notices a group of refugees breaking into the truck stop, searching for food, water, weapons, shelter. The Bradley is concealed but they should get back on the road now. The day will only bring more refugees, each more desperate than the last, and behind them, a flood of Infection.

Anne is waiting for them at the Bradley, hands on hips, her head and shoulders wrapped in rags, surrounded by falling ash. Her shirt is sprinkled with fresh blood. She pulls the rags and bandana down to expose her smiling face. They have not seen her smile before and find it jarring and yet also oddly uplifting. A tiny voice in their heads suddenly tells them that this too shall pass. They will get through this. They are alive, and they can go on surviving.

"Don't give up hope," Anne says.

◆

The Bradley drives along the westbound lanes of the Penn Lincoln Parkway through open, hilly country, passing abandoned cars and files of tired refugees on foot carrying rifles and backpacks and children. The groups of refugees maintain a cautious distance from each other and nobody waves at or approaches the Bradley. The scarred, ash-filled wasteland that was once Pittsburgh recedes the farther they go west; the view here is a brilliant green, virtually untouched.

The vehicle suddenly veers onto an exit, taking it past another abandoned military checkpoint and onto a sunlight-dappled two-lane back road. They pass telephone poles staked at regular intervals and periodic mailboxes and SPEED LIMIT 45 and SCHOOL BUS STOP AHEAD signs. Rolling hills overlook the road from the right, crowded with maple and beech and dogwood. Distant dark figures march singly or in small groups across open green fields. The air is humid and clean and crowded with the sounds of birdsong and insects.

After several miles, the Bradley slows, passing a sign announcing BUCHANAN EVERGREEN FARM and another marked CHRISTMAS TREES before turning onto a long crushed-stone driveway, speeding towards the distant farmhouse and raising a massive cloud of dust. In the living room, they find the desiccated corpses of a large family lying on the floor, smiling and blue and hugging each other, surrounded by empty bottles of pills. They remove the bodies and burn them in the backyard, coughing soot out of their lungs and marveling at the greenery and lazy birdsong. Anne wants to put more distance between them and Pittsburgh but Sarge tells her they will stay the night here. Paul contemplates the fresh graves and the family photos on the wall, depicting generations that owned this land until Infection, and believes the world is slowly becoming haunted. Or maybe we're the ghosts and do not even know we're dead yet, he wonders; survival, after all, has turned out to be a strange purgatory between living and dying. Anne gives Ethan his glasses back, which she forgot she'd scooped up at the hospital, and a fresh T-shirt. She says nothing else, but Ethan, pleasantly numb on painkillers, knows he is accepted again. While Anne unpacks the Bradley, he searches for but does not find his backpack with his family photos, realizing there is now virtually nothing to even note that they once existed. Like the others, he has no home, not even evidence of a past life outside his own unreliable mind. Todd watches the others move about in safety with a smile on his face, biting back witty quips, biding his time. Wendy cleans her Glock and exchanges a long glance with Sarge before going upstairs to take her turn washing in the antique bathtub. The soldiers fortify the house and sit on easy chairs in the living room with a sigh while the others set up the stove and make coffee and drink it slowly in silence, feeling safe for the first time since they left the hospital.

The clock in the living room chimes the hour.

Anne tells them about the refugee camp.

The soldiers she saw on the highway had been attached to the Federal Emergency Management Agency. They had come from a camp. She talked to an officer at the camp on the Humvee radio. It is only a few hours' drive away, in Ohio, in a place called Cashtown.

Sanctuary. A place where they can finally rest. The real deal: A place where they can be finally, truly safe.

The survivors blink at her, unsure how to respond to this news. After everything that has happened, they are happy simply to be alive and clean and fed in this house. The idea that they might finally end this journey is a lot to absorb.

After several moments of stunned silence, Paul says, "Well, Amen."

The other survivors laugh and echo the sentiment.

The night passes without nightmares.

The next morning, Anne is gone.

# FLASHBACK:
# ANNE LEARY

"This is outrageous," she said into the phone cradled between her cheek and shoulder as she flattened a lump of dough with her rolling pin. "Did you call the police?"

Anne had championed the bond to refurbish the park with new playground equipment. If it was one thing she'd learned, it was that playground equipment was not cheap, as in five hundred thousand dollars' worth of not cheap, but she'd negotiated hard—people had a hard time refusing Anne Leary—and gotten the very best. She felt a sense of ownership over it. Now here was Shana calling to tell her that there were two men at the playground acting suspiciously.

"The cops aren't answering the phone," said Shana.

"Our tax dollars at work," Anne said, rapidly cutting the dough into a ten-inch square and then expertly maneuvering the knife to cut the square into strips a half inch wide.

"The phone lines are all jammed up with that thing going on downtown. People killing each other in the streets. It's like the Screaming again. It took me eight tries just to get through to you."

Anne began laying half of the strips on top of her pie filling at regular intervals, pressing the ends into the edge of crust. Afterwards, she would place the other half crosswise across the top, bake it, and produce a perfect blueberry pie with a lattice crust.

"I don't understand what the fuss is about," she said. "They said on the radio it's happening everywhere but if that's true then it should be happening here. *I* don't see anything going on."

"I don't know, Anne. Things are apparently pretty dangerous out there."

"You know how the media is. They sensationalize everything. This is all going to blow over; you'll see. We got past the Screaming. We'll get past a bunch of people trying to take advantage by stirring up trouble. We just got to stay tough until the cops sort it out. And if the cops don't, we will. If the crazies come here, we got to show them they aren't welcome like last time."

"I guess you're right."

Anne looked up at the ceiling as if imploring Heaven, almost laughing. "Of *course* I'm right!"

After the Screaming, the city had filled up with crazies. People deranged by what they had seen, wandering about in shock and anger. Others convinced the world was ending and flailing at their neighbors in panic. Criminal types looking for easy pickings. They were everywhere; some of them inevitably wandered through Anne's neighborhood. People had been scared, staying in their homes, but Anne had toughened them up. They banded together and chased the crazies out.

And this, too, shall pass, she thought. Fear is the real enemy. They just had to stay tough.

"Well, what are we going to do?"

Everybody in the neighborhood knew who Anne Leary was and looked to her to take the lead in a crisis. People didn't just call her to tell her things. They expected her to *do* something. She was treasurer for the local PTA and produced a monthly newsletter for the local homeowners association. After the Screaming, she not only organized the drive to eject the crazies, she also enlisted the other homeowners in her community to get their fallen neighbors to the clinics, take care of their children, and tend their yards and anything else that needed doing. It was hard work but the people who lived here were more than happy to have something they could do to help. Anne believed that a major crisis could bring out the best in people, if you only asked them to step up.

The dog ran into the kitchen and began marching back and forth in front of the glass sliding door connecting the kitchen to the backyard, whining and barking and scrabbling at the glass.

"Hang on," Anne said. "I can barely hear you. The dog's going crazy."

She opened the door and watched Acer take off like an arrow and disappear through a gap in the fence that her husband always threatened to repair, but never did.

"I'm back," she added, scooping up her pie and tossing it into the oven. "We can't have the crazies running amok in our park. Our children *play there*, Shana. If the cops are too busy to help, we're going to have to do this ourselves. Just like last time."

"Oh Anne, don't go vigilante again."

"Me? I'm not doing anything. Big Tom's going, not me."

Her kids tramped by scowling and she followed them with her eyes, monitoring her little ducklings for signs of conspiracy.

"I got to go, Shan," she added. "I have to go vigilante on my kids."

"Tell Big Tom to be careful if he's going out today."

Anne frowned and laughed. "Sure thing. Bye, Shan." Hanging up, she turned on the hot water tap, squirted in some dishwashing liquid, and began filling the sink. "Children, come here!"

Peter tramped back into the kitchen, followed by Alice and Little Tom. They gazed sullenly at their mother.

"Well?" she said, hands on hips. "What's wrong?"

"Dad says we can't go outside today and we're bored out of our *minds*."

Anne turned off the tap and dumped a stack of dirty breakfast dishes into the foamy water.

"Did he now?" she said. "*TOM!*"

Big Tom was in the living room, sitting on the couch watching the news, already an hour late for work. After a few moments, he entered the kitchen scratching the back of his head and looking worried. Her husband was a large man—not muscular, not fat, just *big*. His smile lit up his entire face. People thought he was a natural comedian but they also respected him when he was serious. He was the kind of guy who finished but did not start fights.

"The authorities are saying it's some sort of plague," he muttered. "Things are getting pretty hairy out there."

"Tom. *Tom*. We can't keep the kids locked up like this."

"They're telling everybody to stay indoors, dear."

"It's just more of the crazies. Kids hopped up on drugs."

"It's the screamers, they say. The screamers all woke up, and they're like maniacs."

Anne snorted. "Give me a break. In any case, all that stuff is going on *downtown*, not here. The only thing we got going on *here* is two crazies hanging around the park that I want you to give a good talking to. Go kick them out of there so our kids can go play outside."

"They can play in the backyard," he offered.

"*Tom*. If you were here each day with these little darlings since the Screaming like I have been, you would know that they are wild animals and need space to roam. You cannot keep children bottled up on a beautiful day like this. They will tear the house apart. I am speaking from experience."

Anne suppressed a smile, enjoying their game. She knew he would obey her. He always did. The truth was he loved her more than anything and after a good deal of token hemming and hawing he always did as she said. Anne was the type of person who mouthed off to strangers about their driving, their parking, how they treated their kids in public. She had actually gotten her husband into a fistfight once over her editorializing about a man taking two parking spaces at the supermarket with his oversized truck. Big Tom had apologized after knocking him to the ground.

"I don't think you understand what I'm saying," her husband said with a massive frown.

Her eyes narrowed. He was not playing. He was serious. Well, so was she. When it came to things like this, she was very much in charge. And she could be very, very stubborn.

"Go, Tom. Go be the man."

"You want me to go?"

"Don't go, Daddy," Little Tom said, his voice cracking.

"Don't you say another word," Anne warned him, her voice quiet and deadly. A hush fell over them all; the mood in the house had suddenly become tense. She went on sunnily, "Your father is not working today, so he can help out around the house." She looked him in the eye, accepting his dare. "Yes, dear, I want you to go take care of that problem in the park."

Big Tom stormed out of the kitchen and returned holding one of his shotguns. The kids watched this in stunned silence except for Little Tom, who choked back a long series of sobs.

"Oh, Tom, don't go Rambo or anything," she said. "It's just stupid kids, I'm sure of it. Just give them a stern warning so they leave and don't come back."

Big Tom loaded the shotgun wearing a grimace that was almost a sneer, blinking rapidly. She could tell he was scared and it confused her. The only time she had seen Big Tom scared was their first date, their wedding day and the birth of their firstborn.

"Okay, I'm going, then," he said.

Anne looked at the ceiling, almost laughing, and said, "That's what I've been *saying*."

"Lock the door after I leave the house."

She waved him off, already focused on her next task. Anne had never locked her door during the day and she was not about to start now. If she needed to lock her door, she wouldn't be living in this neighborhood.

After Big Tom left, doubt began to nag at the back of her mind, a little voice whispering, *bring him back*, which she overcame through diving back into the endless housework that constituted her 24/7 job. She washed the breakfast dishes, dried them, put them away. She took her pie out of the oven and set it to cool. Big Tom loved her pie and she almost laughed thinking about him devouring it. He would come back feeling silly about being scared and she would say nothing and put a big piece of pie in front of him with a cold glass of milk. She tried to call her girlfriends to talk about all of these things on her mind, but there was still trouble on the line. Around noon, she made sandwiches for her kids and began to seriously worry.

The kids ate their lunches sullenly at the kitchen table. Little Tom's chin wobbled as he chewed mechanically, watching his mother with big, watery eyes.

"Where's Dad?" Peter said, his voice challenging.

Alice stopped chewing. Little Tom sobbed and rubbed his eyes. Anne, who had been staring out the window wondering that very thing, realized they were all looking at her.

Fear flickered across her face, followed by a smile.

"Dad went for a walk with Acer," she said.

She stood, picked up the phone, and tried to call his cell, but the phones were jammed. She tried again. And again. Always the same. Always that frantic busy signal indicating system failure. The kids studied her closely with worried expressions.

Peter understands what is happening, she thought. Perhaps even better than I do.

"Ha!" she said. The phone was ringing.

Big Tom's ringtone, Leo Sayer and the Wiggles doing the chorus of "You Make Me Feel Like Dancing," sang out from the living room.

Anne slammed the phone down, biting back a nice, juicy F-bomb. That was just like him. He was always forgetting to bring his cell phone.

"Where's Dad, Mom?" Peter pressed.

"Go to your rooms," she said.

"*I want Daddy*," Little Tom screamed, wailing.

Alice buried her face in her hands, sobbing.

"Where's Dad?" Peter said.

"I have a better idea," Anne said. "Come on, get up. You're all coming with me."

"Where are we going?" her boy demanded.

*"You're* going to Trudy's next door. *I'm* going to get your father. You all right with that?"

Peter nodded, almost visibly deflating with relief.

"Then let's go, troops," she snapped. She bent to wipe Little Tom's tears with a paper towel. "You too, big man. Finish your juice first."

The kids got out of their chairs and put their shoes on, Peter helping his brother and Anne helping Alice. Anne noticed how grown up Peter was becoming at just seven years of age and she swallowed hard to get rid of the sudden lump in her throat. Outside, it was a beautiful day, sunny and a perfect seventy degrees. Anne blinked in the sunshine, looking for trouble, but the neighborhood looked the same as it always did. The air was crowded with distant sirens, but there was no trouble here in the 'burbs. Just green lawns and well-kept blue-collar homes and beautiful blue sky. No people either, but they were probably all at work or inside watching the news. Even Little Tom perked up and she had to hold his hand to keep him from becoming distracted. He had reached an age where he was fascinated by anything resembling a rock.

She herded the kids across the street to Trudy's house and rang the doorbell.

A muffled voice: "Who is it?"

"Trudy, it's me."

"Anne?"

"Open up, Trudy."

The door opened and Trudy Marston peered out at them and then past them, scanning the sidewalk and street beyond.

"Everything all right, Anne?"

"Right as rain," Anne answered, resisting the urge to turn around to see what Trudy was looking at. "Listen, friend. I need you to watch my little ones while I go look for Big Tom at the park."

Trudy opened the door further, exposing her haggard face. "Jesus, is he okay?"

Anne smiled grimly. "He won't be after I get through with him."

Her neighbor's voice suddenly became shrill. "What was he *thinking* going out today?"

Anne blinked. "Never mind that. I need to bring him home. Can you watch my kids?"

"I'm sorry, I can't. Hugo is in a bad way. He's been stirring all morning, crying out in his coma. I got to keep a watch on him."

"You know Hugo is in our prayers, Trudy. If he's stirring around on his bed, that's a good sign he'll wake up soon. It's not a coma anymore if he's yelling in his sleep. Take it from me: You know I was a nurse before Peter came along. They'll all wake up soon. We're all hoping that."

An expression of horror crossed Trudy's face.

"You okay, Trudy?"

"Yes, I hope so, too," the woman said, her voice tired and faded. "Anyhow, I got to keep a watch on him. I got to be ready when he wakes up." She laughed harshly. "Even after everything, I just can't leave him. Ain't that a hoot?"

"Well, now you got three little helpers to help you watch. Right, helpers?"

"Yes, Mom," Peter said, scowling skeptically at Trudy.

"This is not a good idea, Anne."

"Come on, kids, get in there," Anne said, hustling her children through the door. She stifled a cough; the house stank like sour milk. Her poor neighbor had really let herself go since Hugo fell down during the Screaming. "Trudy, fifteen minutes is all I ask."

"Please . . ."

Anne looked up at the sky, almost laughing. Why was everybody being so unreasonable with her today? "Come *on*, the park is right over there. It's a five-minute walk. I'll be right back, I swear."

People had a hard time refusing Anne Leary.

She power walked to the park, fueled by her fury at her husband for making her worry like this, and paused at the curb. If there were a couple of crazies lurking about, it might not be a good idea to run into them. She had a forceful personality and was a big talker, but she was physically small and hated violence. Talking tough could only get you so far and she could not back it up without Big Tom around. She surveyed the neatly manicured lawns and trees for any sign of friend or foe. For any sign of people at all. Wind rustled in the branches. The playground stood empty, the swings moving a little in the wind, as if haunted.

"Tom?" Anne said, hating how timid her voice sounded.

Where was everybody? Usually, there were a lot of people in the park on a beautiful day like today, even on a Monday, even after the Screaming screwed everything up.

She noticed a plume of smoke rising in the east. That was downtown. There was a big fire downtown. The sirens crowded in a little closer. As she moved into the trees, she heard a crackling sound. Of all things, she thought. Who would be lighting fireworks at a time like this?

"Tom!" she yelled, feeling bolder. "Tom!"

She crisscrossed the park repeatedly, searching for any sign and finding none. She did not wear a watch, setting her schedule by her routine alone. Fifteen minutes had blurred into an hour. The sirens only grew louder until, suddenly, she realized they weren't there anymore. Everybody seemed to be lighting fireworks downtown. Time blurred again as her rage turned into panic. She felt the day slipping away from her.

"Tom, I'm sorry," she cried, running blindly. "I'm sorry. Now come on out here!"

Anne stopped, sweating and panting. Her shoes were muddy, her pants scraped and torn. The sun hung low in the sky. The last sirens were petering out. She had a sense of some massive unseen battle being fought and lost. The crackling sound was everywhere now.

"*I want my husband,*" she said fiercely, spitting.

A horrible feeling overtook her, shooting through her like an urge to vomit, making her fall to her knees.

"Oh no," she said, covering her mouth with her hands. "Oh, *no no no no no no.*"

Anne rose unsteadily to her feet and ran as fast as she could, wondering if she were too late. She finally arrived at Trudy's door gasping for breath.

"Please," she said, pounding on the door. "*Please,* God."

Nobody came to open it.

She ran to the picture window and tried to peer in, but the sheer curtains obscured her view. A television was on, glowing in the dark interior. She pounded on the window until pain lanced through her hand, forcing her to quit. She briefly contemplated breaking the window and how she might accomplish this. Instead, she ran around to the back of the house feeling like she was about to scream. She had a sense of being out of control.

*If somebody touched one hair on my kids' heads—*

Anne could not bear to finish the thought. Could not bear the idea they might be hurt.

"Please God," she breathed. "Please God, please God—"

The glass sliding door was open. The screen door was closed, the mesh torn away.

That sour milk stench poured out of the house.

"Please," she whispered, stepping inside.

The living room was dark. The TV was on, displaying the rainbow colors and emitting the loud ring of the emergency broadcast signal.

"Trudy? Trudy, are you there?"

Nobody answered her. Anne ran across the room to the kitchen. Three small glasses sat on the table. One still had a little milk in it.

"Trudy, where are my kids?"

There was an unmade bed in the master bedroom and the sour stench in there was so concentrated it made her gag, pushing her back out of the room with an almost physical force.

"Trudy, it's me, Anne!"

All of the rooms were empty. It seemed nobody was home. Where had Trudy taken her kids? she wondered. She needed time to think. She needed to find them and keep them safe until Big Tom came home.

Anne returned to the living room. The emergency broadcast signal continued to grate on her frayed nerves and she moved to turn off the TV.

*Oh my God—*

"No," she said. "No, no, no, no—"

She convulsed, bending over and vomiting explosively onto the carpet.

After several moments of retching and gasping to catch her breath, Anne was able to look again at what had been hiding in plain sight.

The bodies were arranged on the floor by the fireplace. Trudy had died wearing an odd smile, her neck cleanly broken. Peter and Alice and Little Tom surrounded her legs.

Something had mangled them. Torn pieces out of them. There was blood everywhere.

They had huddled around Trudy for protection. They had wanted Trudy to protect them because their mother and father were not there.

No, Anne told herself. Peter still held the poker from the fireplace. They were protecting her. That's my kids. This is just like them. To put somebody else's safety before their own. So brave. My big, grownup boy is so brave. My good Peter. Just like his daddy.

Anne screamed, clawing at her face, until she passed out.

♦

She found herself wandering in the middle of the street coughing on smoke. Paul Liao was calling to her from the driveway of his home as his wife hustled their kids into an overpacked station wagon. Across the street, a body lay on the sidewalk at the end of a long smear of blood. Somebody far away was screaming. Somebody close by fired a gun, shattering a window.

A van approached and stopped. The doors opened.

"I got her," somebody said. "Cover me."

A cop in riot gear appeared in front of her, flinching at the sight of her face.

"*Crazies*," she said thickly, her voice sounding alien to her ears.

"You're safe now, Ma'am," the cop said. "Step right this way."

Another cop stood nearby, sweeping the area with his shotgun.

"Jesus, look at her face," he said. "I thought for a second she was one of them."

Moments later, he began firing, the gun's roar filling the world.

"*Chase them out*," she insisted. She wanted to tell them something else important but could not remember what it was. The noise had scrambled her thoughts again. She was having a hard time thinking. She was fading in and out of consciousness, making hours blur into minutes. She remembered burying her children in her backyard. She remembered the power going out. She remembered digging a grave for herself. She became angry. She wanted to yell at the big cop, but he was gone. It was dark—inside, not outside. She became aware that she was in some type of big room, sitting with her back to the wall, her face stiff and stinging from an alcohol wipe and the wounds on her cheeks throbbing under thick, bulky bandages. A blanket was draped around her shoulders and she pulled it tighter protectively. She sensed the presence of hundreds of people in the room, coughing and whispering and snoring. As her eyes became accustomed to the darkness, she saw their bodies lying on cots and sitting huddled on the ground like her.

"Tom," she said, trying to find her voice. She called out: "Tom? Tom, are you there?"

"Oh Jesus, not another one," somebody groaned.

"Please shut the hell up!" another voice roared in the darkness. "We're trying to sleep here."

"Big Tom!" she cried. "Answer if you can hear me!"

"You're not the only one who lost somebody, lady," another voice answered. "Give it a rest."

There were people sobbing in the dark, talking to loved ones who were not there. Somebody coughed loudly. Nearby, a couple made love on a cot. A man masturbated loudly under a blanket. The tips of cigarettes glowed in the dark. Another man lay on the cool hard floor twenty feet away, huddled around a handful of photos he studied endlessly with a flashlight.

Anne could not remember when she last got some real sleep. She recalled that the last time it happened, she dreamed of a single baby tooth resting on Trudy's mantle. She had not truly slept since then. She stared at the man's flashlight until her vision washed out in a flash of white and she became aware of two men arguing loudly. One of them said it was only a matter of time before the food and water ran out and then they'd be killing each other over the crumbs. The other said the world was ending outside and only a fool would try to make plans that lasted longer than a day.

Anne blinked at the voices. It was daytime, she realized; time had blurred again. Beams of morning sunlight streamed through a row of punched windows near the ceiling. The room was a vehicle service garage. People milled around aimlessly, bartering candy and cigarettes, settling disputes with swift and furious beatings, emptying their waste into a row of portable toilets, washing themselves with sponges and tepid water poured into plastic bowls. The air smelled like old motor oil and human waste and fear. People huddled around radios and argued over the news, then drifted away. Colorful public health notices plastered the walls, orange and red and yellow, reminding her to wash her hands and avoid the Infected and approach law enforcement and military personnel calmly, without sudden movements, and with her hands over her head.

She realized that she was not in some type of government fortress but instead an old-fashioned refugee camp, and a temporary one at that. How long had she been here? How long had it been since her world ended? She felt lightheaded, like she had not eaten in days. She thought of a blueberry pie sitting on a kitchen counter, covered in flies.

"The authorities are in control," a voice said. "Help is coming. Don't give up hope."

The skinny, shell-shocked kid was some sort of government official and he was handing out lists of evacuation centers printed on clean yellow sheets of paper.

"This one's been overrun," somebody said in a disgusted rage. "I was fucking *there*."

"The next one on the list is five miles from here."

"Might as well be on the Moon."

"The only safe place is right here. I'm not going anywhere."

The kid ignored them, continuing to hand out his yellow sheets and deliver his simple mantra of hope with an unconvincing smile.

He held one out until Anne accepted it. His dead face warped into his plastic smile and he said, "The authorities are in control. Help is coming. Don't give up hope. Report any suspicious behavior."

Nobody else seemed to be in charge. The cops who'd brought her here were gone. Even the kind woman wearing a blue Wal-Mart apron who eventually brought her rations appeared to be some sort of volunteer. Then she saw several men working the room, shaking hands and looking concerned and writing things down in a notebook. This ad hoc leadership committee gradually grew close enough for her to hear one of them, a gentle-looking overweight man wearing large glasses, tell people that they had to get organized.

"Why?" a man said belligerently.

A woman sitting on a cot said: "You're just like *them*."

The overweight man blinked, adjusted his glasses and said, "Them?"

"The government."

"But we're all alive because of the government," he reasoned. "They brought us here and gave us food and water, blankets, medical supplies. We're trying to get organized in case the supplies run out and the government can't send us anything else."

"Like I said," the woman said triumphantly.

Anne shook her head in mild disgust. At least these guys are doing something, she thought. She recognized something of herself in them.

"But I *could* use some batteries if you got any you could spare," the woman went on.

Anne noticed an armored fighting vehicle parked at the far end of the garage and decided to take a closer look. Wrapping the blanket around her tightly and hiding her half-full water bottle in her back pocket, she wandered through the dense smells and noises of the camp until she found an empty spot where she could sit and put her back against a concrete pillar with a clear view of the impressive war machine. Three soldiers stood hunched over the engine, arguing in language so technical it was almost foreign. Anne thought they looked more like mechanics than soldiers. She watched them while she slowly sipped her bottle of water. They cleaned engine parts with rags and occasionally studied the crowd around them like engineers looking for cracks in a dam.

She planned to stay close to them. It was obvious to her that the man she'd heard arguing this morning was right: This place would not last very long. If anything happened, the safest spot in the room would be behind the soldiers and their weapons. She hated herself for thinking this. Anne cursed herself for wanting to survive.

She watched them work on their vehicle for the next three days. During that time, the refugee population rapidly dwindled to less than a hundred souls. The cops never came back to bring in more people, and as food and water began to run out, the portable toilets filled to overflowing, and petty crime escalated, many people left to take their chances trying to make it to one of the evacuation centers.

On the third day, the Wal-Mart woman brought Anne her daily ration—this time only a bottle of water and an energy bar.

"Sorry it's a bit meager this morning, love," she said. "But don't worry. We're expecting another shipment later today, I'm told. The government promised."

"So things are getting better outside?"

An expression of fear flashed across the woman's face, quickly replaced by a sunny smile.

"Of course!" she said.

The mood was tense in the shelter. People were furious that the rations had been cut to almost nothing, and were looking for somebody to blame. Mothers demanded milk for babies that screamed in their hunger. Rumor spread that several women at the far end of the room had been raped in the night. Most of the refugees wanted the portable toilets cleaned and the corpses, zipped up in shiny black body bags arranged in nice neat rows against the east wall, removed. Some of the men were threatening each other over accusations of using more than their fair share of supplies. People were crowding around the leadership committee demanding answers. Eventually, the overweight man with glasses fought his way through the mob and approached the soldiers timidly.

"May I speak to the commander?" he said, his voice tight and thin.

"I'm Sergeant Toby Wilson, sir," one of the soldiers said in a booming baritone, extending a large hand. "You can call me Sarge."

The man shook the commander's hand with enthusiasm, beaming at the warm reception.

"Nice to meet you, Sarge. I'm Joshua Adler."

"So what can we do for you, Mr. Adler?"

"Me and some of the other guys, we've been trying to get things organized."

"Uh huh. We've been watching you do that."

"Well, you must know that our supply situation is getting bad. The government said they would be coming back with more. Now, I've drawn up a list of supplies . . ."

The man fumbled with a notebook until Sarge held up his hand.

"Mr. Adler, we have nothing to do with that. We don't know anything about it. We're just here to get our rig working again. It needs professional civilian maintenance. Seeing as that's not going to happen, it's on us to fix it using whatever we can find around here. That's taking time."

"I see. . ."

"We almost got it figured out and we're hoping to return to the field as soon as we can. Getting back where we can be useful is our top priority."

"All right, I understand, uh, Sarge, but maybe you could tell me if you have any news of things on the outside—"

"It's bad," said Sarge.

"Bad?"

"Bad as in really, really bad. Bad as in we are losing this fight."

"So who's in charge?"

Sarge shrugged. "I guess you are," he said.

At the other end of the garage, the doors opened, letting in a blast of cool, clean air and three soldiers armed to the teeth and wearing bulky MOPP suits complete with goggled respirator masks that gave them a vaguely buglike appearance.

"Stay where you are," one of the soldiers announced, his voice muffled by his mask. Anne could not even tell who was speaking from where she was sitting. "Please stay calm."

The first soldier appeared to be the leader. Gripping a pistol in his clenched fist, he walked through the people crowded among the cots looking into their faces, as if searching for something, while the other soldiers followed toting automatic rifles.

Joshua excused himself, signaled to the other men in the leadership committee, and worked his way through the crowd to the soldiers.

"Captain," one of the soldiers said.

The leader turned and raised his pistol. "Sit down, sir," he commanded.

The soldiers standing behind him swept the room slowly with their rifles.

"But we're—"

The Captain slid the bolt back in his service weapon, chambering a round. "Now, sir," he added.

Joshua abruptly sat on the ground with the other men, paling.

The soldiers continued to walk through the crowd, the Captain leading the way, looking each of them in the face before moving on. Everybody was quiet, watching the soldiers, except for a few babies that cried softly in their mothers' laps.

Finally, the Captain pointed at a man and said, "I got one here."

One of the soldiers reached and grabbed the man by the arm, pulling him.

"Where are you taking this poor man?" a woman demanded.

"He's Infected, Ma'am," the Captain said. "Come on, Parker, get him up."

The people nearest the man cried out and shrank away from him, leaving him to struggle weakly against the soldiers. He was obviously sick; his face was shiny and red with fever. Finally, one of the soldiers thrust the butt of his rifle into his head and he fell limp, moaning.

They began to drag him out of the garage.

"Wait," Anne said. "Officer, wait! What are you going to do to him?"

The Captain replied, "Sit down and shut up, Ma'am."

"I think she likes you, Captain," the soldier named Parker said.

"Watch out, she's going to report you to her PTA," the other added, laughing.

"He's just sick," she pleaded. "He's not one of them."

The Captain raised his pistol and aimed it at her face.

"Maybe you're Infected."

A man stood behind the soldiers and approached the Captain. Anne could tell instantly from his black suit and white collar that he was a clergyman.

"Now, hold on a minute, sir," the man said.

The Captain turned, gave the clergyman a quick once-over, and said, "Are you Catholic?"

The man blinked, caught off guard. "No, son, I am not."

"Then I don't give a rat's ass what you have to say."

The pistol flashed in the man's hand, striking the clergyman in the face and knocking him to the floor. Anne, still standing, exchanged a quick glance with Sarge, who stood by his Bradley with his crew, wiping his hands with a greasy rag. The man shook his head slightly.

Anne swallowed her rage and returned to her seat on the floor as the soldiers dragged the sick man out of the garage and the clergyman lay groaning, cupping his face in his hands.

The roar of the gunshot penetrated the walls and rang in her ears.

Later that day, about half of the refugees packed their meager belongings and left the shelter after a long, bloody fistfight between some of the men who were leaving and those who were staying over whether the remaining supplies should be divided up. The Wal-Mart woman ended the dispute by announcing that there were no more supplies. Nothing. Not a crumb. Those who remained were broken people, lying on the cots staring at the ceiling, including Joshua, holding a dirty wet rag against his bleeding nose, one of his eyes almost swollen shut.

The following night was long and uneventful except for people sobbing quietly in the dark. The room stank with the ammonia smell of piss. They were doomed and they knew it.

The next morning, the doors burst open again and a group of men and women entered the garage carrying rifles and pistols and wearing a motley collection of military uniforms. The refugees shrank from them, screaming shrilly.

"Anybody here need a ride?" one of newcomers called out, grinning.

"Sam!" a woman cried, flinging herself into the man's arms.

"I told you I'd find you," he said, tears streaming down his face. "I told you."

"We've got buses outside, enough for everybody," announced another member of the gang, a woman with a bandaged head. "There's a FEMA camp on the way to Harrisburg and we're starting a convoy. If you want in, pack up your things now. We're out of here in ten."

The refugees crowded around asking questions. They must have been satisfied by the answers, because all of them grabbed whatever possessions they had and hurried out the door to the line of commuter buses idling outside.

As the last of the refugees headed towards the door, one of the them called out to Anne, "Last chance, lady!"

She shook her head.

The man waved and shut the door. Anne sighed with something like relief. The atmosphere, previously tense and stifling, became peaceful. The room suddenly seemed so much larger without the others filling it.

"Why didn't you go?"

Anne noticed the clergyman had also stayed behind.

"It shouldn't be that easy," she said.

"You might be right. I'm not sure if I trusted them either."

"No," Anne said. "The others had no choice but to trust them. I have a choice. It should not be that easy."

The clergyman nodded. He approached and sat on a nearby cot with a heavy sigh, touching the bruise on his face gingerly. Anne got a good look at him. He was a big man, with short, white, frizzy hair and a weathered, stubbled face. She guessed him to be in his late fifties.

"What about you?" she asked. "Why didn't you go?"

He shrugged and said, "'Long is the way and hard, that out of Hell leads up to light.' That's a fancy way of saying I agree with you."

"I liked that. Was that the Bible?"

"No. *Paradise Lost.* John Milton."

They introduced themselves. His name was Paul.

The Bradley commander approached.

"I think we've just about got the rig fixed," he told them. "If you don't mind, later on today we'd like to start her up and drive her around a bit. We'll open the service door a little to ventilate, but it's going to be loud and smell bad anyway."

"It's all right," Paul said, wandering off to contemplate the rows of corpses, still in their body bags, which lay waiting for transport that would never come.

Anne said, "Sergeant, how could you be so callous when they were dragging that man outside to be murdered in cold blood? You knew he wasn't Infected."

The soldier shrugged. "I could give you a dozen reasons, Ma'am. Let me ask you a question. Why were you willing to risk your life to save him?"

She thought of several reasons—the man was innocent, his murder was immoral, a society is judged by how well it defends its weakest members—but all of them rang false and hollow in her mind. She snorted. "What was I really risking?"

Sarge smiled grimly and nodded. "That's what I thought. In Afghanistan, when things got really bad, the only way we could get through was to accept the idea we were already dead."

"Jesus," she said, recoiling.

"Those people out there," Sarge said, pointing. "The Infected. They're pretty much the living dead. But us? We're the dead living."

"How can you say we're already dead?" Anne said, panicking at the thought. She thought about it for a moment. "How could you do it? Doesn't it change you?"

"Yes," Sarge said. "It changes you. But." He shrugged again. "You survive."

"Why?"

"Why what?"

"Why survive if it's not really you anymore?"

"Why me? Why you? Somebody's got to live, Ma'am. Somebody's got to carry on. That's all we need to know. That's all we're ever going to know. Somebody's got to live or the whole thing is pointless."

"What is?" Anne wondered.

He blinked in surprise. "The human race, of course."

"That's a lot of responsibility."

"If we don't accept it, we might as well let them win now and get it over with."

He cleared his throat and told Anne how he had taken his unit into the field to test a non-lethal weapon, and how radio dispatches suggested some type of disaster. He and his crew subsequently lost contact with the Army. They were on their own. They had a new mission in mind for themselves. They wanted to return to the mission site and try to locate their lost boys.

"We won't survive out there long on our own," he explained. "We need infantry to protect us. In return, we offer protection. The Bradley's mobility, its armor and cannon."

"What are you saying?"

"Well, I guess I'm saying I want you to join up with us."

"I want to help you, I really do, but I'm not a soldier," she said. "Never been one either."

"I want you to pull together some civilians and run them as a squad. We have weapons. I will teach you how to use them. If we find our guys, then two days, max. Maybe three."

"What about him?" Anne said, looking at Paul praying over the bodies of the dead.

"I think he's suicidal," Sarge said. "But if you want him, you can have him. See how this works?"

"But why me?" she said. "If you knew me, you wouldn't pick me for something like this."

"I am picking you based on what I know. You don't fear death. You're tough; you're not looking for easy answers and for everybody else to take care of you. And you've got a good head on your shoulders. You sat down instead of getting yourself killed helping that man, so I don't have to worry about you welcoming death or even actively seeking it."

"Well," Anne said in amazement. "I can see you've thought this through."

She realized she wanted this. Had, in fact, been sitting here for days waiting for something like it to present itself. The chance to really do something. The chance to fight back and stop the plague in its tracks.

The chance to kill every one of these monsters for what they did to her kids.

"You're a survivor, Anne," Sarge said. "I need survivors."

# FEMAVILLE

The refugee camp appears over the next rise, a sprawling mass of people and buildings covering the land as far as the eye can see. Distant helicopters buzz like flies in the still, hot air. Tiny figures swarm among the houses and public buildings and trailers and tents, a seething ocean of humanity partially obscured by smoke drifting from thousands of cook fires.

The Bradley grinds to a halt and the survivors emerge from its dim interior at a crouch, weapons at the ready. Acting like a combat infantry unit is now second nature to them.

One by one they join Sarge on the cracked road that plunges downhill and straight to the gates of the camp. Their weapons slowly sag in their hands as they forget themselves, overwhelmed by the view. Jaws drop as Sarge passes around a pair of binoculars. They stare at the camp in a mounting daze. It is literally tiring just to look at it.

The camp easily holds more than a hundred thousand people. At its core is Cashtown with its private houses and stores and public buildings and parks packed with rundown FEMA trailers. Beyond the core, the camp encompasses outlying farms, the fields filled with campers and vehicles, even a giant circus tent. And beyond that, entire forests leveled to make room for this teeming horde and its miles of camping tents and shanties. Massive clouds of dust hang over the land like a brown veil. The camp surges against mountainous walls of heaped sandbags, tractor trailers, vehicles, piled office furniture and box springs, all wrapped in miles of barbed wire and buttressed with wood guard towers. The air is filled with the white noise of thousands of people and vehicles, occasionally startled by the distant popcorn pop of gunfire. In the east, a small band of Infected makes a run at the wall through the haze and is cut down by snipers in the towers.

Just two weeks ago, this camp did not exist.

"There it is," Wendy says, her chest heaving with emotion. "The FEMA camp."

"I can't tell if I'm dreaming or having a nightmare," Ethan says.

The sight almost defies belief. It is beautiful. Beautiful and horrifying.

"It's incredible," Paul says, his voice loaded with awe.

Wendy glances at Sarge. "This is good for us, right?"

"Maybe," says Sarge, running his hand over his stubble.

"I can smell it from here," Ethan says.

"We're Americans," Todd says. "We're all on the same side, right?"

"We can't be sure of anything," Sarge tells him.

Steve whistles. "I wish Ducky could have seen this."

To the survivors, the camp represents the Time Before. If they drive into that place, they will rejoin the human race. They will be like astronauts returning home after years in space. But the world will not be the same. The Time Before is gone and anything resembling it is a mirage and possibly a trick. The truth is if they go down into the camp, they will surrender their liberty in return for protection, and they are worried about the cost. Right now they are being chased hard by the devil, but it is the devil they know.

Sarge sighs. "It's a chance. Anybody got any better ideas where to go?"

Nobody does.

"Anne would know what to do," Todd says.

"Anne ditched us, Kid," Sarge says bitterly. "We waited around for two days and she didn't come back. We barely made it out of there alive. She's either dead or on the road. Either way, she already made her decision and has no say in ours."

"*Okay*," Todd says.

"So that's it, then," Paul says, nodding. "We're going in."

Wendy snorts. "We have no choice."

◆

The Bradley cruises down the road past fields filled with the stumps of cut trees and burning piles of cleared brush. Scores of pale department store mannequins wearing designer fashions strike surreal poses across the smoky wasteland, their torsos tied to stakes and old street signs planted at regular intervals, some lying in the dirt among rags and scattered plastic limbs. A hundred yards from the road, several figures in bright yellow hazmat suits load bodies into the back of a municipal garbage truck, pausing in their work to stare at the armored fighting vehicle as it zooms past.

The camp looms close now, piled across the horizon and emitting waves of white noise and sewage smells and wood smoke. The vehicle roars past a concrete pillbox from which the barrel of a heavy machine gun protrudes, swiveling slowly to follow its progress. A man wearing a T-shirt and camouflage pants steps into the road and waves at them, motioning them to stop, but the rig keeps rolling, sending him sprawling into the ditch. Near the gates, more in hazmat suits are tossing body bags from the back of an olive green flatbed truck into a deep, smoking pit. They pause in their work, staring, as the Bradley comes to a halt in a cloud of dust and sits idling in the sun.

The man in the camo pants jogs up panting for air. He slaps his hand against the Bradley's armor.

"Open up in there, goddammit," he shouts.

After several moments, he adds, "If you think we're going to let you into the camp without you telling us who you are, you're crazy. So what's it going to be?"

The single-piece hatch over the driver's seat flips open and the gunner pops his head up, grinning. Moments later, the hatch on the turret opens and Sarge emerges wearing a scowl.

"We're looking for Camp Defiance," he says.

The man laughs. "You came to the right place. And you would be?"

"Sergeant Toby Wilson, Eighth Infantry. I've got one crew and four civilians inside. We were told it was safe here."

"We're still here, ain't we?" The man turns his head and roars, "Open the gates! Got a military vehicle coming in!" He winks. "Welcome to FEMAville, Toby."

The gates slowly grind open, pulled by soldiers with rifles slung over their shoulders, and the Bradley lurches forward in low gear, following a uniformed woman directing them where to park using hand signals. The area smells like diesel fuel and decaying garbage. Other soldiers press in, gawking at the vehicle and its cannon.

Sarge blinks, startled, as they burst into cheers at this symbol of American might.

They are still clapping as the survivors emerge blinking into the sunlight, wide-eyed and smiling awkwardly.

The area appears to be some type of checkpoint and distribution area bustling with activity. The Bradley sits parked between a beat-up yellow school bus and a Brinks armored car. A massive pile of bulging plastic garbage bags awaits disposal next to several rows of body bags. A large truck stacked with cut logs sits next to a cluster of large yellow water tanks, one of which is being coupled to a pickup truck. Men in overalls are unloading salvage from the back of a battered truck covered with a patchwork of tiny scratches made by fingernails and jewelry. Light bulbs hang from wires strung between wooden poles. The Stars and Stripes sways from one of these wires like drying laundry, big and bold, making Sarge suddenly aware of a lump in his throat.

He looks down at the cheering, hopeful boys and wonders if this might be home.

A man pushes his way through the throng, extends his hand and helps Sarge down from the rig. He is a large man with a square build and salt and pepper hair and silver Captain's bars.

"Welcome to Defiance, Sergeant," the man says. "I'm Captain Mattis."

"Sergeant Tobias Wilson, Eighth Infantry Division, Mechanized, Fifth Brigade—the Iron Horse, sir," Sarge answers, saluting.

The Captain grunts. "You're the first I've seen from that unit."

"I'm afraid I've lost them, sir."

"And your squad?"

"KIA over a week ago, sir. Pulling security for a non-lethal weapons test."

"Non-lethals," Mattis says sourly. "I almost forgot we even tried it. Seems like a year ago. You've been on the road with these civilians since then?"

"Pretty much. I trained them, and they did most of the fighting."

"I'll be damned," Mattis says, sizing up the others. "Were you all in Pittsburgh?"

"We got out just ahead of it."

"A horrible thing. I stayed overnight there once, you know, years ago. Loved the rivers and all the bridges. The old neighborhoods. Beautiful city."

"Yes, sir, it was. So what is the situation here?"

Mattis smiles. "You rest up. I'll bring you up to speed after your orientation, Sergeant."

Sarge notices that the grinning soldiers are collecting weapons from the other survivors.

The Captain adds, "Now please surrender your sidearm."

♦

Wendy climbs onto the school bus and collapses into one of the seats, fighting the urge to curl up into a ball. For the last two weeks, she has lived with her Glock always locked, loaded and within easy reach on her hip. She now feels its loss as if it were an amputated limb.

Sarge sits next to her, his hands fidgeting.

"Are we under arrest or something?" she whispers to him.

"I don't know," he says. "They said we have to go through some sort of orientation."

She chews her lip, wondering. Orientation could mean just that— the people who run the camp want to tell them about who runs it, what the rules are, how to collect rations—or it could be a euphemism for something else, perhaps something sinister. Sarge looks worried, not a good sign. The windows have been painted black and covered in layers of chicken wire, making the interior as dark and claustrophobic as the Bradley. And without the protective weight of her gun at her side, she is ready to assume the worst.

The school bus roars to life and begins rolling forward, trembling violently as it passes over a series of deep potholes.

Wendy reaches for Sarge's large hand and clasps it in hers.

"Did the soldiers tell you anything?" she asks him.

Sarge shakes his head. "I don't know who's in charge."

"What do you mean?"

"I mean I literally don't know who's in charge here—FEMA, the Army, some other branch of the government. Those guys you saw at the gate weren't from a single unit. I recognized patches from at least six different outfits. Some Army, some National Guard. The highest-ranking officer on the scene—that captain I was talking to—was a logistics officer in an ordnance company. The only real clue I saw was the flag when we came in. It was a U.S. flag."

"All right," she says. "But if they're Army and you're Army, why'd they take your gun?"

"I don't know, Wendy."

"I don't like this. Not knowing."

He squeezes her hand and says, "I don't like it either."

"At least we're all still together."

Wendy flinches at a loud thud, followed by another. Somebody is throwing something heavy at the bus. It reminds her of the monster bashing their vehicle as they struggled to flee the Pittsburgh fire. She gasps and digs her nails into Sarge's hand, which he accepts without protest. The soldiers at the front stand up, glaring, fingering their rifles. The window across the aisle explodes and angry shouting and dusty sunlight penetrates the bus. Wendy half stands in her seat and catches a glimpse of camping tents and people through the jagged hole.

"Take your seat, Ma'am," one of the soldiers says, a clean-shaven kid with large ears protruding from under his cap. "Please, it's for your safety."

Wendy sits, shaking her head in wonder.

"Volleyball," she says, feeling almost giddy with relief. "I saw some teenagers playing volleyball outside."

"That wasn't a ball that hit us," Sarge says. "Somebody was throwing bricks or rocks at us. Something is wrong here."

"It can't be all wrong if kids are playing volleyball," she says.

"People play volleyball in prison," Sarge tells her.

The bus stops and the driver kills the engine. They sit quietly for several minutes, waiting for something to happen. The heat is oppressive. The smell of diesel exhaust slowly dissipates, replaced by conflicting odors of cooking and open sewage. They hear a mother shouting at her child to be careful. Somebody is playing a guitar.

The door opens and a woman enters the bus carrying a clipboard, her face partially obscured by a green bandana. Her blue eyes glitter against her sunburned forehead. She pulls the bandana down, revealing a young, pretty face set in a bright smile.

Wendy grunts with surprise. The camp appears to be run by teenagers.

"I'm Kayley," the girl says. "I will be your orientation instructor."

◆

The survivors are led into a classroom inside a brick school building. Kayley stands at the front of the room, by the chalkboard, while they take their seats. The window blinds are open, allowing sunlight to fill the space and providing an outside view of several women taking a smoke break while another inventories a pile of boxes.

Ethan pauses at the teacher's desk before finding a seat. His classroom had been like this one, clean and neat but low on budget and behind the times in terms of technology. The main teaching method was lecture using a green chalkboard, erasers and lots of chalk. For a little excitement, maybe an overhead projector with transparencies. He remembers how much he loved the squeaky sound a stick of chalk made on the board as he wrote equations for his students. He loved everything about the job, in fact. That, and his relationships with his family, had defined him.

How quickly things change, he thinks.

How would you solve for $x$?

Answer: You try to kill it.

His finger throbs with pain. He pops another painkiller.

A part of him realizes that he could start over here. The camp appears to offer a second chance. If they provide schooling to kids, maybe he could even become a teacher again. Putting his skills to work here is a duty as real as Wendy's wish that she were still a cop. One might think teaching kids math during the apocalypse would be a waste of time, but the opposite is true. Kids should continue learning, preparing for the future. Otherwise, there is no future and the war against Infection is already lost. The other way lies barbarism.

He will never teach again, however. He knows this. Even if the plague and the fratricides were to end tomorrow, he still cannot imagine it. That part of him is as broken as the world.

The truth is the only reason he is here is because of the slim chance he might find his family among the camp's residents. This hope, as thin as it is, has become his strongest reality. Everything else is illusion. He will keep searching until he finds them. He will search forever. That is what he does now. That is who he is.

Todd flops into the desk next to him and slouches, scowling. "I just can't get away, I guess," he mutters.

"Ready for some algebra?" Ethan says with a wink, hoping to rib him.

"I liked algebra," Todd tells him. "It's school I hated."

A man walks into the room, talks quietly with Kayley for a few moments, and then leaves. Immediately, a group of people enter in a cautious daze.

"You are all survivors of Pittsburgh," she tells them. "You are not different from each other. You are all the same. At one time, you were neighbors. Welcome each other."

The survivors pause, sizing each other up, and nod before taking their seats. The newcomers are filthy and exhausted. One of them sobs quietly as she hugs a sleeping toddler against her chest. Another puts his head down onto his desk and immediately falls into a fitful sleep. Dust floats in the sunlight around them. They smell like ashes.

"Welcome," Kayley says. "Welcome to Camp Defiance. You are safe here, in this room. This is a safe place and you're okay."

The survivors quiet down and look at her hungrily.

She says: "After the Screaming, the Federal Emergency Management Agency established a series of forward operations posts across the country to coordinate Federal support of local authorities. Camp Defiance was one of them, although back then it was simply called FEMA 41."

After the Screaming turned into Infection, she explains, the camp was almost overrun, but word had gotten around about its existence, and people poured in from all over southern Ohio. The refugees helped keep the camp going and now it is run by a mixture of Federal, state and local government people and protected by a mixed bag of military units.

"Today, the camp has a population of more than one hundred and thirty thousand people, and is constantly growing," she tells them, pausing to let that sink in. "I worked in a refugee camp for the Peace Corps for two years overseas. The ideal size for a camp like this is twenty thousand. It's nothing short of a miracle this place is functioning as well as it is."

Ethan suppresses the urge to whistle. A hundred and thirty thousand people is a tiny fraction of the population in this region before Infection, but it represents a chance. Somewhere, in this teeming horde, his wife and baby girl might be living, safe and sound.

Kayley spends the next fifteen minutes describing how they will be processed. Newcomers to the camp must go through a brief medical exam and register, she tells them, to receive resident cards. Food and water may be collected at food and water distribution centers. Skilled workers may be offered jobs by the government paid in gold, and receive priority access to housing and bonus allotments of food and water. The camp also has a health center and scattered health posts, pest houses, cholera camp, schools, markets and cremation pits for disposal of the dead.

"Does anybody have any questions so far?"

"I do," Ethan says. "What kind of records do you keep? I've got family missing."

Kayley nods. "Locating lost loved ones is a big priority for us. Tell the people at registration while you're being processed, and they'll help you out. We keep a record of every person who has ever entered this camp. They also have contacts with other camps in Carollton, Dover, Harrisburg and other places."

Ethan leans back in his chair, satisfied.

"I've got a question," Sarge says loudly, standing. "What are you hiding here?"

Kayley smiles at him. Her face shows no signs of surprise.

♦

The survivors bristle at Sarge's tone. A moment ago, they were disoriented, listening to Kayley in a lethargic daze, struggling to absorb everything she was telling them. Now they are alert and taut as deer that smell a predator in a sudden shift of wind. They watch Sarge and Kayley closely, their hearts racing and their breath shallow as they once again, automatically, tread the tightrope between fight and flight.

After several moments, Kayley says, "Can you be more specific?"

Sarge blinks. "Well, for one, why did you take our guns?"

Wendy glares at Kayley, wondering the same thing and wishing she felt the reassuring weight of the Glock in her hand right now. She feels electrified by urgency and confusion. She has complete faith in Sarge's instincts but he sprang this confrontation without telling her; she has no idea how to back him up.

"Sergeant Wilson, almost everybody in this camp is armed," Kayley is saying. "We all know that Infection spreads like wildfire. If one person got the bug, it might bring the entire camp down. We are on the constant lookout for Infection and must be ready to act quickly if we see it."

Sarge crosses his arms. "I'll ask again, then: Why did you take ours?"

"Your weapons were taken for the time being because, quite often, certain newcomers do not take to orientation. We do not have the means to enable new residents to slowly transition from the dangerous world outside to the relatively safe oasis that we have created here. Some people cannot accept the sudden change and become upset and irrational."

"I can see why," Sarge says. "It's like a police state around here."

"Yes and no. We are actually rather thin on policing. Surely you don't really think this camp could function without the consent of its residents. But it is true that we are a society that is under siege. It is different being here than out there on the road."

"If we are not prisoners, you would let us leave if that's what we wanted."

"You are not prisoners, but neither can you simply come and go from the camp as you please, for obvious reasons. Every time somebody enters the camp, there is the possibility of Infection or some other disease being imported. We cannot allow that."

"You're not answering my question," he says.

"The simple answer is you can leave any time you like. But if you do, you cannot come back. Is that a satisfactory answer?"

"We can leave with all our gear?"

"If a resident decides to leave, they can go with either what equipment and supplies they brought or its equivalent value, which is the law."

"What about our Bradley?" Sarge says, glaring at her.

Kayley's smile disappears, replaced by a hard line.

"I think you mean *our* Bradley, Sergeant. That machine was manufactured for the Army and belongs to the people of the United States. You are a soldier and if you try to leave, your superiors may let you go, or they may decide to shoot you for desertion. I don't know. But I can tell you for a fact that the people in charge here are not going to let you drive out of camp with a multimillion-dollar piece of military hardware that could be used to save American lives."

"This is bullshit," Sarge says. "It's a trap."

"The trap is in your mind, Sergeant Wilson."

Sarge turns to the other survivors and says, "Come on, we're leaving. They can't stop us."

None of the survivors move, not even Wendy, who believes Kayley explained the camp's position perfectly and is now feeling reassured rather than threatened. Sarge gapes at them, sweat pouring down his face, seemingly disoriented and unsure of what to do next. He bumps against his desk and knocks it over with a crash that makes the other survivors flinch.

"It's not safe here," he pleads, his breath suddenly shallow.

Wendy stands and peers into his face.

He says quietly, just to her, "This is a bad place."

The man is visibly shaking.

"You are among friends here," Kayley says. "You are perfectly safe."

Wendy glares at her briefly and says, "Could you shut the hell up, please?"

She returns her attention to Sarge, slowly reaching out until she is touching his face gingerly. She holds his face in her hands.

"Tell me," she says.

His eyes avoid hers until finally connecting.

"I'm scared," he says, taking a deep, shuddering breath.

"I've got you, baby," she tells him. "Look at me. Look at *me*."

The other survivors look away. Nobody judges him. They have all been where he is now. Everybody has post traumatic stress disorder, or PTSD, these days, with its bad sleep, depression, guilt, anxiety, anger, hyper vigilance and fear. Wendy still cannot sleep at night without flashing to the Infected bursting howling into the station. She is amazed that after everything Sarge endured, it is now that he cracks, and here, where he is finally safe.

But she understands. The truth is none of the survivors is comfortable in this place. The very sudden change from survival to safety—not just safety, but society, with rules and customs—is nothing short of an abrupt shock to the system. None of them fully trust it.

And yet it is not evil. It is, in fact, their best chance at survival.

"I'm sorry," Sarge says.

Wendy now believes she understands why Anne did not come with them to the camp. We are all broken, she thinks. None of us may belong here.

♦

Holding Sarge's face, she suddenly remembers the man in the SUV during the morning of Infection, when Pittsburgh woke up to a war zone. Her station had already been overrun and Wendy walked the streets alone, on foot, shrugging off people begging her for help. The cars were snarled bumper to bumper all along the four lanes of North Avenue and were even stacking up on the sidewalk and jamming into the narrow median, their horns bleating like panicked sheep. Others raced through the trees in the adjacent park, skidding in the mud and going nowhere fast.

The Infected ran among the vehicles in the jam, peering into the cars as if window shopping before punching in the glass with bloody knuckles. Wendy saw the Infected swarming over a nearby wrought iron fence, emitting a communal howl that made her heart rate skyrocket and her legs turn to jelly. Although her conscious mind was still in pieces, it registered in the back of her mind that Allegheny General was on the other side of that fence; the Infected were still waking up and streaming out of the hospital's doors even now, like rats.

Wendy unholstered her service weapon and fired once, twice. A man yelped and flopped off of the fence, quickly replaced by another in a paper hospital gown, his legs smeared with his own shit. I don't have enough bullets, she thought.

People were abandoning their cars and running into the park swinging purses and briefcases or holding hands, turning the traffic jam into a parking lot. She turned, distracted by the sickening sound of crumpling metal and a gunned engine straining against an impossible load.

A man was driving a shiny red 4x4 SUV on a lifted suspension, three tons of glass and steel with a little evergreen air freshener swinging from the rear view and a specialty license plate reading XCESS over the standard *visitPA.com*. He was panicking and trying to ram his way out of the press of honking vehicles. The acrid stench of muffler exhaust and burning rubber filled the air. He backed up his vehicle, his face and his mouth working behind the windshield, and then stomped his foot on the gas and rammed into the car ahead of him, shoving it forward less than a yard and jolting himself with whiplash.

Recovering, he backed up again, yanked on the steering wheel, and roared into a Volkswagen Jetta in the righthand lane at an acute angle, the collision twisting the frame and shattering the driver's side windows. The car's driver howled in shock and pain, covered in blood and glass, trying to shield her face with her arms. As the SUV backed up again, crumpling the hood of another car behind it, an Infected man pulled himself into the Jetta's open window, his gown flapping and his legs kicking in the air.

Wendy's stomach turned over and she bent to spit a gob of bile, listening to distant car alarms. The mindless, brutish cruelty of the SUV driver and the rabid Infected was making her feel physically sick. The driver had a cut on his forehead now and looked dazed, revving the engine and bucking his vehicle forward into the car in front of the Jetta, shoving it sideways against the curb and bursting its windows in the sharp impact. The passenger door opened and a woman emerged, wailing and pulling a screaming child out of the backseat. The air filled with a sweet maple syrup smell, ethylene glycol released by a broken radiator. Wendy swallowed hard against another urge to vomit.

"Halt," she said hoarsely, then raised her arm and stepped forward, shouting: "Stop it!"

She marched up to the SUV as the man stepped on the gas. She did not flinch. Recognizing her uniform, he braked with a short screech, stopping the vehicle inches from her knees. He stared down at her through the window, panting for air. His eyes slowly focused with understanding and regret, began to fill with tears.

The cop raised her gun and fired, punching three cobwebbed holes in the windshield. Smoke filled the cab and blood splashed across the glass.

She wished she had more bullets.

Then she is back in the classroom, cupping Sarge's face and looking into his eyes.

She knows what it is like to lose control.

"I've got you, baby," Wendy says. "I've got you."

♦

After a brief medical exam, Todd hurries into the processing center, a hot, confusing jumble of people and tables jammed together under various signs and flags in what used to be the school gym. People sit behind the tables, talking to sitting or standing applicants, while others sit on the floor ringing the room, fanning themselves with pieces of cardboard marked with numbers. A wave of sour body odor immediately envelops him, almost making him gag. It is so hot in the room and there are so many people sweating that a mist hangs in the air, rising on beams of sunlight entering the space through skylights. He spots Ethan at one of the tables but cannot locate the other survivors. His heart races as he realizes they must have gone through processing already, leaving him behind. He had been last in line for the medical exam and apparently he'd spent too much time in the bathroom taking the longest dump in his life sitting on a real toilet that actually flushed, surrounded by four walls in blissful privacy. His thoughts are jolted as a man shoulders him as he walks past, offering a muttered apology.

His first impression of the place is that there is still a huge number of refugees entering the FEMA camp, but he soon realizes that all sorts of government business goes on here, from job applications to replacement of resident cards to reporting crimes, and more. Some of the tables are run by sharp-eyed, clean-shaven men in business suits under American and other flags indicating various agencies of the Federal and Ohio state governments. Todd figures they're the complaints department. You go there and complain, and in return they give you bad news.

He takes a number and finds a spot on the floor, fanning himself like everybody else, trying to keep an eye on Ethan, who has moved to another table, keeping the little stump of his finger elevated as he works the room. Probably looking for his dead wife and little girl. Todd is mentally flexible enough to accept that his father is dead or Infected along with all the other cubicle drones at the office where he worked, and his mother is definitely Infected, having fallen during the

Screaming. He feels sorry for Ethan but living your life like a defective CD eternally skipping during your favorite song is not living.

Eventually, his number is called and he finds himself sitting at a picnic table across from a red-haired woman who looks at him like he just hit her in the face. Slapping an index card on the table in front of her, she begins to take down his information—name, where he lived, social security number, gender, age, height and eye color, nearest relations and a brief medical history.

"You were in high school?" she says, pen poised above the card.

"Yes, Ma'am," Todd answers, using the respectful tone he used with teachers.

"What grade?"

"Senior," he says, worrying in the pit of his stomach that the woman would check up on him and realize he lied about that and his age. But then he notices the stacks of index cards tied with rubber bands being carted by the other bureaucrats, and realizes he can pretty much say anything he wants and there would be no way that she could confirm or deny it.

"Do you want to go back to school? We offer schooling here. You could get your diploma."

"No thanks," he says sunnily, his brain working hard on how to defend that decision.

The woman shrugs, does not care.

"Any job skills?" she asks.

"I've had jobs before but nothing that required skills," he tells her. "I am really good with computers, though. What kind of skills are you looking for the most?"

"Psychotherapist," she answers.

He laughs.

"I'm not kidding," she adds.

Todd opens his mouth, but she silences him by holding up her index finger, the universal sign for *wait a minute*. The woman pulls an old mechanical typewriter towards her and starts pecking at the keys with agonizing slowness, glancing frequently at the index card. She finally yanks a business card-sized piece of paper out of machine, stamps it with a seal, and hands it to him with a thick manila envelope.

"This is your resident card," she tells him, explaining that he will use it to obtain his rations, access the showers and medical services, and apply for other government help. "This is your information packet. In it you will find a recap of your orientation—a map of the camp, the rules you are expected to follow here, and a list of services and where to find them. There is currently a small surplus in shelters so you do not have to build your own; your allotment is marked in yellow highlighter. This is your claim ticket so you can pick up the property you brought into the camp with you. And finally, here are two flea collars. Put one around each ankle. Keeps the lice away."

"Gross!" Todd says. "I mean, thanks."

"Do you have any questions?"

"Just one. Do you have stores or anything like that?"

"There are six outdoor markets. Four are where people sell pretty much anything. Another is for produce grown in the camp, and the last is for meat."

"What's the accepted currency?" he presses. "Is it a barter system, or is the dollar—"

The woman glances over his shoulder and yells, "*Twenty-one!*"

Todd stands, trying to think of something biting, but a family approaches, wild-eyed and holding out their cardboard number to the woman like an offering, and he tells himself she is not worth it. *She is not going to get me down. I survived out there weeks while she was in here sitting on her ass filling out index cards. I have fought and killed to survive.*

He has a sudden flashback to Sarge standing in front of the hospital, spitting tongues of flame and smoke with his AK47 in the dark. He remembers throwing a Molotov into a mob of the Infected. The Bradley smashed through the parked cars, its gun booming. He smiles.

"Ha," he says, and walks away to find Ethan standing near one of the tables, wringing his hands. He asks the man how the search is going.

"Slow," Ethan says with a sad smile, but he appears happy to be trying, and this is something, Todd realizes. At least there is that.

"Where's everybody else?"

"The Army took Sarge and Steve away for debriefing. Wendy got a job as a cop and is heading to where they told her she could live. She gets priority housing being a cop. And Paul is on his way to one of the food distribution centers. He got a job there passing out food."

"Well," Todd says, feeling awkward.

"How about you? You going back to school? They offer that here, you know."

"I don't really see the advantage of learning calculus," Todd says before catching himself. "Oh, sorry, man."

Ethan nods sadly. "It's okay. I don't see the point in teaching it anymore, either."

"I've got big plans, Ethan. I've got this stash—"

"One hundred and eight!" a voice cries from one of the tables.

Ethan perks up. "That's me."

"Well," Todd says, frowning. "I guess I'll be seeing you around."

"Right," Ethan says vacantly. "Take care of yourself, Todd."

Todd collects his duffel bag, weapon and ammunition in another room and walks outside into hazy sunlight, feeling tickled and breathless with excitement.

I'm here, he thinks. I made it.

The street in front of the school is filled with activity. A group of bored soldiers glances at him, sweating in their helmets, and then go back to talking among themselves. They barely look a day older than him, just beefy kids. Several children sit on the cracked sidewalk, drawing with pieces of colored chalk. Another group of kids, orphans of Infection quickly going feral, pull a red wagon filled with empty plastic jugs and bottles. Whatever grass might have grown here is now gone, trampled into dried dirt that floats in the air as dust. A military five-ton truck rolls down the street, ignoring a stop sign, beeping at the lazy crowds. Several men are working on a large machine, their tools and parts laid out neatly on a filthy white blanket. Dogs are barking inside a mom and pop shop across the street converted into housing. A loudspeaker attached to an old telephone pole, dangling a tangle of wires, squawks instructions on how to avoid cholera, followed by an ear-splitting screech. A moment later, a Britney Spears song begins playing, tinny and offering more nostalgia than entertainment in this time and place.

Todd is irritated at the other survivors. They could not even stick around to stay goodbye. You're on your own again, Todd old man, he tells himself. You were doing just fine before joining up with them. You were *ninja*, surviving on your own, as you've always done. You will do it again. The improbable umbilical cord was not meant to last. It had been a relationship born of necessity, nothing more. Now it is time to be a nation of one again.

He consults his map, a virtual city carefully drawn in madman scrawl, his to explore. He identifies the school, situated on a road that forms one of the camp's major arteries used for motorized transport between the central hub and the distribution and health centers. He finds his new home, a speck in one of the endless shanty towns, revealed by a blotch of highlighter. Then he locates the nearest general market, where he intends to launch his career as a trader.

The other survivors are haggard, tired, broken. Just look at Sarge, he thinks, the man who fought a horde of screaming Infected by himself and saved our lives: damaged goods. Todd is young and taut and mentally flexible and much, much more resilient than he looks. If anything, the apocalypse has been almost kind to him. Already lean, he is starting to put on a little muscle and with it, more confidence. He feels powerful. He looks at the kids running by in packs and the soldiers passing around a cigarette and thinks: My generation will survive this. Will be defined by it. And we will define the age in turn.

◆

Paul hitches a ride hanging onto the side of a garbage truck as it grinds down one of the camp's main arteries, raising a choking cloud of dust. The truck has been assigned to collect the dead for disposal. Its sides are decorated with crowded layers of outlandish graffiti, much of it incorporating grotesquely painted skulls and bones. He let the driver bum a cigarette and in return found out why the dead are burned in pits outside the city. The reason, he was told, goes back to the camp's origins, when many people, raised on horror films, postulated that the Infected were zombies—hungry things that rose from the dead. Although it has been disproven, the practice stuck. Even if the people here want to bury the dead now, they cannot. There is simply not enough space.

A rock glances off of the side of the truck with a metallic boom, making Paul flinch. Another sails by close to his head, almost making him fall into the dust. The cab's passenger-side window rolls down and a rifle protrudes, carefully sighting on a target among the tents.

No more rocks are thrown at the vehicle.

The truck lurches over the potholes, trembling in its metal skin. It makes three stops to pick up bodies lying stiff in the sun, their faces pale and their skin flaccid and waxy under sheets of plastic. For years, Americans sanitized death. Few people actually saw the dead in their natural state, bloated and drawing flies with their stench. They saw them laid out on velvet in fine caskets, dressed up in their best clothes, preserved like Egyptians.

The truck finally slows in front of a large wood church. A hand reaches out of the window and points to the front doors.

Paul jumps off, pounds the side of the truck to signal the driver that he can go, and waves. The hand waves back and the truck continues down the road.

Free of the truck's exhaust, the camp's ever-present smells of cooking, wood smoke and sewage return with a vengeance.

He breathes deep, figuring he might as well start getting used to it.

The doors are open and he walks in eager to do something.

Moments later, he finds himself staring down the barrel of an M16 rifle.

"Where do you think you're going, Father?"

Paul frowns. "It's Reverend, not Father, and I'm going to the place where I've been assigned by the authorities to live and work."

"Let's see your papers."

The soldier studies his work papers while the rest of his squad glances at him curiously and then returns to their business. Paul ignores them and takes a look around. The church is filled with children sitting on every kind of chair in front of every kind of table—folding chairs, armchairs, office chairs, deckchairs, ottomans, benches, dining room tables, ping pong tables, nightstands, coffee tables, end tables, drawing tables and poker tables. The pews are gone, probably hacked up for firewood. A long line of sunburned kids holding bowls, spoons and mugs wait their turn to receive stew being ladled out of large vats on the altar in the domed apse, like a scene out of *Oliver Twist*. Their chatter fills the grand nave, rising up to the vaulted ceiling. They chew in the light of windows beautifully patterned with hand-stained glass.

"Hi," a man in clerical garb says, approaching with his hand outstretched. The man is tall and skinny, his shoulders slightly stooped, and wears a neatly trimmed beard. "I'm Pastor Strickland. This is my church."

"Nice to meet you," Paul says, taking his work papers back from the soldier and shaking the man's hand warmly. "I'm Paul Melvin. These kids are all . . . ?"

"That's right. Orphans of Infection."

"So many," says Paul, staring at them. He has not seen a happy, living child in weeks and seeing so many here, eating good food in a safe place, warms his heart.

"These kids must be nourished and protected. They are our future. But they're still wild animals, most of them. Don't turn your back on them or leave your property unattended."

"I'll keep that in mind. But they seem pretty well behaved."

"They have an abiding respect for the supernatural," Strickland says with a smile. "They think if we find the right words, God will end Infection."

Paul grunts, pleased. "That's something I have in common with them. I'll have to ask them what words they think will work."

"I'm sorry, Paul. But you won't be working here. You'll be working down the street at the FoodFair handing out rations to the campers. Hard work, most of it, and thankless at that. Is that a problem?"

Paul shakes his head. He would like to work with the children, but it does not matter. "I just came here to work. I have to wonder, though."

"Why do we need somebody like you to do that kind of work?"

"Something like that," Paul admits.

"Ah, well," says Strickland. "I'll tell you. On a weekly basis, we hand out enough food to give each camper about twenty-one hundred calories a day. They get wheat, beans, peas, vegetable oil, fortified food such as a corn soya blend, some salt and sugar. If the camp gets its hands on some cattle, we can distribute a little beef, but that's not all that often. The campers get no spices and most people can't afford that kind of thing at the markets. Our fare will keep you alive, but it's monotonous, as you can imagine, and people get mad after a while eating the same thing. Here's something else. We try to give rations to women only because they are more likely to pass it on to other family members instead of selling it to buy something else. That naturally produces conflicts. Plus there's the simple fact that we work for the government here, essentially, and a lot of people are resentful."

"I saw people throwing rocks at a garbage truck today."

"They are less likely to throw them at people in our profession," Strickland says. "Does that answer your question simply enough? A lot of people have turned away from God because of what has happened, but they haven't gotten around to blaming us for it yet. Most of the campers see us for what we are: people trying to help."

"That's what I want to do," Paul tells him. "I want to help."

"Then you've come to the right place. This camp needs all the help it can get."

◆

Wendy enters the police station, a graffiti-covered building crowded with shouting people arguing with powerful, burly men wearing a variety of motley uniforms, from correctional facilities officers to private sector rent-a-cops. The building smells like angry men testing each other, a scent she knows well. She senses an atmosphere of simplicity and brute force here. The walls are plastered with wilting public health notices, camp edicts, duty rosters and poorly rendered carbon copies of missing persons sheets. Two bearded officers shove their way through the crowd, loading shotguns. Dogs sleeping on the floor raise their heads sharply as the men tramp out of the station. A man wearing a STEELERS cap, handlebar mustache and CASHTOWN FIRE DEPARTMENT T-shirt directs her to where Unit 12 bunks, the cost for this information a degrading moment of sexual appraisal. He does not care why she wants to know; he probably thinks she is somebody's woman paying a visit. He watches her leave, spitting tobacco juice into a soda can.

She walks down a corridor that smells like an ashtray. The administrative area has apparently been converted into housing for another unit; off-duty officers pad in and out of the rooms barefoot in their underwear, scratching their bellies as they watch her struggle along with her duffel bag. The hallway is partly blocked by boxes of miscellaneous equipment. She briefly wonders if Sarge is okay, surprised by the sudden sensation of butterflies in her gut. He seemed fine when he left with Mattis, but she is worried about him and wonders when she will see him again.

The reality of the situation strikes her just before she reaches her quarters. The camp is overcrowded and space is obviously at a premium. People are jammed everywhere, and skilled workers are expected to live in or near their base of operations. Unit 12 bunks in the detention area; she will likely be living in a jail cell. Pondering the irony of it, Wendy enters the space, her foot crunching on an empty beer can, and takes in her new quarters.

She was right. Eight men occupy the detention area's processing space and six holding cells. A man snores loudly in a bunk while another sits next to him on the floor wearing a pair of boxer shots and cleaning a rifle. A mustached man smokes a four-smelling cigar while filling a plastic cup from a water cooler. Another has a small Coleman going; she smells coffee brewing, rich and strong, which makes her feel strangely homesick. A gray-haired man stops reading his book and peers at her curiously over his reading glasses, a toothpick clenched in his teeth. Wendy suddenly becomes aware they are all looking at her with their lean, stubbled faces. Good ol' boys. She returns their gaze coolly, wearing her game face. Her heart is soaring at the opportunity to be a cop again but she suddenly wonders what it is going to cost her.

"I'm looking for Ray Young," she says. "The unit sergeant."

"And you would be?" the man with the book says.

"Officer Wendy Saslove, reporting to the unit."

The man glances at the others briefly before chuckling.

"How about that," he says, chewing on his toothpick.

"Christ, Jonesy, I could have sworn she was one of yours," a voice behind her says.

Wendy instantly recognizes the mildly sardonic tone. She turns and sees the man with the STEELERS cap filling the doorway, smiling and holding his soda can.

"I'm, uh, working on that, Ray," the young man called Jonesy says, licking his hand and straightening his hair.

Ray spits into the can and says, "Well, Officer Saslove, I guess that's your room right there." He nods, gesturing to one of the holding cells.

"Thank you, Sergeant."

Wendy picks up her bag and takes it to the cell. The toilet is dry as bone and the sink has been removed. Instead, she has a washing bucket with a sponge and fresh bar of soap and a shit bucket with a bag of lime and roll of TP. The bunk looks serviceable enough and will actually rate as four-star comfort after sleeping on the ground for the past two weeks. The walls are plastered with photo spreads of big-chested blondes from porn magazines; those will obviously have to go. The main problem will be privacy in this male zoo. She rolls out her sleeping bag on the bed and then opens her duffel bag, noticing for the first time the name DEVEREAUX written on it in black marker.

After a few moments, Wendy becomes aware that the sergeant followed her and is standing in the doorway to the cell. The others watch closely, wearing half-smiles.

"Officer Saslove, if I may," he says. "It's not that I mind having a pretty face like yours hanging around, but I look at you and I wonder: What are you doing in my unit playing cop?"

She ignores him, pinning her badge to her belt. Ray squints at it and adds, "So what were you, then, a meter maid?"

One of the other cops walks up to the cell and leans against the bars, peering in with a smile.

"Hey, I'm talking to you," Ray says, crumpling the soda can in his hand. The room tenses and Wendy with it. She will eat the sergeant's shit; she is the rookie here, so she expects some unit hazing. But if any of them touches her, if that's how things work in this shithole, she is going to break bones.

In preparation, she takes out her Batman belt and puts it on, her body electrified by the comforting weight of the Glock on her hip. She almost smiles. She pulls her side-handled baton out of the bag next and slides it into place, flashing back to its last use back at the hospital.

"Where'd you get that gear, Saslove?"

"From the Pittsburgh Police Department," she tells him.

He glowers at her, his face reddening. "Is that so? How did you get it, exactly?"

"It's standard issue, Sergeant. I worked patrol for nearly a year."

"You'd better be telling me the truth, so help me. Are you shitting me?"

Wendy stares back at him, saying nothing.

He takes a step forward and she places her hand on the handle of her baton, already planning where she is going to hit him and how hard.

"Jesus Christ," Ray says gently, with something like awe.

The other cops gather around behind Ray. "Pittsburgh," they whisper among themselves, almost chanting the word. "She's a cop." One of them reaches and touches her shoulder lightly, making her flinch, while another holds out a warm can of beer with a friendly wink.

"Welcome, Officer Saslove," Ray says, his eyes big and watery. "And God bless you."

♦

The open air market is set up at the site of the old Cashtown Flea Market on the outskirts of town, and serves as the closest thing to a mall the camp's residents can get. Now situated in the middle of a vast shantytown, the market's boundaries are roughly marked on the west by Christmas lights and light bulbs hanging from wires strung between poles, and on the east by one of FEMAville's many foul canals. These canals were once part of a Medieval-style defense system of staked trenches dug around the old town by the original refugees to stop the Infected, but were slowly absorbed by growth, the stakes removed and burned for firewood, the pits filled with rainwater. Wood planks form bridges over the rank canals, now filled with sewage and garbage and even a few bodies, some always burning, day and night. Solar landscape lights thrust into the dirt mark its edges to ensure night travelers do not fall in. The canals are deadly; if the fall into the toxic sludge itself does not kill you, any number of diseases will.

Todd wanders awkwardly among the crowds of people browsing the wares stacked on the tabletops, as if testing his legs on the deck of a ship. He is not used to crowds. Especially crowds where almost everybody is carrying a gun, axe, hammer, bat or other weapon. The people here are angry and desperate and stink of fear. He feels exposed, vulnerable, a little disoriented with something like vertigo—

that weird sense that everybody knows each other and is aware of you and that you do not belong. It's high school all over again.

Come on, Todd old man, he tells himself. Nobody here gives a crap about you. They have their own problems. Boy, do they ever.

The vendors near him are shouting out products and prices while others are being haggled by customers or chasing away children and beggars. The products include batteries, candles, matches, condoms, cigarettes, hand lotion, knives, sewing thread, spices, seasoned firewood and boxes of useless electronics. Commodities, rarities and plenty of junk. The prices are based on whatever the seller wants— dollars, gold, services in kind, barter—and the market appears to be thriving. Like the earth, capitalism abides. Barter appears to be most popular form of exchange; one merchant is selling playing cards and board games and dice but is only accepting cigarettes as payment.

Nearby, a line of people wait their turn to get into one of a battery of portable toilets. They erupt into spontaneous applause as a truck drags an emergency generator down the road. Electricity means progress. Two men in orange jumpsuits pull the bottom section out of one of the portable toilets, where the waste reservoir is located, mount it on a wheeled cart, and push it up a ramp onto the back of a wagon drawn by a horse.

More than anything, the people here want and need electricity, Todd realizes. That and plumbing. In the shanties where he lives, he saw people everywhere using car batteries, sometimes wrapped together in banks, to power DC devices and AC devices using adapters. One enterprising mechanic has two cars wired together with jumpers and juices up failing batteries as a service. As for water, the only option is to wait hours in line at a government water tank.

Todd walks among the booths, taking notes of merchants and what they buy and sell. Water purifiers, baby supplies, vitamins, tampons, propane, clothespins and lines, toilet paper, garden seeds, weapons and ammo. Sugar, porn mags, chocolate, duct tape, bug spray, soy sauce, bikes, scissors, coffee and tea, candles, jeans, matches, shaving kits, candy, cigarettes, chewing tobacco, manual can openers, laundry detergent. Little bits of comfort and convenience and civilization. Pieces of an America that has fallen down, most of them garbage. Products from other countries that no longer exist. Consumable relics of a past age.

Todd has a lot of DC-powered appliances from the truck stop store that could make life much easier for at least a few people here. They are heavy, though, and liable to break. He wants to dump them in exchange for a different product. The most successful merchants, he notices, specialize in a particular item that everybody needs. The item should be small and lightweight to be easily portable. Something like cigarettes would be ideal but then he would need to be constantly on guard against addicts. Sugar and coffee would be ideal but the sellers are dealing them in plastic baggies, creating a risk of spoilage due to water or infestation. Garden seeds should be a popular item right now but he does not understand gardening.

Something like candles, on the other hand, would be perfect.

"So what are you supposed to be?"

He turns and blinks in surprise as he realizes the girl is talking to him. Time slows as their eyes connect. His heart takes a sudden flying leap. She is a petite fiery thing, her skin white as a sheet, with long, curly red hair that rages about her head like a lion's mane. She looks about fifteen or sixteen, which is his own age. She has a sly mouth and a button nose and laughs easily, her blue eyes sparkling, betraying an appealing brand of feminine insanity.

"I'm Todd," he says instantly.

"I'm Erin," she says. "I asked you what you're doing."

"I'm going to be a merchant," he tells her. "I have some stuff I'd like to sell."

"Really? You should definitely hire me, then."

Todd laughs. "And why should I do that?"

"You're new. I can show you how things work around here so you don't get conned."

He stops laughing. "How do you know I'm new here?"

Erin flashes him a glance that tells him she thinks it is obvious. "Do you know about the gangs? They will try to collect a tax from you."

"How much should I give them?"

"Nothing, you dodo bird," she says. "It's just a con. If the sellers paid every gang, there would be no market. They can't really do anything to you. The sellers look out for each other, and everybody here is armed to the teeth. Now aren't you glad I told you that?"

"Yeah," he admits.

"You need somebody," she points out. "Every day you have to collect water and firewood and cook your food. Once a week you pick up your rations and they let you take a shower. That doesn't leave much time to be a seller. All these sellers have somebody helping them out."

He has to agree she makes a good argument.

"You could do all that for me?" he asks her.

She shrugs. "I'm doing it anyway for me. Might as well try to get paid."

"And what do you want in return?"

Erin smiles as she leans in close, making his heart pound.

"I want in on the action," she whispers close to his ear.

◆

The school gym is hot and crowded and noisy. The tired volunteers and professional bureaucrats manning the tables feverishly write and type information that nobody will read and hand out poorly mimeographed information that few will actually use. The main thing people seem to come here for is decisions, but they appear to be in short supply. After days of working the system to try to find his family, Ethan is beginning to see the processing center as a flea market for dying government. One big going-out-of-business sale. Waiting for his number to be called again by the records people, he wanders among the tables, finally pausing in front of a clean-cut young man under a U.S. flag and a sign that says ASK ME ABOUT RESETTLEMENT.

"Would you like to hear about Resettlement?" the man suddenly asks him.

Ethan shrinks back, shaking his head.

"It's all part of the President's policy for a Fresh Start," the man says. He is clean shaven and wears a business suit with a neatly ironed white shirt and blue tie. "When the pandemic is over, we're going to have to put Humpty Dumpty back together again. This means people who still have assets out there, somewhere, will recover them. Those who have lost everything will be given the means to start a new life. This is Resettlement in a nutshell."

"You're going to do what, then? Tell me where to live?"

"Only if you sign up," the man says with a smile. "If you enroll in the Resettlement Program, we will match you with a good community and give you a job as close to your old profession as possible, respecting of course your preferences, special needs such as any health problems, and surviving social networks. But of course the final decision is yours."

Ethan laughs. "And the incentive is you're going to give everybody a house and a car?"

"Whatever you need to start a new life."

"How can the country afford this?"

"The nation is filled with dispossessed property, sir, previously owned by individuals and corporations. Property owned by individuals who die intestate will be passed on to the nearest surviving heirs in accordance with state and local laws. But in cases where there are no identifiable heirs, the property will escheat to the Federal government for redistribution."

"My God," Ethan says.

The man behind the table is talking about a massive seizure of property on an unprecedented scale, to be distributed to the survivors.

"Not God," the man says. "The Wade Act."

This Wade Act will conflict with numerous state and local laws. With the amount of power and assets on the table, it might even be enough to trigger a civil war.

Ethan does not care about any of this, however.

"I'm here trying to find my missing family," he tells the man.

"Resettlement is about looking to the future, but there will be a full accounting. Every person, every dollar, every asset. If your family is alive, you will find them and you will be able to live together again under Resettlement."

"Good," Ethan says.

"Just fill out these forms," the man says brightly, holding out a clipboard.

"Let me ask you a question first."

"Of course."

"You mentioned a full accounting. How full will that accounting be?"

"The fullest."

"I'm speaking of the dead. We all have blood on our hands."

"Don't ask, don't tell, sir," the man smiles, still holding out the clipboard.

Ethan stares at it longingly.

"Perhaps later," he says.

The man frowns, dropping the clipboard back on the table.

Ethan adds, "Sorry."

"You know, we will survive this," the man tells him. "It's okay to hope."

Ethan says, "Not yet it isn't."

♦

Mobs of people, angry, shell-shocked, dressed in filthy clothes, wander among the densely packed tents and shanties built on grass long trampled into dust.

Ray says this place is going to blow.

"It's fucked up, but it works— barely," he says. "And for now. You know the old saying about America being three days away from a revolution? Here, it's a matter of hours."

Wendy nods. "What are the biggest community problems?"

Ray laughs. "Everything. Wendy, we got people packed in here like sardines. The place is an open sewer that serves gruel for breakfast, lunch and dinner. We have to truck in clean water for half the camp. Outside resupply is obviously touch and go. Then there's the constant threat of fire, disease and of course Infection. Everybody's carrying a gun. We got gangs, prostitution, drugs, con games, rapes, murders, suicides, you name it. All right?"

Just two weeks ago, this place did not exist. There was a sleepy small town here in the middle of eastern Ohio. Outlying farms. Open fields and woods. All of it now absorbed into a camp with the same population as Independence, Missouri and the poverty of Calcutta.

"I get the picture," she says.

"Don't worry about them. Worry about you. The main thing you got to realize is there are a lot of unhappy people in this place who had everything and now they have nothing. They are mad as hell and looking for somebody to blame. Every once in a while some asshole gets an itch to take a shot at a cop. So you keep a sharp eye out there."

"I will, Sergeant."

"My name is Ray. Use it. Dammit, Wendy, you should be calling the shots, not me."

"I'm just fine with the way things are, Ray," she says. "So when does my training start?"

The man snorts. "This is your training. You got a question?"

"Okay. How are arrests processed for trial? Where is the courthouse?"

"Stop right there," Ray says, taking off his grimy STEELERS cap and wiping sweat from his forehead. "I guess I need to explain a few things. Wendy, I know you were a cop back in the real world but this is the far side of the Moon. We just don't have what you want here. It's frontier justice. We're holding this ground by force."

They approach long lines of people waiting for their turn to fill their jugs at a bright yellow water tanker guarded by a squad of kid soldiers with M16 rifles. A cloud of dust hangs over the scene. Ray changes the subject, pointing out landmarks on what will become her night beat—shower facilities, health tent, food distribution center, and a feeding center where new mothers can breastfeed and collect extra rations. The latrine area, a large battery of portable toilets, is especially dangerous at night. Women who come here after dark are often raped. Men, too, sometimes. As a result, many people drop their waste into the nearest canal, and sometimes fall in.

"So what am I supposed to do if I see a crime?" she interrupts. "Just rough them up?"

"If you want," Ray says, placing a pinch of chew into his cheek. "Or you could take them to the Judge, who will probably give them hard labor such as shit disposal. They get an electronic bracelet that tags them. It's pretty much the same punishment for any offense, so only bring in the hard cases you really want punished. The worst offenders get put outside the wall."

"What about proof? Is it just my word?"

"Yup," Ray says. "That's how it is here. You got to understand, though, that our main role is not to solve and punish crimes. The locals mostly do that for us. The people here all watch out for each other. They usually know if somebody commits a crime, and sort it out themselves without our involvement. We're not really in the justice business. Our job is to keep the peace."

"We're not cops," Wendy says, disgusted. "We're armed thugs."

"Yup. You want out?"

She does not even have to think about it.

"No," she says.

"Our unit's shift starts around sundown. Then we get to patrol a Third World shantytown in the dark for twelve hours. Memorize your beat, don't get lost, don't fall in the canals, don't get killed. Especially don't get killed. We need people like you, Wendy."

"I'm nothing special, believe me. Especially for this work."

Ray stops and spits a gob of tobacco juice into the dust. "You don't understand. We need people like you to *survive*. Listen: One day this thing is going to end and things are going to get back to normal. To do that, we're going to need people who can remember what normal was and can make things right again. There are not many cops walking the earth right now. Every time one dies, all those memories of how things used to be dies with them."

"I'll live, Ray. I survived out there for weeks. I'll make it in here. This is nothing."

"Just know the original cops in this town were good men and they died trying to hold this place when it was first being built. Not all of them died by the hands of the Infected."

Wendy smiles at him, touched by his concern.

"I promise I'll be careful," she tells him.

"You do that, Wendy," Ray says, eyeing her sadly. "You do that."

Speakers mounted on poles in the area squawk, *we are winning; ask what you can do to help*, before screeching loudly and resuming a tinny rendition of Madonna's "Like a Virgin."

◆

Paul leaves the FoodFair supermarket, dog tired and enjoying the night air after hours of handing out food packages, shifting boxes and mopping floors. The food distribution center has no air conditioning and keeping the camp supplied is hot, sweaty work. His tattered clerical uniform, recently cleaned and patched, is already getting ripe again. He could use a shave and a haircut. But he did good today. He digs into his pocket for his wilted pack of Winstons and lights one up, sighing. The cool air feels good and he is happy for the opportunity to finally rest. After his smoke, he will brush his teeth and hit the sack with the other workers, lying on his old bedroll with bags of rice as a mattress.

The camp is still noisy but is slowly settling down for the night. The parking lot of the FoodFair is covered in tents and campers and people huddled around their cook fires. He takes another drag and exhales, enjoying the relative peace. He remembers that the last time he had a cigarette like this, Pittsburgh was on fire. The Infected streamed through the cars. He threw a Molotov. He cut somebody in half with his Remington. The Bradley roars in his head.

He stills his mind with a short prayer of thanks that he remains alive to do this good and useful work. Maybe God does not want to listen, but being omnipresent, he cannot help but hear it.

"Is that you, Paul?"

Paul sees a figure sitting on a bench and approaches. It is Pastor Strickland, sitting with one hand cupped around the flame of a candle and the other holding an old photo.

"Do you think it's impossible to still love somebody who is Infected, brother?" Strickland asks him.

"No," Paul says. "I think it's not only possible, but unavoidable."

The man smiles, wiping his eyes.

"But they hate us in return," Paul tells him. "That is the hardest thing to bear."

Strickland rubs tears from his eyes with the palm of his hand. "The love is just as hard." He adds, "You did good work today, Paul."

"Thank you."

"This means something to you, doesn't it? The work, I mean."

"It's the only way I know how to be me," Paul answers, surprising himself with the sudden insight. He wants to think about it more, but his tired mind cannot hold onto the threads.

"There will be a march within the next few days," Strickland says. "A march of Christians trying to make things right around here. There's more that can be done working together than by one man alone. You might want to give a listen to what they have to say. I'll be there, too."

Paul slaps the back of his neck to kill a mosquito. "I'll do that."

They pass the next few moments in silence. Paul finishes his smoke and grinds it out on the asphalt with his boot. Strickland blows out his candle. A dog howls in the distance.

"Can I tell you something, brother?" the pastor says quietly in the dark. "Can I speak to you as a man of the cloth? Will you hear a short confession?"

"Of course."

"I always wondered if you could be a Christian and cry at a funeral. I mean, if somebody is going to heaven, shouldn't we be celebrating? It's the same here. The world is dying. Why are we so sad? Why do we cling to this miserable life? Maybe this is it, Paul. Maybe the Lord is calling us all home. If so, why do we resist the call? Why are we fighting God's will? And why does it feel so horrible? Why does it taste like ashes? Why does it fill us with sadness?"

Paul has no answer, but he understands the essential question. He has asked himself the same question repeatedly in the past.

"I don't know," he says.

Sara would have an interesting answer, he is sure. His mind flashes to the battle between the Infected and the mob and what happened after the Infected overran the last knot of fighters: sketchy images of himself walking down the road, returning home to his wife. But he cannot remember what happened after that.

He is beginning to worry that he may have killed her.

♦

Ethan runs between the shanties, his finger itching and throbbing. He hears his pursuers shouting to each other. He believes he has lost them.

It happened suddenly.

The woman was telling him that the Marines had landed in New Jersey when her friends noticed what he was wearing.

He still wore scrubs from the hospital—the pants, anyway.

They thought he was a doctor.

Ethan spent the last few days at the processing center trying to locate his family, sleeping on the floor and living on handouts. The arrangement was not so bad. The school still has electricity and plumbing, the government's way of demonstrating its strength. In some ways, he has been living in luxury compared to many people in the camp.

They sat on folding chairs, fanning themselves with their cardboard numbers. The woman told him she heard the Marines had landed in New Jersey.

He had already heard the rumor several times while waiting in the processing center. The Marines established bases along the coasts and the Army was striking inland, reinforcing the refugee camps and using them as forward operations bases in the campaign to retake the country.

It sounded a bit wishful, to say the least.

If it's true, then where are they, why aren't they here? Ethan asked, and didn't bother listening to the answer. Rumors about the Army held no interest for him. All that mattered was the search.

While the woman continued talking, he began to notice how attractive she was. He realized that he could always move on. He could find somebody else and start a new family.

He did not want to do that. What was it Paul said to him when they talked about the people who left behind photos of their loved ones? *I wouldn't even know how*, he said when asked if he could ever let go of those he left behind. Right.

Thinking about Paul triggered memories of hours sitting in the dim, hot belly of the Bradley fighting vehicle, rolling through a dying city on screaming treads.

The memory made him feel oddly homesick.

Ethan was wondering how the other survivors were coping when the woman's friends approached. They noticed he was wearing scrubs and asked if he was a doctor. They had a sick friend and they were there to try to get him placed on the list for surgery—a service provided only to the most needy cases in this time of scarcity, as so many medical professionals were either killed or infected in the first days of Infection. The hospital sent them here, only to be told by the government to return to the hospital.

They reminded him that it was against the law for doctors to avoid work. Their eyes were gleaming, desperate.

When he told them he was not a doctor, one asked him if he had been a hospital patient. How could he have survived when the first wave of Infected rose from their beds? Maybe he had the disease but did not know it. Was he a carrier? Was he infecting all of them even now?

Ethan does not remember how things became violent. His memories blur at that point. He may have lashed out at them first; his mind simply blanked out. He became aware of shacks flying by, grim faces staring at him from doorways and over the flames of cooking fires. Lawn ornaments, hanging laundry, buckets and plastic jugs. He knocked something over. Curses filled the air.

He remembers when he used to be a pacifist. At school, kids would occasionally fight, and he would have to get between them and break it up. He hated doing it. Sometimes he would have night terrors over getting punched by a kid. In these visions, he would lose control, lash out and lose everything.

A truck rumbles alongside, filled with men laughing down at him. One of the men, a brown giant in T-shirt and jeans, stands and shouts, "Hey you! You want a job for the day?"

Better to ride than to run, he tells himself. He nods, gasping for breath, remembering that horrible day in the department store, as he ran blindly among the mannequins.

Large, calloused hands reach down and pull him up into the truck. "¿Qué onda?" they ask him.

He sits on the trembling bed of the truck as it lurches over the potholes. One of the men hands him a bottle of water. He takes a drink, wincing at the metallic taste, and hands it back.

"You got a trade?" the giant says to him.

"I was a teacher," he says. "Now I just kill people."

The men laugh, ringing him with their bearded faces. They spit over the side. He can smell onions on their breath. Some of them speak English while others chatter in Caló, an argot of Mexican Spanish common in the Southwestern states. Somebody passes around a flask and he smells distilled alcohol, probably made from the wheat and rice distributed in the weekly ration.

Booze is not the only thing you can make by distilling alcohol from mashed grains. Distilled alcohol makes a good anesthetic, antiseptic and preservative, he knows.

The truck stops in a cloud of dust in front of a large barn and the men jump out. The building is being used as a slaughterhouse. Cattle pace around a holding pen, agitated by the smell of blood. Draped in plastic garbage bags, butchers work on animals hung upside down by their hind legs, draining the bodies, removing the head, feet, hide and internal organs. The ground is soaked with blood.

The giant tells Ethan the beef is cut, wrapped and sent out immediately to the food distribution centers. The men here are paid in meat. A lot of it ends up in the market, bought and consumed fast before bacteria take hold. Most refugees put it into an eternal stew they keep continuously bubbling over fire, along with anything they can find such as wild onions and beans. The bones are fed to the camp dogs—pets brought by the refugees who now can no longer afford to feed them—whose presence is tolerated by the authorities because of their hatred of the Infected, making them good sentinels. The fat is used to manufacture soap and candles and biodiesel.

Other slaughterhouses in the camp process chickens, sheep, pigs. This one, the giant says, handles only cattle—steers and heifers mostly. The men here know cattle, how to stun them with a hammer, how to cut their throats and drain their blood with a knife, how to strip the carcass.

"So what do we do?" Ethan says.

"We move the cattle that comes into the camp into the pens."

"From where?"

"The truck pulls up over there."

"And we move the cattle about fifty feet into the pens? That's it?"

The giant grins down at him. "That's it. We were told some trucks are coming in today. Here comes one now."

The massive tractor trailer trembles, coughing, as it pulls up near the holding pens. The cattle, crammed together inside, bellow sadly.

"*Águila*, boys," the giant says. He winks at Ethan. "Sharp eyes. Like an eagle."

The men take their weapons and form a semicircle around the rear of the truck. Two men clamber up and tie a nylon net in front of the trailer's doors. The driver, sweating in a camouflage JOHN DEERE cap and hunting vest bulging with shotgun shells, gets out and leans against the cab, watching them and biting into a tomato.

"What do you want me to do?" Ethan says.

"*Caile.* I want you to stand right here, *bolillo.*"

The giant moves to the doors, removes the bolts, and flings them wide. He quickly steps out back and to the side. A wave of heat pours out of the trailer. Ethan winces at the rich smell of dung. The cattle push against each other, jostling and raising their heads, lowing. Their eyes gleam at him from the dark.

Ethan wonders why nobody is doing anything. Two of the men continue to hold the net taut, sweat pouring down their faces. He suddenly realizes that the others have moved away from him, stepping back from the trailer.

"*A ponemos chancla,*" one of the men whispers behind him.

The creature lunges hissing out of the dark, claws outstretched. Ethan cries out in fear and revulsion as it smashes into the net and plunges to the ground at his feet, shrieking and straining and reaching for him. A massive stinger protrudes from between its legs, stabbing repeatedly at the dust. The men surround the thing, hooting over their shotguns and holding the net, while two others rush in with spears. They shout obscenities in multiple languages as they thrust their weapons into the monster, which begins thrashing, keening, almost pitiful.

Finally, the thing lies still, dead. The men continue to stab it with their spears until it becomes a bleeding, featureless pile of road kill.

"*Mono,*" one of Chicanos says to Ethan, drawing his finger across his throat. "Hoppers."

Ethan shakes his head, trying to clear it of the blind terror he felt when the thing sprang out of the dark. And rage at being used as bait.

"Now you are one of us," the giant says, grinning. "*Machín.*"

"See this?" Ethan says, holding up his finger. "I was already one of you."

The giant nods, transfixed by the jagged stump, his face paling.

Ethan stares at the thing lying dead on the ground. The men are spitting on it.

"So what happens next?"

"Now we check the cattle for Infection, *vato.*"

The cattle are led into a special quarantine pen. Two of them are Infected. They are easy to spot: thin, silent, listless, staggering a little when forced to walk. A heifer has one of the monkey things growing out of its side while a steer has two, both on its right flank.

"Hoppers," the giant says.

The Infected cattle are separated, killed and dragged to a large, smoking pit behind the barn. The heat there is incredible, rising from the scarred ground in blistering waves. Charred legs stick out of the blackened piles of meat, slowing crumbling into ash blowing away in the wind.

There, the dead cattle are burned with all of the others.

◆

Todd lights a candle in his small, sweltering one-room shack and stares at its intense glow. This candle, he thinks, is possibly the only beautiful thing in this entire horrible place.

Candles would be an ideal specialty as a merchant, he thinks. Everybody needs candles. They are simple, small and necessary. The only thing to watch out for is breakage. That and a match shortage. He might have to sell matches, too.

But he is not going to buy and sell candles.

He has an idea he believes will make him rich. He remembers Philip telling him that a good businessman will buy low and sell high. But how do you do this with a barter system?

The answer may be that you acquire lots of something that is almost worthless now and sell it later on when it is almost priceless.

Winter clothing, for example.

A few people sell winter gear in the market, mostly for scrap value and as substitute pillows and stuffers for bedrolls. Coats, hats, scarves, gloves, sweaters.

Almost nobody here believes Infection will last until winter. They have been here for less than two weeks and many of them have no idea what things are like outside. They believe the rumors that the Army is coming to save them. They believe the government propaganda that things are getting better. Things are not getting better. They are getting much, much worse.

Todd knows the people here will be in for a rough winter. If he can build up a big supply of winter clothes, he can trade them for pretty much anything he wants.

"Knock, knock," a voice says from the doorway.

"Hey, Erin," he grins. "Come on in. Welcome to my humble abode."

The girl walks into his shack and looks around.

"Humble is right," she says. "*Yeesh.*" She holds up a plastic baggie. "I scored some weed. It's not very good, but it gets the job done. You want to get high?"

"Okay, I guess," Todd says warily, looking at the bag.

Erin sits on the ratty carpet covering the dirt floor and starts rolling a joint.

"I am in dire need of some entertainment," she says. "My need is *dire*. You know, before everything went to shit, I was going places. I was one ugly duckling as a kid. And then I got older and I wasn't. Just like that: Suddenly I was popular. I had like eight hundred friends on Facebook. Then the bug comes along and I'm cut off from the world. Sometimes I feel like I don't even exist anymore."

Todd watches her come up for air but she says nothing more, lighting her joint and toking on it carefully until getting enough smoke in her lungs. She hands him the joint and he kisses it, taking little puffs and wondering about the strange, strong smell of it.

"I'm so fucking bored," Erin says, blowing a long stream of smoke.

"I used to do a lot of wargaming with these college guys," Todd offers tentatively. "I'm wondering if there are any wargaming clubs around here. You know, *Warhammer 40,000* . . ."

Erin is staring at him curiously. His voice trails off and time appears to slow. He coughs loudly on the smoke.

She suddenly smiles, beckoning the joint to return.

"I don't know anything about that stuff," she says. "Can we light another candle?"

"Sure," he says, relieved.

"Cheer this place right up. How about beer? You got any alcohol?"

"No, but I have some candy if you're interested."

"Oh *God*, yes."

Chewing on Gummi Bears with an expression approaching bliss, she asks him what things are like on the outside. He tells her about escaping his house during the first day of Infection, surviving on his own, finding the other survivors. Riding in the belly of the Bradley, spilling out to fight and scavenge. The stories are so fantastic that instead of embellishing them he tries to downplay their drama, afraid she will accuse him of making it all up.

Erin stares at him wide eyed. "I wish *I* had done all that," she says, her eyes gleaming in the candlelight.

"I'm not sure if you would. We came very close to dying—well, almost every day."

"Man, it's so *cool*."

"Um," he says.

"Is that how you got that wound on your arm?"

Todd remembers the worm monster lunging out of the dark, its sharklike jaws snapping.

"Yeah," he says gloomily, covering the bandage with his hand. "So how about you? What's your story?"

"I've been here almost since the beginning," she says, then stops.

"What happened?"

"I came to the camp with my dad and I got bored," she mutters, then suddenly brightens. "Let's play truth or dare."

"Okay," he says.

"I'll go first. Go ahead, Todd. Ask me."

"Um, truth or dare?"

"Truth," she announces, sitting primly.

"All right," Todd says. He is not sure if he is high or not from the joint but he wants to think that he is. "Okay, what's the most embarrassing thing that ever happened to you?"

"Oh my God, I've got a *great* answer to that one." Erin starts laughing and Todd smiles along. "One time, in study hall, me and my friends were updating the status on our Facebook pages, right? I had to run to the ladies' due to some women's trouble. That night, my Blackberry started ringing nonstop with these guys wanting to do some really gross things to me. Turns out I'd left myself logged in to Facebook and my jerk friends wrote as my status that I love to give blowjobs, with my phone number."

She is laughing loudly now while Todd continues to smile along politely, wondering why she finds something so cruel to be so funny.

"Oh, man," she adds. "That happens to everybody sooner or later, right? Okay, it's your turn. Truth or dare?"

"Truth," he says, hoping she will not ask him the same question.

"When was the first time you did it with a girl?"

Todd stammers briefly before inventing an elaborate story about his junior prom and how he scored with his date in the backseat of his friend's car. His voice trails off. She can tell he is lying.

"It's okay," she says.

"Um," he says.

His mind scrambles in search of something light and witty to say to recover the mood, but none is needed; Erin deftly rescues him.

"Want to see one of my cheers, Todd? A really good one?"

"Okay," he tells her, feeling overwhelmed.

Erin jumps onto her feet, shakes off a sudden wave of laughter, and then stands erect with her arms stiff and muscles tight.

"Sharp and snappy," she says. "One, two, three, here it is: Go Cougars!" She claps to the beat, keeping her hands under her chin. "Go Cougars! We are the Cougars, hey, we're number one; our cougar roar has just begun." She punches the air. "Roar!" She claps again. "Roar, roar! We are the Cougars, yeah, we'll say it loud; we're stepping up because we're proud. Roar! Roar, roar! We are the best, all right, we're here to win—"

Erin finishes a kick and flops onto the ground laughing. Todd claps his hands.

"Wow," he says, his heart pounding with sexual excitement.

Outside the shack, somebody yells at them to keep it down, making her laugh even harder.

"Let's pretend that was my dare," she says, panting. "Now it's your turn."

"Dare," he says.

"Kiss me."

Todd was hoping for this. Truth or dare, after all, is a kissing game. He moves towards her on his hands and knees, feeling lightheaded and breathless, unsure of where to begin. He has never kissed a girl before. She meets him halfway. It is like falling into a warm pool, smooth and jolting. He kisses her for several moments, holding her shoulders. He probes her tongue with his, wondering if he is doing this right. His right knee, pressed against a pebble on the ground, is beginning to hurt, but he ignores it, afraid to move. His erection strains against his jeans, sending waves of pain and pleasure through his body. Finally, she pushes him away.

He falls out of the kiss, amazed.

"And," she adds, "take off your shirt. I forgot to mention it's a two-part dare."

Still dizzy, he obeys automatically, then fidgets as she appraises him.

"No tattoos," she observes. "Wow. My boyfriend has tats everywhere."

Todd frowns, alarmed and jealous. He half expects a bunch of jocks to enter the shack pointing at him and laughing and congratulating her on setting him up for a fall.

"You have a boyfriend?" he says, trying to control his tone.

"He's one of *them*. Outside."

Well, then he's not really your boyfriend anymore, he wants to say, but holds his tongue.

She smiles coyly at him and says, "Maybe I need a new boyfriend."

He smiles back, thawing quickly.

"Dare," she says.

"You too," he says bravely.

Erin crosses her arms, hesitating with a teasing glance, then pulls her shirt over her head in one swift motion. Todd expects her to be wearing a bra but there is none. Her pert breasts are shining and perfect. Her smooth body burns in the candlelight. He stares at her in awe.

"Dare," he whispers.

"Come here," she says. "Kiss me again."

◆

As Wendy approaches the latrines, she turns her flashlight on and continues warily. Next to her, Jonesy does the same. She prefers to patrol by moonlight, letting their eyes adjust to the dark and becoming hunters instead of mere night watchmen, but the latrine area is dangerous at night even for cops, and a nearby canal is poorly marked by solar-powered landscape lights. A flare arcs into the sky over the horizon and she hears the snarl of distant small arms fire. The pickets have been busy tonight outside the camp. Then the shooting stops as suddenly as it began. Wendy radios in their position to Tyler, the gray-haired book reader back at the station.

*Roger that. You guys be careful, now. Keep a sharp eye.*

She smiles at the men's protectiveness as she keys the walkie-talkie and says, "You, too."

*I most certainly will, young Wendy.*

Another flare arcs over the distant shanties.

"Sounds like a real battle out there tonight," Jonesy says, chewing loudly.

"Give me some of your gum."

"What do I get?"

"Jonesy, my boyfriend could break you in half. And if he couldn't, *I* could."

"Okay, okay," he laughs. "Can't blame a guy for trying."

She pops the piece into her mouth and begins gnawing on it with a vengeance.

Her third night on foot patrol with Unit 12, and she is already bored.

Last night, a little excitement: An explosion on the far side of camp, a flash in the sky followed by a boom and slight shock that she could feel in her feet. Outside her patrol territory, unfortunately. Turns out it was a homegrown crystal meth lab that blew sky high. She finds herself almost wishing something like that would happen here.

Flares burn as they fall across the distant sky. A machine gun begins rattling.

They walk along the edge of the canal, looking for planks that will allow them to cross. Their flashlight beams flicker along the rough ground. Somebody is playing a harmonica in the nearby shanties. A couple moans loudly, having loud sex in one of the shacks.

Jonesy chuckles.

"Guess you're not the only ladies' man around here," Wendy says.

He laughs.

"Here's the bridge," he says. "Watch your step."

They tramp over the planks and find themselves among the batteries of portable toilets.

"Police," Wendy says loudly.

"Police coming through," Jonesy says.

Three days, and still no word from Sarge. Wendy is now worried.

"So Jonesy, how did you end up becoming a cop?" she asks to distract herself.

"Well, Ray started the unit and Tyler and Ray are on the same bowling team and Tyler's my dad," Jonesy answers. "When Infection started I was finishing high school. I was going to college, too. I was going to learn how to be a veterinarian."

Wendy smiles. Tyler was not being protective of her, but of his son.

"Being a vet is a good job," she says.

"Oh, yeah, it's a really good—"

A man suddenly appears in their path, shielding his eyes from the glare of their flashlights.

"Can you all get that light out of my eyes, please?"

They lower their flashlights a little. Wendy places her other hand on the handle of her baton.

"Stay where you are, sir," she says.

"You're cops, right? I thought I heard you say you were police."

"Do you need assistance?"

"My wife is missing. She came out here to use the bathroom an hour ago."

"All right, sir," she says. "Can you describe—"

Her instincts scream, *Fight.*

She wheels, drawing her side-handled baton as Jonesy falls moaning to the ground, a man standing behind him holding a length of pipe. Another pipe glances off the side of her head with a meaty thud and her eyes go black and flood with stars.

She reels, struggling to stay on her feet as the shapes close in.

The training takes over and she moves.

She flails with the baton, smashing one of the men in the face, then backhands the other man in the ear. The first stumbles backward and she pursues, beating him furiously to the ground while the second thrashes in the nearby canal, coughing and spitting.

Another blow to the head.

She falls into a deep blackness.

*Sarge. Sarge, help me*

Wendy regains consciousness, first becoming aware of a heavy weight on her body and a stabbing pain in her genitals. She opens her eyes, looking up into the darkness, and sees the Infected leering back down at her, its face gray and wet with blood, its eyes red with virus.

Wendy screams.

She no longer sees an Infected on top of her, just a man telling her to shut up or he will kill her. She smells his rancid breath, hot on her face. He strikes her savagely once, twice.

She blinks and sees an Infected, and screams again.

His hand clamps over her mouth. She works her teeth around it and bites down as hard as she can. He hits her again, but with little force; she clamps down harder, growling like a dog. Within seconds, the man is screaming and begging for mercy. She feels blood spray down the back of her throat and releases the mangled hand, coughing wetly.

She screams again. And again. But the man is gone.

♦

The crowd of thousands pours down the road past the food distribution center, singing hymns and waving poorly made signs announcing GOD IS STILL WITH US and LUKE 21:11. Paul grinds out his cigarette and joins their ranks. His mind flashes to the suburban mob marching down the road back in Pittsburgh, thronged together with their weapons and shouting their slogans to make themselves feel stronger. Air Force jets roared overhead in a sky filled with black smoke, dropping bombs on distant targets. He remembers how he spoke to them: He blessed them just before the Infected attacked. He told them their war was just.

They march by the camp's feeding center and the pest house and a swing set displaying flags for various government agencies and services housed inside a small red brick building that used to be the town post office. The refugees pause in their daily routines, watching the marchers stream by singing, "Onward, Christian Soldiers." Some of them excitedly join the march while others laugh or shout at them to go make noise and stir up the dust somewhere else. Soldiers squint at the marchers, fingering their weapons and glancing at their sergeants.

God is not very popular these days, Paul realizes. These people here are the hardcore Christians. The true believers. Their faith astonishes him. It makes him feel a bit ashamed. And yet he cannot help but see them as a woman who defends the alcoholic husband who beats her regularly, making excuses for what is essentially psychotic behavior.

"Did you hear?" a man says behind him. "The Marines are in New Jersey."

"Who needs 'em?" another man snorts.

"I heard the Feds are going to try to take our guns away from us after the Army shows up," a woman says. "We'll be defenseless."

"That's just a rumor. Just like the Marines landing anywhere is a rumor."

"I heard it was Philadelphia, not New Jersey," somebody cuts in.

"But what if it's true? Don't they understand the Second Amendment saved this country? If it weren't for the Second Amendment, we'd all be Infected by now. God bless the NRA."

Paul hears babies crying, startled at the sound, flashing back to the giant fanged worm slithering out of the gloom, mewing for food. He marvels that even now, children are being born in the camp. No matter what, it seems, life goes on. Perhaps the human race abides, too.

Near the front of the crowd, a man is shouting into a megaphone. The march is slowing, becoming more congested around several figures standing on the roof of a van in front of the old high school, the nominal seat of government in the camp. Paul continues to push forward, recognizing Pastor Strickland and several other clergy standing behind an overweight man wearing a crew cut, white collared shirt with the sleeves rolled up and massive sweat stains at the armpits, and a bright yellow tie. Paul has never seen him before but recognizes his voice. The man is a popular talk show host on the AM dial in the Pittsburgh area. McLean. Thomas McLean.

"We thought we were invincible," McLean is saying. "We were consumed by money and pleasure and sex. Infection is happening because God is punishing us."

The mob roars its approval, drowning him out.

"They want you to believe we can live without God," Paul hears him say after the crowd settles down. "Without our faith. They want us to ignore God. But God ain't ignoring us, folks. No, sir. God is talking to us loud and clear. And do you know what he's saying?"

Paul holds his breath, straining to hear, wondering who "they" are.

"He's saying we have insulted him, and he's not going to take it!"

The crowd roars. Pastor Strickland and the other clergymen behind McLean nod and applaud, smiling grimly.

"We have insulted him by celebrating the spirit of the Antichrist and we are reaping the whirlwind. Insulted him by allowing feminism to destroy the American family, murder children and promote lesbianism. By allowing homosexuals to destroy marriage and corrupt our children. By corrupting this great nation with our greed, pop culture, liberal universities, public education, separation of church and state, and persecution of Christians."

"No," Paul says. "Not this. Not now."

The crowd is growing increasingly angry. He can feel the energy surge through them like a wind. They wave their signs, crying out to McLean to tell them what to do.

"We must repent for the end is nigh," McLean says. "I think we can all agree that it's pretty nigh. But how does one repent? Do you even know what that word means? It means to make yourself *righteous*. Pure. We must purify ourselves as a nation and forge a new covenant with God."

Hundreds of hands are in the air, waving gently like wheat in a breeze.

"To the atheists, I say, banish them from the camp!"

"Cast them out," the people chant.

"Banish the homosexuals!"

"Cast them out."

"Banish the elitists who look down at you!"

"This is not right," Paul says to the faces around him as McLean continues to run down his list. "God does not want this. God does not want us to hate each other."

"He wants us to hate sin," a woman snaps at him.

"It ain't a rally until the devil shows up," a man observes. "Here he is in the flesh."

"This is deranged," Paul pleads. "Infection has deranged us. Can't you see that?"

"All I see is a nigger with a death wish," the man says with a grin.

"Keep that racist crap to yourself," another man warns.

"God is punishing us for our wickedness," the woman says. "Why is it deranged to think that?"

McLean is pointing at the processing center and shouting.

"Those people in there, they tell us how to live, but nobody voted for them! Now they want to silence me for speaking out! They see me as a threat! They can kill me, but they do not understand that the fire has been lit, that the fire is you, and it is spreading, and we will burn the corruption from the body of this great nation, and an even greater nation, a true Christian nation, will rise from the ashes!"

The crowd surges towards him hungrily. The soldiers guarding the processing center push the people back from the front doors with their rifles, angry and sweating.

"Tell them to pass the Sodomy Law. Tell them loud. Tell them now. Tell them—"

A metallic shriek drowns him out. The crowd pushes, compresses, eventually loosens as people scatter at its edges. Down the road, a Bradley armored fighting vehicle approaches at forty miles an hour, raising a massive cloud of dust. A wreath of wildflowers trembles on its metal chest like a necklace. An American flag waves from one of its antennae. McLean points at the vehicle, shouting into the megaphone, but nobody can hear him, coughing and blinded by waves of dust in the air.

The vehicle flies through the crowd, sending people lunging out of the way into the dirt, and continues on its path.

Paul grins, watching it pass. It is his Bradley, he's sure of it, and it can only be Sarge and Steve driving. He ducks out of the mob into one of the narrow alleys between the rows of shacks, intent on following the vehicle. It would be nice to see a friend right now.

♦

The Bradley rolls past the sentries and into the military compound. Squads of soldiers, sweating in their helmets and uniforms, admire it as it passes. The Bradley slows as it turns onto Main Street, whose small retail stores and upper-story apartments now provide barracks, mess and headquarters facilities. The street is filled with soldiers wearing different uniforms, merchants and mercenaries, prostitutes and drug dealers, civilian officials in business suits and olive green five-ton trucks unloading troops and food and ammunition. A long line of soldiers waits patiently in front of a water tanker. Even here, the command structure is confused, with many different Army and National Guard units mixed together, large numbers of raw recruits, and with several different headquarters displaying their loyalty to the United States, State of Ohio and/or Commonwealth of Pennsylvania. One banner hanging from the barracks windows announces simply, PRAISE THE LORD AND PASS THE AMMUNITION.

The Bradley slows again and executes an abrupt turn into the service garage. The grease monkeys instantly surround it, hoping something is wrong, itching to work on its engine again. They love the machine. There are so few of them left operating on American soil.

The hydraulic ramp drops and Sarge emerges, holding Wendy in his arms.

Smoke drifts in the air, reeking of cordite. On the other side of the garage, a squad of recruits practices firing M16 rifles at paper targets set up in front of a wall of sandbags. The loud firing quickly tapers to respectful silence as they catch sight of the Bradley's commander carrying the beautiful sleeping woman into his quarters.

◆

Todd enters FEMAville's military compound, marveling at the barbed wire and chaos, asking around where he can find the man commanding the Bradley.

They laid in the shack on their backs staring up at the ceiling, sweaty and naked and panting. For the first time in his life, he felt truly accepted. She had seen him naked and he had come inside her and now they were bonded and he would love her until the day he died. His body continued to shudder with the aftershocks of the incredible explosion of pleasure. The shack was filled with her unique musky smell. She lit up the remainder of her joint and chattered about her iPod and Blackberry and Facebook and how she wanted to exist again. Todd nodded, barely listening, studying the curves of her body and feeling strangely envious of her effortless beauty. He was already sad that she would have to leave and he might never have her again. He was suddenly starving. Moments later, she asked him if he wanted to do it again, and immediately went down on him, making him come again in her mouth. After the third time, he passed out.

When he woke, Erin was gone, and so was his stash of electronics. His capital.

Suddenly, he had nothing.

She left him an enigmatic note that read simply, *Sorry. You are very cute.*

He thought about his options all morning. He could try to find her and get his stock back or he could forget about it. Confronting her would be problematic. To put it mildly. Todd is terrible at confrontation, plus he believes he might be in love with her. He can feel the agony of wanting to see her again slowly overtake the anger he feels at her robbing him blind.

Screw this, he told himself. I know a cop. I'll get her to help me. The cops will get my stuff back, and I'll forgive Erin and we'll be together again.

He knows he will never have her, that he was used. But he cannot stop himself from hoping.

By the time he reaches the military compound—where he believes he will find Sarge, who in turn will be able to tell him where Wendy is—he has replayed the events of the previous night dozens of time in his mind. He has imagined many conversations they are yet to have. The angry one where he asks her why she used and hurt him, forces her to take a hard look at herself, and makes her cry over her misdeeds. The calm one where he gazes upon her coldly and tells her he forgives her and pities her, and then wishes her a nice life. The happy, highly improbable one where she brings his stuff back and they fall into each other's arms.

The steady crackle of gunfire at the perimeter of the camp intensifies, reminding him that his personal problems are insignificant compared to the ever-present threat facing the people here.

The garage is filled with soldiers sitting on the hard cement floor writing letters, reading books and making coffee on Coleman stoves. Chickens cluck in a series of cages against the far wall, next to neatly stacked cordwood. Todd smells cordite and coffee and chickenshit. The soldiers are being oddly quiet, frequently glancing at the office in the corner where Sarge has made his home. He treads carefully among them, ignoring their hostile stares, still muttering to himself as he knocks on Sarge's door. No answer. He pounds angrily.

The door opens and Sarge steps into the entry wearing his camo pants and a T-shirt, glaring at him, his expression instantly softening with recognition.

"Hey, Kid," he says. "Good to see you."

Todd flushes at hearing his old nickname.

The soldier thrusts out his hand, and Todd shakes it.

"You too, Sarge."

"What brings you out this way?"

"I got some bad news. Can I talk to you for a minute?"

"Come on in, then. I have some bad news, too, Kid."

Todd stops in surprise at the sight of Paul and Ethan standing over a cot where Wendy sleeps fitfully, softly moaning.

♦

Wendy wakes up with a massive headache and an overwhelming sense of dread. The small room is filled with men staring at her. Sarge presses a cool, damp cloth against her forehead and looks at her with an odd mixture of love and fear. Paul, Ethan and Todd are here, and so is Ray and all of the cops of Unit 12 except for Jonesy and his dad, their faces lighting up at seeing her awake. Ethan looks like somebody punched his lights out, grinning with a black eye. Somebody is asking her how she is feeling and she struggles to concentrate on the voice. Her mind has been swimming in and out of consciousness and she wants to wake up. She is not even sure she is awake now. If this is a dream, it is a good one; she feels happy having Sarge close and strangely safe being with the other survivors. Odd that she should spend the two worst weeks of her life with this group of people and suddenly feel so bonded to them. They are her people. She remembers how, at the hospital, she began to think of them as a tribe.

She wonders if she is dying.

Sarge is asking her if she needs anything. Does she need water?

After she drinks, she asks them how she got here. Her voice sounds funny and she thinks there might be something wrong with her ear. The men glance at each other, avoiding her eyes. The truth is she remembers nothing. Whatever happened to her was so bad that they cannot bear to say it out loud. Ray sits on an ammo crate next to her bed and tells her that she and Jonesy were attacked. Jonesy has a concussion and is in bad shape. She got banged up pretty good but physically she is fine. Wendy takes this in and wonders why she cannot rise from the cot. She feels oddly feverish. She cannot shake the feeling that she is dying.

You should see the other guys, Ray says with a grin, nodding with respect. You really did a number on them. We caught two of them. We know who the third guy is and we'll have him in the bag soon. You don't worry about them, Wendy. We'll take care of it. They deserve to die for what they did and we're going to take care of it.

Ray places her badge on the pillow next to her head.

We found this at the scene, he tells her.

Her head is pounding. She feels confused. Her dreams were filled with nightmares, and now she is wondering if some of them were real.

Ray asks if she has a problem with them taking care of things the Defiance way.

Wendy surprises herself by saying clearly, "Do it."

She leans over the side of the bed and vomits onto the floor at Sarge's feet. Moments later, she is plummeting into a nauseating darkness lit briefly only by a few tiny sparks.

◆

The Unit 12 boys, smiling like wolves, leave the room in single file to deliver justice to the men who attacked their people. They nod to Ray, who is staying behind to look after Wendy, as they pass by with their black shirts and bullet-proof vests and guns.

Wendy tosses and turns on the bed for the next few hours while Sarge dabs at her face with a wet cloth. As evening approaches, soldiers bring in steaming bowls of beef stew and the survivors sit on the floor in a circle to eat by candlelight.

"Just like old times," Paul says, chewing. "Except for this good food."

"Must be nice to have a job that pays in raw beef," Ray says.

Ethan grins. "You don't know what I had to do to earn it," he points out.

"Something dangerous, from the looks of your face," Sarge says, squinting at him as if trying to figure out a puzzle.

"It's nothing," Ethan tells him happily. "Some people at the government center thought I was a doctor and attacked me. I ran, found a crew unloading cattle, and worked the day."

"Ah," Ray says in understanding. He knows about the cattle crews and how they use people as bait for the monsters that infect the animals.

"When I got back to the government center, the same people were waiting for me and gave me this," Ethan answers, pointing at his face and laughing.

Todd laughs with him and says, "Why are you so happy about it?"

"I'm happy because I think I may have found my family."

The other survivors glance at each other and offer weak smiles.

"That's good news, man," Ray says.

Sarge touches his shoulder and adds, "Yeah, it's good, Ethan."

Ethan glares at them. "I'm serious."

"And I'm taking you seriously," Ray answers carefully, bristling.

"I spent several days at the government center. The records people found one Carol Bell in the camp, but it wasn't my wife. I kept pushing until I finally convinced somebody to check some of the other camps. Turns out there is a C. Bell and two M. Bells at the FEMA camp near Harrisburg. Three days after Infection, a C. Bell and an M. Bell arrived on the same day."

He studies the faces of the other survivors for a reaction.

"It sounds hopeful, Ethan," Paul says, nodding. "I mean it."

"It sounds *awesome*," Todd tells him.

Ethan turns to Sarge and says, "I was wondering if you could take me there. There, or as far as you can."

◆

Sarge believes it is appropriate that the other survivors are here with him again, as he has never really left them. His mind has been plunging into the past, against his will, during every still moment, reliving the horrors of Infection, the Screaming, Afghanistan. The worst is when he suddenly finds himself standing in the dark alone in front of the hospital, shooting the Infected swarming across the parking lot while every atom in his body screams at him to run. He surfaces from these terrifying flashbacks drenched in cold sweat, his heart clenched in his chest, refilling his lungs with a sudden gasp. He is not stupid. He knows he is suffering heavily from post-traumatic stress. He also knows that getting back out into the field will cure it, at least temporarily.

"I might be able to take you to Steubenville," Sarge says.

"What's in Steubenville?"

"Bridges."

"The Infected of Pittsburgh," Ethan says, nodding.

"What are you guys talking about?" Todd says.

"That big fire that chased us out? It also chased out all the Infected," Ethan explains. "They're walking west, straight to the bridges. Straight to us. Right, Sarge?"

Sarge nods. "I'm leading a mission out there to blow the bridges. Specifically, the Veterans Memorial Bridge. Six lanes across the Ohio River."

"You can't help but hear them," Paul adds. "They've been attacking the camp ever since we got here. The gunfire has become almost constant, day and night. After a while, it gets to be background noise. If they get inside, we're done."

"We're the last refugees that made it to the camp from Pittsburgh," Sarge says.

"Can the Infected swim?" Ray says.

"Our intelligence says they can't," Sarge tells him. "If we blow the bridges, they'll be stopped cold at the river."

"What they'll do is go north and south."

"That's not our problem."

Ray shrugs. "You're right. It's not."

"The migration will be deflected and that's all that counts as far as we're concerned."

"I want in," Todd says. "Let me come, Sarge. Please."

"I might as well join in, too," Paul says, eyeing him hopefully. "I could be useful."

Sarge shakes his head in mild disbelief. The truth is he would be happy to bring them on the mission. The boys he commands are good but they do not know what the survivors know. Frankly, he is surprised that they would want to leave the safety of the camp to go back into the jaws of the beast. And after just a few days, no less. Was it not the point of their journey together, after all—to find this sanctuary, and try to live a normal life?

"It's going to be incredibly dangerous," he tells them.

He remembers driving through Steubenville, the town eerily quiet. No sign of life, not even a dog barking. The Infected are there, all right. And with many of the Infected of Pittsburgh migrating west, the place is going to be swarming.

"I'm coming, too," Wendy says from her cot.

"Wendy!" Todd says happily.

The men launch themselves to their feet as she stands painfully, visibly trembling, touching the back of her head and wincing. She shrugs off their hands and walks to where they were sitting, taking a place next to Sarge and accepting a drink of water in a plastic cup.

"Well, then I'm going, too," Ray says.

"The hell you are," Sarge growls. "You're not one of us."

"But she's one of *us*. If she goes, I'm going. It's that simple. I made a promise."

"Yeah?" Sarge glares at him. "To who?"

"To a lot of fucking dead people," Ray snaps back.

"Ray is coming with us," Wendy rasps.

Sarge scowls but says nothing.

"Are you all sure about this?" he says.

"Yes," the survivors murmur, looking down at their bowls.

"What about you, Wendy?"

"You were right," Wendy says. "It's not safe here for us."

"Can you do it?"

"You're not going without me."

"All right," he says.

The room falls silent as they consider their reasons for wanting to go.

"I hate it here," Todd says finally.

Ethan says, "I actually love it. But I have to get to Harrisburg."

"We'll get you as far as we can, Ethan," Sarge tells him.

"It will be good to get out of here for a few days," Paul says. "Maybe I'll go all the way to Harrisburg with you. This place is unclean. God doesn't live here."

"Where exactly does he live, Preacher?" Ray asks quietly.

"Where? Out there, friend. With *them*. They are his agents."

"Get your sleep tonight," Sarge tells them. "We're training tomorrow. The morning after that, we're going to drive out there and blow a hole in that bridge."

He adds, "I hope this is what you want."

# FLASHBACK: REVEREND PAUL MELVIN

He remembers seeing the half-eaten remains of the children defiling the altar of his church, blood running down its sides like the afterbirth of some grisly sacrifice to a pagan god. He remembers his shoes squishing on the wet carpet, stepping over the bodies of his congregation surrounded by clouds of buzzing flies. He remembers the mob marching out of the haze singing and waving their Bibles and banners and weapons. He remembers how they hung the Infected on a traffic light at the intersection of Merrimac and Steel, how they demanded that he bless them, how he told them their war was just. He remembers the screams, the popping guns, the newly Infected lying twitching on the ground, the final shouting as the last of the mob made a stand and were overrun in the smoke. He remembers telling them not to be afraid as they died.

He remembers walking home through the smoke while the screams rose up from the city all around him. He remembers walking home intent on letting Sara infect him so that they could be rejoined. He remembers finding his house on fire.

Like Job, Paul lost everything he loved.

As with Job, God allowed it.

# THE BRIDGE

When the survivors left Pennsylvania, they crossed a sliver of West Virginia, a piece of ground stabbing north like a spike, before finally entering Ohio. The Veterans Memorial Bridge connects Steubenville, Ohio and Weirton, West Virginia—six lanes of modern superhighway carrying U.S. Route 22 across the Ohio River. Nearly twenty football fields in length, the cable-stayed bridge consists of steel girders and beams supporting a composite concrete road deck, the entire structure suspended by cables fanning out from the two support towers, a common design for long bridges.

Before Infection, thirty thousand people crossed this bridge every day. Now it is a funnel for more than a hundred thousand Infected moving west away from the still-burning ruins of Pittsburgh.

♦

The Bradley roars east on Route 22, leading a convoy of vehicles including several flatbed trucks stacked with explosives, armored cars and four school buses packed with soldiers and fitted with V-shaped snowplows on their grilles.

The rig slams into an abandoned minivan and sends it spinning onto the shoulder of the highway without breaking its stride. The crash makes Wendy flinch.

"We're going to practice a rapid scan," Sarge says.

Wendy blows air out of her cheeks and nods. She moves her left hand to wipe sweat from her forehead and bangs her elbow again.

"Mother," she hisses. Sitting in the commander's seat directly adjacent to Sarge in the gunner's station, her body is almost

surrounded by hard metal edges. Not much room to do anything
except work the joystick that controls the turret and weapons systems.

She peers into the integrated sight unit, which provides a relay of
what Sarge sees, overlaid with a reticle to help aim the Bradley's guns.
The highway slices through the rolling hills to the horizon, flanked
with green. Smoke is still pouring out of Pittsburgh, darkening the
eastern sky. The horizon shimmers and pulses with heat waves.

"Hey," Sarge says. "You're sightseeing."

"It's hard to take my eyes off the road."

Sarge smiles. "You have to get used to the fact that somebody else
is driving. While Steve will obey our commands to stop and go and so
on, we are a self-contained world up here, just you and me. You help
scan and identify targets, and I'll track and kill them."

"Yes, sir," Wendy says.

"I'm not a sir. I work for a living, Ma'am. Now let's do a rapid
scan with overlapped sectors."

"With who, what?"

"That means I'll be scanning roughly the same ground ahead as
you. First, scan center out, near to far, then left and right to center,
near to far. I'll be scanning far to near."

Her gum cracking, Wendy scans the highway ahead and identifies
two abandoned vehicles in the grassy median. They are passing a
billboard on the right that tells her to tune in to *Channel Seven News at
Eleven with Janet Rodriguez,* Janet grinning confidently down at her in a
power suit with her arms crossed. Beyond, power lines and trees.

The opposite lanes of the highway are occupied by a long column
of Infected that stare grimly at the rig as it rolls by on its grating treads.

"Identified," she says.

"Confirmed. Range?"

"Fifty meters?"

"I'm asking for the range to the nearest target."

"I thought that's what I was giving you."

"See that billboard up there on the other side of the highway?
That's about a hundred."

"Oh, then twenty, twenty-five?"

"Bingo," he grins. "You're learning fast. You should be proud,
babe."

"That's Private Babe to you," she answers, turning and flashing a
smile.

"What can I say, girl. You do look good in cammies."

"Settle down, Sergeant," she laughs. "This Army uniform is like
two sizes too big for me."

"You wear it like a dress."

"A tent, maybe."

Wendy laughs lightly, feeling good for the first time since she kissed him at the hospital. Sarge is a good man. He gives her precious moments in which she can forget about Infection and everything else. She believes she could easily fall in love with him if they live long enough.

The Bradley trembles slightly with the stresses generated by dozens of moving parts. She can feel the beating heart of the engine, turning the force of controlled explosions into the raw horsepower needed to turn the treads and propel the vehicle's twenty-five tons. The vibrations flow through her body, reminding her that she is riding a metal bull with the strength of five hundred horses and a mind of its own. And yet she feels powerful sitting here in its brain. More in control than she has ever felt, in fact. She is in an armored box with wheels, somebody else is driving, and she's got the big guns. She laughs again as she considers there are few better places one could be in the middle of a zombie apocalypse.

The exhilaration she feels, however, is tempered by a growing weight on her chest. Running the rig is a lot of responsibility. The soldiers, the other survivors, and all the people back at the camp will be counting on her to make good decisions when they hit the bridge in ninety minutes, and she simply does not have enough training or experience to do it right.

She is scared.

"You ready for more?" Sarge says.

I'm ready for a hot bath with real soap, scented candles, some Alanis on the CD player and a tall glass of red wine, she thinks.

"What else you got?" she says.

She is still wondering why she wanted to come on this mission, but another glance at the man beside her in the gunner's station reminds her. They are a tribe.

♦

Todd smiles at the almost surreal sense of déjà vu he is feeling at being back inside the hot, noisy, dim interior of the Bradley. He has butterflies in his gut, the humid air is dense with the smells of nervous sweat and diesel combustion, and he has to pee. Just like old times. It feels oddly right. The big difference is Anne is gone, Wendy is up in the front with Sarge, and there are two new faces in their unit—Ray

Young, the rent-a-cop with the hard eyes and handlebar mustache, and Lieutenant Patterson, the combat engineer with the buzz cut and earnest, clean-shaven face.

"Once more into the breach, huh, Rev?" Todd says with a laugh, hoping to show off his easy familiarity with the group to the newcomers, but the two men either did not hear him over the Bradley's engine or are simply lost in their own thoughts. As usual, nobody cares.

Paul smiles weakly and nods, but says nothing. Todd looks at him and realizes how grounded he feels being here with the other survivors. The Bradley feels like home. And yet he still does not know these people very well. He suddenly wants to talk to the Reverend about something important, something philosophical, man to man at the edge of the abyss—the nature of faith during war or whatever—but he cannot think of where to start such a conversation. A little more grounded, but he is still floating, away from others as well as himself.

The survivors' role in the mission is to help clear the bridge and then keep Patterson safe because the Lieutenant is going to blow the bridge using more than two tons of TNT and C4.

The engineer told them that cable-stayed bridges are a little harder to blow a hole in. The cables fanning out from the towers pull to the sides instead of up like a suspension bridge, requiring a stronger deck to compensate for the horizontal load. That means more force will be needed to blow a hole in it that the Infected cannot cross.

What's more, they will not have time to attach the charges under the bridge for a bottom attack. Instead, they will have to lay the explosives directly on the road deck, tamp it with a hill of sandbags, and blow off the concrete to expose the steel reinforcements. A second round of charges will cut the steel rods and beams. It will be a lot of work and take a long time.

Here is what will happen: After the bridge is secured, the trucks will pull up and workers will unload the explosives in piles across the eighty-foot-wide, six-lane bridge. These piles will be laid out in two lines covered in sandbags used as tamping to direct the force of the blast down into the concrete. The engineers will apply shaped C4 charges to the exposed steel elements.

Then, boom. The unsupported piece between the two blast lines will fall into the Ohio River and the resulting forty-foot gap will stop the Infected from crossing.

They have to do all this while potentially holding off a horde of Infected at both ends of the bridge.

"Hey," Todd says to the combat engineer.

The glazed eyes flicker and focus.

"Hey, what?"

"Why forty feet?"

Patterson grins. The transformation this brings is almost alchemical. A moment ago, he looked like a hardened killer on death row waiting for his lawyer. Now he looks like a frat boy about to explain how he spiked the professors' punch at the party.

"Mike Powell," he says, his accept deep Louisiana.

"Oh yeah," Ray says.

"Who's Mike Powell?"

"He set the world record in the long jump back in the nineties," Ray says.

Patterson nods.

"Almost thirty feet," he points out. "We're going to do forty—just in case one of those little Hopper sumbitches can beat old Mike Powell's record."

Todd grins with the other men, nodding, suddenly filled with awareness that history is being made today. It's the end of the world but a new one is beginning. He cannot help but feel excited. It's epic, *ninja*, like living in a video game.

He has already forgotten the brief, crushing sense of death he felt back at the hospital when Wendy held her Glock against his head and Ethan counted down to zero. You made it this far, Todd old man, he tells himself. You're lucky. You're good. Hell, you're practically immortal. You are earning your place in the new world. There will be historians in this new world, recording the heroic deeds of people during the dark time of Infection for future generations to understand and respect.

The bridge they are blowing is the Veterans Memorial Bridge. What buildings and bridges and monuments will they build to honor our sacrifices? What day will they set aside for our memory? They will look at us as the Greatest Generation, the people who fought Infection and rebuilt the world. Every war has a turning point. Ours is here, now. He thinks about John Wheeler and Emily Preston and the ghosts of his high school. Most of them are by now certainly Infected or dead. But not me, he reminds himself. I was chosen for a reason.

Maybe this time he will reap the rewards when he returns. Maybe he will get a little more respect. Erin was impressed by his tales of survival and the wound on his arm but ripped him off anyway. Inside the camp, he felt powerless, small, his life reduced to stories nobody could truly believe even in these times. Out here, he feels powerful, somehow more real, part of something again. He would never say such a thing out loud to the other survivors, but he is here because he wants to find himself.

♦

Paul signed up for this mission on impulse, but he is old enough to know that nothing happens purely that way. There is always a reason.

It is not loyalty to the others. He feels safer with them, but not really safe, and certainly not very safe out here, in the lion's den. He loves them in his own way with whatever love he has left to give anyone, but they can make their own decisions and take care of themselves.

It is not disgust with Pastor Strickland and his ministry of bitterness and regret. He does not approve it, but he also has no interest in fighting it. Strickland still loves the Infected that he lost but hates people he does not understand. A kingdom divided will be ruined and a house divided cannot stand, as Jesus taught. There have always been lost sheep like Strickland and McLean, and there always will be.

It is not even a simple desire to find a better place to live. If he continues on with Ethan to Camp Immunity near Harrisburg, it will be as filthy, hungry and violent as Defiance. When they were leaving, the people were cheering and blowing whistles and shooting into the air. The rumors that the Army was coming had achieved a critical mass. But nobody cared about the convoy of vehicles leaving the camp, filled with troops ready to sacrifice everything to save them all.

If God can appear cruel and hypocritical and vindictive, well, we are all made in his image, he reminds himself. God should have told Job that he had no right to question him because as bad as God is, people are even worse. When the chips are down, the best and worse is on full display.

The funny thing about the story of Job is that Job never questioned Satan. In Hebrew, Satan has two meanings. One is the Adversary. The other is *ha-Satan*, the Accuser. In either case, he is an Angel of the Lord. Maybe Job did not question Satan because he did not have to do so. If God is everything, he is also Satan. The Adversary. The Accuser. Creator of Heaven and Earth.

The fact is Paul hated leaving only a little less than he hated staying. Perhaps that is why he is here. Anne had the right idea, he tells himself: Just keep moving. He feels like he finally understands her decision to abandon them.

If you keep moving, they can never get you. You might even outrun yourself.

Stay still, and curse the day you were born.

We try to live with as little pain and as much pleasure as possible. But pain makes us realize we are alive. We truly live one moment to the next when we live with pain. When pain stops, we become afraid. And we remember things we do not wish to remember that are themselves painful.

Long is the way and hard, right, Anne?

The Catholics believe there is Heaven and Hell and between them a place called Purgatory, in which souls are purified and made ready for Heaven through a period of punishment. Similarly, there is a state of existence between living and dying: survival.

These days, God has no use for charity and good works. God demands everything now. These days, the Lord only calls those who have been baptized in blood.

And that, he realizes, is why he has come. Not to be tested, but to put an end to these tests.

"I came naked from my mother's womb, and I will be naked when I leave," Job said upon hearing that his family died and all his earthly possessions were destroyed. "The Lord gave me what I had, and the Lord has taken it away. Praise the name of the Lord!" Sara, I will be with you soon.

◆

Ethan remembers holding Carol's hand while she pushed Mary out into the world, counting between pushes, trying to pour all of his strength into her by will alone. He had always wanted children but felt ambivalent about the amount of responsibility they entailed. He wanted kids to be like Blockbuster videos, rentable and returnable within a week. Something he could manage over time, not maintain every single hour of every single day. The idea of wiping shit and vomit and changing diapers for the next few years was overwhelming. Mostly, he was worried about his relationship with his wife. They had a good life and he did not want to see it spoiled.

"It's a girl," the doctor told him.

"It's a girl," he said to his wife, his heart bursting with pride.

Carol cried with relief and joy, still holding his hand.

Later, the nurse asked him if he wanted to hold his daughter for the first time.

"Yes," he said without hesitation.

The woman handed him the tiny swaddled creature and his heart opened. A visceral, almost painful love surged through him, pouring out into the child in his arms.

Change diapers? He would *eat* this kid's shit, he realized.

Anything, he pledged. Anything for you.

This person will die without me. But more than that: Everything I do to this child from now on will reverberate through the rest of its life. He never felt so needed. So responsible.

"Your name is Mary," he told her in a singsong voice, not caring how it sounded.

From that point forward, nothing mattered except family.

They are going to the bridge to blow a hole in it and then he is going to travel two hundred miles to Camp Immunity near Harrisburg. He is going to have to get there on his own this time and it will be very difficult, if not impossible, to do it. Carol and Mary might as well be in Australia. And yet he has not felt so close to them since Infection started. There is a chance *they exist*.

The operation itself appears equally difficult. Two school buses loaded with troops will lead the way. The buses are forty feet long, which is almost exactly the span of each set of lanes on the bridge. They will drive to the end of the bridge and block it, creating a wall of firepower against the Infected. The Bradley will follow at a walking pace with the survivors and another squad of soldiers, clearing the bridge and setting up the charges while another pair of buses parks behind them, sealing both entrances against the Infected.

The combat engineer and his people will set up the charges, strip the concrete, plant the next round of charges, and then begin the countdown. The soldiers in the buses will make a run for it. Machine guns will cover their retreat. The final charges will blow.

Mission accomplished. Bravo, bravo.

Impossible.

A million things can go wrong, not the least of which is that the Infected might brush them off the bridge with ease. Monsters walk the earth now. The bridge might be packed with giant worms, swarming with malevolent little Hoppers, or even worse, occupied by the terrifying Demon that kicked the crap out of the Bradley and almost burst their ear drums with its wailing.

He will not even be able to launch his journey to Immunity on the West Virginia side of the river. He is going to have to find a boat. Even that seems impossible to him. But he will do it.

He will do anything, kill anybody, sacrifice everything, to find his family again.

♦

Sarge is glad to be back in the Army doing his duty, although he is not sure who he is actually working for at the moment. Captain Mattis is regular Army but got the operational orders for the mission from the provisional government of the Commonwealth of Pennsylvania. The Federal government nationalized the Guard while Ohio claimed control of Federal troops currently fighting on its soil. The refugee camp is run by FEMA, at least nominally, with people from different levels of government claiming jurisdiction over everything.

Even here, in the field, things are not perfectly clear: Sarge is in charge of security, but Patterson, the combat engineer and a first lieutenant, is nominally in charge of the entire operation. Mattis gave him a half-strength, watered-down National Guard infantry company for the mission, two-thirds under Sarge's direct command for the assault on the Veterans Memorial Bridge, the remaining third to be deployed for a separate operation to destroy the smaller Market Street Bridge a few miles to the south. The northward Fort Steuben Bridge had already been demolished the summer before the Screaming, apparently. The soldiers are weekend warriors for the most part, supplemented by volunteers from the camp, but most of them are well trained, disciplined and equipped, and some have even done time in Iraq.

In the end, it does not matter to him where he got his orders. The mission is sound and he is simply happy to be back in the field commanding troops. Out here, ringed by death on all sides, appears to be the only place where he can feel truly calm. He is terrified by what this means. He is glad Wendy came along because he is not sure he is going back when this is all over.

"Identified," Wendy says, adding, "What the hell is that thing, Sarge?"

The giant hairless head totters on spindly tripod legs. It suddenly stops and drops a load of dung that falls onto the highway like a wet bomb. Grimacing with a wide mouth and oversized, bulging eyes, the thirty-foot-tall monster leers down at the Infected streaming around its legs.

"*Shaw chonk*," it says, its deep voice booming through the air.

Suddenly, a long, thick tongue lashes out, wraps around the torso of an Infected woman, and pulls her up into its cavernous, gobbling mouth. Chewing loudly, the thing chortles deep in its throat, the heavy bass sound vibrating at its edges like an idling motorcycle.

"*Shaw chonk roomy lactate.*"

"Jesus Christ," Wendy says.

In any other time, the vision of this monster tottering down Route 22—its skinny legs supporting a bloated, improbable sphere of mottled flesh with its grotesque, almost human face—would have suddenly and irreparably damaged Sarge's mind. Today, it only fills him with instant revulsion and hatred. The thing is a trespasser on his planet and must be destroyed. Anne used the perfect word to describe these things: abominations.

Sarge gives the general order to halt the convoy and tells Steve to stop the Bradley.

"What are we going to do?" Wendy says, her voice quiet and breathless.

Sarge switches to high magnification for a closer look at the thing. The monster's grinning face fills the optical display. Revolted, he quickly switches back to low magnification.

"*Roomy lactation!*" it bellows across the landscape, eyeing the vehicles.

"We're going to kill it," Sarge tells her.

He estimates the range to target at two hundred meters using the rule of thumb method of picturing a distance of a hundred meters and ranging to the target in hundred-meter increments. He adjusts the RANGE-SELECT knob.

"Two," he says absently.

He presses a switch on the weapons box, illuminating the AP LO annunciator light, indicating selection of the twenty-five millimeter gun with armor-piercing rounds firing at a low rate of fire, about a hundred rounds per minute.

"Line up the shot, Private Babe," Sarge says.

Wendy presses the palm switch on her joystick with her fingers, activating the turret drive and releasing the turret brakes, then puts pressure on the stick. The turret responds immediately, beginning its rotation. The reticle centers on the monster's legs.

"Now give me elevation to center mass on the thing's hideous goddamn head."

She feathers the stick until the reticle is centered between the monster's eyes.

"Got it."

"You're drifting."

"Sorry."

"Don't say sorry; stabilize."

She pushes the drift button, stabilizing the turret.

"Good job."

"Sarge, if something should happen—"

"Nothing's going to happen," he says, his eyes glued to optical display. He presses the arming switch for the cannon. "But if you really want to know, I love you."

"So we'll be together no matter what."

"No matter what, if you want me," he grins, adding: "*On the way.*"

He depresses the trigger switch and the Bradley's main gun begins firing.

"Tell me what you see," he says.

The rounds arc up the highway, the path illuminated by tracers. The thing is moving again.

"Um, lost?" she says, meaning she thinks the rounds are passing over the target.

"Correction," he murmurs. "I'm taking over the turret."

He corrects the elevation and starts shooting again, leading the lethal fire into the beast using the tracers. Giant cigar-puffs drift lazily away from the rig. The rounds, designed to penetrate Soviet tanks and concrete bunkers, enter the monster's skull and burst in flashes of light, sending geysers of blood and brain rocketing high into the air.

The Towering Thing screams shrilly and stumbles, weeping and groaning, until it topples to the ground trailing black smoke, the remains of its head splashing across the lanes and into the median. One of the legs twitches briefly, and then it is still.

Despite the noise of the Bradley's engine and systems, they can hear the soldiers in the buses cheering. Sarge's heart pounds in his chest. These things die just like anything else.

"Target destroyed," he says, turning his head to smile at Wendy, who beams back at him.

"Holy crap, that was exciting," she says. "I think I'm addicted. And I think I love you, too."

"We're going to get through this," he tells her, smiling. "We're going to win."

His smile suddenly fades. The truth is a part of him hopes that they never win. The truth is he wants the war to go on and on and on, because he can never return to peace.

◆

The Bradley hums, idling after the shooting stops. Sarge gets on the intercom and tells them they just destroyed one big, ugly monster. Ray glances across the smiling faces and wants to scream at them for being complete morons. They are driving to a place where the big, ugly monsters will be thick as fleas. They are going there by *choice*; they are idiots.

The idea of driving onto that bridge and being greeted by the entire Infected population of Pittsburgh fills him with pure, bowel-evacuating terror. America has become a killing floor and there are things out there that want to eat you. They will eat you while you are still alive and then you will be dead and you will never see the sun again or kiss a girl or laugh at a joke or drink a beer. Ever again. Forever.

And nobody will give a shit about your famous last words. These days, if you're lucky, your friends will burn you in a pit. If not, then you're food.

Only a crazy lunatic would want to put himself into that situation.

These motherfuckers are crazy.

No, he tells himself. *You're* the looney. You're here because you made a promise, which you actually did not literally make, to a lot of dead people, who are, well, *dead*, to make things normal again, which means asshole cops back being asshole cops, and if it's one thing you hated from the Time Before almost as much as credit card debt, it's *asshole cops*.

These maniacs don't know any better, apparently; you do. Which makes you an even bigger fool.

He swallows hard, fighting the urge to retch.

Todd leans towards him and says charitably, "It's going to be okay, man."

"Shut up, kid," he says.

Just because you're suicidal does not make you any braver than me, he thinks. In my time, I started fights over anything from noble causes to petty grievances, and more often than not I ended them. I fight to win and I fight dirty. Bravery has nothing to do with this. This is about living and dying. There is nothing in between. You make a choice and that is your choice.

Cashtown had so many ne'er-do-wells like him that the few upright citizens were hard to tell apart from everybody else unlucky enough to have been born there. Once, the town prospered in steel and timber, but like so many places in America, it fell into ruin due to overseas competition and decades of betrayal of the American worker by big business and the country's politicians. People passing through left with impressions of rusting, abandoned steel mills, smokestacks and rail yards. Deteriorating housing drenched in American flags. For years, it was just one town in a depressed region where people lived check to check with as much pride as they could muster.

Ray worked as a rent-a-cop for a self-storage facility and frequently got into trouble with real cops. He drank, he smoked, he brawled, he broke things, he screwed anything with two legs. He lived in his mom's basement and broke her heart with bad behavior and odd jobs and general lack of a future. Probably the only decent thing he ever did was volunteer for the local fire department.

When the Screaming happened, he was sleeping one off. He found his mother dead hours later. She had caught the Screaming while taking a bath and drowned, all alone. There were so many dead that the mortuary could not bury her. The county zipped her up in a shiny black body bag, tagged her, and drove her away in a truck for burial in a mass grave—to be dug up later and buried properly when things returned to normal. Of course, they never did.

During the morning of Infection, he was driving home from his shift when he saw a pack of lunatics in pajamas tackle and tear apart a child fleeing on a bicycle. Suddenly, there were people fighting everywhere. The people who ran the bakery were looking out the window of their store, pointing and murmuring to each other and trying to call somebody on the phone. As Ray drove by, he saw another pack of pajama-wearing lunatics crash through the window, lunging for them.

All Ray could think at the time was, *I don't want that to be me.*

The truck radio shouted at him until he turned it off.

He drove home and loaded his rig with everything he could get his hands on. Food, beer, liquor, cigarettes and dip, jugs of water, packets of Kool-Aid, burritos and TV dinners. He restarted his truck, turned on the radio and flipped across the shouting voices until he found the local AM news station, which promptly began emitting the emergency broadcast signal.

He turned off the radio. It's better this way, he told himself. I don't want to know.

He drove back to the storage facility, locked the chain-link fence behind him, and then sealed himself inside one of the storage sheds with somebody else's dusty furniture.

Ray stayed in there for five days until he ran out of booze, the last set of batteries failed in his flashlight, and he could no longer stand the stench of his own waste.

He opened the garage door and emerged into a brave new world.

The camp was already sprawling, bursting out of Cashtown until it reached the self-storage facility. Some of the storage units were being plundered to make room for refugees. He stood there for fifteen minutes, blinking in the sunlight with his mouth open, trying to understand it, his head pounding with the worst hangover of his life. After what he had seen on the first day of Infection, he had thought he would find the town abandoned by the living. Instead, he found a thriving refugee camp with the population of Boulder, Colorado.

Not a very noble way to survive that first deadly week of Infection, but the point is he *emerged*. The point is he *survived*.

There is no honor in survival, but life goes on and life is everything. Nothing else matters. And anybody who thinks differently is a fool—a fool who probably won't live very long.

Most of his friends were dead. The town had five governments. Four families were living in his mother's house, which had already been looted top to bottom. Some of them he recognized as his former neighbors. Many of the locals had tried to cash in, selling land to the government and basic necessities to the refugees at outrageous prices, trading everything they had for a pile of paper money that rapidly declined in value until it became virtually worthless. Some of the more important and civic-minded locals, however, became entrenched with the government. They knew Ray and trusted him and they needed to beef up community policing fast.

So Ray became a lawman and, in the process, a true believer in making the world right again. He was good at it. His only regret was that his mother was not alive to see him do it.

When he found out Wendy was a Pittsburgh police officer, it had been like meeting an angel. The news of the burning of the city had hit the camp like a thunderbolt. People walked around in a daze, unable to comprehend it. By the time Wendy showed up at the police station, the fire had already become a legend. That made her something of a miracle, rare and precious.

Which is why he came, to protect her. The part of Ray Young that he has been finding out is good believes that if he can protect her, he can help make the world right again.

As for the part of him that is bad, the part he knows all too well, that part also wants to see the world return to normal. Ray is tough and morally ambivalent, he can be a bully and violent on a whim, but he has no wish to live in a world in eternal fear of being wiped out by a horde of diseased, homicidal maniacs. He longs for the day when he can get drunk on payday, throw a bottle through a window, and take a swing at honest cops who come to arrest him. He was a loser back in the day, that is true, while he is an important man now. But he was a loser who was certain to live a long life of petty amusements in a town he loved. He wants the world to get back to normal: a world where beer is manufactured and sold cheaply in mass quantities, tobacco farmers are free to harvest their crops unmolested, and women are loose and have easy access to birth control.

He came for reasons both selfless and selfish, but none of that matters now.

Now that he is here, all he wants to do is live.

♦

The numbers of Infected multiply as they approach Steubenville along Route 22, the Bradley breaking their bodies with sickening thuds, the buses sending them flying with their V-shaped highway truck snowplows that had been retrofitted onto their grilles. They bypass the town along the north, their view of it obscured by a treed slope that gradually turns into a concrete wall. The fronts of the vehicles are splashed with blood; the windshield wipers are working full time. The Bradley crashes through a guide panel mounted on a sagging overhead gantry and announcing ROUTE 7 SOUTH STEUBENVILLE, smashing it into flying green shards that flutter and scatter across the highway. The Infected race towards the buses, squealing and pounding on their sides painted with special messages: HELLO, NOW DIE and NONE SHALL PASS and INSTANT CURE! INQUIRE WITHIN.

Sarge says into the intercom, "We're approaching the bridge. Stay frosty."

Wendy glances at him with wide eyes, her face pale and pouring sweat.

"Eyes forward," he says, then adds gently, "You're okay, babe."

"This is different than before. This is not just survival. This is a mission." She shakes her head briefly before returning her attention to the ISU. "We're fighting a war now."

"Don't matter what you want to call it. Either way, people's lives are riding on what you do, so you make sure you do right. You do the best you can."

"It's too much this time. I'm scared."

"Only crazy people don't get scared. Being scared is perfectly normal. You just have to control it so it don't control you."

"How?"

"You take things one step at a time. Each minute as it comes."

She nods, licking her dry lips. "Okay," she rasps.

"Baby steps. Right now, all we got to do is drive."

The bridge appears in the distance on the left, growing larger by the minute. Sarge glances at the instrumentation, pleased that none of the critical annunciator lights are lit up or flashing at him, which would indicate a problem with a vital system. He activates the intercom.

"Get into your battle rattle," he says, trying to sound upbeat. "We'll be in the shit in less than ten and back home in a few hours."

No macho cheering or theatrical complaining comes back to him from the passenger compartment, just cold silence. He reminds himself that this is a different kind of war. A war of fratricides. A war of genocide against people they once loved.

Nobody wants to cheer in this kind of war until it's over.

The bridge looms on the left, dominating the view against a gray sky that darkens towards the horizon like a distant storm. Waves of heat ripple at the horizon's edge, Pittsburgh continuing to give up its ghost. The appearance of the bridge itself, a wonder of modern engineering appearing suddenly after miles of empty country, is almost as startling as the memory of the fire. An overhead road sign declares EAST 22 NORTH 2 WEIRTON PITTSBURGH. The convoy slows as it comes together in single file, exiting for the interchange.

Honking loudly, a line of Brinks armored cars and flatbed trucks at the tail of the convoy breaks off, continuing south along Route 7 into Steubenville. These troops are headed to the Market Street Bridge, just a few miles to the south of the Veterans Memorial Bridge, an old light rail suspension bridge built in 1905 that was later upgraded into a two-lane crossover for vehicles. Seven thousand cars and trucks crossed that bridge every day before the end of the world. Now it is used only by monsters.

The Bradley rolls onto the bridge. Sarge sighs with relief.

The operation has officially begun.

♦

The two leading buses race ahead to the other end of the bridge, knocking down Infected along the way while the rest of the convoy slows and stops. The other two buses deploy laterally across the Ohio side, forming a steel wall blocking access to the Infected. Immediately, the soldiers in the buses begin shooting out of the windows, cutting down the Infected who were following the convoy. The Bradley sits on the asphalt, idling. Inside, the survivors listen to the occasional pop of rifle fire as soldiers on the bridge take down stray Infected.

*Oh, Jesus, oh Jesus Christ*

Sarge keys his handset.

"Negative contact, Immune 2. Say again, over."

*There are thousands of them*

"I repeat: Negative contact, Alex. How copy, over?"

Over the Bradley's idling, Sarge can hear the splash of small arms fire from the other end of the bridge nearly six hundred meters away. Wendy flinches at the sound, then returns to scanning the bridge for threats. The Immune 2 unit, comprising the two buses that moved ahead, are supposed to plug the West Virginia end of the bridge by creating another steel wall. Once both ends of the bridge are sealed by buses manned by combat troops, Sarge and his force will walk the bridge from one end to the other, clearing it.

Then Patterson and his engineering team can do their work.

*We're trying to set up the buses but they're everywhere, Sarge. Not just the Infected but the monsters, too. Hoppers. The giant heads with legs. Elephants with worms growing out of them.*

"Copy that," Sarge says.

"Should we go and help him?" Wendy says.

"Our job is to clear the bridge," Sarge tells her. "Alex's job is to secure the other end."

*I think we got it! Yeah, he's got it. Holy shit, we're in place. We're in place, Immune 1.*

"I copy, Immune 2. Great job, over."

*We'll hold them here as long as we can, over.*

"Hang on. We'll see you in a few minutes, out."

*Roger that, out.*

Wendy activates the Bradley's intercom system before Sarge can reach for it.

"It's time to go, guys," she says, fighting to control her voice. "I just wanted you to know that I love all of you. Good luck and come back safe."

Sarge nods.

"You heard the lady," he says, and presses the button to drop the exit ramp.

♦

The survivors dismount the vehicle, stepping into May sunshine. Nearby, a squad of National Guard and two machine gun crews watch them fidget with their weapons while wearing expressions of barely concealed disdain. Covered by the Bradley, they are all going up the bridge together. Their job is to clear it of anything breathing so that Patterson and his people can do their work. The big five-ton trucks, loaded with tied-down boxes of TNT and C4 covered in plastic tarps, stand idling, surrounded by large, burly men waiting for their turn in the game. Patterson walks over to them and shouts instructions. Immediately, the men begin taking off the tarps, exposing enough explosive to rip the bridge in half.

Todd checks his M4 carbine and waits for the order to move out, chomping at the bit for some action. He saw the way the Guard were looking down their noses at him and wants to show them what he can do.

The firing at the other end of the bridge suddenly increases in volume. Todd wonders what those men up there are seeing, what they are going through.

Paul nudges him, blowing air out of his cheeks.

"This is going to be a shit storm, boy," he says. "You stay close to me."

"I'm not worried, Rev," Todd says with a smile. "If God is with us, who can be against us?"

"That's what I'm afraid of," Paul answers. "I think God might be on *their* side."

"Got an extra smoke for me, Preacher?" Ray says.

"Here you go, Ray."

"Thanks. Feel that breeze. Man, that feels good."

While the two men smoke, Todd moves away a little, irritated. Between their smoking and all the exhaust hanging in the air from the idling vehicles, he is starting to get a headache.

Gunfire crackles in the distance. The survivors crane their necks and squint at the Market Street Bridge, clearly visible to the south. Vehicles and tiny figures are moving on the road deck. The crackle becomes a steady pounding roar. Sparks flash along its length, tracer rounds streaming to contact. Several pale figures fall off the bridge and into the muddy waters below. A rocket explodes at the far side, a flash followed by a deep boom and a mushroom cloud.

There is a hell of a fight going on over there. The other force is in action.

Todd fingers the handset the Army gave him for the mission and keys it with a squeeze.

"Uh, Sarge?"

*Todd, unless this is an emergency, get the hell off the commo, over.*

"Sorry about that, Sarge."

Todd hesitates, but cannot help himself. He is already committed. And he cannot resist using the radio.

"I was just, uh, wondering when we're going to get moving," he adds. "Um, over."

*You move when I tell you to move. Out.*

Todd smiles. He heard Wendy laughing in the background.

Moments later, Sarge gives the command to advance.

*It's show time, folks.*

◆

The Bradley begins crawling along the bridge, keeping pace with the Guard unit led by Sergeant Hackett, fanned out across the left three lanes, and the survivors spread out on the right. On the far right, near the edge, Paul looks down at the brown torrents far below. The water seems a good place to be, he muses, especially if the Infected cannot swim. A man could get a boat and disappear. He thinks about how the Ohio is formed by the Allegheny and the Monongahela meeting at Pittsburgh, and travels all the way here; downstream, it feeds the Mississippi. He asks Todd to swap weapons for a moment and uses the close combat optic to get a magnified view of the far shore. It is swarming with Infected as far as the eye can see. Corpses and small islands of plastic garbage float in the water, collecting in piles on the riverbanks. The Infected gather at the water's edge, drinking among scores of bloated corpses washed up onto the mud.

Paul lowers the rifle, feeling sick, and hands it back to Todd.

"You look like you saw a ghost, Rev," Todd says. "What's going on over there?"

"The usual," Paul tells him.

Behind them, Ray says, "Hail Mary, full of grace," repeatedly until doubling over, vomiting loudly onto the road.

Sergeant Hackett frowns at the survivors and shakes his head.

Todd flushes with embarrassment and hisses at Ray, "Come *on*, man."

Ray wipes his mouth, gasping, and says, "Fuck this."

"Contact!" one of the soldiers calls out.

The Guard begin shooting. The Bradley slows even further, almost coming to a halt. The survivors slow their pace as well, waiting until the threat is eliminated.

"Clear," the soldiers shout. The motley little army resumes its advance.

*Ray is right to be scared*, Paul thinks. *The hordes of hell are waiting for us at the other end of this bridge.*

As if reading his thoughts, Ray says, "You don't look too scared, Preacher. What's your secret?"

"There isn't any secret, Ray."

"You think if you die, you go straight to Paradise to be with the virgins, right?"

Paul smiles and answers, "No, boy. I'm not scared because I'm already dead."

Ray stares at him in disbelief for several moments before shaking his head. "You people are fucking crazy."

"*I'm* not crazy," Todd says.

Paul notices Ethan frowning as if trying to solve a difficult puzzle. The Reverend pauses, raising his shotgun. He knows that look well. Todd sees them and shoulders his carbine.

"What you got?" says Todd.

Ethan suddenly roars, "Heads up!"

His voice is drowned out by a flurry of screams and gunshots and curses. Paul looks up in time to see a flash of pale gray flesh. He pulls the trigger and the shotgun discharges with a burst of light and sound, bucking hot in his hands. The little creature flops to the deck, rolling and hissing and bleeding. Paul aims quickly and fires again. The Hopper explodes, leaving a trail of smoking gore splashed across the asphalt.

He turns quickly, sensing motion in the corner of his eye, and cracks another of the little monsters in the skull with the butt of his gun. The thing stumbles away, reeling with vertigo, squealing with confusion and pain until Ray Young pumps several rounds into it with his pistol.

Killing the Infected is hard because they are people. These monsters are something else. Demons. When Paul kills them, he feels he is doing God a favor.

He scans the area with his shotgun, but sees no other threats. The gunfire around him sputters.

"Cease fire, cease fire!" Hackett calls out.

"Man down!" one of the soldiers cries.

"We need a minute to take care of our people," Hackett shouts at the survivors. "What you got?"

"We're all okay here," Paul tells him, waving.

The Guard pause after this announcement and glare at the survivors with open resentment.

"Guess they thought we'd all be dead or something," Paul says.

"Sorry to disappoint them," Todd grumbles.

"The Hoppers were up in the cables," Ethan says sheepishly, shrugging. "These cables that hold the bridge together. They were up there waiting to drop down on us. A pretty basic ambush."

Paul nods. "Good one, boy."

Ray laughs, his face as white as a sheet, and spits on the ground. "Batshit crazy," he says. "But you seem to know your stuff. I'll give you that."

♦

Sergeant Hackett pulls a can of spray paint out of a leg pocket, shakes it vigorously, and sprays a bright orange X on the back of one of the two men in his squad who were stung by the Hoppers. The man nods, accepting his death sentence. He will keep fighting but he will have to be killed when it is all over.

The other soldier was apparently stung several times and lies curled up on the ground with his face clenched in mortal pain. He does not appear to be able to move. Ethan looks at him and wonders what must be going through his mind right now. Wonders if the man can feel Infection proliferating in his blood. Can feel his body slowly being converted into an alien life form.

Hackett crouches, talking to the man, patting his shoulder. Then he stands, unholsters his nine-millimeter, and shoots him in the head with a loud report. The other soldiers tense and Ethan thinks, this is it, they're going to shoot him now and go home, but Hackett growls at them to get back in line and prepare to advance, and they obey.

The Bradley revs its engine and resumes its slow crawl to the center of the bridge. Ethan glances at the other bridge to the south, now almost concealed in a haze of smoke lit by muzzle flashes. As the survivors pass under the overhead WELCOME TO WEST VIRGINIA sign, the remaining Infected stream toward them in a flying horde, howling.

We kill them and the bridge is ours, Ethan tells himself. This is it.

He raises his rifle, but Paul pushes the barrel down.

"What?"

"Wait," Paul says, watching Hackett.

The sergeant has called for a halt and to hold fire until his command.

"What's going on?" Ethan says.

"He's afraid of hitting the bus and killing our own people," Paul tells him. "We're going to let the Infected get close and take them out with aimed shots."

The Infected are bolting down the bridge, arms splayed at their sides. It takes every bit of strength Ethan has not to empty his rifle at them. Or run like hell.

"Hold the line," Hackett cries.

This is ridiculous, Ethan realizes. There are too many. If they get close, the survivors are going to have to make almost every shot disable one of them.

He sees no old faces in the swarm. The virus is a harsh mistress, driving its hosts to constant exertion in its never-ending effort to spread Infection. The bodies of the old failed long ago. There are also no children. The Screaming spared the children but Infection did not; the Infected refuse to spread the virus to them, preferring instead to kill and, if they need food, eat them.

What is left are healthy adults who were once Americans and had lives. He sees a man running at him wearing a tattered business suit, his tie still neatly knotted around his throat. A Sikh with a long beard, dressed in a turban and greasy mechanic's overalls. A cop still wearing his bulky Batman belt, dead radio and all. A beautiful naked woman with a gray face and the remains of a hospital gown dangling from her wrist.

A wave of stench washes over them, the characteristic sour milk stink of the Infected.

"Give the order," Ethan murmurs.

"He's got this," Paul says.

"Why is nobody firing?"

"Don't panic," Ray mutters. "If you start panicking, I'm really going to panic."

"Give the goddamn order already!"

"FIRE!" Hackett screams across the highway.

The line erupts with a volley and the Infected collapse in a red mist and haze of smoke. Ethan blinks, caught off guard, and fires his first shot, shooting the mechanic through the throat. He adjusts his aim and puts two into the woman. He backs up several steps, firing at the businessman, missing until finally shooting out his knees and putting him down.

The line trembles. Suddenly they are all running, streaming back towards the Ohio side of the river, firing as they run, trying to keep distance between themselves and the Infected.

"Halt!" says Hackett, holding out his arms.

The soldiers show good discipline, stopping and firing upon the remaining Infected. The air fills with noise and smoke and cordite. Ethan keeps running. For a moment, Ray runs alongside him and it feels like they are racing. Then Ethan is abruptly jerked back. He struggles, fighting against the hand grabbing at his shirt.

"Fire your rifle," Paul shouts in his ear.

"Leave me alone!" Ethan screams in a panic, wrenching out of Paul's grasp and spinning in time to see the swarm bearing down on him, hands outstretched, their howl and sour milk stench turning his legs to cold jelly.

Paul's shotgun crashes in his ears and a man wearing pajama bottoms collapses in a heap.

Ethan feels drained and he can no longer run. A part of him wants to sit and let the Infected take him. His mind flashes back to Philip, who sat in the cinders of a half-burned convenience store in Wilkinsburg after seeing a newspaper with an old date.

He pictures his daughter's face.

He screams and fires. The cop's face explodes and the man continues running, almost decapitated, until collapsing to the ground at Ethan's feet.

◆

The team returns to the center of the bridge. The survivors walk among the twitching, dying bodies in a slight daze, as if through a dream, their shoes soaked through with the blood of the dead. Killing is exhausting work, draining on all levels, leaving them feeling numb. The wounded Infected crawl after them, coughing blood and growling, until finished off with mercy shots given without a second thought.

The machine gun crews set up at the edges of the bridge, aiming their weapons towards West Virginia. One of the soldiers sneezes loudly on the sharp tang of cordite hanging in the air. There is a sea of Infected on the other side of the two buses up there and if that line fails, the MG teams and the Bradley will become the main line of defense, holding off the horde until the engineers can finish the job.

The five-ton trucks are already backing up towards the center line, men clambering along their beds, cutting into the boxes and dumping piles of sandbags on the road.

Ray sighs loudly, feeling strangely blessed. He has been ambushed and rushed and he is standing next to a bunch of morons fooling around with more than four thousand pounds of high-grade explosives, but he is still alive. When Patterson tells him to grab some sandbags and start distributing them along the two lines in the road he drew with chalk, he is almost grateful. Mindless labor he understands. He is perfectly fine with that. A little work won't kill him.

"Yo, Ray. Ray. *Ray Young.*"

He turns and sees the Bradley commander gesturing from the open hatch of the vehicle.

"You need something, Sarge?"

"I've lost contact with Sergeant Horton. He's in the right bus. I need a runner to get up there and report back on what's happening."

"Christ, Sarge, you can hear the firing from here. They're still there."

Sarge glowers and Ray glares back, setting his jaw, feeling mean. He is afraid of death, yes, but not of fighting. He never backs down when it comes to a fight.

Anytime, Sergeant Wilson, he thinks. Anytime you want, you let me know.

"Ray, there's blood on the windows," Sarge says. "I need to know if he's got casualties. I need to know what he's got in front of him. I need to know if he needs ammunition."

Ray understands bullying very well. Sarge is not being a bully. It's a reasonable request.

"All right, all right," he grumbles.

"You sure it's okay? Sure you don't mind?"

"I said all right, I'll go."

"Then move your ass, shit for brains!"

Ray grins, checks the magazine on his M16, and starts jogging. After fifty feet, he is already flagging and wheezing a little, his lungs starting to ache.

Christ, Ray, he thinks. You need to get back into shape.

He feels a hand on his shoulder and almost screams.

"What's up, dude?"

"What are you doing here, kid?"

"Thought you might want some company."

"Why don't you just do it and I'll go back?"

Alarm crosses Todd's face.

"Sarge wouldn't like that. Come on, it'll be cool."

*It'll be cool.* Crazy, stupid kid.

They slow as they approach the bus. Several of the windows are sprayed with blood on the inside. Two of them are open and gun smoke drifts lazily out of them. Dark shapes are moving inside. The constant pop of gunfire is so hot and loud here that it almost feels like a physical barrier.

Ray and Todd glance at each other.

"What do you think?" Todd shouts at him.

"I think we should get this over with."

Ray pushes open the bus doors and climbs aboard, looking down the aisle and coughing on the smoke. The aisle and seats on the right are filled with soldiers, firing and reloading and roaring obscenities. Dead men occupy several of the seats on the left, their eyes staring at nothing. Empty shell casings clatter onto the floor, already covered in brass and links. There is an atmosphere of madness here. The soldiers wear wild expressions, like they've completely lost it.

But they are holding.

He is about to grab one of them when he sees Sergeant Alexander Horton sitting in one of the seats, his eyes bulging with fear and his chest torn out and dripping onto the floor, dead as a doorknob. Mission accomplished, now let's get the hell out of here.

Todd taps him on the shoulder and points.

Ray looks past the nearest soldiers and sees the horde.

It surges towards him in a vast shrieking swarm, an endless freak show of monsters and zombies converging on the bridge. He spots packs of Hoppers with their absurd walk, occasionally leaping to sting one of the Infected. Giant leering faces swaying on bony stilted legs. Titans waving their tentacles, bellowing. And flowing among them, mindlessly marching and occasionally serving as food for the monsters, thousands of Infected waiters and students and housewives and cashiers and typists and investment bankers.

He wakes up outside the bus, running, gasping for air, trailed by Todd.

Paul rushes to meet them halfway. They fall to their knees together.

"Talk to me," he says.

"He freaked out," Todd says. "Paul, there are like *a million* of them over there."

"Ray?"

"Tell your boss that Horton is dead," Ray gasps. "In fact, one out of four soldiers on that bus is dead. And every Infected bastard from Pittsburgh is beating at their door."

♦

Sarge sits on the Bradley's turret, aiming his binoculars at the school buses at the end of the bridge and chewing his lip. They have been on the bridge for over an hour, anxiously watching the engineers do their job. Patterson bangs on the armor to get his attention and tells him that he is almost done setting up the charges. The TNT is arranged in two lines in front of the Bradley. All that remains before the show, the engineer explains, is finishing the tamping and pulling back the wires for each series of explosives to where they will be detonated.

Twenty minutes, he says.

Roger that, LT.

The distance between the Bradley and the end of the bridge is about three hundred meters. Sarge has the Bradley's battlecarry—pre-selected range and ammunition—set up, establishing a kill zone around the buses. He looks at his watch nervously, sweating in the afternoon sun.

He sees Todd, working with the other survivors and Guard to pass sandbags along a human chain, and waves.

*Yeah, Sarge?*

Sarge smiles. For a moment, he forgot he has radio communication with the survivors.

He keys his handset and says, "Todd, I want you to go up to the buses and tell those boys we need twenty more minutes from them, over."

*Cool! Todd, out!*

Todd snatches his carbine and takes off at a sprint.

He hears a colossal crash of thunder and looks south. The center of the Market Street Bridge, shrouded by a drifting cloud of black smoke, is collapsing into the Ohio River.

The soldiers let up a ragged cheer. Sarge grunts with satisfaction. Half the mission is over. But it will not be successful until they finish the job and destroy this bridge.

He returns his binoculars to the buses. He sees fresh streaks of blood on the windows, the dead propped up in the seats, as if waiting for their next stop.

Just hang on a little longer, he thinks. He marvels at the bravery and endurance of the men inside those vehicles. He cannot even imagine what they must be going through in there.

The engineers are shouting in alarm. Sarge shifts his gaze and sees one of the Towering Things leering down at the bus, ropes of drool leaking between its massive teeth.

The monster's tongue lashes out. After several moments, it pulls the broken body of a National Guardsmen into its chomping mouth. The monster bites down, chewing greedily with a blissful expression, its eyes closed and leaking tears. The creature is so happy it is crying.

Another Towering Thing appears on the right, chortling. Its tongue lashes out and a man screams.

The bus is *moving*.

"Todd, get back here now," Sarge says.

*But I'm almost there, over.*

"Get back here now," Sarge roars. "The line is breaking."

The gunfire sputters and stops. Soldiers emerge from the buses and race towards the safety of the machine guns at the center of the bridge. One of the monsters lashes out over the roof of the bus and grips a fleeing soldier by the ankle, yanking him up and into the mouth, the man screaming and firing his weapon until the teeth crush his body into paste.

The bus is moving, swinging open like a door. Something big is pushing it. Tentacles wave in the air behind the vehicle. One of the Giants. A limb as thick as a tree trunk, knotted with thick, pale muscle, emerges. Moments later, the behemoth pushes its way past and lumbers onto the bridge, bellowing like a foghorn.

"Prepare for action," Sarge says into his handset. "Hold the line!"

So close, he thinks. We are so close to winning this.

He drops into the telescoped seat, lowers it, and seals the hatch.

*Immunity 1, this is Immunity actual, over,* he hears over his headset.

"Go ahead, LT," Sarge says.

*I still need fifteen minutes, over.*

"You got your fifteen, out." Sarge shouts, "Get those MGs up!"

Moments later, the .30 cal machine guns placed at the edges of the bridge start firing, the tracers streaming down the causeway and converging on the bellowing titan, which staggers back a few steps, its massive head trembling. The Infected swarm around the feet of the monster, racing towards the center of the bridge.

"Hackett, I want that MG fire focused on the foot mobiles," Sarge says.

*Roger that, Sarge.*

"What about us?" Wendy says.

"On the way," Sarge says, squeezing the trigger.

The rig shudders slightly as the cannon fires, BUMP BUMP BUMP BUMP BUMP, empty shell casings spilling down the Bradley's chest. The HE rounds crash into the Giant and the area around it, exploding in a series of flashes.

"Target," Wendy says, letting Sarge know that his aim is good. "Target."

"It's like shooting at a barn," Sarge mutters.

*Immunity 1, this is Immunity actual, we're about ten from detonation. How copy?*

"Solid, LT," Sarge says. "Ten minutes to detonation."

The Giant collapses, shivering, gushing blood.

"Target destroyed," Wendy announces.

*Good work*, Steve says from the driver's station.

"Mark the time, Wendy. Officer or not, if the LT is not ready in ten, I'm going to put my boot up his ass."

Smoke billows at the end of the bridge. The horde comes running out of the smoke, throwing themselves into the machine gun fire, driven by their endless rage.

"Shifting fire to area target," he murmurs, switching to the coax MG. "*On the way.*"

Sarge keeps the reticle in the same place, fires a burst of ten to fifteen rounds horizontally across the target area, then another diagonally, then another horizontally, in a repeating Z pattern.

"Jesus," Wendy says, almost retching.

Hundreds of rounds fall among the ranks of the Infected, cutting them down like wheat under a scythe. The bodies collapse in groups, often in pieces. Smoking fingers and hands and heads and feet and legs fly through the air in a bloody mist. Just as often, the bodies literally disintegrate under the withering machine gun fire, flesh and bone exploding wetly across the asphalt.

Ten minutes, Sarge reminds himself. Ten minutes is a long time. But we can do it. The soldiers and the survivors can handle the Infected, while the Bradley can handle the larger monsters.

He freezes, wincing, as the Bradley fills with a hellish roar that he remembers all too well.

♦

The monster's screaming cascades across the bridge. The shooting sputters for a moment as the soldiers and survivors flinch in primordial terror. The screaming fades and the firing resumes while the engineers begin removing sandbags and rows of TNT blocks in front of the Bradley. The rig revs its engine and trembles like a bull stomping its feet.

"What in the hell is that?" Ray says.

"We don't know," Paul tells him.

"But you've met."

"Yeah, we've met. We call it the Demon."

For several moments, nothing happens. Thick clouds of smoke hover at the end of the bridge in a thick haze, concealing the buses and the Infected. The Infected have stopped coming for the moment. Then the monster screams again, rending the air with its pain and drawing the smoke clouds into strange swirling patterns.

Todd catches a glimpse of a massive horned thing. Then it emerges, a thickly muscled mass of armor and spikes and giant horns instead of eyes set almost directly over its wide chomping mouth. Enormous membranous wings. Todd can feel each of its steps sending a tiny vibration up his spine. The thing is so ugly and terrifying that his eyes glance off of it.

The Bradley's cannon begins firing. The Demon shudders, stumbling under the blows, but does not appear harmed. It screams, blanking out Todd's mind for a moment, literally eliminating his memory of the last few seconds, and advances. The smoke follows it in swirling patterns, clinging to its limbs.

The engineers have removed the array of charges from the Bradley's path and Patterson is shouting into his mike. The rig jolts forward. Todd reads BOOM STICK on the side of its turret as it roars full speed towards the Demon, its cannon pounding.

"What are they doing?" Todd demands, running after the Bradley and waving his arms. "What the hell are you doing?"

Paul grips his arm and pulls him back. "Let them go, Todd."

"No! They'll be on the wrong side of the bridge when it goes up!"

The Bradley disappears into the clouds of smoke swirling at the end of the bridge. The thick haze lights up with flashes of cannon fire, the reports echoing back as booming thunder. Then it is gone. The engineers are already returning the charges to the road.

"No!" Todd screams. "No!"

Waves of Infected pour out of the smoke, squealing and howling.

"They had no choice," Paul shouts into his ear. "Patterson's not ready and we don't know what that thing can do to us. We've got to finish this, boy!"

One of the behemoths lumbers towards them, groaning under the MG fire, then roars and gallops forward blindly with a sudden, heart-stopping burst of speed until crashing through the rail and falling into the river below.

Ray appears at their side, shooting.

"Fire your fucking guns!" he cries, emptying his rifle into the swarm.

The Towering Things step ponderously among the Infected, their giant faces grinning.

*"Shaw chonk?"*

*"Roomy lactate."*

*"Shaw chonk mute chonk."*

"Fire in the hole!"

Trailing a line of smoke, an AT4 rocket streams from the Guard unit, scoring a hit on one of the Towering Things. The top of its head suddenly erupts in a geyser of blood and brains.

"Holy shit," Todd says in amazement.

He drains his magazine, reloads, fires again.

Hoppers drop down from the cables onto one of the MG teams.

"They're above us again," Ethan yells into the noise, firing into the air.

"Got it," Todd says, adjusting his aim to shoot at the things clambering up the cables. Moments later, two of the creatures fall to the ground with a wet, meaty sound.

The soldiers are screaming and shooting their rifles as the Hoppers leap into their midst, fangs bared and stingers erect. Ethan sees more climbing the cables.

Ray tugs on Paul's arm. "We got to fall back or we're screwed."

"You go, Ray. I'm not moving until this bridge is down."

"You may already be dead, Preacher, but I'm not."

"You will be if we don't blow this thing, understand? We all will!"

Todd glances behind them and sees the engineers running after the retreating five-ton trucks, joined by some of the soldiers. Patterson is backing away slowly at a safe distance, uncoiling wire. He waves at them. The charges are in place, tamped, primed and ready to explode.

Hackett blows his whistle, calling the retreat. It's time to blow the bridge.

Another AT4 missile zooms down the span, detonating on the far side. A score of Infected disintegrate in the blast, raining blood and flesh on the rest. A severed arm comes to a skidding halt at the survivors' feet.

"Now can we go?" Ray asks.

The survivors turn and sprint after Patterson, who is already splicing the firing wire to the blasting machine rapidly with expert fingers.

Several engineers are waving at them.

"Fire in the hole!" they shout.

"Get down, get down!"

Ray tackles Todd to the ground as the blasting machine sends an electric pulse through the firing wire and each of the electric blasting caps wired in series in the TNT.

The blasting caps explode, detonating nearly a ton of dynamite in the far right lanes.

The bridge erupts behind them with a cataclysmic peal of thunder. The bodies of the survivors leave the ground as the shockwave hiccups through the bridge. The massive jolt tears the cables, sending them flying through the air like the metal tentacles of a colossal beast, causing one of the towers to shift and slump. The sky goes dark overhead as a massive wave of dust billows over them. Then another section of TNT erupts, sending a second shock wave through the bridge. The ground bucks under them again, and for a moment if feels as if they are all falling into the water.

After the third explosion, the bridge falls silent. Todd raises his head and looks behind him, coughing on dust. The world is dark and filled with swirling particles and he cannot see five feet in any direction. His ears ring loudly. Through it, he can hear the tramp of thousands of feet, sense monstrous shapes moving through the clouds of dust, searching for them. The Demon screams, the sound vibrating through the concrete deck. The Bradley's cannon booms in response.

"We did it," he rasps.

"Almost," Ethan says. "That was the stripping charge. Now we have to go back and finish it."

◆

The Demon punches the Bradley with a crash that reverberates through the hull and the bodies of the crew. The thing is constantly circling the vehicle one step ahead of the turret. Wendy presses the fast turret switch, increasing the speed of its response, and wrenches the joystick, suddenly bringing the monster's body into view. As the reticle passes over the Demon's spiky flank, Sarge fires the cannon point blank with armor-piercing rounds. The monster stomps away with a series of deep booms, roaring in pain. They catch a glimpse of its tail terminating in a spiked ball, then it is gone. Moments later, they hear the Infected pounding everywhere on the hull, trying to get in. The LO AMMO indicator light pops on and begins flashing. Sarge overrides the system, but has no target.

"Where is it?" Wendy cries. "We almost had it!"

*boom boom boom boom boom boom*

The Demon is rushing them from the right on stomping feet. Wendy yanks on the stick, pulling the turret as fast as it will go. The monster roars and punches the hull and she blacks out for a moment, seeing stars. When she comes to, she cannot remember why she is here.

"I have no shot!" Sarge tells her. "Move the turret!"

She frowns at him. Why is he yelling at her? Suddenly, she remembers. She pulls on the stick. Sarge fires again and curses. The sear indicator light is blinking.

"What's wrong?" she says.

"Misfire!"

Sarge presses the misfire button, returning the 25-mm gun bolt to the cocked position, but the sear light continues to blink.

"It's still jammed," he says, staring at the instruments in helpless rage.

"What now?"

"Now . . ."

*boom boom boom boom boom boom boom*

"Look out!"

*BOOM*

The next punch makes her vomit against the instrument panel.

"Sorry," she moans, wiping her mouth and wagging her head to fight the continuing nausea.

"What?" Sarge says. "What's going on?"

"What do we do now?"

"Where's Randy?" he says, laughing.

"Sarge, knock it off!"

She shoves at him twice, hard. The Bradley commander stares at her blankly, then shakes his head to clear it. He presses a button and another light pops on. Wendy recognizes it. Sarge is dropping all of their smoke grenades at once.

"Steve," he says into the intercom. "Reverse! Steve! Back the hell up!"

*Wilco, Sarge.*

The rig jolts backward on screeching treads as the Demon stumbles through the thick white smoke, screaming, looking for them.

"We still got the TOW," Sarge says.

The monster emerges from the smoke, its head bobbing as if smelling the air, and then roars and charges them.

"Fire it now!" Wendy screams.

"We can't," he tells her.

They hear a series of thuds from behind as the Bradley slams into the Infected during its retreat.

The Launcher UP and TOW indicator lights are on. The TOW launcher is deployed and ready to fire missiles from its firing tubes. The MISSILE TUBE 1 indicator light is on, indicating its missile is ready to be fired.

"It takes sixty-five meters to arm," Sarge explains. "We need distance."

"Go, Steve, go," Wendy says, virtually praying to the driver to go faster.

The Demon gallops at them, its enormous wings outstretched and flapping, dissipating the smoke in seconds and fully revealing its monstrous form. Suddenly, it stops, jerking its head back to lick the bleeding wounds on its flank.

Sarge presses the arming switch for the TOW.

"Put the reticle center mass on that abomination and keep it there."

The monster rolls lithely back to its feet and resumes its chase.

"Come on, come on," Sarge adds, sweating.

"We need more distance."

"Yeah," he says. "Yeah, we do."

Wendy looks over her shoulder but there is no back window, no rear view mirror. Somewhere, behind them, Patterson blew two cratered trenches into the bridge, each more than two meters deep. She is not sure the Bradley will be able to drive over them. If the rig falls into one, she is not sure they will be able to get it back out.

The thought fills her with claustrophobic panic.

"Um, Sarge?"

"*On the way,*" he says, and presses the firing switch on the gunner's right control handle.

The TOW missile flies down the bridge and strikes the Demon in the chest in a fraction of a second, detonating in a burst of light.

"Target!" Wendy shouts, laughing and crying.

*Cowabunga!* Steve says.

The MISSILE TUBE 1 light is flashing. Immediately, the TOW system indicator lights burst across the board: TRCKR, CGE, PWR SUP. The TOW system is failing across the board.

The monster lies on the bridge keening and thrashing in a widening lake of thick black blood, one of its wings broken and flapping, one of its arms dangling by a few ropes of cartilage.

"I think we killed it," Sarge says, blowing air out of his cheeks.

"Thank God," Wendy says. "What now?"

Swarms of Infected pour around the dying demon, racing towards the Bradley.

Sarge selects the coax machine gun, arms it and puts his finger over the firing switch.

"Now we hold them off here as long as we can," Sarge tells her, adding, "*On the way.*"

♦

The soldiers gather around Patterson and Hackett, filthy, their faces drawn and tired, their eyes wild, their hair and uniforms plastered with sweat and coated with white dust. Several wince and massage body parts where they have been stung and are even now gestating another generation of monsters.

"It's just us now," Hackett says. He reaches into his kit, pulls out the can of orange spray paint, and throws it over the side.

The survivors gather at the edge of the crowd, looking in. Paul coughs on the dust, feeling a hundred years old, tired in his bones. He removes a wilted-looking cigarette from his battered pack of Winstons and lights up, sighing.

Hackett spits on the ground and glares at the lieutenant. "LT, I need an honest-to-God, no-shit assessment on what it's going to take to finish this."

"I need thirty minutes up there to lay the second round of charges," Patterson says.

Hackett nods slowly, apparently weighing fight or flight.

"They're coming, Sergeant," one of the soldiers says.

"Sergeant, if it's all the same to you, I'd like to say," another tells him.

"Me, too," says one of the engineers.

All of the men who have been stung want to stay and do their duty. They have literally nothing else to live for. They know that within several hours, they will be dead.

They want to die for something.

"We still got the Bradley up there," one of them says. "I can hear it shooting."

"And the MG," another offers.

"I still got a few rounds left for the AT4."

Paul blinks, realizing that most of the men here have been infected. They are dying. For them, the search for the meaning of life is over. Now they want to find meaning in death.

"We also don't have a lot of bullets left," Ray points out. "What are we supposed to kill them with?"

Hackett ignores him. "Your orders, sir?" he asks Patterson.

"I want you to get my team to the center of the bridge and hold it for thirty minutes."

"Yes, sir."

"Hooah," the soldiers shout with hoarse throats.

They scramble for one of the five-ton trucks and climb onto the back among the boxes of shaped C4 charges, sitting with their legs dangling over the sides, rifles loaded with safeties off.

The truck revs its engine and starts down the highway with a burst of exhaust, speeding towards the onrushing horde. Paul stands on the back, leaning over the roof of the cab, blinking as the dust rushes into his face.

"You may want to start praying again, Ray," he says. "Say another 'hail Mary.'"

"I gave that up," Ray tells him. "I think you were right."

"What about?"

"God's on their side, Preacher."

"Something's working," Paul says, smiling grimly. "You're still alive, aren't you?"

Ray snorts.

The air fills with the pop of aimed rifle fire as the truck wades into the horde and the soldiers begin clearing the bridge.

At the center, Hackett blows his whistle and the soldiers jump down from the truck and charge. "Go, go, go!" he roars.

The soldiers fan out, covering the MG, giving it time to deploy. Moments later, the air fills with its staccato bark. A rocket streams into the open mouth of one of the Towering Things, exploding inside the massive head, smoke pouring from its eyes and mouth as it topples to the ground. The dust is settling and they see the Bradley among hills of dead and dying Infected, its coax machine gun still chattering, sending waves of Infected toppling to the ground.

The engineers drop ladders into the trenches and begin placing the charges, Patterson priming them with blasting caps connected by firing wire unreeled from a cardboard spool. The soldiers hurdle the trenches and deploy in a firing line, occasionally shooting but letting the machine guns do the hard work for now.

The minutes tick by.

The Bradley suddenly stops firing.

♦

The vehicle is either suffering another malfunction or, more likely, is simply out of ammo. The endless horde surges around it, rushing towards the soldiers. Tentacled titans and towering froglike things and hopping monkeys and squat crablike creatures with enormous clacking scissor hands mingle with the Infected—thousands of them, needy, wanting, hungry.

Hackett roars an order. The soldiers stand and fire in a volley that sends the front ranks of the Infected crashing to the ground in a lake of blood.

"Reloading!" the MG crew calls out.

"Pour it on, boys, and make it hot!" Hackett roars, his M16 popping.

Tracers stream through the smoky haze in a pounding roar of gunfire. Todd aims center mass at a woman running at him and fires a burst, knocking her over. He spares a quick glance down the line and sees fewer than twenty tired men screaming like maniacs and firing rifles. Beyond, at the edge of the bridge, the MG team feverishly reloads its gun.

He aims at a man running at him in hospital scrubs and fires again. His vision shakes; the man falls. Nearby, Ray shoots on full auto, the rifle spitting empty shell casings and puffs of smoke, while screaming every obscenity he knows. The rifle suddenly jams. He throws it away, still roaring his endless string of profanity, and yanks two handguns out of their holsters, emptying them at the horde that is now less than twenty yards away and coming fast.

The Hoppers leap into the air with hisses, landing on several of the soldiers and sending them toppling back into the trench. A tongue lashes down, wrapping around the machine gunner and yanking him roughly into the air to land in a salivating mouth.

The Infected are dropping like flies while the rest close the remaining distance and surge against the firing line with a general howl.

Their horrible sour milk stench fills Todd's nostrils moments before he feels himself shoved roughly to the ground. Shoes and bloody bare feet slam into his body. He glances up and sees the hateful faces of the Infected glaring down at him, shrieking.

It's not fair, he tells himself, gasping at the lancing pain. He wishes he had never come on this mission. He wishes had had stayed. It's not fair. It's so stupid.

He curls up into a ball, covering his head with his arms. The Infected scream down at him.

Their chests explode and they flop to the ground in a smoking ruin.

"Don't you touch that boy," Paul roars, chambering another round and firing. Instantly, more bodies collapse all around Todd, spraying him with blood.

"*ROOMY*," one of the monsters bellows over their heads.

"Don't you touch that boy, I said!"

"Get him up," Ethan says, rushing in with his rifle.

"We'll cover you!" Ray says, firing with both fists.

Todd opens his eyes, his vision blurred by hot tears, and sees Paul's face.

"Hey, Rev," he rasps.

"You're all right now, son. I'll get you out of here."

They hear a rumbling sound they can feel deep in their chests. Paul suddenly gasps, his eyes wide with recognition.

"You all right, Rev?"

Paul smiles weakly.

"God bless you, Kid—"

He suddenly lurches high into the air and into the gaping maw of one of the Towering Things, which bites down with a sickening crunch, chuckling deep in its throat.

"No!" Ray screams, firing his pistol up at the thing.

"The legs!" Ethan calls to him, shooting at the Infected. "Shoot it in the legs!"

"Rev?" Todd says, trying to stand, his eyes flooded with tears.

Ray nods and rushes at the Towering Thing, shooting down the Infected running at him until standing almost directly underneath the monster.

"Die, you piece of shit," he says, taking careful aim and shooting out one of the thing's knobby knees.

The Towering Thing squeals, its leg collapsing under its enormous weight, and falls into the horde with a meaty splash.

Another sound pierces the air.

Craig DiLouie

Hackett is blowing his whistle.

♦

Ethan and Ray and Todd leap across the trenches, trailing clouds of dust, the Infected spilling into the open pits behind them, squealing and clawing at the walls. Todd stumbles on the other side, screaming for the Reverend, Ray half dragging him.

"Go ahead, I'll cover!" Ethan says, turning and walking slowly backwards while pouring lead into the snarling faces of their pursuers.

On his left, Hackett and several soldiers run toward him from the opposite lanes, chased by a group of Infected. He slaps a fresh mag into the rifle, chambers a round and fires several bursts, cutting down the pursuers.

I think I'm finally getting the hang of this, Ethan thinks, and turns again to provide cover fire. Constantly aware of the other survivors, he wonders where Paul is, and feels a sudden stab in his heart as the fact of his friend's death strikes him again.

He lowers his rifle for a moment, panting with exhaustion.

"I'm sorry, friend," he says, thinking: I hope you're in a better place.

Hackett collides with him and he feels the air rush out of his lungs. The world spins and he hits the ground hard. His rifle is gone.

"Jeez, Sergeant," Ethan gasps. "You okay?"

He feels a boot strike his ribs, knocking the air out of him again. Another sinks into his back, sending a lancing pain up his neck. The soldiers are standing over him, kicking him.

*They're Infected,* he realizes.

Hackett slowly rises to all fours, groaning.

"Run, run, run," Ethan hisses at him.

Hackett turns, snarling, and bites into Ethan's ankle.

Ethan screams, flailing. The pain is incredible. He remembers the pistol on his hip and unholsters it, snapping off the safety and squeezing two shots through Hackett's skull. His eyes stinging with tears of regret, he looks down at his torn ankle smeared with blood and saliva.

The soldiers have stopped kicking him.

The virus has entered his nervous stream and is already flowing into his brain. Within moments, he loses control of his limbs and his body begins twitching. The pain in his ankle recedes as his body responds to Infection by flooding his brain with endorphins.

The soldiers growl, grinning wolfishly, and then run after the others.

Probabilities. He was a math teacher. He understands probabilities. It works like this: You take enough risks on a long enough timeline, and you will probably lose. It's that simple.

He looks at the gun still gripped in his hand. Despite the weakness and spasms, he retains some control of his body. He should end it now, before he becomes one of them.

He raises the pistol slowly to his head.

Infected begin to race past, snarling, their feet slapping on the wet asphalt and splashing through puddles of blood. Ethan slowly raises himself onto his elbow and aims the gun at them, firing methodically. A running figure spins like a top before toppling to the pavement.

His hand suddenly flops back to the ground, the gun forgotten.

The world is bathed in shades of red, terrifying and beautiful.

The first wave of despair passes through him. Now he understands why the Infected cry out at night. They are filled with sadness. Incredible, impenetrable, inconsolable sadness.

The sadness of memories of an entire life just out of reach.

The sadness of slaves.

Then the rage begins. The pure hatred.

The hunger. The need.

The urgent, directive hum of the Brood.

Ethan hisses, spraying spittle, struggling to stand. He knows there are things on this bridge that have not yet received the viral gospel.

There they are, murdering his people, each death an extinguished vector. He sees figures advancing towards him, running and shooting. Small arms fire crackles across the bridge.

A woman stands over him now, looking down at him wearing a sad expression. She holds two smoking pistols in her fists.

His face contorts into a hideous grimace.

"Anne," he growls. "Good to see . . ."

The small moment of pleasure passes almost instantly. He glares up at her with hate, trying to push himself off the ground. She falls to one knee, meeting him halfway.

"Ethan, listen to me," she says close to his ear.

He shakes his head and snarls. "Go . . ."

Within moments, he has already forgotten who she is. All he knows is that she is a terrifying monster in the eyes of the Brood. A monster that destroys vectors for the Brood. A monster that is a threat to the Brood. A monster that must be tamed by becoming a host for the Brood.

*Assimilate*, the Brood hums. *Assimilate and grow in safety in a fertile host.*

The monster says: "Your family is still alive."

The red veil suddenly lifts and he gasps as the faces of Carol and Mary flash through his mind. He sees Mary in a bathing suit running through a series of sprays in a water park, Carol laughing as she unpacks lunch on a picnic table.

"Mary," he growls deep in his throat.

Mary turns and rushes towards him.

"Daddy!" she squeals.

The sun in his eyes, so bright.

What a perfect day that was.

Ethan's head bursts as Anne pulls the trigger.

♦

Todd staggers through hell, shouting for Paul and Ethan while the engineers retreat with pistols and crowbars and baseball bats, forming a tightening protective circle around Patterson, who struggles to connect the firing wires to the blasting machine, the right side of his face swollen to twice its normal size.

Help is arriving. Fresh troops have formed a ragged line and are shooting into the ranks of the Infected, which break apart under the withering fire. The soldiers are from the two buses they left behind at the Ohio end of the bridge. There are civilians here, too, whom he does not recognize. He wanders among the Infected, which drop bleeding to the ground around him.

He shouts the names of his friends.

*Get down, get down*

*Fire in the hole*

The trenches in front of him erupt in a blinding flash, followed by a deafening crash. A massive tremor buckles the bridge, knocking him off of his feet to land hard on the asphalt.

He struggles back onto his hands and knees, feeling lightheaded.

*Come on, kid*, a voice says, tiny and distant.

He blinks and sees Ray Young frowning down at him, his mouth working, his STEELERS cap smoking. The man hauls him roughly to his feet.

The garbled, muffled sounds of the world rush into his ears with suddenly clarity.

"The bridge didn't blow! We got to move! You hear me? It didn't blow!"

Todd turns and sees a Giant lumbering towards him, bellowing its foghorn call, stomping the ground, its tentacles swaying like whips.

"We got to get out of here!" Ray tells him.

They failed. It's over. And his friends died for nothing.

"Come on, kid!"

The horde continues its mad rush across the bridge, led by the titan.

Todd collapses to his knees, dragging Ray to the ground with him.

"No!" he says.

"Come on!"

"No! No!"

He pushes the man away from him, scrambling on all fours, and stops to shake his fists at the Infected, screaming and crying.

"You killed my friends! I fucking hate you!"

"We're going to die here if we don't move," Ray pleads with him.

Todd stands shakily, shrugging off Ray's hand again, and unholsters his pistol.

"You killed all my friends and now I'll kill you!"

Todd aims his pistol at the behemoth crashing towards him and fires, screaming. Ray appears next to him, screaming his head off, firing with both hands until his guns click empty.

The Giant lunges into a gallop, roaring, filling the air with its stench.

Within moments, the monster looms over them.

And falls through the earth with a groan.

The broken section of the bridge detaches cleanly and tumbles seventy feet until swallowed by the waters below. The monster falls with it, lowing plaintively and flailing until crashing into the river.

Todd raises his fist, whooping like a savage as the Infected continue to run at him, toppling over the edge into the river below, shrieking like bats.

"Ha!" he screams at them. "Ha! That's what you get!"

He finally falls to his knees among the rubble and bodies, crying hysterically.

"You killed my friends," he says.

I didn't know you very well, he thinks, but you're the only ones who really knew me. You listened to me when nobody else did. You saw me. You depended on me. You accepted me.

Like nobody ever did.

"All for a goddamn bridge," Ray says in disgust. He drops his pistols onto the road and walks away shaking, leaving Todd alone.

Moments later, Anne kneels next to the boy and puts her arm around him. After some time, he curls up into a ball on the ground, his head on her lap, and falls asleep.

In the distance, over the stomping feet and snarling breath of the Infected hordes, she hears the metallic scream of amored treads.

◆

Ray sits on the corner of the edge of the bridge among the dead and dying, his feet kicking in empty space, looking down at the river. He briefly ponders the water, the clouds, the sun hanging low in the sky. The wind whistles through the gap, sweeping dust into the water. Across forty feet of open space, hundreds of Infected still crowd the other side of the span, moaning and reaching out to him as if pleading. He resurrects a mangled cigarette from the crushed pack in his shirt pocket and lights it, inhaling deeply and blowing a long stream of smoke. A cigarette never tasted so good. What I wouldn't give for an ice cold beer, he thinks, almost salivating. Ice. Cold. Beer.

Life is good. It's even beautiful.

And way too short.

The pain in his side is incredible. He can feel the virus growing there, converting his cells into a monster waiting to be born. One life ends, and another begins.

I'll fight it, he vows. And maybe I'll win.

He heard that the Hoppers grow right out of your body as if it were topsoil, sucking it dry, and then eat what's left when they are born, the way baby spiders in some species consume their own mothers after they hatch. By that point, you're so drained that all you can do is watch.

It's a lousy way to go. He'd rather die of bone cancer.

The first time he does something really good in his life, he has to die for it.

A noble sacrifice. Right. Big fucking deal.

We ain't the three hundred Spartans, he thinks. There ain't no legends being born here. The country is filled with heroic chumps sacrificing themselves for a future that will be dominated by all of the ignorant, selfish assholes who hid and did nothing. In a week, most of the good citizens of Camp Defiance will forget all about it. And even if they didn't, even if they built a goddamn pyramid here in my honor, I'd still be dead. I gave my life when all that matters is staying alive.

It's too bad. I really wanted to see what I could do.

I was just starting to feel like I had some potential as a human being.

# EPILOGUE:
# ON THE ROAD

Sarge and Wendy sit on the Bradley's warm metal skin on a thickly treed hilltop overlooking the desolation that was once Steel Valley. Sarge inspects the scorched land with a pair of binoculars while Steve stands guard nearby with a rifle. They see no sign of life, Infected or otherwise. The entire region appears to be dead, barren. They will be driving past Pittsburgh today along a southern route and they need to take a look at the road to see what is ahead. To the northeast, the city is still smoldering and blasting heat into the sky like a massive furnace and bleeding its toxins and rubble into the Ohio River. The land is carpeted in gray ash and cars half melted into the road.

They are refugees forced from everything they consider home, nomads living on whatever they can find. But mostly they are survivors. They are good at surviving because they are on the road and they are still alive. They have done the things one had to do to survive. They are going to Camp Immunity, near Harrisburg, to find Ethan's family and tell them that he is dead and that he never gave up searching for them. That he never gave up hope. His little girl has a right to know who her father was, how he died so that thousands might live.

They do not intend to stay in Immunity. The only sanctuary they trust now is the Bradley.

Wendy runs her fingers along the deep scratches in the turret made by the claws of the Demon. The grooves remind her of the empty spaces inside her that appeared when she learned Paul and Ethan were dead. It is still unfathomable to her that they could die, even in this dangerous world. They had become larger than life in her mind over the past weeks, closer than family. Now she feels their absence like an amputated limb or a missing gun. Her mind still wants assurance they are there, covering their sectors, with her world being a little safer because of it.

Sarge touches her shoulder. Wendy wipes her eyes with the palm of her hand and tries to smile.

"They live here," he tells her, touching his heart.

"It should have been me."

"No," he says. "It shouldn't."

Wendy looks down at the charred wasteland that was once a thriving city and wonders why she is alive when so many died. She does not see anything special about her. She cannot accept that she deserves it.

Sarge adds, "They didn't die for nothing. They died so that many more could live and that's the noblest way to die."

She squeezes his hand and sighs, feeling strangely sick and empty, starving but unable to eat anything, her mind searching for its own sanctuary.

Maybe she will find it on the road.

The Bradley was not trapped on the West Virginia side of the river. The vehicle has an inflatable pontoon that encircles the rig and can turn it into a boat propelled by its treads at four miles an hour. But they did not go back to Defiance.

Anne radioed to tell them the mission had succeeded. She had been leading another group of survivors to the camp, taking them through Steubenville for supplies, when they heard the sounds of battle. She found the soldiers at the buses on the Ohio side of the river arguing over whether to abandon their position and support their comrades. Anne rallied the soldiers and led both them and her team of survivors in an assault that bought Patterson enough time to finish blowing the charges. Just what Wendy would expect her to do. She is a natural leader.

Anne said she was going to take Todd back to Defiance with the other survivors, and then head back out to find more. Todd said he wanted to go with her.

After breaking radio contact, Sarge told Wendy and Steve he could never go back. That he could never feel safe there. That the only place he could stand being is here, on the road.

They agreed instantly to come with him.

"I believe in you, Toby," she says.

"It's just us now," he tells her.

"We'll find others and start again."

"A tribe, right?"

He puts his arm around her and she snuggles close, her eyes glassy.

"A tribe," she agrees, and sighs.

"We'll be together."

"No matter what."

Odd that they should reject the security of the camp for the brutality of the road, which just claimed two of their friends. They know it is insane, but they feel safe out here. They understand it. And strangely, they feel they must go on facing it in order to continue earning the right to be alive when so many died.

Survival, it seems, is also a state of mind. And it carries a steep price.

"Sarge!" Steve calls out.

"What's up?"

The gunner grins at him. "Listen."

The pounding of rotors in the distance, growing louder.

Sarge and Wendy turn and see five black objects moving slowly across the sky in formation.

"God," Sarge says, raising the binoculars to his eyes. "I can't believe it."

"What is it? Toby, what is it?"

He lowers the binoculars slowly, smiling in a daze. "Chinooks. Big helicopters, troop carriers, moving west."

"How? Who are they? Where are they going?"

"It's the Army, babe. The Army. Here, take a look."

Sarge hands her the binoculars. She watches the helicopters move across the sky. There is an elegance to the ungainly beasts that she finds inspiring.

"See that?" he says, sounding wistful.

Behind the first formation, another approaches, five black dots in the sky heading west.

Wendy nods, swallowing hard. Tears roll down her cheeks and she smiles.

"Look at them go," he adds.

America's far-flung armies are coming home.

The fight is not over. It is only getting started.

The counterattack has begun.

# THE INFECTION

The world is rocked as one in five people collapse screaming before falling into a coma. Three days later, the Infected awake with a single purpose: spread the Infection. A small group—a cop, teacher, student, reverend—team up with a military crew to survive. But at a refugee camp what's left of the government will ask them to accept a dangerous mission back into the very heart of Infection.

## BY CRAIG DILOUIE

ISBN: 978-1934861653

## PETER CLINES
# EX HEROES

The plague of living death spread around the globe. Despite the best efforts of the superheroes, the population was decimated, heroes fell, and the city of angels was left a desolate zombie wasteland like so many others.

Now, a year later, the heroes lead teams out to scavenge supplies, keep the peace within the walls of their home, and try to be the symbols the survivors so desperately need. But the ex-humans are not the only threat left in the world, another group has grown and gained power.

And they are not heroes.

ISBN: 978-1934861288

Made in the USA
Lexington, KY
02 November 2011